The Wolf and The Lamb

The story of Mary Cole, 5ᵗʰ Countess of Berkeley

Volume 1

1783 - 1799

*Though you teach a wolf the paternoster, he will say "Lamb!
Lamb!"* Aesop.

Cover Design and Document Preparation by
myITfixed.co.uk

ISBN 978-0-9556877-1-6

New Eve Publishing
Great Britain

When Mary Cole, a butcher's daughter, caught the eye of Lord Berkeley, it was as flint to tinder. A libertine and a forsworn bachelor, he was taken aback that the Catholic-reared beauty refused to be his mistress. Within weeks he'd brought her family to bankruptcy. When, still, she eluded him, he devised a theatrical plot to abduct her.

It was then that he knew he could not let her go.

Aided by his corrupt chaplain, Hupsman, the Earl duped his 'shepherdess' with fake nuptials.

Tumbling to the truth, Mary became passionately committed to gaining her eldest son's birthright. With an astonishing grasp of pastoral economy, she repaired the Berkeley fortunes while a succession of children compounded her plight.

Her estranged sisters, meanwhile, were moving among the *glitterati* of Pitt's England and the New America and their scandalous activities had to be curtailed at the highest level before a legal knot was eventually tied.

Upon Hupsman's death, the temptation to affirm the 'first marriage' proved too strong for the Earl and Countess and they conspired in a criminal act to 'find' the registry. The upshot was a sensational trial in the House of Lords in 1811 whose repercussions were to shake the foundations of the Berkeley dynasty for ever and put Mary's life at risk.

Was that marriage a sham? Or was it a timeless truth?

Family Ties

Clove Hitch

A Gordian Knot

The Knot of Heracles

Family Ties

Prelude

"I have been as much sold as any lamb that goes to the shambles!"

Often she had watched them in the fickle days of spring, skipping about the lush meadows of Gloucester, exulting in the gift of life. Steadily they grew fat and independent of the placid ewes, unaware of the shadow of the butcher's blade, or that they were destined for some rich man's table.

That was long ago, when Mary was a slip of a thing and Pa kept The Swan Tavern at Barnwood and grazed livestock there. He used to send his meat into the city of Gloucester and numbered among his customers many of the great houses of the Vale. They were well-known, the Coles. Folk grumbled about their airs and graces, but William Cole was a respected tradesman who never sold anyone short. He was proud of his three lovely daughters, of whom Mary was the youngest, and had high hopes of his fourth child, his namesake, Billy, despite the shameless way the women of the household mollycoddled him. His wife, too, was a comely body who earned pin money by nursing sick and newborn infants and saw no contradiction in this humble occupation and that state to which she aspired. "For," observed she, "high birth or lowly, tis nought but an accident. Nobility of character is what signifies." Mary possessed a natural reserve and took this dictum to heart, but her sisters were wanton and Cole was relieved when his eldest, Ann, took up with Will Farren, a likely fellow in the same trade as himself, and went to live in Butcher's Row, Westgate, in wedded safekeeping.

Life was simple then. The sun always seemed to be shining. Mary delighted in picking nosegays of sweet peas and lavender from her father's garden and went capering off to school with them, adding poppies and buttercups and Queen Anne's lace along the bridle way.

But in the year 1783, when Farmer George was King and Mary was full-grown, the recent death of old Cole marked a dramatic change in the family's fortune....

One

"Faith!" cried Susan, who loved to mimic her betters. "What a woman of the world I shall fancy myself living in London!"

Her mother, perched on the edge of a shabby sofa, burst into a fresh fit of weeping. "Heartless wench! How can you say such things with your poor father only buried these five days and the bailiffs at the door?" She wiped her eyes and proceeded to blow her nose noisily on the corner of her apron. "Believe me, Mr Parsons, we was never in such straits afore. Never!"

"Calm yourself, dear lady," begged the attorney. "Miss Mary, be good enough to fetch your Mama a noggin of rum. Twill nicely stiffen her nerves."

Mary obeyed, glad of something to do. Activity helped to dull the grief. She could not conceive of a life without Pa, who had been the sun of her existence, and did not know whether to envy or pity her sister who took it all in her stride. Two years ago, when the Cole finances were more threadbare than usual, Susan and Mary had been obliged to leave Mrs Clarke's boarding school in Gloucester. Susan was rising sixteen and Mary eighteen months younger. Their home was rented and in order to attract high-class patrons (not notably the most prompt in settling their bills) Cole's income had been stretched to give the business an illusion of prosperity it could not sustain. Mary had learned to cook and clean and sew and keep accounts in earnest. Billy was always ailing and Susan not as helpful as might be wished. Although she delighted in saucy backchat and was much at home behind the bar, she considered her talents quite wasted in that West Country backwater and lived for the day some well-heeled nobleman would come in off the highway with a craving thirst! Now, Mr Benjamin Parsons, whom Pa had long supplied with plump game and choice cuts of beef, had come in charity to disentangle William Cole's affairs and make arrangements for the future.

His widow and Billy were to live with Ann Farren above the shop in Butcher's Row. From there, Mrs Cole could look about for nursing and sewing work to earn her keep. Meanwhile, lodgings had been taken for Susan and her younger sister in London where it was felt that opportunities of good posts in service would abound. Susan was unduly elated at the prospect of freedom, but Mary did not relish being a stranger in the city.

When she returned to the parlour, the stout lawyer was saying: "Your landlady, Mrs Fraser, is a God-fearing soul and will provide that strict moral guidance so essential in the absence of your own dear mother."

"Lud, Mr Parsnip," Susan brazenly disabused him, "we were never used to saying our prayers!"

There she was wrong, for Mary was diligent in her devotions which were conducted in secrecy. This was partly to spare herself Susan's scorn and partly because Catholic belief, in which their mother had been reared, was distinctly uncomfortable in those days when Culloden was a living memory and the Gordon Riots were daily currency. It had taken three Protestant kings from the Court of Hanover to quench notions of the Mother Church and make sure that Catholics did not combine and were kept out of Civil Office.

Billy sniggered at Susan's cavorting and Parsons glowered as though he itched to put the rebellious young creature across his knee. He eyed Mary with a good deal of sympathy, wondering how two such dissimilar girls would fare on their own.

"Miss Cole," he addressed Susan, for he was not disposed to call her by her Christian name and she was the elder, "you must understand that your chances of a position might be severely limited by the two of you remaining together. Perhaps...."

"What, live in separate households! Poor Mary would never contrive without me to protect her!"

Parsons expression was that he scrupled to believe it. He regarded Mary with an enigmatic air which brought a disconcerted blush to her cheeks. "For a young lady of fifteen summers, she is uncommonly self-possessed." This Mary took to mean 'strong-willed' but later thought that she might have done him an injustice.

"I should prefer to stay with Susan, Mr Parsons. I don't like to see our family further scattered."

So the matter was settled and next day, wrapped in thick cloaks, the girls took up their bundles and climbed aboard the Gloucester stagecoach which left The Bell Inn at dusk. Economy seats on the outside had been booked but, providentially, two inside passengers failed to appear by the time the coach was due to leave and the sisters were able to beg seats under cover. A thin rain was falling and the tavern lanterns were creaking in the wind. Their mother sobbed and clutched Billy's arm, determined that Fate should not snatch him also from her.

They travelled through the night at a fairly smart pace. The wheel-rims of the vehicle were extra wide. Coaches so equipped were granted freedom from tolls because they helped to compact the road surface. On the steeper inclines, every fit person had to pile out of the vehicle and trudge to the summit, being sure not to lag far behind. Clouds sped across the night sky as sleepy towns and villages rattled past in the opposite direction. Torchlight glistened on the rain-lashed windows filmed with human breath.

"Farewell to dull old Gloucestershire," Susan said.

"I shall miss the ploughed red fields and the beechwoods in any season."

"Fudge! Nothing exciting ever happens in Gloucester. We shan't find dashing husbands there!"

"Husbands?" echoed Mary as though this were an alien notion.

"I despise Ann for throwing herself away on that shifty Farren. She's a fine-looking girl and could have had a far better catch."

"She will always eat meat."

"Lord, how humble you are!"

"I would rather marry an honest tradesman than a wicked peer, even though he might cut up well."

"Give me the wicked lord any day," retorted Susan, "and I will teach him to do my bidding, wedding ring or not!"

Mary wriggled uncomfortably, thankful that the faces of their fellow passengers were lost in shadow. The reek of musty leather, tobacco and unbathed bodies was stifling, but as the night wore on, they grew accustomed to it. At length, Susan dozed, but Mary could not. Only as dawn broke over Hounslow, suffusing the sky with opal beams, did the knot of apprehension inside her begin to dissolve. They had come through the storm and the windmill on the deserted heath stood motionless, towering above a cautionary gibbet. A fiery sun, like a link boy's flare, kindled between the naked trees. Soon a dome gleamed through the far mist, and steeples craning above a miscellany of pantiles, thatch and crooked gables. Mary shook her sister. "Look! The city!" Susan squinted blearily through the mud-splashed window and promptly nodded off again.

The nearer they got, the slower their progress. The turnpike was choked with wagons of every description; dawdling cattle and panic-stricken geese were being driven to market between punishing goads. But, punctually, on the stroke of nine, the driver drew rein outside the Gloucester Coffee House in Piccadilly and, clutching their few possessions, the girls set foot on untried ground.

"I swear I shall faint from hunger and thirst before long," Susan cried above the clangour. "Let's find a cab to take us to Mrs Fraser's."

"Can we afford it?" asked Mary anxiously.

"In London one must do things in style!"

"We have lodgings to pay for."

"Do stop fretting, Sis. We shan't be in them above a couple of days. All these fine mansions must be clamouring for servants. Oh, did you ever see so many crested carriages!"

Young bucks of rank and fashion with powdered hair and embroidered coats were laughing and gesturing above the bull's-eye panes of the Coffee House. While Mary was unnerved, Susan was mightily amused. A burly, weather-beaten Quaker who had journeyed on top of their coach, obviously used to the rigours of travel, kindly summoned a cab for them and informed the driver of their destination. Mary thanked him warmly. "God be with you, lass," he whispered and gave her hand a reassuring pat.

They jogged and crawled by turns through the winding alleys and came shortly to Whitecross Street where they were ushered inside Mrs Fraser's quaint oversailed cottage by the good lady herself. She was a small, buxom individual, childless, whose reddish hair was threaded with silver. For all her piety, she was a cheerful soul ready to think well of mankind. The sisters did not hesitate to trust her. Even Susan, who was prepared to do battle with anyone who tried to control her, found her disarming. Of Fraser there was no sign. He was a Major in King George's army serving in America and his longsuffering wife had not seen him in several years. His Majesty was obstinately clinging on to his dominions and, though it was more than a twelvemonth since General Cornwallis had surrendered at Yorktown after the British defeat by the French at Chesapeake Bay, the peace treaty was still unsigned.

The guest room was spotless. The girls sluiced their hands and faces at the washstand and then, as Mrs Fraser had bidden, went down to the kitchen where she laid a neat gingham cloth on the table and plied them with bowls of frumenty, spiced ham and coffee. Then, after a reviving nap, they wanted nothing so much as to learn their way about London and discover what work there was to be had.

Mr Benjamin Parsons had warned them that it would he easier to find independent vacancies, and he had been right. Advertisements were duly penned and inserted in the *Morning Chronicle*. For three days in a row, the Coles trudged the streets, rapped on countless doors and fled from a drunken butler brandishing a poker. Never, even in the depths of her later misfortunes, was Mary to feel the portals of privileged folk so relentlessly closed against her. Surely someone in the whole of the capital needed a brace of serving girls!

Their spirits and their shoe-leather quite worn down, Mrs Fraser proposed a cheering diversion. "Now here's a thing, lassies, to make your faces blithe," announced she, waving some deckle-edged cards.

"A masquerade at The Pantheon!" Susan exclaimed.

"Oh ma'am, how excessively kind," Mary said in delight, "but you should not have put yourself to such trouble."

"And why not," she twinkled, "when I've long sought an excuse to go there myself?"

Susan bemoaned that they had no disguises to wear.

"For my part," Mary said, "I shall be more than content to sit and watch."

And so on Shrove Tuesday evening, they made their way to Oxford Street and mounted the steps of the building reputed to have the most gorgeous interior in London since Wren built St. Paul's. It was a popular place and had been hailed as a 'winter Ranelagh' when it opened. Mr Wyatt, the architect, had adapted the design from something similar in a far-flung corner of the Byzantine Empire, but no one knew that at the time and he was considered a genius, that was before he was seized of a craze for the Gothic and ran riot all over England with his towers and battlements!

To girls fresh from the country, it caused a sensation. Their landlady herself gasped in disbelief. It was richly carved and gilded, just like a cathedral. Under a vast dome, the main hall was encircled by a wide balcony supported on marble pillars and decorated with a frieze depicting scenes of Valhalla, all brought to life by a galaxy of candles. Statues posed in niches about the walls and green and purple lamps created a mythical gloom for the merriment of the masque. A quadrille was beginning and the dancers, an assortment of characters from history and fable, pointed their toes in unison. Harlequin was accompanied by his Columbine; Robin Hood partnered Good Queen Bess and Nell Gwynn was honoured by Othello whose boot-polished visage had no need of a mask. Many of the ladies wore simple dominoes: eyelet-holes gleamed above scarlet mouths emphasised by black patches and complexions made pallid by litharge of lead.

Stationed upstairs, Mrs Fraser and her charges sipped lemonade and watched the fun, but before long, some bold rascals were calling them to come down.

"How I dislike being a wallflower," Susan complained. "I've a mind to join them and so should you, Mary."

"We've no costume to put on."

"What a damp you are! You've no sense of adventure!"

Their chaperone smiled and seemed to approve. "Tis but a foolish spree, child," she said soothingly. She was prevented from saying more by the appearance at her side of a sturdy Highlander who bowed and requested the favour of an introduction. "I am James Perry," he informed her," removing the mask from an honest-looking face, "a student of law lately entered at the Inner Temple."

"And a forward fellow indeed," added Mrs Fraser with a touch of arch humour. "That's a Cameron tartan you have on, for I was one myself before my marriage to Fraser."

"Tis true, I've no right to the colours," James Perry admitted cordially, "you must put down the liberty to admiration of your stalwart clan."

Having begun on this agreeable footing, Mrs Fraser was content to let him whisk the girls into the fray. He was personable and courteous and she quickly warmed to his Gaelic charm.

Mary went reluctantly, Susan's reproof ringing in her ears. Mr Perry borrowed a couple of pitchforks and sunbonnets, decking them out as haymakers and the elder Cole went prancing about the hall chased by a golden-masked Apollo who roared: "Make hay with me, my beauty!"

Mary tried hard to enter into the spirit of the evening, but was ill at ease. So many false identities! Milliners' assistants passed themselves off as fine ladies and Dukes' daughters as opera-girls. So many bold advances! Faces with a fixed anonymous leer sprang forth from a netherworld shade. Some of the revellers were dancing a boisterous *allemande* and were rolling about the floor and kicking one leg in the air as if they had tumbled out of a Rowlandson cartoon. It was all as far removed from the Lammastide reels in the barns of the Cotswolds as it was from the sedate minuets in the drawing rooms of Mayfair.

Sensible of these feelings, Mr Perry steered Mary by the elbow into a corner where they sat down on a bench. She must have seemed as starched and sober as a Puritan to his sophisticated eye, but she had never been able to pretend to be what she was not. She preferred simple clothes, muted colours, and could not forget she was in mourning. Nature had not fitted her to pose and posture, though she might admire a well-bred lady in the pink of fashion as heartily as any man. "Miss Cole, what troubles you?" he besought her gently. "I perceive that yours is a bright and happy disposition, yet none of this is to your taste."

"Oh sir, if only I were really haymaking back in the West Country!"

"Och, is that where you'd rather be?" he said, amused. "Those lily-white hands were not made for labour."

Whether he mocked her, she could not tell, for though her hands were pale and slender, they were ingrained with the tell-tale grime of potato peeling and blacking sessions upon the kitchen range. She explained how poor Pa was laid to rest not a month since, and that her mother was as destitute as any widow could be whose husband had been engaged in a competitive trade. She told him how she and her sister had searched high and low for employment, but it seemed that they must part and go different ways. "Our purse is already run out," Mary ended dolefully, "and there is no one to whom we can turn."

This pathetic appeal was not intentional: the anguish of manifold loss in that moment overwhelmed her. The shadow of the workhouse loomed. Mary saw the two of them transported to some grim cotton mill under dour Northern skies where they would never see the light of day nor England again. For Susan, it was a wry joke: she refused to entertain the possibility for a second. Her sister's austere integrity astonished her. Did Mary not understand how boldness would well repay in this world's coin? It was the falterers who were left to underwrite the losses.

James Perry was moved by Mary's sincerity. He shuddered to think of the snares and temptations to which impecunious young females in the city would be exposed. "Fret not, lassie," he said roundly. "I'm not entirely without good friends. A word here and there and we shall see what can be done."

In an access of gratitude, she seized both his hands. "How kind you are, dear Mr Perry!"

"Do me the honour of calling at my chambers in Clement's Inn the day after tomorrow. And keep that smiling countenance. It suits you well."

That night, Mary slept with a lighter heart.

On the appointed day, the girls presented themselves at James Perry's address. It was late afternoon on a glittering day and the light was fading in a blaze of rose-tinted bronze behind the buildings. They hoped to find their lawyer friend enjoying a respite from his books and had chosen their time accordingly. Cheeks aglow, they ran up the winding staircase and paused outside his door, suppressing a giggle before knocking. They need not have hesitated, for he swept them in with an effusive welcome, bade them sit by the fire and called for chocolate and muffins. He could not afford tea, he told them, and hoped that they would not look for such luxuries when they came to visit him! Currently, he was editing a newspaper called *The Gazetteer* in order to finance his studies.

Mary discarded her muff. "You're a journalist, Mr Perry?"

"I have been many things, Miss Cole," he replied. "When my father's business ventures failed in Aberdeen, I turned to acting, a course not crowned with success: I'd a heavy brogue I've since chaved to tame! Then I came to London to try my luck as a hack."

Susan yawned and cast a lacklustre eye towards the well-thumbed volumes piled up on the desk. "I was never of a studious turn of mind," she owned. "I swear it took me a twelvemonth to master my hornbook."

"Feint the danger of you becoming a bluestocking, then!" The lawyer retrieved the newspaper he had thrust down on his chair when he answered the door. "Now the *Morning Chronicle*.... There is an admirable publication. Candid! Fearless! No unctuous toadying to the Monarchy."

"You must be a Whig, Mr Perry?" Mary said, pleased to have overheard the gossip of her father's cronies.

"Why, certainly! And proud to have made the acquaintance of Charles James Fox and the playwright, Mr Sheridan, men with the sharpest minds."

"But have you met the Prince of Wales?" Susan wanted to know.

"Depend upon it, I shall! He is chief-like with Fox and those politicians who abhor the way he is kept imprisoned in Buckingham House and needs the dispensation of the King every time the daftie chooses to appear in public. Far from bridling him, it makes him run wild."

"Oh do tell!"

Perry was not sure that he ought to enlarge on the follies of this flower of the Hanoverian dynasty upon whom all his hopes for the future were founded, especially in the presence of canty wee lasses. The dietary regime of George III angered him. "Well, I suppose the embroiling with Mrs Robinson is no secret...."

"Oh," broke in Susan, "she is a very great actress, is she not?"

"Second only to Sarah Siddons, and a celebrated beauty. The Prince first met her three or four years ago when she played Perdita in *A Winter's Tale* at Drury Lane and was enchanted by her."

"Love at first sight!"

"Feuch! He cast off a certain damsel of the Court there and then. If Mary was Perdita, he was to be Florizel. But, of late, I fancy there's a change in the wind. Mrs Robinson takes her position a shade too seriously, something such fellows are apt to find tiresome."

"And will His Royal Highness now discard her also?" asked Mary, reflecting wryly on the lot of women.

"Who cares a fig for that," put in Susan, "if one has been the mistress of a Prince?"

"You're a couthie soul, Mary," said the lawyer, moved to drop the formalities, "but don't waste your pity on Mrs Robinson, for she holds all the aces. She's a bond worth twenty thousand pounds and a large bundle of billets from the Prince. Such assets go a long way towards mending a broken heart."

Had the sisters been of gentler birth, Mr Perry would not, perhaps, have introduced this delicate topic, but it served to open the younger girl's eyes. She had listened intently to the conversation, unaware how these illustrious names were to exert a powerful influence over her destiny.

Their companion went on to say that he thought the day of the Whigs not far hence. The present Coalition could not last. Fox and Lord North were ill-assorted bedfellows, the one being the King's man and a Tory of the bluest dye, the other a confirmed partisan of the son's camp. Fox was all for the Commons electing its own Chief Minister. He was a witty, eloquent, thick-set little man in a hurry who had quickly amassed a band of supporters. Judge how flattered the young Prince was to be courted by so charismatic a person, as engagingly shabby as the Prince was impeccable. However, the real impediment was the Earl of Bute, said the lawyer. His lordship was well past the peak of his career but in former times had been the King's tutor and had instilled some rigid notions of monarchy.

They were interrupted by an elderly servant who shuffled in with a tray of refreshments which he set down on the games table by the sofa. "That will do nicely, Wheeler," Mr Perry nodded, spearing a muffin with his toasting fork and thrusting it towards the fire. "Enough of my ranting, ladies! You've not come to hear me discourse on the government, though what I do have to tell you is not unconnected with Bute. Regarding your search for situations, I might have found the very thing! The grapevine is a remarkable plant."

"Where? With whom?" Susan sounded wary.

"With Lady Talbot whose husband is a friend of Bute's. They live in Berkeley Square and need a couple of housemaids. You are from Gloucestershire, so it was the neighbourhood of first choice."

"Dear Mr Perry, thank you!" Mary cried. "We will go tomorrow, directly after breakfast."

The muffins were scorching hot and delicious and all three tucked into them eagerly. Outside, the last embers of a setting sun died and the glow from the hearth deepened.

What Mary could not have known was that these were the last moments of unalloyed pleasure she was to know in a very long time.

Mary's first impression of Berkeley Square came sharp as a premonition. She marvelled at the sun-dazzled Venetian windows of its august houses, the lawns and laurel groves where Daphnis and Chloe might have roamed, the soft echoes of an Arcadian retreat where doves chirred and doorbells created a happy assonance of their own. It was all so different from the Southwark Street of the sisters' lodging-place and the bustle of Piccadilly only a stone's throw away. There the peddlers of gew-gaws, primroses, linnets and brooms, broke into shrill cries and the organ-grinders vied for alms. Chairmen cut across the pedestrian and coach-drivers came to blows.

In Berkeley Square, the carriages came and went in an orderly fashion, keeping to the left. A knife-grinder plied a lone trade and all the scullery maids in crisp aprons and caps ran out on the cobblestones to have their cutlery honed. "Fancy!" marvelled Susan. "When you think of the way Pa sometimes used the doorstep!"

Going into service was like starting out of a dream, or of being reborn. It was a world of unfamiliar values and customs where polished manners disguised a dissipation that had little in common with the ribaldry of the Taproom of The Swan Inn. Life was lived strictly by the clock, not the sundial, and the 'London Season' had a meaning of its own.

The girls were interviewed by Lady Talbot's termagant of a housekeeper. Mrs Thwaite was a Yorkshire woman with steel-grey hair scraped into a bun and a tongue that would have 'clipped clouts' in James Perry's idiom. She was jealous of her dominion below *and* above stairs. This brusque daughter of Calvin was accustomed to quote the more vengeful texts of Scripture to keep the maids in check and looked the hopeful pair from the provinces up and down as though reluctant to be impressed. "You've no references, I see."

"No, ma'am," Mary said earnestly. "This is our first employment."

"Rely on men to vouch for you, do you?" was Thwaite's tart response.

Not until later did Mary understand the full meaning of this innuendo, but her sister was goaded to retort: "To be sure, we'd not be here if we did!"

The housekeeper bridled, but it was plain that she quickly conceived a grudging respect for Susan. "There's no hanky-panky goes on under this roof. It's aching backs and calloused knees and three square meals a day. Seven guineas a year the mistress pays to keep you in pins and worsted stockings."

Seven guineas a year! It sounded a fortune. But oh, they worked hard! Within days, bruised shadows circled Mary's eyes. No sooner had their heads touched the cambric pillows and the night-soil carts had come rumbling into the Square, than they awoke to the first rays of dawn and another day of backbreaking chopping and mopping, mending and scrubbing, wringing and polishing, ironing and starching. Before breakfast, there were rooms to be swept, ashes to be raked, fires to be stoked up and drawn with great bellows, churns to be heaved and rolled off the milk wagons. Hard work had never daunted Mary, but her unaccustomed body protested at so barbaric a rhythm.

Susan fared better but was work-shy and resented being told what to do. She larked with a footman and earned a reprimand from Mrs Thwaite. Jackson, the butler, and Tabitha, the cook, looked at one another over the griddle. Notwithstanding, Susan was emboldened to address the master of the house, whom she encountered twice on the main landing, with a hint of coquetry. He was a distinguished fellow and she could tell that she did not displease him. A subtle contact had been made. Mary begged her to behave in a more seemly fashion and not to flout Mrs Thwaite whom they relied on for bed and board.

"Who cares a button for that?" Susan said with a defiant toss of the head. "I don't mean to be stuck here for long. It's not servants they want, it's slaves. Anyway, the old battleaxe mightn't find it so easy to be rid of *me*. I've a strong notion, the Earl could be induced to miss me, what with Lady Talbot and the boys away in Ireland and no one to warm his bed!" They had yet to meet Lady Talbot. There was a Joshua Reynolds portrait of her in the hall, cast as Pallas Athene, the Greek goddess of wisdom, learning and the Arts, which showed her to be as remote as she was beautiful.

"For shame, Susie! I know you're chaffing but...."

"Am I? I'm not a prude like you, Mary. I was born to have lovers. There are pleasanter ways than this of keeping body and soul together."

The teasing strain had vanished from Susan's voice. Her sister saw that she meant it. Isolated from their own community, the new pressures had brought into relief the differences between the two of them. Mary's head was throbbing with the onset of a chill. "We were brought up to be honest and decent," she protested weakly. "You'd break Mother's heart if she could hear you."

"Well, she can't! Anyway, Mother'd be the first to turn a blind eye. Your fine scruples are all very well when there's a man to provide for you. It's time you accepted the world as it is. God helps those who help themselves."

"The Bible says it's the meek who inherit the earth."

"Oh, that old fustian put about by Mr Wesley to keep folk in their place! I'm sure the citizens of Gloucester rue the day they turned out to gawp at the meddlesome old fool."

"Mr Parsons says that there will be an uprising in France because the rich grind the poor down. He says there will be bloodshed and that the same might happen here but for Mr Wesley teaching people not to want what they can't have."

"I want my blessings in this world, not the next! Listen Mary, you'd do best to own that tis men who call the shots. If we're not to be helpless creatures at their mercy, we must learn to shake the dice to our own advantage. Play their game and you can have anything, *be* anything, you want. For I swear you're too pretty to rot below stairs. You'll end up marrying a footman and living in a poky cottage by the Thames with a clutch of brats around your skirts!"

Susan liked to strike poses, but Mary was seeing her in a new light under the city skies. How could she explain that it wasn't the influence of any ranting preacher, not even their mother's edicts, it was the grain of her own nature she felt compelled to obey? How could goodness be worth anything if one donned an outlook, like a garment, to suit the occasion?

Mary's eyes smarted from the heat of the kitchen fire where they sat darning hose while the brawn pies baked and Tabitha searched the market for fresh artichokes. "His lordship has a certain look in the eye," Susan smirked at some private joke as she held her needle up to the light for threading. "If I didn't know better, I'd say he was in thrall to my charms!"

"Surely he wouldn't tumble one of his own chambermaids!"

"Wouldn't he! If half the whispers I've heard be true, he's aiming in every particular to fill his Uncle's shoes."

The late William, Earl Talbot had been a hot-headed blade in his youth, ready to leap to the defence of the crown. He was a staunch supporter of Lord Bute who had been an intimate friend of the King's late mother, Princess Augusta. Once, this had landed him in a duel with the degenerate John Wilkes, Member of Parliament for Aylesbury, who had slighted the Scottish peer in his acidulous journal *The North Briton,* but the pair had ended up swearing eternal friendship.

Susan bent closer, quite taken up with her theme. "John Wilkes is one of the monks of Med'nham. They worship Satan and chant the Lord's prayer backwards. Did you ever hear of such a thing! Tis rumoured," she muttered darkly, behind her hand, "that they fornicate with young virgins upon an altar. Judge then, whether this family is more a paragon than the Coles!"

"Susie! That's powerful wicked! God could strike you dead for speaking so!"

"Our betters," said Susan airily, enjoying Mary's shocked expression, "are no better than they should be. Why should we wait on the like?"

"We have no choice."

"Well, for my part, I mean to be one of them. When milord discovers I'm indispensable to his comfort, he'll set me up in a snug town house and shower me with gifts and fine gowns. Yes, I'll take a leaf out of Mrs Robinson's book! When he tires of me, he'll have to buy me off and I'll take a new name and play the beguiling widow!"

"But have you no conscience? No pride?"

"They, dear sister, are luxuries for those with a bank balance. I shall acquire some pride by and by!"

By now, Mary's head was hammering. She felt faint and began to shiver feverishly, despite the heat pulsing from the grate. She could not train her eye upon sewing any longer. Mrs Thwaite despatched her to bed before supper, giving her opinion that the girl would mend fastest with sleep and a mug of her own special hot toddy.

Thankfully, Mary yielded her cramped limbs to the creaking truckle bed and lay still while the dizzying patterns inside her brain subsided and the draft took effect. She was deeply asleep when Tabitha shambled in with her battered candlestick and kicked off bunion-strained shoes worn down like careening skiffs. Scarcely had the wick been snuffed, than cook lapsed into stertorous slumber. Thus, neither remarked the absence of the elder Miss Cole, or the hour she crept stealthily to bed.

At the first servants' bell, while it was yet dark, Mary pressed herself into action, feeling a little improved, but her sister stubbornly refused to rise at so uncivil an hour. "Susie!" hissed Mary, "the Thwaite will snap at your heels all day if you're late! We'll be turned on to the street without a character!"

"What a little fishwife you're becoming." Susan stretched languidly. "Anyway, I don't care."

When she eventually deigned to appear below stairs, she looked like a cat with cream. There was something unfamiliar in her bearing. Every movement bespoke confidence. She was in a sportive humour and could not contain herself when the two of them were stripping sheets in the Earl's bedchamber.

"There's no telling how his lordship begot so many creases in one night. I swear his linen was as crisp as parchment yesterday."

"It is not of the slightest concern to us."

"Wouldn't you *die* to know?"

"Indeed not."

"Well, I happen to know he entertained a certain lady...."

"Of questionable virtue no doubt," said Mary flatly, refusing to be drawn into the conspiracy.

"So that is how you regard your sister!"

The great fourposter bed divided them. Mary was stunned. "You jest, Susie. Tell me you jest."

The appeal fell on deaf ears. "I was never more earnest. And I won't play the innocent maid led up the garden path. Give me *some* credit for honesty!"

According to Susan, Talbot had arranged to dine at White's the previous night with the Duke of Queensberry, that hideous old cullion with a sinister squint and a keen eye for supple young flesh. He had suggested to the Earl that afterwards they repair to an address in Bond Street where he might introduce a pair of comely wenches. However, old Q had succumbed to an attack of gout, a consequence of a diet of eggs, jellies, veal cutlets and other highly seasoned meats with which he was plied at two-hourly intervals of the day and the night. Sooner than pursue these pleasures alone, his lordship elected to go home and eat a light supper in his room where he was waited on by Susan with whom he had been amply consoled. She told Mary that a Persian rug had caused her to miss her footing and that she stumbled against a sofa. The master swiftly came to her aid, declaring that he never could resist a fallen woman!

Mary feared that their dismissal was now inevitable. It was only a matter of time before heads wagged and fingers were pointed. But, within days, Susan had given in her notice. There was to be no more serfdom for her! She said she intended to stay with relatives in Lincolnshire for a while, but Mary was sceptical. Who could be satisfied with the empty skies of East Anglia when they craved the excitement of London? That her sister could so lightly abandon her was indeed hurtful when they had gone to such lengths to find work together. How quickly the furnace of servitude had highlighted their contrasting characters. Well, Mary would not bolt like a frightened fawn: she would prove that she could be independent of her family and did not need to rely on a man.

As the weeks wore on, Mary struggled with mounting exhaustion. The primrose light of spring gave way to the sunflower light of summer and the plane tree leaves deepened from peridot to jade, but they belonged to a world trapped behind glass. Hardly was there time to put her nose out of doors. She began to question the value of a self-reliance which severed her from her family and native county. In London, life was organised in such a way that rich and poor were forced apart. Even the farrier, the chandler, the butcher, were intimately known by their betters in the country. At the beginning, Berkeley Square had overawed her, but now she saw it in a different light. The bastions of the rich kept the poor in constant bondage. Wages in the capital were higher, but the penalties and pitfalls were legion. There was no escape. Mary had no money. Her only hope was to explain her situation to James Perry and, to that end, she forfeited her few precious hours of rest one Thursday afternoon to call at his lodgings, walking from Berkeley Square to Clement's Inn in the City.

"Why, Mary, I have been wondering how you were faring," was his amicable welcome. "Come in and sit down."

"Please do not think me ungrateful for your kindness, Mr Perry," she said, "but Mrs Thwaite at Charles Street drives us very hard. Work eats up the whole week. We don't even go to church on Sunday."

"Well, well, I cannot pretend to be very surprised. Your sister was here, last Friday fortnight."

"Susie!"

"Extremely disaffected with her lot. I was entertaining a distinguished Member of Parliament from Nottinghamshire at the time, I recall. They seemed to get on very agreeably together. She did not want to return to Gloucester, so I persuaded her to go to your relatives in Lincolnshire and gave her the fare."

"Then she has gone to Folkingham as she said. That was most charitable, Mr Perry. I hardly know what to say."

Relief swept over her at the news that Susan was safely boarded. Perry saw that his young visitor was overwhelmed, not incensed as her sister had been. He felt her pitiable reluctance to seek help, especially since her sister had made a prior plea.

"You do indeed look fatigued, Mary, if I may say so."

"I did not dream it would be so hard to find domestic work in London. A lady – a complete stranger I met in the street – offered me training in a milliner's shop. I wonder if I should try it."

Instantly, Perry said: "No! That is not a good idea. A young lady from the country…. There are pressures. *Temptations*."

Mary was startled by this almost authoritarian reaction. She was good at sewing. "You think it wrong to pander to the vanity of women like Susan?"

He took her hand and gave it a paternal pat. Had she been out to manipulate him, she could hardly have done it with more effect. He was feeling in an inner pocket for his purse. Her situation disturbed him acutely. More, perhaps, than was merited.

"Look, take this. Go home to your mother – that is my counsel. See what awaits you in Gloucester."

Two

"They shall never get the marriage chain around my neck!" swore Frederick Augustus, 5th Earl of Berkeley, echoing the sentiments of his boon companion, the Prince of Wales.

Not even for the sake of a venerable posterity did he mean to sacrifice the bachelor freedom he'd cherished for the better part of two score years. Fred preferred not to tax his brain at all with speculation upon the future, but to abandon himself, with a sublime singleness of heart, to the pursuit of pleasure. His days were spent hunting stag and fox, or trying to recoup a dwindling fortune in the Clubs of St. James's, and his nights in hunting daughters of the *demi-monde* and other fair damsels reckless enough to cross his path. Upon the violincello, he displayed a rare talent, which he seldom indulged save in the most dilettante fashion, scraping away with the best of them in the band of the South Gloucestershire Militia of which he was Colonel-in-Chief.

His pedigree was as impressive as that of his illustrious friend and boasted a long line of nobles who lived hand-in-glove with the Throne, so it was as natural as breathing that he should discover in its latest scion a mind that was gratifyingly in tune with his own.

He was fond of relating how he was twenty-first in descent from Harding the Dane, a fierce Viking raider, come over with Swein Forkbeard, who fell on the south-western shores of England and subdued its inhabitants long before the time of the Norman Conqueror. Canute, Swein's son, might have failed to stem tides (that was reputed to have taken place on Berkeley's own estate at Bosham in Sussex!) but the seed of Harding was to prove a power in the land. Over a century later, Robert Fitzhardinge, a shrewd merchant of Bristol and Mayor of the town, sought the favour of his monarch, the red-maned little firebrand, Henry II, by lending him vast sums of money. The Royal Treasury was emptying faster than revenues could fill it after the domestic strife of the usurper, Stephen's, reign. He had made promiscuous gifts of land to his followers and Henry's first mission was to summon his council and rampage through the country forcing the new barons to surrender their tenure and all domains rightfully belonging to the Crown. This done, he turned to reward his own votaries. Not least among them was the prudent Robert who was granted lands in the verdant vale of Berkeley and a charter to build the castle of his choosing.

A crude fortress rose, complete with motte and bailey, high above the loamy banks of the Severn, rough-hewn in appearance, as though it had sprung from living rock. It was built of spice-pink sandstone and slate-grey tufa that merged into an eerie lavender at twilight when wraithlike mists stole up from the river. The marauding Welsh and Norse and French would think twice before laying siege to the place, especially when the water-meadows below its terraces could be flooded at will by a cunning system of sluices. They were lords of all they surveyed, the progeny of the good Squire of Bristol. They became Barons by Tenure for eleven generations and, thereafter, Barons by Writ, taking their name from the Vale of their provenance. If they suffered reverses, they were apt to come up smiling before long. 'The mercy of the Almighty,' it was said by one diarist of their fortunes, 'takes this family by the chin and keeps the head from drowning.'

It was George, the 9th Baron, who pleased that merry monarch, Charles II, and was rewarded with an earldom and a secondary title, Viscount Dursley. It seemed he could do no wrong for when James II succeeded his father, George was given the Lord-Lieutenancy of Gloucester and membership of the Privy Council. Despite that, the crafty fellow turned coat when his sovereign's star was in decline and vowed allegiance to William of Orange should the doughty Dutchman cross the sea and claim the Throne of England. George's conveniently malleable conscience saw him restored to the Privy Council and he died in 1698 bequeathing Charles, his son, an array of laurels and a foothold to gain even more.

James the 3rd Earl, distinguished himself by becoming First Lord of the Admiralty and the fact that he was in cahoots with George I was indicated by the audacity of a hare-brained scheme to kidnap the Prince of Wales and transport him to America when the lad was an acute embarrassment to his father. The plan was not adopted but was discovered among the King's papers after his death. Needless to say, this Lord Berkeley could not expect to prosper further under George II!

The 4th Earl was Augustus, Colonel of a Regiment which advanced on the Jacobites in the '45 Rising but never engaged them. He was a liverish fellow who imagined himself at death's door from one ailment and another and his early demise, when Fred was only ten, was ascribed to the use of quack medicines.

Assuming his father's honours at so tender an age did nothing to deflate Fred's self-importance. In contrast to his parent, he was known to be physically brave and early on learnt the knack of placing himself in dangerous situations to gain attention. He ran rings round his mother who packed him off to Turin Academy when they despaired of him at Eton, but that did not answer, for he became a libertine and a gambler whom no prospective Mama-in-law dare allow across her threshold. A Maid of Honour to the late Augusta, Princess of Wales, his mother had been pretty Miss Drax whose own charms had never been solely reserved for her husband. It was not to be wondered at that Fred should shun the matrimonial yoke and strike out on his own.

But Fred was proud of his heritage, though he took it for granted and did not bestir himself to assume the role of curator. He never paused to consider what his stewards and bailiffs might be doing behind his back, or to listen to the plaintive voice of his tenantry whose hovels were in dire need of repair.

Fred's life was a rollicking round of gaiety and devil take the sobersides who reminded him of his duties!

"Your love of dissipation," bellowed the King, "has for some months been with enough ill nature trumpeted in all the public papers!"

He was confronting his eldest son, a handsome young dog whose easy grace often perturbed him, after a cannonade of acrimonious letters had gone flying from one end of Buckingham House to the other.

"Your Majesty has his enemies, too," ventured George with an insolence thinly disguised by courtesy.

The Brunswick eyes bulged alarmingly. "Now the Cabinet invites us to discharge your debts. We are told you might reasonably expect one hundred thousand pounds a year at your coming of age. A shameful waste of taxes! Why, sir, in your position I managed on half that amount. Eh! So did y'grandfather."

"If I am to have an establishment of my own...."

"What's that you say? An establishment! A lair to plot treason with your Whiggish friends!"

"I cannot be seen to live under Your Majesty's domestic governance any longer."

"An establishment, eh? You shall have Carlton House. Make do and mend as the Queen and I have had to do all these years."

"Carlton House!" echoed the dismayed Prince. "No one has lived there since Grandmama died. The timbers are rotten and the walls are running with damp."

"It needs only a lick of paint and a stick or two of respectable furniture. For I don't suppose you shall get more than fifty thousand a year to squander on your wine and y'women, to say nought of your jewellers and tailors. You've made an unmitigated ass of yourself over that giddy actress, Mrs Floosie-by-candlelight!"

"Robinson," corrected George junior stiffly. "Rest assured, that is all over now, sir," he said, suppressing a smile at the memory of how divinely Lady Melbourne danced and how dashing he felt in her company, what discrimination she had when it came to the Arts and how her tastes so admirably concurred with his own.

"Glad to hear it. Uncommon glad. A tidy penny it's costing the nation to pension her off. You'll know better in future, what!"

A roof of his own! It would mean space and freedom. What matter if the place was a shambles? No tradesman in the land would refuse to help him transform it. And what matter when the accounts got paid? It was for George and England! He would turn that old pile in Pall Mall into a palace fit to rival the Court of St. James's.

In the summer of 1783, a few months after Mary Cole had returned to her sister, Ann Farren, in Gloucester to stitch clothes for the children and serve in Will's shop, the Prince of Wales turned one and twenty and made merry in celebration of his long-awaited liberty. Carlton House was not yet renovated, but Henry Holland, the architect who lived in the pockets of the Opposition, was desirous of executing the Prince's designs as speedily as may be and got a team of workmen to roll up their sleeves and achieve miracles in no time. By November, the place was improved out of all recognition with fine pillars and pediments amid velvet plains of new turf. The puritan symmetry of its outlines belied its gorgeous interior. Some said it was the most opulent building in England and not inferior to Versailles or St. Cloud. It had porphyry columns and gilded plasterwork and chandeliers that would have beggared an Emperor. Well, the Prince thought to show it off to the world and next spring held a magnificent *levée* there. Mr Fox was there and Mr Sheridan and

Mr Burke and all the sharp fellows who hoped to ride into office on his back. Long ago, Colonel Lake, his principal equerry, had warned him not to set too much store by the friendship of ambitious men, but George was young – he was flexing his wings – and it was sweet to be deferred to by the pungent wits of the day who had a happy knack of conceding how hard done by he had been as a result of the King's miserly regime.

Another guest at the party was his Uncle Cumberland who had been banished from Court for a torrid affair with Lady Grosvenor during which some incautious letters had been exchanged. These brought many a royal flush to his brother's cheek and cost a tidy sum to retrieve. The Duke had fallen further into disgrace by uniting himself with a commoner, the widow, Anne Horton, a gay and scandalous creature who was reputed to have lashes a yard long and a sense of humour twice as broad which necessitated the washing out of one's ears after an hour in her society. Cumberland House was the haunt of the Opposition where many a Whiggish plot was hatched and the Prince of Wales was drawn to it like a magnet. The Cumberlands were mightily amused to subvert young George from his father's fusty command. The Duke would set up his faro-bank of an evening and announce:

"Don't punt more than ten guineas, and no tick." His nephew had no objection to being fleeced of his blunt in such congenial surroundings and put it about that he wished to be invited to informal card-parties and suppers, for he heartily disliked pomp and display when it came to socialising.

But if ever George, Prince of Wales, had occasion to doubt his followers, there was one person he could always rely on for unbiased support, and that was Fred Berkeley. They were birds of a feather, he and Fred. The Earl was approaching forty, almost of the King's generation, but lacking a philosophical turn of mind, had not matured in wisdom and was game for any frolic his youthful patron might care to devise, from the masked seduction of some unsuspecting female in the shadowed walks of Vauxhall to inflating the National Debt at Newmarket.

That spring, Fred forsook his Regiment and went bowling up to Town in time for the spree, sprucely presented in his dress uniform of crimson with blue facings, gold buttons and braid, and white breeches. Now that the Treaty of Versailles had been signed and the war with the Colonists was over, the South Gloucesters were disbanding, although the sergeants, corporals and fifes remained embodied. The collapse of the Coalition, just before Christmas, had brought in a makeshift Tory administration headed by the brilliant younger Pitt. The Whigs had laughed it to scorn and forecast its doom before the mince pies were eaten, but they were proved wrong and a general election in March had given Pitt the mandate he needed for a long term in office.

The Prince hailed his confidant without ceremony. He was in a benevolent mood and indisposed to be discreet. Enough vintage champagne had been uncorked to sink a fleet which lent a misty enchantment to the universal admiration for his talent and taste, his exquisite furniture and early Dutch masters. Fred Berkeley, who hardly knew his Vermeer from Van Dyck, wasted no words of compliment. To him, Carlton House was a sumptuous new venue for gambling and Bacchanalian revels.

"Your Aunt of Cumberland is in fine form tonight," he observed, accepting a glass of Chambertin from a periwigged footman. Like most men, he was fascinated by the amorous eyes and mischievous tongue of the Duchess.

"It breaks my heart that the King will not receive them at Court," said the Prince. "What could be more exemplary of all he holds dear than the connubial felicity of Cumberland House?"

"Buff and blue, sir, that's the trouble. Makes him see red!"

His Royal Highness guffawed at this allusion to the Whigs. "She don't care a rap, God bless her, but Uncle Henry does. Tis not in the natural way of things, a rift in the family. I don't mind telling you, Fred, when I think of that accursed law they brought in after the Cumberlands' marriage, it puts me in a passion."

It was mainly on account of his brother's *mésalliance* that the King had introduced the Royal Marriage Act in 1772, forbidding a Prince of the blood, or any descendant of George II, to marry a commoner, or indeed to marry at all under the age of twenty-five, without the King's consent. Thereafter, the sanction of Parliament must be obtained. Chatham, the Great Commoner, who had served His Majesty faithfully for years, thought it a high-handed measure and went so far as to say so. But the King swore to remember the dissenters when choosing future ministers, and the bill found its way on to the statute book.

That day, the Prince had had reason to reflect at some length on this piece of legislation. He wondered whether he dared let Berkeley into his confidence after the solemn oath the pair of them had taken to remain footloose. Edging closer to his guest, he glanced furtively about the room.

"I was at Covent Garden the night before last."

"At the Opera? Pray what did you see, sir?"

"Why, I saw the most exalted vision of womanhood," said the Prince in tones of rapture.

"You don't say so! A beatific *Alceste*? No, don't tell me, a ravishing *Constanze*?"

"Confound you, Fred, you're being devilish obtuse! She was in the *audience*, in Lady Sefton's box, a distant cousin of some sort. According to the *Morning Herald*, she is the cynosure of 'a new constellation in our fashionable hemisphere'."

"And am I permitted to know the identity of this mysterious beauty?"

"Her name is Maria. Maria Fitzherbert. She's a widow twice over, poor woman, and not yet thirty."

"You've certainly a taste for the riper charmers."

"And you for the sweet and tender! A regular wolf in sheep's clothing, that's you, Fred."

The Earl pondered this and, devil take him, fancied it an apt metaphor. It conjured up a virile, predatory image, which was not displeasing. "By my life, that woman queening it in my castle at Berkeley must go! I begin to tire of her pettish ways."

Mrs Bayly, the lady in question, had been so long a fixture in his rambling stronghold by the Severn, that he had come to regard her as one of its archaic features rather than one of its ornaments.

"A handsome draft upon your bankers will console her."

"Great heavens, it will!" Lord Berkeley's martial resolution was, nevertheless, quick to desert him when he thought of the day of reckoning. "At least, it *would*. Haven't your ready backing, sir."

"Damme, Fred, with that fellow Pitt at the helm and in league with the King, I'll not have a feather to fly with by the end of the year!"

"Taxes," brooded his lordship. "Rum, brandy, tea, all the basic necessities of life! The very light of day is taxed! We'll none of us have any credit if Fox don't spike his guns."

"A man of principle, Fox," asserted the Prince. "Resigned over the Royal Marriage Act when he was at the Admiralty."

"A good thing you've no desire to hitch your cabriolet. At least that piece of mischief won't affect you."

That the Heir Apparent had a moral obligation to provide for the Succession did not weigh heavily with the Earl when he considered the Draconian expedients necessary to achieve it. His royal companion looked discomfitted. The diamond star on his left breast twinkled and flashed in the soft radiance of multiple candles and his already florid complexion deepened a shade. The three eldest of his sisters gazed down benignly from the Gainsborough canvas he had commissioned for his new home. Only Charlotte was heeding him with a faintly wry smile as if she anticipated some precipitate folly. "It's Maria," he admitted sheepishly. "Had you but seen her! Her skin is as soft as a peach and her eyes as blue as Dresden. She has the most wonderful mane of pale bronze hair...."

"Ye gods, you've been mixing your liquor!" cried the Earl, aghast.

"Fred, she's truly divine. I must have her to wife!"

Frederick Augustus gaped, drained his glass in one draught and looked at once for another. His nerve thus fortified, he attempted to reason, albeit inarticulately, with his errant friend.

"Can't....can't do it, *George*. Consider! Tis a sin against nature, saddling oneself with a spouse."

"My heart is well and truly engaged."

"Said so about Perdita and Mary Hamilton, *and* that flighty Vernon romp."

"I assure you that this is not in the same case. Please refrain from mentioning Maria in the same breath as those lemans."

Lord Berkeley could only desist, thunderstruck at so reckless a breach of their sacred pledge. That enshrined legislation would have to be overturned if the Prince persisted in this abject idiocy was the minutest particular of the situation, as far as he could see. So soon after the Prince had acquired his emancipation, the fickle fellow was to place it in jeopardy. No more wild escapades! Farewell the pleasures of the flesh! What kind of female was it who had inspired sacrifices of that order? A ray of hope then penetrated these funereal deliberations when it occurred to the Earl that young George P. was so used to having women at his beck and call that the lady's feelings had probably not been consulted. Was she even aware of his?

"I take it," he said with as much tact as he could muster, "that your Maria favours the attachment."

"Hang it all, Fred," rejoined the Prince, "I've only known her a couple of days!"

It was towards the end of 1783, when the West Country winter began to bite, that Mary Cole first set eyes upon her future husband, although she was quite unaware who he was. The redcoats would come into town for supplies and turn all the heads of the eligible women. They would go strutting along Westgate, laughing and joking, and would linger to peer into Walter Mayer's window, the jeweller over the way from Farren's shop, where they purchased trinkets for their sweethearts and brought them across for her sister's approval. They were often to be seen loafing around the shop door. Ann, though married and the mother of little ones, had a raffish sense of humour and loved to play the worldly-wise arbiter of discernment. Will Farren raised no brow: he could not afford to. One didn't offend the likes of Lord Berkeley, nor his colleague, Dan Willy, the yeoman farmer to whom Farren owed money. He'd no head for accounts, Will, and Mary quickly perceived that his business was mounted upon credit the same as her father's had been towards the end. In Butcher's Row, competition was fierce and mainly confined to the custom of simple folk. Will was not so keen a judge of steak on the hoof and a fine saddle of lamb as Cole had been and had neither his reputation nor character. Mary often pictured him, dapper as a duke, in his striped apron and straw hat, advising cooks of busy kitchens how to *fricassée* beef or spit-roast a hog to the best advantage. Whereas Will Farren's heart wasn't in the trade. He had pretensions to more intellectual pursuits and would say that when he was out of the wood, he intended to study law.

But it was Ann's neglect of her children which grieved Mary most. Henry, the baby, had entered the world on the heels of his brother, Liam, and both were in need of unremitting attention. Motherhood had given Ann no bloom; it had drained her of any fortitude she had.

"Won't you come and kiss them before they go to sleep?" Mary cajoled.

"Not now!" said her sister, preening her tarry curls in front of the looking-glass. "They'll throw up all over my new percale."

Ann had some of the prettiest gowns and tastes beyond her station. Her husband smiled indulgently upon her and swallowed his dismay at so improvident a call upon his resources, for her temper was apt to be short nowadays, and perhaps she did have a part to play in placating his creditors.

Whilst Mary patched and darned and turned sides to middle, Ann sent for copies of *La Belle Assemblée* and left them strewn about the parlour to impress the gentlemen she invited in to take tea. The journals might have imparted a subtle gentility to Chippendale's craft but did nothing to enhance the modest chattels turned on the lathe of John Boucher in Bell Lane. Ann adopted a more passive attitude than Susan and chose to believe herself a gem trodden in clay which circumstances had denied its deserved setting.

In vain Mary pleaded with her to remember the children. They were Ann's stake in the future, all she had. She would gaze deep among the linen frills of the cradle, or at her cherry-cheeked, nut-brown first nephew engulfed in slumber with his curled fist against the pillows, and wonder at the miracle of life, sprung seemingly from nowhere, and its dependency upon inconstant mortals. She would watch the baby grow pink, then puce, with colic from the buttermilk which formed the chief of his diet. Ann protested the indignity of putting a child to the breast – she had a morbid fear of being sucked dry – and soon the yield dried up and was gone just the same. Nor was she willing to pay for a wet-nurse. Mary would put the baby against her shoulder and pat his back to relieve wind, then dab her wrists and forehead with lavender water, for the sour odour of nursling vomit tended to cling. The gentle motion of the rocking chair would soothe him to sleep. It was like a defence against the world, Mary thought, a piece of armour, cradling a child in her arms, as though he absorbed *her* vulnerability.

Mrs Cole, too, chided her eldest daughter for her extravagant ways, but was seldom in the house two hours together. She slept at Mary Medlicott's, down by the pin factory, whose little son was sick of a consumptive fever and needed more care than his harassed mother could give. She also worked for Mrs Horseman at the Post Office close by and helped with the sorting of bye-letters and cross-letters, and the organising of fresh teams of horses for the diligences carrying the mail. The whole postal system had been under review in Parliament and Samuel Palmer's plans for increased efficiency were being tried.

Susannah was fond of Mary and Mary of her. The good woman generously paid over the odds for Mrs Cole's services. They were lately widows together and could parley bravely about days that would never return.

Billy, at this time, had left school and was apprenticed to Mr Parker, the surgeon and apothecary, where he kept the Day Book and learned to distinguish between a scalpel and lancet.

"He'll be much in his element," Will Farren approved, never a man to make fine distinctions. "Butchery's in his blood!"

As the weeks slipped by, Mary was conscious that something had loosened her from the city of Gloucester. Despite her experience in London and her longing for home, there was no happy niche for her there. She trod with caution, saw with warier eyes, was quick to scent danger. Even Gloucester itself had a changing face. In her absence, they had dismantled the top half of St. Nicholas' spire because it leaned at a precarious angle and the way to heaven had become oblique. By way of apology, a celestial crown now adorned the truncated tower and altered the skyline. Gloucester had been the seat of government in the Dark Ages long gone. Kings were crowned in St. Peter's Abbey and the coin of the realm was copiously minted. Once there had been a royal palace guarded by men-at-arms who valiantly overpowered the Danes and sent them packing into Wales. But the forces of Canute had later prevailed, and after that, those of William the Conqueror. Soon this ancient capital of Mercia was abandoned in favour of Winchester and London.

Thus kingdoms must founder when there is no Head to rule them. Pa had passed on and with him the old way of life.

Mother was the only anchor in that uncertain period and, outwardly at least, seemed unchanged by widowhood. Mother – and the red, iron-rich soil of the Vale which Mary never wanted to leave and had a strange yearning to till.

Meanwhile, Ann Farren grew petulant, her husband poor, and the babies cried.

It was into this microcosm over which Mary had gained some degree of mastery, that Lord Berkeley made his incursion in gold lace and heavy regimental boots.

One misty November afternoon when the merest wafer of sun had vanished and the rhythmic click of the crib on the bare floor had lulled both the nursery's occupants to sleep, Mary moved to the window embrasure to take up her sewing. A pile of her brother-in-law's shirts awaited her and many of the buttonholes begged repair which was a particularly wearisome task. Lifting her needle to the light and threading it, she chanced to glance down into the street and there espied the familiar clique of officers, stunningly bright among the drab cloaks and broadcloth of Gloucester's bustling citizens. To her astonishment, she saw that they were all gazing up at her window in demonstrable amusement. The highest-ranking, who had an air of diffident heroism about him, stepped forward and kissed his hand to her, doffing his hat in a sweeping bow. His build, fairly tall but inclined to portliness, was not that of some courtly swain accustomed to overblown manners, so that he appeared a trifle ludicrous. Perhaps it was because of this that Mary felt peculiarly touched: her whole being blushed and she shrank, with a vague gesture of acknowledgement, from the panes.

The half-hour sounded its warning chimes, an inevitable downbeat stroke.

Just then, Ann's tripping step could be heard on the stairs. She burst into the room, beaming breathlessly. Mary had rarely seen her so jubilant.

"Only fancy! You've made a fine conquest! There's a gentleman in the parlour who wishes to meet you, Mary."

"I....I can't come now," Mary faltered, conscious of her patched skirt and the unruly locks escaping her neat lawn cap.

"Take off your apron and come as you are. You always look prettier when you're flustered."

"Who is he? What can he want?"

"His Lordship of Berkeley, no less! As to the rest, we shall see!"

The Earl of Berkeley! Had it indeed been he who had saluted her just now? Though the gentleman's identity was unknown to her, the reputation attaching to it decidedly was not. "Pray make my apologies. I am not well today."

"Nonsense! You'll come down if I have to sling you! The Lord Lieutenant of the County waits upon you and all you can do is take a fit of the vapours!"

Henry began to toss and frown, Liam to whimper, and all Mary's crooning was undone. Frustration tied her protesting tongue. Will appeared in the doorway, his pale eyes glinting like a nervous rabbit and full of importunity. He was a short, obsequious man who had not the presence to make up for what he lacked in stature. Why had Ann married him? His apron was soiled; raw fetor of blood hung about him and introduced a primordial note to the innoxious smells of the nursery.

"You'll take no 'arm, girl. He's a nice-mannered fellow. Come down and work your charms on him, on *both* of them. I beg you won't vex Cap'n Willy, for there'll not be a farthing to spare in the kitty by the end of the week."

What could be more natural than a social visit to pass the time of day, Mary asked herself briskly? If she was angry at Will's incompetence and her sister's feckless ways, the children could not be forgotten. Her acquiescence could mean bread in their mouths, crusts for Henry to cut his teeth upon and milksops for Liam's supper. The Captain might even stretch Will's credit. She fumbled to loosen the strings of her apron, smoothed the folds of her gown, and followed Will downstairs, dumb as a lamb before the shearer. Henry's forsaken howl rent the upper room behind them and Mary was torn in two by an irrational sense of innocence betrayed.

Will fussed and fawned over the introductions, then shot off into the shop, vowing that his customers would by now be forming a queue halfway down Westgate. "Praise be!" cried Willy, mindful of promissory notes. Mary skimped a curtsy and looked Berkeley in the eye with a most appealing candour. "I'm honoured to make your lordship's acquaintance. Yours, too, Captain," she managed steadily.

"So you are the fair Dorcas on the other side of the glass," the Captain said.

"Egad! You've a flowery turn of phrase, Willy."

"More decorous, perhaps, than your own, my lord. 'Delectable jade,' wasn't that how you put it?"

The Earl coloured. "Stop playing Tom Fool," he commanded with some asperity. "Referring to a piece in *Mayer's* window!"

"His lordship, you'll appreciate, Miss Cole, has a fine eye for a gem."

Daniel Willy's keen grey eyes shone mischievously. Mary gathered that his pointed, and not entirely tactful, remarks were intended as a gentle warning. He apologised for the intrusion and disclaimed any responsibility for bringing the meeting about. His Colonel-in-Chief had spotted Mary on several occasions at her needlework and, knowing his comrade's dealings with the Farrens, had requested an introduction, which the gallant Captain had firmly refused. "What, expose an honest maid to your toils? I'll not answer for that, Colonel or no!"

Yet, for the life of her, Mary could not see in this bulwark of a man, blanking out the draught from their shrunken sills, anything to excite her fear. On the contrary, with his disarming touch of buffoonery, he seemed the kind of fatherly fellow a woman might instantly trust. His distinctive features were good-humoured, his high brow calm, quite a contrast to the spare handsomeness of Willy whose fatal chivalry was far more beguiling. Lord Berkeley's eyes were an unusual shade of blue which defied clear description. Periwinkle, Mary decided. The sorcerer's violet.

"Mary, be good enough to offer the gentlemen a dish of tea," chivvied Ann, bidding their guests make themselves comfortable and not wait for the ladies to sit down. They tossed their bicorne hats on to the dresser and spread themselves upon Ann's newly-brocaded sofa.

"Mrs Farren has a nice sense of priority," observed Willy, stretching out his long legs before the fender so that the pinchbeck buckles of his shoes gleamed like molten gold in the firelight. "The coffers might echo but the tea-caddy don't!"

This insinuation of debt did nothing to mortify Ann. "Why, I swear, Captain, those heifers you sent last month were all rib and no beef."

"Bless you, ma'am, I'm a man of business and can't afford to give my fatlings away!"

While Mary lodged the kettle safely on the fire and took down their best china from the cupboard, Ann disappeared to fetch lardy cake.

"Miss Cole," began the Earl, "you've been away in London, I hear."

"In service, my lord, in Berkeley Square."

"Indeed? And was life there agreeable?"

"No, sir. I badly missed the country."

"I'd lay odds," ventured his lordship, "that your situation formed your view."

Did Mary imagine it, or was there some purpose in the drift of this exchange? Captain Willy was watching with avid interest. Mary scooped out the tea, trying to control her shaking hand.

"The work was hard and the hours long. London's a lonely place, sir."

Lord Berkeley leaned forward. Something complex was encoded in the Viking eyes. Mary's heart leapt. An intimation of the unknown brushed against her....and was gone. In a single moment, she left girlhood behind.

"Come now, what have the provinces to offer a winsome girl compared to the attractions of the Great Wen?"

"We were merry as crickets at Barnwood."

"Some pretty frocks, a smart equipage to cut a dash in the Park, a servant or two to do your bidding and you'd change your tune, I'm sure."

"This is where I belong," replied Mary soberly, although she did not feel quite at home.

"Westgate does not deserve you, by God!"

The blackened kettle hissed and sang. She turned her face to the fire and the heat was intense. "I like the society of those who earn bread from the land and the loom and strive to keep the Commandments."

Captain Willy stifled a snort at seeing his colleague put out of countenance. Berkeley shuffled in his seat. He was used to light-minded females who giggled at his mordant wit and did not unseat him from composure.

"You are of this Evangelical persuasion sweeping the land, perhaps?"

"Indeed, no, sir. Mother was a cradle Catholic: her family were Jacobites. To be truthful," added Mary, "she is a little lapsed since then. She had us christened in the Parish Church."

"Uncommon glad to hear it!"

It was when Mary said with such devastating simplicity: 'I try to tread the path of virtue,' that Fred knew he must have her. The feeling was like a razor wound. In the beginning, it was not the urge to topple her that smote him; it was the wanting to cherish her unworldliness. *He needed it for himself.* This strange and sudden alchemy had invoked a place where they were equals. He admired Mary for being undaunted by his rank, for the welcome steel of her character. The Dowager, his mother, had imposed no discipline upon him, being signally unacquainted with the concept herself, and his favourite sister, the bubble-headed Lady Craven, was of much the same mould. The Earl could take neither seriously, though he doted on both.

But on that dim November afternoon, in the butcher's homespun parlour, his conditioned brain did not tumble to the truth.

"And does virtue pay the bills, Miss Cole?" he asked.

"We make shift."

"Forgive me, but your brother-in-law is not – shall we say? – in good odour with the merchants of Gloucester, nor with the farmers who supply him. Were they to foreclose...."

There was no mistaking the Earl's intentions now. Mary noticed his stubborn chin and his complacent expression. She wanted to hammer against his breast with her fists, to rail against her sisters who played into the hands of such men and perpetuated their grip. Why, even here, the black pulse of the world throbbed while the babies looked for succour. The water was bubbling and the kettle-lid trembled. She took a folded cloth and grasped the handle, steam rising about the chestnut spirals of hair. "Tis to be devoutly wished they don't, sir!"

"Why be bonded to fortune, Mary? There is another way."

She turned a dovelike gaze upon him that was tinged with sadness. "God will provide," she answered quietly.

"Even he needs his instruments," commented the Earl. "Come, let us be in charity with one another."

"I'd find that easier, my lord, if you did not press your attentions."

"Then I shall cease, Miss Cole, if it pains you," he said. "I shall strive not to put myself into a taking over your debts if you don't!"

It struck Mary that Ann's absence was overlong and that she had probably devised it so. The suspicion that there was a conspiracy under the family roof made Mary feel even more vulnerable and alone. While the tea brewed, she made her excuses to leave the room and find her sister with the cake.

"Upon my word!" exclaimed the yeoman, laughing. "I think your lordship has met his match!"

When the Earl of Berkeley left the narrow, timbered house in Westgate, his emotions were in ferment. His masculine pride, his ancestral pride, had taken no small blow. (Doubtless he would be the butt of many a private joke at the barracks for having fallen victim to the principles of a butcher's maid.) But worse, an unaccustomed sense of loss vexed him. It made him sorely dissatisfied inside his own skin. He had glimpsed a haven from himself he did not know existed and had therefore never recognised the urge to seek. His happiness lay in the manifold diversions of his lifestyle whose only penalty thus far was the taxes imposed by a Treasury anxious to sink the National Debt after the American War. Nothing had ever been denied him. Lands had been granted his forebears as their due, but here was a state that neither money nor affiliation to a cause could buy.

He could not banish Mary from his mind. Her presence filled every crevice of his being. He could hear her voice laced with the creamy lyricism of the Southern Cotswolds. She had a very different disposition from her sisters and was better spoken, conducting herself with an air that was both sedate and natural. What haunted Berkeley most was her expression when he and Willy turned from the door. She was standing sideways with both hands pressed against the doorpost, looking after him, almost wistfully, as if he alone had injured her faith in the ultimate goodness of human nature.

How he would reconcile all these feelings, he had no idea. He only knew that he must retrace his steps and find paradise, though he did not perceive it in quite those terms.

Farren continued to hang up his feathered game like a blind in the window. The taint of the slaughterhouse was stronger than usual. He sawed and hacked at his carcasses, severing bone from bone with a purblind persistence that eluded him in everything else. The sound of offal slithering and slapping into pails could be heard in the living quarters, and water being drawn from the pump to swill the yard of spilled blood. It went swirling in a cordon of lurid red down Westgate dyke.

Mary had had the nerve and the unwisdom to rebuff the mighty Earl of Berkeley whose influence was second to none in the county, and the household was hostile.

"You high-minded prig!" stormed Ann. "You've everything to gain! Think of the children!"

"No!" Mary cried, stamping her foot. "You think of them for a change! I tend them and mend for them and all you can do is flaunt yourself before weak-minded men! Must I pay the price of that?"

Jealousy and anger contorted the elder girl's lively features. Her Romany-dark eyes glinted meanly and Mary saw how soured she had become by living with a husband she had quickly learned to despise, in a trade that was unromantic and could not be made to show a healthy profit.

"Think yourself lucky, my girl! Faith, if his lordship had designs on me, you'd not see me for dust! He'd not be sporting with coy virgins!"

Mary crammed her fists over her ears. "I can't bear to hear you speak so, with infants upstairs and a husband below."

"That cock won't fight when we stink with bills. Left to you, we'd end up in the Poorhouse. Only give me half a chance to turn a wealthy man's head!"

"But you promised at the altar to be faithful to Will."

"Tis a pretty enough notion when you've the wherewithal, but the rankest moonshine when you haven't. You'd not find Will creating a stir, I can tell you, if such fortune as yours came my way."

"Hush, Nan," said Mary in a stricken whisper. "Don't you fear the wrath of God? Adultery be mortal sin."

Ann backed off with a shudder of distaste, as though her sister were a beggar-woman clamouring for a bowl of gruel at the back door. "I'll have none of that religious cant in this house, thank you, Miss."

"But marriage is a Holy Sacrament. That's what Reverend Longden called it when you and Will were wed. He said it was a symbol of Christ's union with the Church."

Ann met this with a grimace of profound revulsion. "You're mad! You should be locked away."

She turned on her heel and went from the room. Mary made to pursue her but the door slammed so that any gesture of conciliation froze before its rigid laths. Upstairs, Henry protested the need for sustenance or a dry breechcloth, or both, and Mary didn't know which way to turn. She couldn't talk to her mother, for the poor woman had grief of her own (though Ann vowed she'd be showing her petticoats before long.) Why, when Mary sought everyone's welfare, had life turned against her? Not only in London among the frivolous rich, but here, too, in the bosom of the lowly Cole family, was virtue neglected and the decencies forgotten. She tried hard to excuse the expediency stemming from a horror of debt, but was not convinced that good could ever spring forth from evil.

Christmas brought an occasion for goodwill and Mary strove not to think of the last one, when Pa had presided at table, a great fire blazing under the canopy in the oak-beamed kitchen of The Swan. They had spit-roasted a haunch of venison, raked hot potatoes and chestnuts out of the ashes, and had wanted for nothing. Several days later, he was dead.

Susan sent no word of her doings, but Cousin Ann from Thornhaugh in the Lincolnshire wolds wrote to her Aunt, Susannah Cole, to say Susan had gone up to London to seek a new post and had not informed them of her whereabouts.

"She'll be up to no good, the vain hussy," her mother prophesied. "I'd not dare lift my head if we was all back at Barnwood."

"Give over," Ann said. "Let her do as she pleases while she may. Heaven knows marriage is a hard-pinching boot."

At this the widow dissolved into sobs, never far from the surface. "Your poor Pa was a good un, Nan. He'd have sold his last shirt to keep you in ribbons.

Ann went to the cupboard and brought out a fine decanter, full to the brim, and poured out a fulsome quantity of flame-coloured spirits. "Here, sup that and be grateful."

A mere whiff caused the widow to revive. "A nice old cognac," she approved, "and all of seven shillings the bottle! Where did you get this?"

"My Lord Berkeley," replied her firstborn in a supercilious tone, casually patting her topknot. "He sent a half dozen bottles."

Mrs Cole blinked and half-choked as the brandy slipped down without the lingering appreciation it deserved. "Nan, he never! Mighty be here, you'd best watch your step! He's been the ruination of many a poor wench, that one. You'd think with a ring on your finger and a nursery full of trouble...."

"It's not me, Ma. It's Miss Prim-and-Proper and she won't so much as bat an eyelid in his direction."

"Lord Berkeley's been setting his cap at our Mary? You're bamming!"

"Indeed, I am not."

"Well, I never!" Mary watched the conflicting emotions play alternately upon her mother's face and was disheartened that she did not instantly leap to her defence. "I'm sure he'd not meet a finer female anywhere to grace his establishment," speculated she. "Think on't, a ladyship in the family. We'd be beforehand with the world for evermore!"

"Oh Ma, stop this wild daydreaming!" Mary burst out. "How can you suppose that he means anything so honourable? The Earl of Berkeley wed a butcher's daughter!"

"Mary is quite set upon casting herself as the downtrodden heroine in a melodrama," Ann sighed. "She won't see it as the greatest good fortune which might be turned to her advantage....and ours. Now, if she had an ounce of Susan's wit...."

On St. Stephen's day snow fell inches deep and sealed up the weatherboards on all the street doors. It gathered like cotton wads over the cobbles, piped the galleried courtyards of the New Inn and effaced the lacy carvings on the north side of the Abbey. It made hieroglyphs of the signboards in Butcher's Row and turned to something unspeakable when the slouch-eared hogs, fattened on whey, trotted, squealing, to market. During the week that followed, the conduits froze and the only water supply was snow gathered by the pailful and left on the kitchen range to melt.

Trade slumped. Folk kept their own hearths and simmered the bones of their Yuletide fare. Lord Berkeley could have wished for no better ally than the elements, for Will bemoaned his loss of custom and muttered resentfully about Mary's wrong-headedness. Ann, on the other hand, entirely lost her glower. Her manner softened and Mary began to be at ease now that the officers did not come.

In fact, it seemed that Ann had made a resolution to acquire some wifely skills and a concern for the welfare of others. Cheerfully, she busied herself making her mother and Mrs Medlicott a mutton pie. She spent a whole day with her bunches of dried herbs, poring over a herbal, to make a posset for the boy, Tom, whom the excessive cold had caused to relapse. Her youngest sister did not question it. It was what she had long hoped to see.

After supper, on New Year's day, Ann bade Mary leave the dishes and pans and take her offerings down to the Medlicotts' cottage. "A change of air won't go amiss, for you're grown over-pale of late," she said, bundling Mary into a cloak and setting a pair of pattens before her.

So, carrying her basket, Mary slipped out into the night. The air was diamond-sharp and the ground crisp as sugar underfoot. Stars powdered the sky, countless as the descendants of Abraham, and she wondered what 1784 would bring. The snow made a ghostly twilight of the darkness. Hardly a soul roamed the streets at that hour, although some of the shops were still open and the soft incandescence from their windows made sparklets dance across her path between deep shadows.

At the lower end of Westgate, the shops were closed. Mary quickened her pace past the darkened doorways. She could hear singing in the Abbey, a heavenly chant, hushed and distant, like a half-remembered promise.

Seconds later, she was startled by the clatter of hooves, the careering of wheels: a black landau turned out of Upper Quay Street, confronting her with dazzling lanterns. She winced as it passed, churning up mud and snow, to charge in the direction of the High Cross. In the vanishing light, she caught a fleeting movement some paces ahead. Stepping out into the road, she hurried on, wondering whether it was cutpurse or whore. Then Mary saw that the figure was a man wearing a misshapen Kevenhuller pulled down against the cold. He was huddled in a greatcoat and limped with an explicit jerk, stabbing his staff into the snow with such a curious absence of feebleness that Mary could only suppose he must be a very determined old character. "Give alms, kind lady," he waylaid her. "Take pity on a poor soldier wounded for King George at Saratoga."

"Oh sir, I have nothing to give. My purse is empty. But wait, I will run to my mother and beg a crust of bread and some cheese." She heartily wished that the mutton pie were hers to give him.

The next moment, he unbent his queer posture and thrust down his staff, the gruff West Country accents abandoned. "A crust! You would give me a crust? Why, Mary, you shall give me a lot more than that, for I am not so humble a dog as to gather the crumbs from under your table!"

Mary recognised the voice of Lord Berkeley. Instantly he seized her with the aid of an accomplice who materialised from nowhere. Her basket was snatched from her grip; the stars pitched above her and the towering walls of Westgate swerved upon their foundations as she was caught up and carried away, kicking and protesting, but nobody heard her cries. Her captors took her into a narrow lane where a carriage awaited. They bundled her inside and Berkeley clambered in after her. The door snapped shut, its blind already down. "Mary, Mary, I must have you! Will have you!" he rasped, his mouth bearing down on her own so that she thought she would suffocate. He wrenched at her mantlestrings, his weight crushing her and his skin chafing like sandpaper. Every atom of her being was focused on resistance.

"Please," she implored, "please let me go. I am not the answer."

It was an odd phrase to come from the lips of someone so young. Berkeley loosened his hold upon her a fraction. "How can you know that?"

Against all reason, Mary felt an uprush of pity and tenderness to see a nobleman of the realm expose raw and unrequited passion. Despite Berkeley's superior power, the fear drained out of her. A deep intuition told her that she had a moral ascendancy to which his sensibilities would yield.

"Fornication's a powerful wicked thing!"

"Mary, do you not understand? You could be mistress of my castle with no one to usurp your authority, for I shall never marry. You need have no fear of that!"

"And when you are done with me, what then? How should I return to my own kind with my reputation in tatters?"

"Christ, wench, you could have been ruined under a haycock by some common farm hand! I would take care of you."

"I shan't ever submit to you, sir, not of my own free will!"

"Oh, but you shall," he said thickly, his strong hand grappling with her bodice, closing in a spasm of agonised pleasure upon her breast. She gasped with pain. His breath burned upon her stinging lips. "I could take you here in this carriage, if I chose, but I shan't. I shall prove to you that I've some regard for your person. It profits me nothing to cause you distress. But, believe me, my sweet Mary, I will yet have you on your knees begging me to take you." So saying, he flung wide the vehicle door. "Pegler, give the lady her basket and send her home to her mother. Let some lusty cowherd take joy in deflowering her!"

Weeping now and faint with shock, a dishevelled Mary found herself deposited in the street while the carriage rapidly forsook the scene. Even though she had escaped lightly, she felt unclean and absurdly drenched in the guilt of Eve. Still more baffling was a sense of something akin to remorse at having inflicted injury. Hastily, she gathered her clothes around her and hurried away. Flurries of snow were beginning to whirl through the air and bewilder her vision. Presently, she caught sight of the flares glimmering on the Post Office wall. Sobbing with relief, she stumbled up the Medlicotts' porch step and jangled the bell. There were stirrings in the depth of the house. She could hear Tom coughing. Mary Medlicott opened the door, her round, motherly countenance sane as a fresh-baked Sally Lunn. "Oh, Mrs Medlicott! I'm so glad to see you!"

"Why, look you, Susannah, tis Mary, for all the world as though she's been wrestling with Satan himself. There, pet! Come on in. Shake out your cloak and sit by the fire. I'll make you a mug of chocolate."

"Mercy me, child! What ails you?" cried Mrs Cole. "You look as though you've taken a fright."

By the safety of Mrs Medlicott's hearth, Mary stammered out her sorry tale. Her mother grew alarmed and her friend fumed with indignation, stout pillar of the Southgate Meeting founded by Mr Wesley that she was. "He threatens to ruin us," Mary whimpered. "Ann and Will and the children an' all. I won't go back there. She's in cahoots with the Earl. As it says in the Good Book: *a man's enemies be those of his own household.*"

Snowdrifts hindered the mail and an unaccustomed quietude fell on the house. Tom's colour was high and his eyes limpid with fever. Mary took turns with her mother at his bedside, sponging his brow and removing the red-clotted rags after each bout of coughing. Mr Parker came and roundly condemned Ann's meddling. "Witches brew!" he bellowed and emphasised his disgust by pouring the foul-smelling decoction into the chamber pot. He had brought a jar of leeches and applied them to the boy's chest to draw out the harmful humours. When he packed his instruments into his bag, he left a bottle of strong paregoric to ease the patient's cough. Mrs Medlicott could not pay him there and then. The cost had risen steeply since the introduction of the new patent laws. She would have to bury her pride and call upon Parish Funds.

Mrs Cole watched the writhing creatures fix upon Tom's skin and become gross and sluggish. "Tis a shameful thing when poor sick mortals have to bear the brunt of the war. What do we want with colonies across the sea when we can't even feed the folks in England?"

"We must suppose," Mary said, "that the new law is to protect us from remedies like Ann's which are sold for gain."

"Which reminds me," her mother went on, "I didn't see fit to tell you before, Mary, on account of your being so upset, but that tall officer was round at your sister's yesterday, calling in debts."

"Captain Willy! What did she say?"

"She told him she hadn't a penny piece that wasn't spoken for. Will stood behind her, wielding his meat cleaver over a side o' mutton and I'll vow the Captain thought twice afore pressing his claim!"

"He made no more ado?"

"No such thing! He told her they must pay a guinea a week until all's square."

A guinea a week! That was a princely sum to the Farrens, but a generous concession on the Captain's part.

"Perhaps Lord Berkeley has repented his oath," Mary surmised hopefully. "Or perhaps the Captain will have no part in his treachery."

"He'll foreclose if they fall behind. I don't know how they'll manage, I'm sure," her mother rambled on, "what with all the farmers swooping down on Will at once and refusing to let him have any more beasts. He can't afford to buy in the Gloucester market with the other butchers bidding high. Then there's that fancy French madam who runs up Ann's clothes dunning her for the price of a bonnet and gown. And the coal-heaver looking for eight shillings the half-ton. Your poor Pa went to the grave, sore at his failure. He died of a broken heart, so he did. I'm thinking twill be just the same for our Nan and she's only been wed these two years." Mrs Cole sniffed and rummaged in her sleeve for a handkerchief, avoiding her daughter's gaze. She slumped down on the cane-bottomed chair, rocking herself to and fro. "Tis a hard life. My poor hands are calloused and my bones weary and there bain't a brass farthing to show for it. We never come through the tunnel into the sunshine."

Mary quavered in her shoes and her breath would not come. So it *was* happening: the net was tightening about her. She would always remember the details of that room, starkly rendered in the bare grey January light falling through the windowpanes. The pale linen, the beams and the bedstead darkened with age, the scarlet stains of disease, emblems of life and death.

"I'd best make some oatmeal broth for the boy," the matron said, "or he'll not keep body and soul together."

She shuffled off in the wrinkled old shoes that were so much a part of her person, goaded by necessity into keeping a grip on life. She was fumbling in the patch pocket of her apron for the snuff she kept in a twist of paper and sniffed behind doors, or among the sage bushes at the back of the privy. Watching her, Mary's heart was as heavy as lead.

When all was quiet, the boy turned his raven head on the pillow, at peace now that the spasm had subsided. The spectre of a smile softened the budding features that prematurely wrestled with pain. The liquorice-black eyes had a peculiar lustre. "I had a dream, Mary, of a land where summer is endless and the swallows never fly away."

Mary sat on the counterpane and listened while he told of crystal streams that were sweet for slaking thirst, of petal-skinned children who held out their hands to him. They didn't have to climb chimneys or wind shuttles for the weaver's loom, or grope about in the darkness under the earth to bring coal out of the mines. The wild animals did not prey upon one another and the people were happy. Their doors were never locked.

"That's how it was in the Garden of Eden," Mary told him, "before Eve ate the apple and let the Devil loose."

"You gottoo tell them...." Tom whispered fiercely. Anxiety brought on another bout of wheezing: Mary helped him to sips of his mother's honey and lemon mixture. "....tell them I don't want to be in the shadows. I want to be with Pa and Aunt Hughes from Llandrindod Wells who used to send me plum candy at Christmas. Let me go easy. I'm all right."

"Hush now, tis the fever talking. You must grow strong again and be a comfort to your mother."

Tom stared at Mary accusingly. He had trusted her with his dream and she was not on his side. A hollow raking cough erupted from the depths of his ribs. Mary tried to take him in her arms and soothe him. His small skeletal body burned beneath the clammy flannel nightshirt and, for one transient moment, she experienced his predicament, stranded as he was between two ways. "I'll tell them, Tom. I promise I'll tell them."

The cough subsided into a rasp. The child exhaled a halting sigh, a sudden aching weight against her. She released him gently to seek a requiem among the pillows, blinking back scalding tears.

Mary heard her mother's tread upon the stairs and turned to meet her at the door, unable to speak. Susannah's face was flushed above the steaming bowl of gruel as Mary had seen it flushed countless times from stirring over the fire, bearing the heat of the day. Words churned senselessly around her head, but her tongue could not lay hold upon the right ones. She took the tray. In apprehension, her mother searched her eyes, as she had not dared to do half an hour ago when they were speaking of debt. "God 'ave mercy," she blurted out, crossing herself. "I know what you're going to say."

"Mother, I must leave, go where the Earl cannot find me. Surely, he'll not hold us to ransom when his cause is vain."

Lord Berkeley's cunning measures were biting hard. Will was summoned to appear before the Magistrates at the next Quarter Sessions. Though Mary forgave Ann the intrigue which had hastened her downfall, Ann would not forgive Mary for choosing the course least likely to prevent it.

"You always was a good girl," Susannah said stoically. "Not like your sisters playing fast and loose with anything in buckskin breeches."

They were strolling by the docks. Cargoes were being unloaded from ships borne in on the spring tides. Wind whistled and jingled in the forest of rigging which meshed a pearl-white sky. Pigtailed sailors worked nimbly to stow and store, the scent of tar and other lands upon them. At Gloucester, the East Indiamen and sea-going cutters would transfer their goods into barges or shallow-draft frigates to travel upstream of the Severn into the Midlands. Sugar, spice, tobacco and cottonseed were exchanged for ironware from Coalbrookdale and the raw mineral for the local pin factory, fine porcelain from Staffordshire, timber and cereals from Worcester. This traffic relied upon the flood water coming down from Wales to bear it along, for the bulkier ships could not navigate higher than the Berkeley Pill and it had been mooted that a canal be cut between Gloucester and Berkeley, though the cost of such an enterprise was no small obstacle.

"What choice have I but to put myself out of Berkeley's reach?"

"But where shall you go? There's no avoiding him in this county, nor the next."

"Mrs Horseman tells me of a position at a vicarage in Kent with a salary of £6 a year. As postmistress she is in a way to learn these things. She thinks it would suit me perfectly."

"That's a tidy wage for the country," considered Susannah.

"About right for a lady's maid."

"Well, but you've had no training for that."

"I'm as fair a needlewoman as any seamstress, Mother. Mrs Horseman says I'm to go to Mr Whittick in the town who will give me lessons in how to dress hair."

"And who's to pay for that, may I ask?"

"Mrs Foote, the vicar's wife. Isn't that kind?"

"Don't count your chickens, my girl. You've still to be hired."

"Oh, but that is quite settled," Mary assured her, beginning to chuckle. "Mrs Cheston from the Southgate Meeting has bought my earnest and has booked a seat on the London and Dover diligence for next Friday. Mrs Foote's sister lives in Gloucestershire and she is Mrs Cheston's friend."

"Well, I'm staggered, blessed if I ain't! You've tied it all up and your longsuffering Ma the last to hear of it!"

Thus, at the breaking of dawn, on a sober Friday morning during Lent, Mary gathered up her bundle once again, made her farewells, and set out for Boughton Malherbe on the Kentish Weald, and Mrs Foote, her new employer.

Three

"The bird has flown! She is gone to France! Oh, to kiss the soil of Calais!"

George, Prince of Wales, was pacing his apartments at Carlton House in great agitation, having received an enquiry from Lord Berkeley, just returned from his country seat, as to the welfare of Mrs Fitzherbert. So the rumours had substance!

"Why?" responded the astonished peer, justifying his sister's nickname for him of Milord Pourquoi. "*What for?*"

"She took fright at the strength of my ardour. She refused my hand when, I swear by heaven, she is the partner of my soul." The Prince lowered his voice in contrite mood. "To tell the truth, Fred, I did give her quite a scare. I had swallowed a quart of brandy. I was beside myself, you understand, lost to all reason, in the utmost despair...."

"Trust me, sir, I take your meaning."

"Ran myself through with a rapier! Near as dammit pierced the heart! I sent for Maria and vowed to tear my bandages off if she wouldn't have me! There and then, I slipped a ring on her finger, should I not pull through!"

"The deuce, *George*! A close shave!" The Earl paled and fell to thinking how it might have been a Frederick to punctuate the run of Georges under the nation's crown. (The Duke of York was known to be the King's favourite.) Could the passions of a moment have such awesome power to subvert destiny?

"This Catholic thing is a cursed millstone," said the Prince.

"Religion," mused his companion gloomily. "It's pretty much fouled up the course of history. What shall you do?"

"I've a mind to go after her. Live abroad for a while, close up this house, economise. That is how I have put it to His Majesty. He won't hear of it, of course. He says if I forsake my responsibilities here, I will lose the goodwill of the people."

"Your popularity *has* been assiduously nursed."

"In any case, that will be lost – my Whig friends will grow cool – if the King has his way."

"Oh?"

"He complains of my debts. I've not done with enlarging this place: it has run through a fortune, but how am I to perform my duties if my salary is not commensurate with my position? My father promises to help, provided I turn coat and favour the Tories!"

"A dastardly thing when a fellow can't follow his own conscience!"

"He has always hated me since the age of seven."

Berkeley let rip a roar of laughter. "Forgive me, sir, but that being the case, you'd do well to steer clear of the Berkeleys! Puts me in mind of my grandfather, James, the 3rd Earl, who devised an outrageous scheme for having your grandfather transported to the Americas and conveniently lost, such an encumbrance was he to George I!"

"The hubris of the man!"

"It is well chronicled, I assure you. It probably accounts for why my grandfather was not re-appointed as First Lord of the Admiralty at your grandfather's accession!"

"Well, bless me, tis not only Popery drops a spanner in the works! Remind me, exactly, on which side were your esteemed ancestors at Culloden?"

"Suffice to say, we Berkeleys have no head for treason," grinned his lordship, with as much truth as ambiguity. "As for the Cloth, sir, *it* don't see us if we see *it* first!"

"Whereas dear Maria is wedded to the Church and I am wedded to the State."

His lordship's mind did not run upon spiritual matters and his heart would not assent to such abstractions as a Deity uncommitted to providing a good hand at cards. Since his friend, George P., had persisted in dedicated pursuit of Mrs Fitzherbert, Fred had been made acutely aware of the painful torments of conscience suffered by those adhering to Roman Catholic doctrine. ('Hell-begotten Jacobines' HRH had called them.) It had been impossible to breach that good lady's honour. Maria was, as she so trenchantly observed, not good enough to be his wife, but too good to be his mistress. The approval of both King and Parliament regarding her status as a commoner was the least of it. To add to his plight, the Prince was forbidden to marry a Catholic unless he forfeited his right to the Throne, and that would have been a perfidious thing. It seemed impossible that the new star of the Hanoverian line should be denied his life's desire by a religious chauvinism on both sides of the fence.

The conversation had begun to stir up feelings of unwonted empathy in Berkeley. He was beginning to bind himself into the same dilemma with a female half his age and of a far humbler station than Prince George's widow. This was terrain he had neither trodden nor owned in his two-score years of experience, and it was nettling. He had a sensation that the very portraits slung about these damask walls, safe in their own pastoral idyll, were mocking him.

"I really don't comprehend....I don't *see*."

"What is it, Fred? You look as though you are trying to fathom calculus."

"Why, by all that's famous, are you set on marrying this lady? Can you not make her a duchess and have her live at Court? Commitment is not the prerogative of marriage: it is a private undertaking. I trust that is the active principle in these forensic deliberations."

The Prince slumped down on a feather-backed chair. "If only it were so simple, but true love should not run smooth.... Maria would see no honour in what you suggest. It is not *merely* the Constitution, Fred. The lady has scruples! Her beliefs will not allow her to live, as she sees it, in sin."

"The fact that you will be the first gentleman of Europe and not your own man.... The fact that an oath of allegiance to her monarch is required...."

"....is not germane to the issue. My status counts for nothing in this! What the Vicar of Christ dictates must be obeyed. We are speaking of mortal sin and eternal damnation. You have no idea of these Papists!"

Frederick Augustus let go a lengthy sigh. The phrase: 'my status counts for nothing' stung on the raw and might easily have applied to him. "Oh, I think I am gaining a fair idea, sir. The measure may be different, but fate has dealt me a similar conundrum."

"You, Fred! What can you possibly want that you can't have?"

"There is a young lady...."

"And you swore you'd never marry! We both did."

"Oh, this is not in quite that league...."

"By the pain on your face, I must beg leave to doubt it."

Berkeley hastily collected himself, irked by his own weakness. "The artful little vixen has run to earth. But I shall find her. I shall flush her out. See if I don't!"

It wasn't long before Mary heard the first cuckoo call, aloof and libertine across the Kentish meadows. Nomad sheep, turned loose from their winter quarters, foraged amidst the blond rye grass where sea holly sprouted and the lark built her covert home. Mary loved the sound of the wind moaning across the marshes, the restive main gnawing away at the land's fringe like a silver beast, and tales of smuggling told in tarred, weatherboarded cottages at eventide. It was true enough, for all he was a clergyman, that the Reverend Mr Foote suffered no deprivation of his favourite cognac, despite Mr Pitt's killjoy taxes.

Kent was a different world in which Mary recaptured some of the lost joys of childhood. Mrs Foote was a kindly mistress, easy to please. Anne Powell, the housekeeper, with whom Mary shared a bedroom, introduced her to the neighbourhood and was her constant companion on woodland strolls. Aconites, wood anemones and celandines gave way to drifts of indigo as the bluebells flourished and the vetches peeked into flower. The sun was as bright as a pollen-pad and showers made the earth sweet and left glassy spherules suspended upon the waxen-leaved laurels and the spiny bifurcations of juniper boughs. Cracks appeared in the speckled aquamarine of blackbirds' eggs, bursting with the regeneration of life.

Slowly the seasons turned. Sloes swelled on the blackthorn: ladysmocks, buttercups and marsh marigolds came into bloom. The hedgerows were spangled with frail pink dog-roses when the first hay-crops were scythed and the women and children turned out to do the tossing. The corn's plaited ears filled out and went by degrees from bleached green to gold. In September, the barns were bursting with grain, the hop-kilns emitted a new pungency, and the throbbing strains of frolicking lingered long into the night. At dawn, responsible dairymaids scrubbed out their butteries and shelved the best cheeses for winter. There the rind would coarsen and the mould multiply in the fissures of each muslin-clad moon, stored and matured until the cheese factor should come on his rounds the next spring and sniff out a price from his sample cores. The local cheeses were not so widely-sought as those made in Gloucestershire which many agreed had no rival on earth.

Each Sunday, between morning worship and the bell summoning servants to the kitchen to contemplate a huge crown of lamb, or a mackerel pie, Mary scribbled a letter to her mother, though the replies were spasmodic. Susannah had an unsteady hand, poor soul, and feared that the written word would betray her lack of learning. Will had been put away in jail and Ann was forced to move out of the shop to a snug property on the corner of Bell Lane and Southgate. (Where the rent money came from, Mary did not know, but could only conjecture that Will's brother,

Ellis Taylor Farren, who had lived next door to them in Westgate, had come to her aid. After all, he was, at that time, a bachelor and had no family of his own to support.) Mr Parker was regimental surgeon to the South Gloucesters and Billy had thus had some dealings with Lord B.

Equally disconcerting, in its way, was the news of Susan. She was in the rudest health and had turned up, bold as you please, bedizened with feathers and gew-gaws, driving a sleek phaeton, a black tiger perched up behind. 'Imagine it,' her mother wrote, 'it fair took my breath! The neighbours turned out to gawp, saucer-eyed.' Susan had married a Mr Turnour who was in a fine way of business up in the West End of London, to the great envy of Ann.

Detached, on the far side of the country, the news reached Mary like a muffled echo. She was glad to have no part in it, but as the shadows of dusk deepened, she could not stave off the yearning for home. She was happy in her new life, at peace with everyone and everything about her, but she was in exile.

With a willing heart, she helped Mrs Powell preserve the taste of summer in damson cheese and quince jam. They brewed ale and cider, pickled walnuts, polished apples and stored them away in wooden racks in the loft. Between sewing for her mistress and accompanying her upon charity visits about the village, Mary was a good deal occupied that autumn and had no leisure to repine. In the fields, hosts of excitable gulls followed in the wake of the plough teams. The whistling plough-boys kept their sights dead ahead, steering an even course, so that the ground was cloven with new furrows, neat as cord.

Then, on the second Friday of Advent, when preparations for the festive season were well under way, the pleasant rhythm of Mary's life was interrupted by a missive from Susan. She would always recall how bitterly cold it was that morning: the water in the ewer was trapped under ice and the windows so feathered with patterns that the rime on the trees couldn't be seen. Susan exhorted her sister to give a month's warning, to let bygones be bygones and to come to London to live with her. They would be as happy as larks together, she said, just as they'd been in the old days. She had married a wealthy gentleman with investments in the City whose long absences left her free to do as she pleased. She could not bear to think of Mary enslaved in service when she was able to provide for her.

Mary was elated to hear from Susan in these terms, but had misgivings about living in London. Having failed with Ann, the chance of mending the rift with Susan was doubly appealing.

Surely Susan would not have sent for her had she not repented of her profligate ways. Within the space of an hour, she handed Mrs Foote her notice, showing her the letter, and wrote to her sister asking that she be good enough to send the fare.

A week passed and no reply came. Then, one morning, Mrs Foote summoned Mary to her bedside, pushing an awkwardly phrased, and hopelessly misspelt, communication into her hand.

In it, Susan begged Mrs Foote to release her sister the week after Christmas as she was 'obliged to go in the country the week following' and wished to see Mary before she left. Mary cringed at the stilted sentences which were a brave attempt to demonstrate education. And where was the money for the coach?

Her mistress pressed her hand sadly, "My dear, I shall miss you. Your happy chatter has brightened many a dull morning."

"Ma'am, I've no wish to leave, not on my own account, but I must go to my sister."

Mrs Foote regarded her charge with a vaguely troubled air. Climbing out of bed and releasing a mass of wiry curls from her lace nightcap, she put on a wrap and settled upon the dressing-stool to converse with Mary's reflection. "Of course you must go. Only I beg you won't get out of the way of reading your Bible and saying your prayers."

"Truly, I've no taste for London."

"But this time will be very different from the last. Your sister is well established and will be able to chaperone you. You will meet a variety of interesting people. Dr Johnson, for all he's a gouty, ill-tempered fellow, says that when a man is tired of London, he is tired of life."

"Well, I daresay he never came to Boughton Malherbe, ma'am, nor to Barnwood, either!"

Mrs Foote responded with a mirthful twinkle and presently observed: "Charles Street? That's Berkeley Square, is it not? Why, I recollect when the late Lord Berkeley of Stratton laid it out, years ago, during the reign of George II."

How the journey to London should be financed, when Mary had only two gowns and two petticoats to her name, greatly exercised her mind. Hesitantly, she confided in Anne Powell. The good woman promptly took down a blue ginger jar from the mantelshelf, a fairing some sweetheart had bought her long ago, and poured out a heap of coins, like manna, silver and copper and gold, on the counterpane. She put a sovereign and a half into Mary's hand and pressed her fingers over them.

"Take it," she insisted. "We'll say it's a loan. And when you become a fine lady, I'll remind you of it."

Escorted by Challoner, the gardener, whose task it was to collect the post from nearby Lenham, Mary booked a seat on The Union, gathered her few possessions together, and on New Year's Day, 1785, set out in drenching rain for the capital.

"Upon my honour, it gave me no pleasure to see that snivelling butcher brought to the Assizes and put away. I did not think twould be necessary."

Having completed their business in Gloucester, Lord Berkeley and Captain Willy had repaired to the King's Head for a dinner of roast potatoes and beefsteak in the inglenook of the fireplace.

"You are not responsible for his debts, my lord. No more am I."

"Common folk are getting too fine a conceit of themselves!"

"If I may say so," remarked Willy, staring into his tankard of porter, "you grossly misjudged your prey. She's too fine-strung a creature for your snares."

"I feared she might be immured in some nunnery," brooded his lordship, thinking of Maria Fitzherbert. "Still, a parsonage is not a port to be stormed!"

"The Goodwife Farren has too loose a tongue."

"Boughton Malherbe! The little minx! Do you know, Willy, I can hunt all the way from Berkeley to Piccadilly on my own lands, but Kent is Sackville territory. The sport south of the Thames is reputed to be unrewarding!"

The Captain strove to keep command of his countenance. He was immensely cheered that his Colonel's delicate quarry had managed to elude him and hoped that he would now concede defeat. Willy could not, for the life of him, see what sport was to be had with an unwilling partner.

"There is another filly in that stable," he said guardedly, "not quite so high-bred, but well-looking. Whatever happened to her, I wonder?"

Lord Berkeley's eyes sparked with the intimation of a smile, but he made no reply.

Skidding and scrambling, the coach lurched towards London, riding the ruts opened up by the weather, gaining the highway and leaving the Weald far behind. For Mary, it was strange to be turning back into the old path, old and yet new, approached from another direction. That escape in the 'garden of England' had so little connection with what went before and what came thereafter.

It was just after six-o-clock in the evening when The Union pulled in at The White Bear in Piccadilly. Through a curtain of rain, the link-boys trailed flames through the darkened streets, mirrored dimly in the wet pavements. The hawking shouts of ostlers competing for custom rose above the milling crowds. Aching from cramp and damp, Mary alighted and was pulling her hood over her hair when there came a tap on her shoulder.

"Miss Cole? Is it Miss Cole?"

Wheeling round, she confronted a familiar face, glowingly disembodied beside the hurricane lamp he was holding up.

"John Gwinnett! What are you doing so far from home?"

"I'm here to meet you, Miss Mary. Mrs Turnour sent me. I run footman for her." He took hold of her carpet-bag and bade her follow him.

"Susan is become a rather grand lady, I hear."

"Out of the top drawer, you might say. Set up very nicely, she is, Miss."

His artless pride in her success was touching. John Gwinnett and his brother, Theo, had been good friends of Billy's. They'd gone to Mr Cooke's school together, in the Oxbody Lane in Gloucester, and used to walk all the way there each day from Barnwood, chalking their names on the gateposts as they went and leaving signs which peddlers interpreted as an invitation to trade with the unwitting residents. They'd talked of becoming pirates on the Barbary Coast, if the Royal Navy didn't press-gang them first!

Bent against the weather, they arrived in Charles Street where Susan greeted her sister in all the paraphernalia of a fine lady going to the opera, a gown of bronze-green damascene and shoes to match.

"Lud, Mary, you're soaked!" she cried, bestowing the merest accolade in order to keep her careful *toilette* intact. "I'd have sent a carriage for you, but we're on the point of leaving for Drury Lane."

She introduced her aide, Mr Edward Howarth. He was a friend of her husband's, she said, who did office as escort when Mr Turnour was absent. He wore a brilliant diamante waistcoat and his pale, girlish curls were made yellower with turmeric powder. Teddy was a scribbler of mannered sketches whose plots relied heavily on mistaken identity. He proffered Mary a limp hand, as though mightily amused at his own affectation.

"Y'sister looks a trifle peaky, methinks. A night at *The Beggar's Opera* would be a splendid tonic."

"How convenient we have a box!"

Mary's opinion was not sought. Her sodden cloak was whisked away and she was duly swept into the parlour and plied with tea and sundry dainties. She protested the shabbiness of her gown, a durable homespun in an unappealing shade of mustard. Susan's response was to frogmarch her to her boudoir and, while Mary freshened herself with Hungary Water, to tear many lengths of black lace, at sixteen shillings the yard, from which she conjured a fichu and panniers for her sister's bodice and skirt.

"There! You look a perfect angel," she announced when her task was done. "You will capture the hearts of all the gentlemen and turn their ladies green with envy."

The cheval-glass threw back a strange and dejected image. "I look more like a devil than anything," was Mary's conclusion. She loathed artifice and was out of her depth. The degree of affluence in Charles Street had taken her aback and Susan's welcome was not what she had hoped for. It was as if they had no shared past, at least nothing that her sister was prepared to acknowledge. There were a myriad questions upon Mary's tongue but, lacking privacy, she had to content herself with asking when she would meet her new brother-in-law.

Susan glanced at her uneasily. "All in good time. Indeed, I do not know, for he is gone to....to Liverpool on some tiresome mission."

In the flurry of preparation, Mary quickly forgot the day's exertions. Going to the theatre had become a mundane event for Susan who had a box for the winter season. Everyone was in a fever of anticipation because Dorothy Jordan had come over from Dublin and was to play Peggy in *A Country Girl*. Reviewers were lauding her performances in the north of England.

They had not settled on their gilt and velvet chairs above five minutes before they were joined by a couple of Susan's friends, a young widow, Mrs Jemima Devine from Virginia, and a stout baronet, Sir Thomas Kipworth. He occupied a chair next to Mary and went out of his way to engage her in conversation. She was not ungrateful, for while the rest of the group were amicable, they were bound in a coterie which did not include newcomers. At curtain-up, Mary was soon transfixed by the colour and comedy of John Gay's rollicking tale of Polly Peachum and

Captain McHeath, her highwayman lover. To her delight, she found that some of the melodies were familiar and her fears that it might be a high-brow presentation full of characters from mythology proved groundless.

At the end of Act I, a great chandelier was lowered from the ceiling and relit to intensify the light shed by clusters of candles around the balcony. Susan took the opportunity to scan the audience for notable people.

"Why, I swear," she declared, "that's his lordship of Berkeley in the opposite box. Fancy!"

In alarm, Mary seized the opera-glass from her. Susan was right! The convex of that philanderer's brow, the mulish jaw, were indelibly scribed on Mary's mind. She distinctly saw him adjust his own glass and train it full on their box so that somewhere in the midst of the auditorium their line of vision must have fused and blurred.

"Teddy, do go and invite him to join us," Susan ordered.

"Indeed, Mr Howarth, you must not!" Mary cried.

"Don't be absurd, Mary," her sister chided. "Do you imagine he's still eating his heart out for you?"

Mary reddened. She imagined no such thing, but did not think the Earl a man to take a snub lightly. Wasn't this he who had been instrumental in putting their brother-in-law away?

Mr Howarth hesitated, glancing from one to the other. "You will find him quite affable, Miss Cole, I assure you," he said graciously, and disappeared before she could reply.

Moments later, Berkeley's presence filled the box. He was turned out in dashing style in the dress uniform of his regiment, gadrooned with ells of gold braid, a gleaming scabbard at his side. He appeared to be acquainted with all the members of the party and greeted them with his curious brand of retarded charm, turning to Mary last and bending over her hand in mock gallantry. The hilt of his sword flashed.

"So you have elected to throw in your lot with the urban savage, Miss Cole? We've none of your worthy country ways here."

Spurred by the thought of Will Farren in Gloucester jail, she surprised herself by responding in kind: "Though you do not disdain the humble folk ballad as a means of diversion, I see, my lord."

Mary vowed to herself that she would not be baited, she would not live under this man's dominion. If she had to, she would shame him into respecting her.

"I believe you are much altered since we last met," observed the Earl lightly, with the finest trace of appreciation.

"A little wiser, perhaps."

Just then, the central chandelier was dowsed and hoisted up, the hubbub dying away with the icy clink of its pendants. The orchestra took up the melodramatic theme of revenge and love blighted. The Earl made to take his leave, but Susan detained him.

"Your lordship might care to take a bite of supper in Charles Street after the performance."

"Obliged to you, Mrs Turnour. Esteem it a favour."

With that, he bowed and made his exit, leaving Susan to resume her seat with an air of satisfaction.

The curtain went up on Act II.

Supper was a lavish array of cold delicacies. Mary marvelled that her sister's fortune ran to providing such a table. Laid out were pheasants and partridges, quails' eggs in pâté, frosted fruits, mince pies and table creams. They were waited on by John Gwinnett and Soubise, the young slave of ten or eleven who had travelled down to Gloucester with Susan last summer. His rolling eyes, black as molasses, remembered another culture, the tattoo of rituals more potent than the posturings of European civilisation.

The evening, nevertheless, was not a success. The champagne punch and the converse quickly went flat. Sir Thomas drank enough to sink a man-o'-war and, lamenting the death of the great lexicographer, Dr Samuel Johnson, whose society he had frequently enjoyed at The Mitre Tavern, fell under the sofa where the company left him to snore prodigiously. Susan babbled away to Jemima Devine who vowed she just adored the neat little shepherdess gowns that were coming into fashion. Then the new white muslins brought over from the West Indies were discussed, and the inadvisability of applying ceruse to the complexion because its lead content was discovered to pit the skin and turn it yellow, particularly when exposed to the warm vapours of the mineral springs at Bath. Edward Howarth took out a lacquer toothpick case and, selecting a fine tool of coral, embarked upon some molar excavation. Lord Berkeley bemoaned his diminished revenues for the year just gone and, turning to the subject of the chase, stated that nothing would induce him to part with his staghounds. He was proud of the Berkeley Hunt's long tradition and had seen the wearing of saffron yellow coats re-instated. Queen Elizabeth had once ridden with the Berkeley and had slaughtered so many deer in her host's absence that he had been moved to a daring protest but had backed down when Lord Leicester, the monarch's favourite courtier who coveted a large portion of the Berkeley acres, claimed he could prove good title to them!

"I remember," mused Frederick Augustus, turning towards Mary in an almost confidential manner, "not long after the King's Coronation, we were hunting the Silkwood covert with the Beaufort, on the trail of a fine red stag, but the animal eluded us and cut short our sport. All of a sudden, up leapt a fox which took to the open and gave such a capital run that from then onwards the hounds were steadied from deer and encouraged to fox."

"You were not disappointed, sir."

"The fox is a wily customer and gives excellent chase, but the stag's a noble beast worth the outwitting."

This remark took root. To Lord Berkeley, the stag was a symbol of his own class, revered and half-despised, and the war he waged upon it, upon himself, engrossed him to his death-bed.

Mary stifled a yawn. "Pray excuse me, it has been a long day."

"I fear I grow tedious," he said. "You, no doubt, would rather speak of the theatre?"

"I must own I know so little about it. Of opera, nothing at all."

"The thing about opera, Miss Cole, is that it celebrates sentiment at the expense of the plot. But much can be forgiven a clumsy device in gratitude for a triumphant ending. Don't you agree?"

She stalled, unsure of his meaning. Tired as she was, instinct warned her that this was no throwaway comment. She sensed that he was enjoying some private joke. Upon his own ground, Berkeley had all the advantages and was not slow to exert them.

It was with immense relief that Mary heard his carriage announced. The gathering began to disperse. He had offered to see Mrs Devine and Kipworth, who had gone to the theatre by chair, safely home. John Gwinnett helped him to haul the baronet, with all the seemliness of field-hands heaving a sack of potatoes, into the yellow equipage drawn up in the street. The American lady was installed at a decorous distance and Susan waved them off. The door shut, she let out a yawn in a grand arpeggio.

"I hope you'll do nothing so rash as to invite that fellow here again," Mary said with a shudder.

"Who, Kipworth? He's an incorrigible old soak, to be sure."

"No, Lord Berkeley. I find him unsettling."

Mr Howarth, divested of waistcoat and cravat, was scavenging among the remnants of supper at the side-tables, a gnawed leg of game in one hand and a slice of apple tart in the other.

"Tis Mr Turnour's wish to know people of consequence, ain't it, Susan? His ventures require it."

"I'll not turn his lordship away on account of some childish pet of yours," Susan informed her sister. "He lives in the neighbourhood."

Mary fell silent. Stretched nerves had left her aching in every muscle and sinew. "I must bid you both goodnight. At this moment, I want nothing so much as my pillow."

It was strange to be waited on by a maid. Lydia Sharpe was extremely young then, fourteen at most, and yet she had a canny grasp of life. The daughter of an Islington tailor and one of numerous progeny, she had inherited some of her father's dexterity with a needle. Mary was ashamed of her darned hose and underlinen, flimsy from long use and overwashing, so she sent the girl away as soon as the sheets were turned down. The deep feather-bedding was bliss.

How long ago and far away Boughton Malherbe seemed. Was it only this morning she said her goodbyes at the rectory? Why had she forsaken it so lightly when she could never be at home here? It was like blundering into a stage performance, the colours fable-bright, the gestures extravagant, the characters larger than life, without any part in the script. The conversation put Mary on edge, with all its subtle innuendi, as though the real pulse of things was to be found there. The truant husband must indeed be favourably connected in the world of commerce since no affluent family was spoken of. According to Susan, Soubise had been given her as a present by Mr Turnour's uncle who was Captain of a merchantman carrying sugar, spices and rum from the West Indies. When the boy brought in coffee in the morning, Mary quizzed him about his life in England, anxious that he should not be pining for his homeland. He could have been forgiven for distrusting her query, but answered with enthusiasm that he liked the household. Most of all he liked to listen for the barrel-organ on a Saturday morning and to laugh at the japes of the grinder's button-eyed monkey. "Missus kind," he told her. "Lydia say: sharp tongue, pigeon chest, heart of gold!"

Mary refrained from bursting into laughter. "And is your master kind also?"

Soubise frowned and his eyes rolled comically, like marbles, from side to side. "Ain't no mas'r here, Missy. 'Less you be countin' Mr Howarth."

Mr Turnour's travels must be more extensive than Susan had implied.

In the breakfast parlour, Mary found her sister behind the first copy of *The Universal Daily Register* and a discarded dish of herrings. She had on a morning gown of the bluest Canterbury muslin. As she leaned to pour coffee from the silverest vessel Mary had ever seen, commissioned, Susan boasted, from the workshops of one, Hester Bateman, her fingers flashed scornful fire at the pale winter sky.

"Take whatever you fancy," she invited, nodding towards the sideboard where several dishes had been kept hot over a charcoal tray.

"All this just for the two of us!"

"Teddy's the appetite of a hog in the mating season."

"Teddy?"

"Yes, I'll warrant he'll be on the doorstep before the half-hour strikes, bemoaning an empty larder or the sudden demise of his landlady. Journalists are always starving, you know."

"It's odd that your husband is content to let him play the squire while he's away. And you new-married."

"Good lord! Teddy's no eye for females!" Susan was about to say more, but thought better of it.

"How does Mr Turnour earn the income for all this?"

"What does he do?" Susan paraphrased, wildly scanning the columns of the close-printed journal. "Why, he works for the East India Company, buying and selling."

"I've heard tell they deal in.... Oh, calico, silks, ebony, sandalwood, exotic things."

"Ivory, indigo and tea. Commodities of that sort. ....In exchange for slaves," Susan added to consolidate the picture.

"Slaves!"

"They're captured on the West Coast of Africa and sent to the plantations of the West Indies, or brought through the Middle Passage to Liverpool before being transported to America."

Mary stared open-mouthed. "But that is the most abominable wickedness! A trade in human beings! Do you mean that you profit from the misery of those poor wretches?"

"Oh, eat up your breakfast and stop playing virtue outraged! They're being rescued from savagery and made civil. It surely don't signify."

Mary quickly lost the appetite for her breakfast. She glanced about her at the toad-like contours of the French furniture, the cold Wedgwood blue walls, and loathed them. She was not far from loathing her sister's society, either. Susan's alabaster beauty could be cruelly dispersed by an ugly phrase, a vulgar grimace. For the second time in less than twelve hours, Mary repented her decision to come to London. Even the aquatints on the walls conveyed no sylvan nostalgia. They were grotesque cartoons, or else depictions of street life against a background of mausoleum-like architecture.

"I must go down to Gloucester soon. I haven't seen Ma in months."

"Indeed you won't!"

Mary was taken aback by her sister's vehemence. "Why ever not?"

"If....if my husband were to return without any warning, as he's apt to do, you'd miss him."

"There's not a single portrait in these rooms. Don't you keep a miniature of him?"

Susan had promptly returned to her perusal of wholesale merchandise in a bid to curtail the discussion. "*Winter cloaks and sable muffs,*" she quoted. "*Italian tiffanies at 18d the yard. Florentine waistcoats of the very best....* My, my, this is not to be missed!"

"I must try to mend things with Ann. She might need help with the children."

"Ann's well despite being in the family way."

"Ann's with child?" The sense of being out of touch with the family struck Mary forcibly. Her mother had been spare with information in her letters.

"She swears it was conceived the night before they locked up Will. Ma's not convinced."

"But how will she make ends meet with another mouth to feed?"

Susan folded her newspaper and laid it down on the table. "Don't bother your head about it, Mary. Suffice to say I receive a regular draft upon some obliging fellows in Lombard Street. To be sure, it keeps me in silk garters and champagne!"

"Nothing's the same since Pa died. It's as though the olden time never existed."

"What a sentimental little fool you are! Look, if it pleases you, I'll fix on an evening when we can enjoy a quiet supper and reminisce to our hearts' content. What do you say?"

Mary's eyes lit up. "Shall it be roast fowl and sausages?"

"Like at The Swan? Whatever you desire."

Lately, Lord Berkeley found himself pondering overlong the entanglement of his royal friend. He had fancied himself an impartial mentor to Prinny (as Georgiana Devonshire and Frances Jersey were wont to call HRH), but this latest *impasse* would not be easily resolved. It was immensely disquieting that a fellow's heart could overrule his head and bring him within an ace of staging his own demise in order to milk every drop of pity from the object of desire and secure her consent to be bedded. To cap it all, it appeared to have had the reverse effect!

Whereas the fourth Earl had had a studious interest in dramatic literature, Fred was susceptible to the ironies of the plot, a consequence of having no work to do and of a chequered intimacy with a number of ladies of the Thespian profession. He was so much a product of the laws of intrigue and manipulation that the theatre did not strike him as unduly artificial, but purely a stylised portrayal of the situations around him. His Berkeley sister, Elizabeth, who had abandoned her husband, Lord Craven, was at this moment cavorting about France and Italy, and pretty much half the Habsburg and Ottoman Empires, in search of adventures in which to star. A lady noted for her Herculean tally of indiscretions, she had long favoured the French Ambassador, the Duc de Guines, and was most at home at the French Court, which Fred put down to Louise de Kéroualle, Charles II's mistress, having been their forebear. Lady Craven had written a play or two herself. Sheridan had produced *The Miniature Picture* at Drury Lane, though scarcely to resounding acclaim. Undoubtedly, she was an enchantress, and was much admired by Walpole among others, so that Fred had been moved to declare rashly that he would never marry unless he met a woman like her. Her frequently-aired view that monogamy was a narrow way of thinking chimed well with the philosophy of her devotees who adored her for that daring which entailed no costly recriminations. (As for Georgiana, Fred's other Berkeley sister, she had been widowed by Lord Granard and had since taken up with a clergyman. Fred supposed there had to be some skeletons in the Berkeley cupboard and kept his distance in the same way he kept silent about the Bishop who had produced shoots on the ancestral tree two or three generations back.) His half-sister, Mary, was married to the Marquess of Buckingham and possessed an unfeminine preoccupation with government. Their estate at Stowe was both a monument and a hotbed of political ideology. When Fred surveyed the gallery of portraits in the reception hall, up the staircase and along the landing at Spring Gardens, he was moved to acknowledge that they were a fine-looking bunch, the Berkeleys, but they struck him now as infinitely dull. None of them had the serenity of Mary Cole, nor her beauty. His thoughts were so engrossed by that face, it had become the only place he could call 'home'. And he was shut out.

Dammit, he was tumbling into a trough of misery to have fallen for a woman so opposite to Lady Craven in every point of character, that he wondered what was happening to him. Perhaps his brain was going soft? If he could not be said to exercise control over his own life, he had always been able to *contrive*.

Clearly, a new gambit was called for. Strolling to the window of the house he shared in Grafton Street with his friend, Captain Isaac Prescott, he idly flicked aside the tulle curtain and watched a fine-sprung town chariot bowling along pursued by a shifty guttersnipe. He knew the kind. They were on the lookout for a pampered lap-dog of some rich female they could hold to ransom.

Then an audacious idea began to crystallise in his mind.

During that first week of 1785, Mary forgot all her qualms and began to relax in her sister's company. To do things for the sheer pleasure of doing them, to run about London in bronze boots and a cloak of brown beaver against the frost, was a joy not to be lightly dismissed. This jack-in-the-box burst of happiness was so exhilarating that she didn't dwell on the faulty premise on which it was founded. What use to bother one's head about things one couldn't change? Life, as those old Flemish weavers knew, was a complex mesh of heterogeneous strands, darkness and light intertwined in a grand chiaroscuro. Too strong a tension and the thread snapped.

So Mary threw her work-a-day shoes on the kitchen range and watched them burn. She left off her homespun and put on a gown of violet linsey-woolsey, soft as down. Her taste did not run to the extravagances of Susan's garb – polonaise flounces, laced and boned stomachers tiered with bows – but her feminine heart delighted in her new lightweight clothes. Further gowns of dimity and merino were purchased for her, and one of mulberry taffeta edged with blonde lace to wear in the evening; bleached linen, silk petticoats, a pomander fragrant with lavender. Susan propelled her into a cordwainer's at the top of Old Bond Street and demanded some shoes of the best Spanish leather and a pair of satin slippers studded with rhinestones to go with the taffeta. Mary wore them to Drury Lane to see Mrs Siddons in *Venice Preserv'd* where Susan pointed out the youthful Duke of Kent, a real-life Prince. He was about to be sent off to Luneberg in Hanover to train as a soldier. She said that his elder brothers, the Dukes of York and Clarence, were already in Germany. The former was a soldier and the latter a sailor who had served under Admiral Rodney towards the end of the war. Mary recalled talk of Admiral Rodney in the Foote household, who had saved Jamaica from French rule. Apparently, the King wanted the Royal Dukes out of country, for he was anxious that they should not fall under the baneful influence of the Prince of Wales who was the scourge of the Government and who gambled and caroused and ruined the fair sex as though his days were numbered.

"I've rather a wicked fancy to meet him," Susan owned. "Of course, Berkeley lives in his shadow, so there is always a chance!"

Berkeley was not mentioned again and they did not run into him. Ranelagh and Vauxhall were closed for the winter, but the sisters drove about the Royal Parks at the hour of the promenade and giggled when some supercilious old Dowager looked down her nose. Mr Howarth took them to Astley's Circus where they were in raptures of fear at the acrobatics on horseback. Most nights brought a flock of friends to Susan's drawing room to gossip and devour the sweetmeats of her bounty. She aimed to cut a dash and she succeeded. One of the guests was James Perry who twice accompanied them to Covent Garden Opera.

All this excitement, the fresh places and faces, took a toll on Mary's energies and she requested that they have the promised quiet supper together.

"We can flower our new muslins and recount our childhood adventures." She had half-expected Susan to plead the dullness of this pastime, but no complaint was forthcoming and it was planned for the following Friday.

That afternoon they went for an airing in Hyde Park. Susan was in high good humour. A natural whip-hand, she urged her skittish mare to a canter through the narrowest spaces and Mary did not flinch. She trusted her sister. It was fun to watch the rose-and-honey buildings go streaking by through a mossy web of branches. They arrived in Charles Street to a roaring fire and sipped ginger wine, toasted their toes and closed the curtains early. Mary was glad to have postponed her visit to Gloucester and that Mr Turnour had not materialised to spoil their *tête-à-tête*.

They brought out their workbaskets and began to embroider their gowns with chains and French knots. The blithe spectre of William Cole was more absolute than at any time since his death. It would not have surprised Mary to see him stride into the room, planting his fists aside his waist and demanding to know why it was necessary for Will Strain, his journeyman, to deliver Colonel Kingscote's sirloin and sweetbreads by way of The Dog and Duck!

At nine-o-clock, they tucked into their roast fowl supper. Soubise came in bearing a huge Monteith punch bowl with all the goblets lodged around its crenellated rim.

"Faith, child, we're not expecting a regiment!" Susan exclaimed. *"Not quite."*

"Contain best rum, Missus," Soubise recommended. "Cook make it just right. Soubise taste!"

"Scram you saucy blackamoor and take your impudence with you!"

Pleased with this cheerful abuse, Soubise made off and, gaining the safety of an exit, peered from behind the door. "Cook say: Chile, when you be washin' all the treacle off that grinning face? Soubise say: When you be washin' all that flour off yours!"

In exasperation, Susan flung a wishbone across the room. "Disappear, fiend! Or I'll put a voodoo curse on you!"

The girls burst into a gale of laughter, already a little tipsy from the wine. Mary remarked that such mischief would have been unthinkable from most servants, but Soubise, apart from being painstaking about his tasks, had a nice sense of where to draw the line.

"He has pluck," Susan agreed. "He don't need charity. He'll make his fortune in English society. Only the good-for-nothing crave pity."

No sooner had these words left her lips than there was a vigorous jangling of the street door bell. A blast of chill air swept through the room. Lydia screamed and shrieked for Soubise to run for the Watch. A violent commotion broke out in the hall where John Gwinnett threw his hefty farmer's bulk into the fray.

The dining room door crashed open and two ruffians burst into the room, unshaven costermongers in tattered coats glistening with molten snow.

"What in the name of heaven...!" demanded Susan, seizing the poker. "Get out of my house, you blackguards, or I'll run you through!" The taller grabbed her wrist and jerked back her arm. "John! Look for a neighbour, a passer-by, I entreat you!"

"Spirited filly, ain't she, Zeb?" leered his accomplice, supping noisily from the punch ladle. "Tis the vine talkin', that. Don't you reckon, my pretty?" He fixed Mary with his salacious gaze. Her heart was hammering against her ribs. "Now which one of you fine gentry-morts is Mrs Turnour?"

"I am, you villain! What's it to you?"

"Well now," says he, picking up a silver salt cellar to weigh it in the palm of his hand, "we hear, Mrs Turn*our*, that you've been running up tick to the grand tune of one hundred guineas." The scoundrel clicked his tongue in mock disgust. "Zeb, here, and me is werry concerned about this, see. Werry concerned. Ain't that right, Zeb?"

"Right, guv'nor."

"We got our glims on a 'andsome reward."

"Reward," Mary quavered. "Reward....for what?"

"Either you pays on the nail, Mrs Turnour, or we marches you off to the spunging-house without more ado. Them's our orders."

"Upon my word, fellow," Susan rallied bravely, "do you suppose I have no friends in high places to put down scum like you? There's not so much as a half-crown in the house!"

"Let's seize her, then, guv! Off to the Bridewell!"

"Unhand me, you barbarians! Unhand me this instant!" Susan tried to wrench herself free, but her assailants had her anchored fast by the elbows.

"Oh sirs," Mary implored, "have mercy! Take the candlesticks, the cutlery, anything you desire, but spare my sister. Where should we find a hundred guineas at this hour when the banking-houses have closed their doors?"

Just then, they heard Lydia shouting to a passer-by: "God be praised!" she was heard to cry. "What a blessing your lordship was going by."

A whirl of snowflakes came over the threshold and the shape of Lord Berkeley filled the doorway. He came in with a purposeful stride and swung off his hat. In a paroxysm of relief, Mary ran to him, sobbing, ran from that invaded room, from the cherished image of Pa and familial concord, ran and stumbled on the hem of her gown at his feet.

"My lord, my lord, two ruffians are holding my sister to ransom and we have not a shilling between us. Only give them what they demand and you shall do whatever you will with my own person!"

For a second, an interminable second, he made no sound. Against Mary's cheek, the broad-bosomed hand was trembling. "Mary," he said in an anguished whisper, looking down at her with moistened eyes, as though he had straddled time and eternity to reach her. "*Mary.*"

The truth broke in upon her as the cage snapped shut. It was all a feint! The walls veered from the perpendicular and she swooned into merciful darkness.

Clove Hitch

Four

'Let none claim that it is only upon love we mortals are doomed to exist. Love, labour, friends and fortune may come and go, but a proper self-respect is the staple of the soul.'

Thus Mary confided in the journal she had started to keep as a means of quelling the tumult of her grief. Her thoughts revealed a meteoric ascent to maturity. Seated at the davenport in her bedroom overlooking the pale façades of Mayfair under a canopy of grim sky, every hopeful impulse was dashed. She was stricken with grief to the point of fever. Her throat was swollen and painful. Dr Denman called daily to administer a febrifuge. He patted her hand kindly, as though she had the vapours, and told her she would be right as a trivet in no time, healthy young woman that she was. Berkeley did not know what to do next. He was as unprepared for such a contingency as for his reaction. Above all, his instinct was to protect her. He was thoroughly ashamed of his vile behaviour in Gloucester and wanted Mary to believe that he had acted under duress and out of character. This nymph from the sticks made him want to prove himself! (Hell's teeth, the quick-tempered Mrs Bayly had never exercised such a hold over him!) Berkeley saw that no good would be gained from foisting himself upon Mary. He must bide his time, show patience, humour her. Win her!

Mary did not know whom or what to believe. It terrified her to contemplate the intricacies of Berkeley's obsession. What did a man who had everything believe she could give him? Was it her very resistance that had driven him wild? Was it that she had invoked the right to withhold her virtue? Whatever it was, he was plainly proof against her tearful pleading for release.

"I swear I shall make you unhappy and shan't amuse you half so much as a lively opera-dancer."

Berkeley roared with laughter. "You've a warm turn of phrase for a God-fearing vestal! Nay, Polly, if I'd wanted a milksop maid, I'd have looked in a dairy, or a painted coryphée, the Green Room."

"Pray don't call me by that name!"

"That's what some call you in Gloucester. I've heard Will Lane call you that."

"The maltster's apprentice?"

"'There goes Polly and Billy Cole,'says he. 'She's a fine wench, and Billy....ah well, bless you, sir, Billy's-a-dying since he went to live in the house of that old clyster-pipe, Parker'."

"They say that Billy is idling!" As her only son, Mrs Cole had encouraged his chronic delicacy. 'Billy's ever so poorly,' she would say, "and not in any way to learn his books."

"Lane's a fund of information, I'll say that!"

Mary burst into a fresh fit of weeping.

"How long will you keep me a prisoner? What will become of me? With my reputation in tatters, I shan't be fit to return home."

"That is not how such things fall out, sweetheart," Berkeley said. In one chivalrous gesture, he shook out a folded lawn handkerchief from his pocket. "Come, dry up your tears. The future is rosier than you think. We shall deal famously, you and I."

The echo of his words hung on the air. He got up and poured whisky which he tossed off in one draught, stunned by the enormity of this concession. Future? He had never in his life considered the future for two minutes together! "I must go. I've an appointment at Tattersall's."

Mary looked at him beseechingly, wanting some kind of resolution and, perversely, hoping not to be left alone with her misery. To be hermetically sealed with a cook, a butler and a maid, having no *entrée* anywhere in the neighbourhood, no companions but turbulent thoughts, was a sentence in itself.

"Will you be dining here tonight, my lord?"

He paused, registering the wistful note in her voice. "I shall suppose that to be an invitation, Mary. Thank you, I will. I must see that you eat up your dinner and regain your strength."

During those bewildering days, the scale of her sister's deceit had made its impact. There *was* no Mr Turnour as far as Mary could see. Susan's establishment was financed by Berkeley for the sole purpose of gaining his way. Her willing connivance had earned her ample reward and a sly satisfaction in teaching Mary a lesson. Possibly she felt that Mary *owed* the Coles this eminent connection. It would be in her power to change *all* their lives for the better if she played her trump card: her fatal desirability in the Earl's eyes. She could seek redress for Will Farren who had borne the brunt of his sister-in-law's pride. A sense of responsibility for Ann and her children began to trouble Mary sorely. The little ones did not deserve to suffer.

That day, she fretted long about the lot of women. It could not be denied that the ancient *droît de seigneur* of feudal times still operated beneath a veneer of good manners. A man need not spare a moment's hesitation for his arrogance in assuming that any woman he chose was there for the taking. Barriers could be trampled down at will without a grain of guilt. Stories abounded of poor wretches who had swung on the gallows for want of the price of a loaf. Yet this Lord of the Gloucestershire Vales, and much else besides, could pillage lives in a bid for amusement. Susan had been right about one thing: there was no changing the *status quo*. Women were powerless against it. How hard it was to do what was right! As she pursued this line of thought, Mary realised how jaded Berkeley's palate for life and love must have become to want to keep her hostage.

"Oh, how I wish I could go back to Westgate and scrub floors and sell chitterlings!" she cried, casting a pair of drowning eyes up to the ceiling when Berkeley returned.

"This is bound to go hard with you," he said with unwonted grace. "Soon you will appreciate what a lucky young lady you are. You shall have anything your heart desires. Anything!"

"Then I beg you will see Will Farren freed."

"Do you imagine I reap any pleasure from his being in jail?"

"You saw his debts called in."

"He incurred them! I did no more than hasten the reckoning. In truth, that sister of yours was the worst investment the poor chub ever made. I'd have turned her out to beg crusts long ago! Odd's life! Don't you understand I've obligations of my own, taxes to pay, tenants who owe a backlog of rent and squeal about roofs that let in the rain?"

"At least you will never know the indignity of being sold!"

His lordship sighed heavily. "I'm no saint and am capable of great foolishness, I'll allow, but I'm not so callous a rogue as you fancy. Mrs Farren and her family are by no means in want."

"How so?"

"Because *I* pay the rent and that's where a fellow feels the pinch worst, in his pocket! You must understand, Mary, that nobody's all black or white. The saint has the devil on his back and the reprobate is not incapable of selfless deeds."

"Oh! I don't know anything any more!"

"Since it pleases you, I will obtain Farren's release. I hope it may put an end to their call upon my purse!"

Mary was vastly relieved and thanked him profusely, but did not dare follow this up with another petition for her own release.

Berkeley had told her that if she tried to escape, he would pursue her to the corners of the earth and nothing so far caused her to doubt it.

The point was well-made when he visited her next day, bringing a bright canary in a gilded cage which he said had sung so sweetly in the Covent Garden market. He bade Harriet stoke up the fire and fetch tea and fondant cakes.

"I have been the most miserable of fellows today. Polly, I have used you ill...."

The uplift Mary felt was instantly apparent. "You mean...?"

"That *incident* in Gloucester....and the maladroit trick that brought you here. Forgive me, dear heart. I'll make amends." In great agitation, he dropped on his knees and buried his face in the folds of her skirt. "You must know that I dote upon you...!"

Mary looked down upon his powdered head, momentarily overcome by the vehemence of his sentiments.

"My lord," she said softly, "I want no man at my feet. Don't put me on a pedestal, for that is the way of tyrants."

"But I am in agony!"

"'Tis a will-o'-the-wisp that makes you wretched and not worth breaking your heart over. Please, if you care for me at all, let me go. Let me return to Gloucester and begin again."

"Heaven forfend!" Berkeley thundered, rising from his knees in a blaze of passion. "Do you think I have this day been pacing the streets in distraction, unable to deal a steady card or throw a straight dice, for naught?"

"Then would that I were ugly and scarred with smallpox and my own person!"

The Earl turned upon her a frown of the most vivid pain. "Do you hate me so much, Polly?"

Wrung of emotion, she surveyed the countenance whose features were not unpleasant and whose owner was probably no more selfish than most of his breed. Tears were slipping down her cheeks. "No, I don't hate you. Can't you see that it's the situation I abhor? It forces me to live in a way which offends against decency. I was brought up with as firm a sense of propriety as females of your own family."

And there's the rub, thought Berkeley. Mary would have been appalled by the piebald reputation of his mother, the Countess Dowager, to say nothing of his sister, Elizabeth. Nor was he likely to mention that Georgiana, had run off, in contempt of her ward, with an uncouth Irishman on the night she was presented at Court. He was titled which covered a battery of faults. Even now, into her second marriage, Georgiana was continuing her indiscretions under cover of that pious repute afforded by union with a man in Holy Orders. Her only sin, in her brother's eyes, was that she possessed neither the style nor the daring of Lady Craven.

"What you must understand, sweetheart, is that I have raised you to a new station. It ain't as though I've a wife. You and I will go about together in society. You cannot be presented at Court, nor introduced into the houses of the *bon ton*, but there are many venues, frequented by those same persons, where you will be accepted as a lady as long as you are under my protection."

Mary knew how to comport herself and wanted only a fashionable wardrobe. With beauty, intelligence and wisdom beyond her years, Berkeley conjectured that she would be the talk of the town before long.

Her suitor, Mary thought, was as merrily illogical as the rest of his gender. While women were regarded as prized jewels, the taking was cheap. She was called upon to betray the very essence of her self-worth as if it were nothing. He could not know how she wrestled with a fiery conviction that she was implicitly to blame; some lethal flaw in her make-up must have triggered this lunacy.

For all her demurrals, a strange bond was growing between captor and captive as the days slipped by. The lodging in Princes Street to which he had taken her was neither her home nor his, but a meeting ground. The Earl was Mary's only visitor so that the object of her distress was the sole comforter for it. Had she begged Lord Berkeley never to cast her off, he might have tired of her within a month. As it was, the perverse seam in his nature was tantalised by the glint of gold in rock. The world itself was cast in optimism and the notion that he might lose sight of that was fearsome. Mary absorbed his disenchantment with his unfulfilled existence without realising that it formed a large part of her pain.

During dinner together on Shrove Tuesday, when venison pancakes were served and a fair quantity of Burgundy drunk, the Earl joked: "You won't wish me to wear a hairshirt tomorrow, I trust, Mary."

"You are beyond redemption, my lord," she replied with a hint of mischief.

"It is vain, then. I might as well go to the devil."

"I'd like to go to Mass at St. George's tomorrow. Shall you come?"

"And tempt God by having ashes daubed on my for'ead! I think not. I shall trust you to intercede for my soul."

"Then I'll light a candle for you."

He had purchased a most exquisite cameo for her that day, an ivory relief of the head of Aphrodite mounted on lapis lazuli. She had left it on the pier-table when dinner was served and, afterwards, he caught her running her fingers over it in tentative appreciation. Stealing up behind her, he lay his hand over hers, making the fingers interlock. He was pressing gentle, heated kisses against her nape.

"Say you'll not banish me to Grafton Street tonight."

"My lord...?"

"Send Harriet away, I beg. Tell her no warming-pan will be needed!"

The next minute, Mary was caught up in a lavish embrace that fetched up a wild confusion of feelings such as she had not dreamt of. Whilst her head protested the wickedness of treading this path, her heart wanted to claim the comfort of intimacy with another human being. How nicely-judged was the tenderness of this blundering good-for-nothing, after what had gone before, when she so yearned for a kind soul to field all the trapped grief. Despite her straitlaced ideas, she was not proof against the stealth of nature. The fear drained out of her, the iron melted.

"Oh dear, what is to become of me?" she whispered as the hold finally loosened.

"Polly, my darling," Berkeley said in a tone rich with discovery. "I do not think you require instruction in the arts of the paramour. To be yourself is enough."

For the first time ever, she was aware of the hand of destiny leading her where she would not go. It was goodbye to bread and dripping and the sweet meadows of childhood.

"Good God and all the saints!" swore Susannah Cole, crossing herself as indemnity against the consequences. "What! Our little Mary? That be the most shocking thing I've heard since Jack Seton went to the gibbet for keeping a Jesuit up the chimley!"

"I tell you it's true, Ma," confirmed Susan, pulling off her kid gloves. Her hectic presence filled the tiny parlour of her sister's house in Southgate Street, Gloucester, whither she had hastened by post-chaise. The ostrich plumes on her modish bonnet rippled and quivered in the draught. "Twas the price of Will's freedom. Ann, at least, should be grateful to her."

Ann was not overjoyed by the news. She leant lethargically in the doorway with arms crossed above her swollen belly. "That's cooked our goose and no mistake. Berkeley will put paid to his favours."

Their mother began to sniff and sob. "Our Mary gone to the bad! Was anything more insupportable?"

"Do give over, Ma," Susan bade. "Matters could be a deal worse."

"She was such a good girl. Not flighty like you and your sister."

"Well, we're the ones with the wedding rings! See!"

Ann sauntered off to make fennel tea, sighing audibly.

"This is not in the way of things," wept the matron. "I was bred up with Christian *principalities*. She's no daughter of mine!"

Susan had untied her bonnet, thrown down her cloak and was squatting beside her mother's rocking chair. "Then tell her so!"

"The filly's bolted! It won't change anything now."

"Actually, it might. Think on't, Ma. There's another side of the coin."

"It won't undo her ruin."

"Write to Mary, setting forth how upset you are. You didn't expect such a thing of *her*. Tell her you cannot countenance her as a daughter and don't want to see her again."

"It might bring her to her senses, I s'pose."

"It might put her association with Berkeley on another footing altogether."

The dame gaped: her jaw dropped wide-open. "You don't mean...?"

"He's besotted with her!"

"Mighty be here! There'd be some gravy in that. Just think...."

"Believe me, Ma, I have done. And so should Ann, instead of whining about being paid off."

"An answer to all our prayers. You always was a good girl, Sue. *At heart*."

So saying, the Widow Cole wiped her nose on her apron and got up from the chair, begging sixpence from her well-off daughter to run down to Pytt's for some decent stationery. If her missive were to fall into the Earl of Berkeley's hands, which was as much its intended destination as her daughter's, she would wish it to make an impression. Susan, she had to admit, was not a great scholar, and neither was Ann. (Ironically, her youngest daughter was the only one who had developed a proper command of the language at Mrs Clarke's Boarding School.) Some literary guidance from Susannah's friend, Mrs Horseman, at the Post Office would be needed and a promise of undying silence!

In the oak-panelled saloon of Brooks's Club, over coffee and curaçao, the Prince of Wales finished reading a copy of the *Racing Calendar* and fell to speculating upon what could be achieved after a lucrative week at Newmarket. In an ambience created, as at Carlton House, by Mr Henry Holland, it was easy to picture the kind of transformation that might be wrought upon the farmstead he had bought down at Brighton last year. A Grecian pediment framing mythical figures above the front door – his fancy rather ran upon Prometheus as a subject - maybe some triple-light bow windows, a stick or two of Sheraton or Hepplewhite, and he was convinced that he and Maria could live as cheaply as one and would be the happiest pair of lovebirds alive. If only he could lure her back to England and into a wedded estate blessed by the Church! It would, of course, be a morganatic marriage, not one recognised by King and Constitution.

"I shall never marry for the succession. My resolution is taken on that subject. I have settled it with Frederick."

His comrade of Berkeley was shuffling a pack of cards from which the lower numbers had been removed in readiness for a rubber of piquet. There was about him a distracted air which did not augur well for a game of chance. The reference to his namesake Frederick Augustus, Duke of York, who was parading soldiers in Germany, only focused his mind on the understanding he had reached with *his* younger brother, George Cranfield Berkeley, conversely the Prince of Wales' namesake.

"And I have promised *my* brother that his line shall be my heirs. Now there's an infant on the way - Emily's doing her stuff with wonderful promptitude – all's set to go sideways."

"Good breeders, the Lennoxes, but that's just as well since you've no wish to go tying the knot."

"If, however, I should seek a more durable arrangement...."

His Royal Highness did not rank this a circumstance worthy of mental exercise. "They'd have to drag you to the altar by the hair!" His eyes abruptly widened with a keen and lively interest. Hadn't Berkeley mentioned some little charmer before? "Damme, fellow, I do believe you're love-struck!"

Something very like a blush warmed the Earl's visage. "The devil of it is, she's of no family. Sister's a thorough-going rake."

"Berkeley, if that don't beat all!"

The Earl glanced uncomfortably about him. "I do urge upon Your Highness that circumspection you would expect from me in so sensitive an affair. Like Maria, she is a creature of unimpeachable conduct and has made herself ill with anxiety over her present situation."

"Which is as your mistress, I presume?"

"She is quite the loveliest thing you ever saw," rhapsodised Berkeley. "She has character, bearing, a certain...."

"*Je ne sais quoi?*" The Prince found it amusing to see Fred struggle to label niceties of feeling and noted the absence of hunting cant from his vocabulary. "Well, how the tables have turned! Fred Berkeley seriously ponders making an honest woman of his sweetheart!"

"But wedlock," mourned his friend, "is so final a step."

"Well, your marriage would not be called illegal, an affront to Church and State. Whereas, if I don't pre-empt the situation, they'll saddle me with some ugly German mare. The King keeps me penniless in hopes of inducing me to settle down. I daresay I shall have to sell my house, my jewels and plate, to scrape enough together to flee to the Americas and live in exile."

His lordship was shuffling the cards over and over again, making skilful waterfalls. Presently, he heard himself say: "A religious contract would be better than none. It shows good faith." He cut for the deal, offering the pack to his royal companion.

"Maria will not consent to live with me without the Sacrament, but how am I to obtain that when it will not conform to the laws of the land?"

The Prince drew the Knave of Hearts and his opponent, the Ace of Spades. Berkeley dealt the cards with a practised hand. "What infernal mischief is made of the need for ink and parchment," he said.

"Carte blanche!" declared the Prince, rapidly counting out a hand which included no King, Queen or Knave. "That's ten. And four aces, *quatorze*."

Lord Berkeley nodded his congratulations at the opening play. "As for myself, sir, I do enjoin upon you the closest secrecy."

"Rest assured, Fred, your fix is as safe with me as mine is with you. Ultimately, I'm not sure I dare trust Fox with the Maria question."

"He knew what to do about Perdita."

"Yes, but the form here is different. Lucky fellow, he's set up very cosily with Lizzie Armistead out at St. Anne's Hill."

"Which is more than you can say for Sherry."

They fell to discussing the Irish scallywag and his disastrous elopement with the beautiful soprano, Elizabeth Linley, for whom King George himself had a tender spot. Sheridan was a man of sparkling wit and capability, but all too few achievements, save for a handful of astringently comic plays. His prodigal style and a string of shallow affairs left him constantly under the threat of bailiffs.

It was a coincidence, then, that the two friends should run into him an hour later in the lobby of the Club. "Ah, Sherry," the Prince accosted him, "we were just debating whether you are a rogue or a fool."

"Why, faith," replied the playwright blithely, taking each by the arm, "I believe I am between both!"

Mary had missed Morning Mass. She felt in burning need of Absolution for, in the end, she had yielded to her lover. To say there had been an element of complicity would not have been far from the truth. What did that say about her immortal soul? At the same time, she was filled with a blossoming tenderness towards humanity itself. Inexplicably, she forgave Lord Berkeley and felt a surge of responsibility for him. He was more than twice her age, but there was something about him of the orphaned child handicapped by lack of caring supervision.

Intent upon lighting the promised candle, Mary crossed the busy Square and mounted the steps of St. George's, going in through the porticoed West door. The church was deserted. Her footfalls echoed in the welling silence. This building was so different from the crude Saxon stones of St. Mary de Lode where Mary had been christened and where, some said, Lucius, a second century King of Britain, had been buried. St. George's was temple-like, with linear proportions borrowed from Greece and Rome, and designed by a pupil of Christopher Wren. In the sanctuary, seven silver hanging lamps transmitted the faint red glow of harbour lanterns. Above the altar was a painting of the Last Supper, showing Judas stealing quietly out of the door while the clamour of disciples hung on their Master's words. "Oh fool," muttered Mary. "To have let my wanton sister deceive me! I should have trusted Ma." She was smitten with distress when she thought of her mother. It was even worse than sinning against

God! Slipping a penny into the box, she added her candle to the chorus of flame beneath the statue of the Virgin. But no words would come. She was deceiving herself if she thought the situation could be made good.

The second post arrived and was handed to her on a silver plate. The staff were punctilious but tended to treat Mary with a deference that smacked of the satirical. Heart pounding, she stared for a moment at the childish handwriting spread across vellum as fine as you'd find in a palace. Mother! How did she know this address? Was she forewarned of her daughter's downfall?

Oh Mary! (it read)

Your sister has whispered your disgraceful setup and I can't hardly believe it! How could you do it? You was always brought up decent and taught to read your Bible of an evening the minit you'd done with your horn-book. That you, of all folk, are come to this! It vexes me sore to say it, but I can't look upon you as a daughter no more. The perticklers of your household arrangements forbid it, what with no marriage lines and no ring on your finger. His lordship must have taken leave of his senses if he thinks you suited to such a life. Twere better you was walled up in a Convent. I tell you, Mary, my poor heart is broken in two. To be widowed and then to lose you is grevious and I should not be surprised if 'tis the end of me.

Your longsuffering Ma.

"Oh Susan! Was it not enough to betray me!" cried Mary to the rag-rolled walls. "Couldn't you have spared Ma? She'll never know it wasn't my fault!"

When Lord Berkeley returned at five-o-clock, she was shedding tears in torrents. Her pretty face, buried in a cushion, was unappealingly blotched and she was in no frame to bewitch him. He picked up the letter by her feet and scanned its sentiments, his brow contracting darkly.

"Meddlesome mare!"

"I am undone," sobbed Mary. "I don't belong anywhere."

"You belong here! There is no going back."

"No! You do not know how repugnant I find it to live with a man who is not my husband. The shame! Only give me hemlock to blot out my misery!"

Berkeley was normally unmoved by feminine outbursts, but this one cut him to the quick. Fear lanced through his vitals, more than fear; desolation. To sup the waters of the Lethe would have been welcome in such a state. What was happening to him?

"Then, by God, we'll be married!" he heard himself vow.

"I...I think you are gammoning me, my lord," Mary gulped and snuffled indecorously. "Pray do not!"

"No, I'm in deadly earnest, Polly." The Prince of Wales was contemplating a marriage tailored to personal circumstances. Why shouldn't *he*? The decision taken, Berkeley came alive. His mind went racing ahead and the Nordic eyes were swivelling towards her and away again. "We must preserve the closest secrecy, of course. The Dowager's in feeble health and already halfway to the happy hunting grounds!"

"This is foolish talk...."

"Then there's brother George....Oh lord!" Berkeley groaned. "There's a confounded thing!" He began to stride the length and breadth of the room, as if assessing its dimensions. "George was married last year. His wife is a Lennox and they're next door to royalty. My grandmother was a Lennox. She was a granddaughter of Charles II. If the King had had his way, the Queen would have come out of the same stable, but he was dissuaded from it for political reasons and took a German princess instead."

Mary watched him, persuaded that it was a flight of fancy. It was a cerebral exploration of feasibility, not intent. "I am dizzy with your meandering," she complained.

"Yes, this must be kept off the record. Your sister's dubious mode of living would render it absolute ruin for our connection to be known before she is respectably settled."

"Haven't you forgotten my lack of birth?" Mary submitted archly.

The regular creak of Lord Berkeley's boots faltered. He made a pretence of studying the gold and azure geometry of a Canaletto, but appeared to find the disciplines of the Age of Reason unrewarding. "Cardinal Wolsey was a butcher's son."

"Oh, I wish you will stop tormenting me with these fantasies. How could the secret be kept?"

"If nuptials are the only way to appease your conscience, lady, then you shall have them! Hupsman, my chaplain at Berkeley, will take care of matters. I'll travel down to the country next week and, when arrangements are made and the due process of law satisfied, I'll send for you. We'll be quietly married, away from London."

Mary held her breath, not daring to trust this epic *volte-face*. Did Berkeley really care for her enough to make this sacrifice?

Her mother had taught her that the essence of humility was to feel inferior to no one as a person, but to know her station.

"Then I should be restored to my mother's affections," she said happily. "My reputation is saved!"

Berkeley was solemn. "My dear, I regret that may not be as you wish. The step we are taking is to acquit you before Heaven, mere men must judge as they will."

"I don't understand."

"If we're to keep the marriage dark, you cannot be known as the Countess of Berkeley...." (any more, thought Berkeley, than Maria Fitzherbert will become The Princess of Wales).

"What then?"

"We must devise some mode of address that befits your position without giving away *the truth*."

"I certainly can't be Miss Cole."

"No."

"So even my own family must not know?"

"I fear not. They'd be calling in favours for ever and a day. I'm not Croesus, Polly. Your brother...."

"Billy?"

"I'd hazard he knows how to keep his lip buttoned," said his lordship, wondering what manner of disbursement would best ensure silence. "We might invite him to witness the match?"

"Oh yes!"

"But I insist most emphatically that you cut all communication with your sister, Susan. The word is that she consorts with a distinguished Silk."

"A colleague of Mr Perry's, no doubt," said Mary suddenly flaring up. "I'll never forgive her! Never! Had I listened to my mother...."

"Let's not pursue lost causes. Go and prepare yourself for supper and we will be in good humour with one another."

When she had gone, Berkeley sank into a chair in a trance. A strange inner trembling had overtaken him. He had stumbled into an area where the compass needle sprang awry. Life without Mary was unthinkable, but how had a frippery female led him so far astray? This sublime madness must be what poets extolled, what opera struggled so preciously to convey. He hadn't cottoned on to the idea that it was actual and crucial, prompting responses that were reckless.

Well, he had pitched himself overboard now!

Five

But for some neglected works upon estate management, the shelves of the gloomy library at Berkeley Castle were crammed with titles testifying to a love of travel, theatre and heritage rather than the cutting edge of literature and learning. It was here, on the Ides of March, 1785, that the Reverend Augustus Thomas Hupsman was undergoing an uncomfortable interview with his patron.

"Do as I ask and all will go merrily as a marriage bell."

"A ripe choice of phrase, my lord, if I may make so bold." Hupsman mopped the pinheads of swear glistening upon his upper lip and brow, his glass eye, the result of a riding accident, protruding rather more than his good one. He was an obsequious scoundrel, close to Berkeley in age, of gaunt build and concave aspect, with waxy-looking hands that itched to explore the forbidden contours of the female form. These featured in many a torrid daydream against his ill-chosen career and his prudish wife.

"Take heed, if there be any breach of confidence, it will be curtains, Huppy." The Earl crossed his throat with his forefinger. Hupsman fidgeted, unclear whether there was more than his appointment at stake. Lord Berkeley had been known to kill a highwayman in cold blood on Hounslow Heath on a journey from Cranford. He had seized the villain's pistol and pointed it back at him, having tricked the fellow that there was someone behind him.

The clergyman bowed. "As you say, my lord. The....er....ceremony you have in mind is to take place, when, exactly?"

"March 30th, early in the morning. I must return to London speedily thereafter.

"I will attend to it with all despatch. A suitable form of words, you say?"

"Keep it simple."

"Begging your pardon, but your lordship did instruct me that the certificate was to be burned the same day?"

"I did so. It will render your own sleep much sweeter to know that it is dealt with. And Hupsman...."

"My lord?"

"Find a witness."

"A witness, my lord?" croaked the cleric, running his finger inside his choker.

"Naturally! The bride's brother will be present but we shall need another party to act as clerk."

Hupsman's earthworm lips formed an astonished "Oh."

"Don't stand there gaping like a fish, man! If we're to keep the matter quiet, there's no use asking Tom Pruett or John Clark to do the honours. Might as well announce it in the *Gloucester Journal*."

"But whom...? How can we be sure to engage silence?"

"That's your funeral, Hupsman. I'll leave it to your imagination. This is a private celebration but we must rehearse the correct procedures."

"Indeed so, my lord."

"My advice is to import an outsider, someone suitably anonymous."

The devil, they say, looks after his own and, that same day, the answer dropped into Hupsman's grasp like a ripened plum. After supper at the rectory, he escaped from his carping spouse and sauntered down to the Berkeley Arms for his quart of ale. The inn was a forum for the debating of local topics, the playing of dice and 'shove ha'penny' and the transacting of commerce. He considered it part of his parochial duty to take the pulse of its activities from time to time. He would have been astounded had he not found old Seth Tulliver sucking on a long-stemmed pipe and holding forth to a veteran audience upon his salad days as a midshipman in the last King George's Navy. In another corner, Joseph Pocock, the Salt Officer, was deep in a game of cards with Squire Pritchard. The Squire's spaniel, squatting on a barrel-stool of his own, leapt on to the table and licked at the frothy overspill from his master's tankard.

Through the hoary atmosphere, Hupsman noticed a couple of strangers in broadcloth and starched ruffles sitting in the circle of firelight over bowls of turnip soup. Emma Winterson, the landlord's daughter, was poring over the wares of a hawker. The fellow's shoulders were weighted with a string of pots and pans. A tray strapped around his neck exhibited pins and trinkets, thimbles and patches, ribbons and lace, anything to tempt the heart of a frivolous lass.

"Don't, dear child, go frittering away the profits of the house," he counselled.

The tinker snorted. He looked pinched and hungry. His bloodshot eyes, smarting from heat and smoke, were long accustomed to biting winds.

"Come, zur, a man must eat bread. Devil the trade I've had this day."

"And they're such pretty ribbons, Reverend," Emma enthused. "Just the thing for trimming my Sunday bonnet."

"Consider the lilies of the field, child. They neither toil nor spin, yet Solomon in all his glory was not arrayed like one of them." Even upon his own ears, Hupsman's sing-song piety grated. "Aye, give the fellow a sale. He could do with a square meal by the looks of him. Have you come far, sir? I divine you're new to these parts."

"Indeed, your worship, foxes have holes and the birds of the air have nests, but Dick Barns has nowhere to lay his head. Last week I was in Tewkesbury town and sheltered in the cloisters of the Abbey. I've trudged on, sore of foot, these six days since, buying victuals at the farms, sleeping in haylofts."

"Pray, unload your wares and take some refreshment. I'm Augustus Hupsman, vicar of this parish. Emma, fetch mulled wine to warm my guest and ale for me."

"Thank ye kindly, parson. I'll not say no."

The percussion of unwieldy pans and utensils being put down caused Tulliver's crew and Joe Pocock and crusty old Pritchard to glare in concert.

"I perceive," ventured Hupsman craftily, "you are a man of some little education. Can you read and write?"

"Why, I reads the sky and the hedgerows and the cottage gates. Dick Barns can make out a milestone's numbers thirty paces hence. I knows my trade and that a fool may prosper where a wise man scorns to tread, but as for book-learning, ah no, zur. Schooling's for gentlefolk."

"And when was the last time you slept in a bed?"

"Maybe, twas Agnes' Eve in yonder Black Mountains. I might find a grand house where the cook's a Christian and sends me to sleep with the grooms, so long as I dowse myself under the yard-pump. Faith, zur, there's naught mortifies the flesh half so true as that!"

Hupsman eschewed this Spartan advice with a scowl, feeling slightly abashed that this bucolic dreamer had the measure of him. "And what say you, Dick Barns, to several nights on a feather mattress and a clean suit of clothes and suppers a-plenty?"

"Nay, zur, I'm a simple soul who asks only bread and cheese and a bale of dry straw."

"In return, you have it in your power to grant me a favour. Come."

Hupsman led his humble acquaintance to a recessed bench by a small latticed window and explained his tight spot in careful phrases. "A second witness, you see, is required by law and my principal is insistent on utter concealment."

Barns shuffled the brim of his hat through his fingers in an agitated manner. "But, zur, I cannot write my name."

Capital! Hupsman thought. He will not be able to read the registry. We will situate him at a distance from the proceedings so that no names are distinct. "No matter. All you need do is make your mark on the appropriate line. But mind, not a word of your business in this town, or it will not go well with you."

"I'm not easy, parson.... Tis folk like me as end up in ditches with their throats slit."

"Afterwards, you may make yourself scarce."

Dick Barns' bovine gaze disconcerted Hupsman. There was a gritty streak of independence in the man he had not bargained for. "Listen, fellow, in addition to your board and lodging until next Wednesday se'nnight, I'll give you a golden guinea for your trouble. There!"

Dick Barns smelled the spit-roast suckling pig, an even greater temptation than money. "Well, seeing as how you're a man of the Cloth...."

"Excellent. Landlord! A room and some supper for this wayfarer."

Winterson was scooping out a careful firkin of millet from one of the rolled-back sacks on the taproom floor and raised his brows, as did some of the patrons of his respected hostelry. The two gentlemen by the fire glanced up, then resumed their dialogue in an undertone. The innkeeper had been watching them and reckoned they were set fair to jaw for the rest of the evening which meant they might wish for accommodation. It was just the sort of custom he wanted, a touch of class and a free hand with the gratuities, valets to ensure boots weren't worn in bed and a modest revenue from horsekeeping! So he was not best pleased to have Parson Hupsman demand a bed for a vagrant.

"Acting the Good Samaritan's all very fine, Mr Hupsman," he said, "but I've my trade to consider."

Hupsman's jowls reddened with anger at being crossed by a publican. "Are you saying, Winterson, that there's no room at the inn? You, of your abundance will not offer shelter to this poor traveller? Why, some have entertained angels...."

"Aye, Noll, that's a fact," cried Seth Tulliver roguishly. "What about the bonny Flossie Fortnum with the peachy bosom?"

Winterson flushed at the mention of this lady of less than impeccable repute who regularly made discreet use of his rooms.

"Well, maybe there's an attic room...."

"Here is a shilling on account," said Hupsman, replete with the smugness of one conforming to biblical example. "I'll settle with you fair and square next time I come."

So saying, he crammed on his shovel hat and took his leave of the Berkeley Arms, the crimson hose sheathing his baluster calves an absurd contrast to the sober weave of the rest of his garb. He was aware that parishioners mocked him. An inn full of clout-shoes, tax collectors, harbourers of loose women, and he had had to spend his way into their good offices!

In London, Mary waited in suspense. The only way she was going to redeem herself in her parent's eyes was to hint at her new-found status and enlist confidence in the overall integrity of her position. Surely her mother would understand how injurious Susan's *ménage* was to advancement in good society.

Then, one morning, a letter came bearing his lordship's frank. Mary was to take the stage to Oxford at dawn on the 29th and to travel from there by post-chaise to Newport in Gloucestershire, spending the night at the Stagecoach Inn. Billy would meet her there at daybreak and together they would walk across the fields to St. Mary the Virgin at Berkeley where his lordship would join them.

Mary passed a restless night at the halfway house on the Bristol road, consoled that outside and beyond was God's own country. The peculiar greenness of those meadows, after a twelvemonth's absence, filled her with joy. The sheer reprieve from her trapped life in London! Today was her wedding day! At dawn, she threw back the shutters and watched the sheep graze the common and suckle their lambs beneath bands of mist. A pair of hares were spoiling for battle on a thistled knoll. The eastern sky was tinged with willow-herb pink which every shepherd knew promised rain. She would need stout boots and her fustian cloak for tramping across the fields.

She dressed hurriedly and was binding her hair before the looking-glass, when she heard the clopping of hooves in the stable yard and ran to the window. It was Billy riding a roan mare lent him by Peach, the maltster. Scampering downstairs, she rushed out to embrace him.

"Billy! I'll swear you're grown a hand or more!" She adjusted his necktie, which irked him a trifle. He was taller than any of them, taller than Pa, and had the wilting stoop of a plant which has outgrown its strength.

"You're an eyeful," he grinned. "Lord, my sister the Countess of Berkeley!"

"Hush! Someone might hear. How's Ma? And Ann?"

"Will's home. Ann's a belly as big as a pumpkin and Ma vows it's twins. Mr Parker's mighty curious to know what goes forward. Last Friday, Berkeley marched in and desired him to release me for a day. Just think, I'll be the brother-in-law of an Earl!"

"Come on, Billy, help me over the stile. I'll race you to the next one!"

Reaching the wooded slopes below the great fortress of Berkeley, Billy stopped, creased with stitch. "Fancy! You'll be mistress of all that."

They climbed up through the wood, through a shingle of beech mast, and came out near the grave of Dicky Pearce, the Earl of Suffolk's fool and the last court jester in England. It was one of the curiosities of Berkeley that the bell-tower of St. Mary's Minster was divorced from the church some distance, its predecessor the relic of an old abbey which had sent out priests to evangelise the heathen during the dark ages. The town had been an important Saxon Borough a millennium ago and had boasted its own mint. On the graveyard path, Lord Berkeley greeted them and hustled them hastily into the porch. He was not easy about oaths made in the House of God and wished the affair to be over and done. Axe marks and bullet holes from a Cromwellian siege riddled the door which could be secured by an ancient draw-bar against enemy attack. The tracery inside resembled a small cathedral, but something pagan lingered in the air; glowering gargoyles kept a vigil over the devotions of the enlightened faithful as though, despite the testimony of generations, they scoffed at any proposition of the Divine.

Arriving at the church on shank's mare like some village hoyden, it was not to be expected that Mary would feel as a bride should. Her skirts were sodden and her locks untethered. She would have liked Psalms and sacred canticles, the prayers of the devout and the goodwill of her friends. But beggars couldn't be choosers and her protector had agreed to have the union sanctified.

They were a sparse assembly for what might have been presumed to be a momentous event, just Billy, Mary, Lord Berkeley and a rough-and-ready stranger with ruddy cheekbones and ruminant eyes. He wore an ill-fitting coat and his grubby neckcloth was rasped by an ill-shaven chin. Great heavens, Berkeley thought, some troglodyte from a peat bog! Couldn't Hupsman have found someone more in keeping? That Reverend gentleman came down the nave with stealthful tread and none of them noticed him until he was upon them. He looked Mary up and down with salacious interest: she took an instant dislike to him.

"The bride and her brother, Huppy," announced his lordship succinctly. "Pray begin at once."

They arranged themselves before the Altar, but outside the medieval rood screen surmounted by the great Berkeley crests. The priest opened his prayer-book and rambled through a curtailed version of the service in a tone of dismaying tedium which made a travesty of its meaning. The groom fumbled in his pocket and brought out a ring made of antique rose-gold. Then Hupsman bound his embroidered stole around the hands joined on the Bible and Berkeley visibly twitched and trembled, as though his doom on the gale had been decreed. He assured himself that this elaborate farce could have no real meaning and was entirely under his control.

The next moment, they were pronounced man and wife together and the thing was clinched. They took turns to sign the register, already prepared and laid out on a table, the meek and silent stranger last. He laid a crooked cross upon the parchment, his knobbly, coarse-grained hand struggling to steady the quill.

"Who was that poor man?" Mary asked when Hupsman, taking a hasty leave of them, ushered him away.

"A tradesman who can be trusted to keep his mouth shut," was Berkeley's curt reply.

No bells pealed in celebration when they came out of the church into the rain. They hurried across the courtyard, into the Morning Room of the castle, once its chapel, where his lordship demanded champagne with his breakfast and loosed off the cork himself in an impetuous frame of mind.

"Well, here's to the reckless deed!" he laughed.

"To the pair of you!" Billy seconded.

Mary watched the silvery bubbles rise in a thread and break upon the surface of the wine and tried to feel a lightness of heart to match the occasion. Her husband made no stir to introduce her to his ancestral home which was as foreign to Mary as the tombs of the ancient pharaohs. There was something wild and archaic about the sombre chambers, overlaid by a patina of culture. In the Morning Room long sweeps of tapestry clad the surly stone. These told the stories of Isaac and Rebecca and the destruction of Sodom, dissertations in thread that doubtless went unnoticed by the occupants of the castle. The vaulted ceiling timbers were inscribed with verses from Revelation and Mary was daunted by this immense weight of tradition against which she must pit herself.

"I've been thinking," said the Earl to Billy, "Mary cannot be known as the Countess, nor yet as Miss Cole. She must have a new name. And, therefore, so must you when you are among us."

In his own mind, Billy decided that this was immaterial now that he had annexed wealth and influence. "Whatever you say, my lord."

Berkeley was looking upwards for inspiration and alighted on the beams decorated with the cinquefoil Rose of England. "Tudor, yes! Mary Tudor! There is a famous appellation!" It was a surname commonplace in the area, probably the result of some Welsh incursion long ago, and would have an authentic ring of antiquity. (The Widow Cole was of Welsh extraction.)

"My lord, no!" Mary protested. "Threadbare though my learning is, I know that Mary Tudor was a cruel Queen."

"There was another lady of that name. She was the by-blow of my eminent great grandfather, the Stuart King, Charles II. Another little Catholic! Her sons were staunch Jacobites and the youngest, Charles Radclyffe, was the last person to be martyred on English soil!"

"I think you are making sport of me, my lord, to furnish such a recommendation!"

"You cannot deny the name has dignity and breeding. It will flatter your newfound estate very well."

The Earl was not to be overruled. His chin jutted adamantly and the schemer's eyes danced to some tune of their own.

"Then I must go as William Tudor," Billy concluded.

"Yes, but not in Gloucester, I think. It is imperative that you continue as before. Tomorrow you shall go back to mixing potions and keeping accounts."

"Go back to Mr Parker's?" Billy was crestfallen after his first heady encounter with champagne. "Surely, Berkeley, you can find me a better post?"

"No, sir, I can't! And I'll thank you to know your place. If you don't do as you're bid and hold your tongue about this day's doings, you'll not see a penny of mine!" He snatched up his riding whip and flexed it against the palm of his hand, glancing about him irascibly and cursing the tardiness of the servants who were preparing breakfast. "Now, we shall all partake of our modest wedding fare, then your sister and I will be leaving for London."

They say that the marriage ring is the last link in the chain that in primitive times bound a wife, like a bondservant, to her husband. Mary's was as slippery as goose-grease. Lord Berkeley plucked it from her finger and, pressing a gold chain into her hand, bade her thread it on that and wear it beneath her bodice. "Next to your soft white bosom," he gloated, "where I alone shall have the privilege of admiring it."

By way of a honeymoon, the Earl took Mary to Kew and to Hampton Court, miracles of botanic symmetry after the backwoods of Berkeley. Hampton Court had an expansive maze through which few found their way unpiloted. Berkeley prophesied that they would make old bones in that place and never be found and never be free. Future generations would stumble on their remains and speculate upon their fate and their folly. After half an hour, he hollered for a gardener he'd seen tending the tulip beds to come and give some direction from the dais in the centre. A well-bred voice echoed in reply, but no one appeared. Amazed to find themselves close enough to the perimeter to need only the simplest instruction, they emerged to confront a tall, well-upholstered young man who erupted into a paroxysm of glee. His hair was teased and frizzed. He wore chamois breeches and a dark blue kerseymere coat with gold buttons as big as medals, a lawn kerchief white as the driven snow and a lapel radiant with diamonds, but none of these things was as imposing as his person.

"Fred Berkeley, by all that's famous! And who is your fair companion?"

The Earl made a low bow. "Your Royal Highness, what a happy surprise! May I present Miss....Miss Tudor to you?"

"I....am greatly honoured to make your Royal Highness' acquaintance," Mary stammered, curtsying deeply. Her knee-caps were quaking.

"Miss Tudor, the honour is all mine," he responded gallantly and drank her in with an appreciative eye and an expression in which sympathy and fascination were commingled. Instantly, she was at ease and knew, despite his rank, that he would always be her friend, a contemporary spirit. "You're a lucky dog, Fred. Luckier than you deserve," said the Prince. "But what brings you here?"

"The desire to see something of our culture. Miss Tudor has a fondness for such things."

"Then, madam, you must be congratulated upon effecting a most salutary change in Berkeley! Have you seen the State Apartments?"

"Oh yes, sir, the housekeeper kindly admitted us. They are splendid."

"My family seldom visits Hampton Court. The King won't come within hallooing distance, not since my great grandfather boxed his ears in the Queen's Drawing room for some mischief when he was a boy. Discerning fellow, George II! But, pray, come down to the river and join our party. We are taking tea *al fresco* in a covered boat."

"Good grief, George, you must be disguised, for there's an Arctic gale blowing!" expostulated Fred.

They stepped aboard the *Leda* to an uproarious greeting and Berkeley introduced the Countess of Jersey and Georgiana Devonshire, Mr Charles James Fox and Mr Richard Brinsley Sheridan, Colonel Whatley who hailed from Gloucestershire. There was also another woman, an unassuming little creature called Mrs Armistead who was Fox's mistress. She was elegantly dressed in contrast to Fox who had a number of buttons hanging by a thread and a prayer. Though she did not go in for the adornments of Her Grace and her ladyship, Lizzie Armistead's subtle wit thrust her into equal focus.

Mary was surprised to find herself easy among this company. As Miss Tudor, a friend of Berkeley's and a guest of the Prince, they welcomed her without demur. She began to understand that the Earl's choice of address had been both clever and delicate. The unmarried state was meant to confer a pristine sense of honour whereas, had she been *Mrs* Tudor, the implication would have been transparent. It was one of the Prince of Wales' qualities that he took everyone as he found them and did not concern himself with birth and breeding. Wit and character were his benchmarks. His Royal Highness toasted the 'fugitive angel' he longed to make his own and gazed wistfully in the direction of Richmond Hill.

Mary was to look back on those few days filled with air and light and blossom buds as through a magnifying glass. For, soon, she was sentenced to a further spell of seclusion in different lodgings in St. George Street, Hanover Square. Thus began a nomadic pattern which lasted for some two years with the object of avoiding prattling tongues.

She endured it for a week, two weeks, three. And then a tumult of misery crashed in upon her and a fever raged. She wept with shame at being taken for a mistress instead of a wife. Again and again, she relived the horror of that night of her abduction, felt tainted and consumed with guilt, vainly wanting virginity restored. The Earl did not know what to do. He grew kinder with the passing months; his attentions in the bedroom were sporadic, but full of solicitude. He had no experience of tending ailing females. Moreover, the doctor's remedies did not appear to be working. One night, he lay awake in the adjoining room, listening to Mary whimpering weakly into her pillow. He went through to her, lit candles and lodged himself upon the bed.

"What's this, Polly? What's this? How's a fellow to sleep? Your eyes have been swollen these three days and your beauty quite spoiled."

She shuddered out a half-stifled lament. "I'm homesick! Homesick! Homesick!"

"Well, I have been giving the matter some thought...."

"Homesick for what is lost and gone, for what will never be."

"Ah Polly," sighed the Earl, "that is the human condition. There's no help for't, not that I can see. The notion of limitless choice is a trick done with mirrors."

He was forty that year and looked older in the dusty glow which muddled shade and tone. The slump of his shoulders bespoke one weighted with cares. In odd moments of contrition, a melancholy mood would surface and drive him to seek escape in the next irresponsible whim.

"Tis like living in a cruel fairytale, being a Countess."

He took her hand and chafed it encouragingly. "Now you must go down to your friends and relations in Gloucester, breathe some West Country air and recover yourself. Spend the whole summer with them if you desire. In the morning, you can write to your sister and tell her when to expect you."

"My lord, thank you! You can't guess how much I have missed them all!" On a wave of gratitude, she put her arms about his neck and kissed him, a blandishment he received with cynical amusement. "You have demanded everything I have to offer, but you have never looked for love."

"How could I?" he answered tersely, tearing her wrists away. "You are young and beautiful. My tender years were fouled by a knowledge of mankind long ago. I think no one truly loved me in my life!"

"Then I shall hope to learn the trick of it," Mary said in a small voice.

She was up before breakfast to scribble a letter to Ann on a sheet of Berkeley's best notepaper. Further consideration prompted her to pen another to Billy, so that he should show no surprise at the length of her stay and remember he was obliged to keep their secret. After weeks of masquerading as Miss Tudor, she dared to sign herself Mary B to her brother. Both letters she addressed to Ann's house rather than let his lordship's frank fall under Parker's eye.

What Mary did not foresee was that her eldest sister, who, when they were younger had asserted some authority over her siblings, would take it upon herself to open Billy's correspondence.

She was no longer a jailbird's widow. Will was restored to a modest way of trade around the corner in Westgate. He had taken on Jimmy Roberts again, a Sergeant in the North Gloucestershire Militia, who ran about delivering orders and fetching sheep out of the meadow.

Mary was apprehensive as to how she would be received by her mother. Nowhere was the onus of silence more cumbersome than this. She stood on the doorstep between a ballast of presents and her excitement vanished before Ann's apathetic stare. Another bout of breeding had caused her to run to fat and had defined the inchoate violence within her. According to the laws of nature, the opposite should have been true, but Ann saw little profit in procreation when her fine gowns must be laid aside and she was tied to the nursery.

Behind her, in the depths of the parlour, darkened by low beams, Mrs Cole walked the tiniest addition, a nameless girl, back and forth against her shoulder, the child blazing up in protest at the intrusion. Henry took fire and peered wrathfully from her skirts, trailing a 'comfort rag', while Billy strode in from the kitchen with a handful of bread and cheese and sporting the gun he'd been cleaning which he used for shooting snipe when he went out with Roberts of an evening. Though they didn't live over the shop nowadays, the miasma of the shambles still lingered about the rooms.

"Well, mayn't I enter? I'm no apparition."

"I suppose we must curtsy to my fine lady now?"

"Curtsy? No, of course you must not."

"You'd best come in." Ann moved from the doorway and allowed Mary to step down into the rush-matted parlour. Mary glanced expectantly from one to the other and the hope of a welcome drained out of her. The exclamation of delight at her new niece died upon her lips. "Ma? Billy?" It was cold for May and a paltry fire spat peevish sparks into the thick uneasiness. They were tongue-tied, not knowing what to make of the situation.

Her mother spoke at last. "You've come a long way, Mary."

"Aye," Billy said, craning to see out of the tiny window. "Where's your grand coach, Sis? When Susan comes, she drives down in a flash phaeton."

"But I've no coach. I travelled by stage to The Bell as arranged. You might have looked for me there," Mary added uncertainly.

"By yourself?" Ann mocked.

"Indeed by myself. I'm quite used to it now."

"We may suppose a coach with servants in livery is too fine for the likes of the Coles and the Farrens."

"But I have no coach," Mary insisted, dismayed by such antagonism, "no means of transport at all."

"Don't gull us with that, *Lady B.* You're ashamed of your inferior connections."

The leaden drop of the wall-clock's pendulum measured an eloquent silence. Billy had betrayed her! He shrugged helplessly.

"It's not my fault, Sis. Ann opened your letter."

"Lest it be urgent," Ann interposed hastily. "Billy was out with Mr Parker at Chater's Farm, bleeding the old man of his brass. He usually sleeps at Parker's."

"It bain't a lie, Mary?" begged the Widow Cole. She settled the baby into the cradle and rocked it in time with the pendulum.

"Upon my oath, Ma, I cannot answer you. Depend upon it, I have done nothing wrong. You must have confidence in me as you used to do."

The refts of tension across her mother's brow relaxed. "You always was a good girl," she affirmed in her special voice.

"Too good for this world," observed Ann tartly.

Mrs Cole made some tea and brought out a drizzle cake. Soon the atmosphere changed and they were Coles together again, their differences forgotten. Billy had put down his gun and joined them but was at odds amongst a parcel of gossiping women and quickly made an excuse to be off. He slept at the apothecary's house that night and Mary did not see him again until supper the following evening. The weather was cool, but fresh with a hint of lilac. Mary said that if he was going down to the meadows to look at the lambs, she'd go with him. He did not object, so she put on a shoulder cape and walking boots.

"Last time we did this, it was the day of your wedding," Billy remarked.

There was an awkward pause. "Billy, have you told them?"

"I'd no cause to go telling them, had I, when Ann saw that letter?"

"How foolish of me to be so careless! Oh, you can't imagine...! Deep down, I longed to reassure Ma."

"It's hard to tell what she's thinking."

"So they're not aware of when it took place, or that you were a witness?"

Billy's complexion turned the colour of naked osiers. "They pestered me and prised it out of me. You know what they're like. There's no mending it now, Sis."

They stepped across a wooden footboard over a ditch, slippery and rotten with a bright orange fungus sprouting in the rough grain. Leaning against a stile, they watched the ewes crop buttercups and listened to the litany of bleating lambs. Mary did not know whether to feel gladness, or regret. Billy chewed on a stalk of rye grass and said nothing. He was only a boy who regarded it all as a game.

"That airing's done you a power of good," said Mrs Cole to her daughter when they returned. She was taking a pair of tongs to haul boiled muslin out of the copper. "You looked so pale and poorly when you came, I wondered if you was in the family way." She got a firm negative for her answer. "Praise be!" she muttered, glancing at Mary, her eyes hooded with a burden of wisdom.

"Wouldn't you be pleased?"

"Well, Mary, youm wearing no ring. What's a body to think?"

Why, Mary wondered, had her mother sought confirmation of her marriage when she had heard Billy's account of it?

97

Six

"This is a tiresome business, Prescott. I can settle to nothing."

The Captain regarded his host's half-eaten plate of kidneys and bacon and deduced that something serious was amiss. Berkeley had been distant and on edge for several weeks and had volunteered no reason. They had known each other since their early days at St. Marylebone School, but the Captain was not a man to look for confidences. His claim that he went through the world in a straight line and did not concern himself with other people's business had stood him in good stead. His own recent history he was not prepared to share beyond the spare facts. There was an abandoned wife and small son living at Kew who, though well taken care of, were seldom visited. At the time of the marital split, Berkeley had invited his friend to look upon *his* house as his own. At first, the Captain had resisted, thinking it might cramp his style, but Berkeley had been routinely about his own affairs and their lives quickly fell into a mutually agreeable pattern. On furlough from his naval duties, Prescott shifted between Grafton Street, Cranford House and Berkeley Castle with almost the same regularity as his peer.

"You certainly seem all at sea. I conjecture there is a lady in the case."

"I was never in such a coil. But I cannot speak of it. The circumstances are rather intricate."

Captain Prescott buttered some toast, thankful that he had ordered his life differently. "Mrs Bayly, if I may so observe, hardly gave you a moment's concern."

"You weren't there when she got her marching orders," said the Earl ruefully. "She'd have called me out if she'd been a man!"

Mrs Bayly had been consigned to the tender mercy of the Captain who fielded her ejection with the utmost diplomacy, then turned his attention to sea-faring. "In my opinion, she is a good woman. Most companionable."

"Don't tell me you felt sorry for her, Prescott. You've no idea how I had to sweeten the pill."

"After last year's returns, I can see that would have been a blow, but it sounds to me as though you are laying another trap for yourself."

"I must go down to Gloucester at once."

"My dear fellow, you have not long returned!"

Later that morning, the Earl set out for the country, leaving Captain Prescott to contemplate the whirlwind of his departure. On this occasion, he did not intend to go down to Berkeley, but to seek rooms at The King's Head in Gloucester. He had received intelligence that Mary was ill and that Mr Parker had been called in to prescribe elixir of vitriol for a raging sore throat that was either the cause or effect of some deeper malady. Having gone to her relatives, she seemed to be sickening rather than recovering.

It was not until dusk the following night that he presented himself at the Farrens' door. Mary had retired to bed, but one guttering candle on a wooden chair gave out its glow-worm light. At the creaking of the door, she stirred and raised herself.

"My lord! What brings you here at this hour?" she said in a croaking whisper.

"I could not risk coming at any other! How are you, Polly? I perceive you are very drawn." He embraced her gently and touched his lips to her forehead. She was hot and slightly damp through the thin chemise.

"Mr Parker cannot tell what ails me. It has been severe enough to confine me to the house these two weeks. I feel as though I've swallowed caustic."

The Earl looked out of place wedged into the small cottage room. "I have passed some confoundedly miserable days in London, Polly...."

"I hope Harriet is remembering to feed and water Daffy and let him out of his cage now and then," Mary rasped. "He'll have no one to sing to. Oh, don't speak of London!"

"Well, you don't belong here! As soon as you are better, perhaps...."

"My lord, I beg you won't tax me with this now. I must bide awhile. There's the baby's christening in June."

"And is Susan to attend?"

"'Tis a family occasion," Mary shrugged. "I can't avoid her altogether when she does not know we are married."

"I concede it is hard for you to discern where your loyalty rests. Polly, there are things....I cannot speak of. Trust me to know what is right in this."

"What things?"

"Do not press me. I'll not be drawn." Berkeley held up his hands and his tone was firm.

Mary besought no further. For the most part she preferred to remain in ignorance. She was ashamed of her sister's permissive ways and fervently hoped their mother would not learn the truth.

Mrs Cole seemed convinced that it was Susan's rise in the world that had aided the Berkeley espousal.

The children slept soundly. Farren had long gone to The White Hart next door for a jug of ale. The low hum of women's voices drifted up the staircase. The absurdity of having a peer of the realm on the doorstep looking for favours, like a tramp seeking shelter, defied belief. When Berkeley took his leave and descended the narrow steps into the parlour, Mrs Cole got up to meet him and earnestly counselled:

"I hesitates to say so, my lord, but you'd best leave by the back door. There's folk still abroad in the street."

"Top marks for sentry duties, ma'am. I'll thank you and bid you goodnight. Mrs Farren."

"What a rigmarole!" Ann huffed when he had gone.

"I can't make head nor tail on't, Nan."

"If Mary's good enough to be his wife, then he should have the courage to own it!"

"Well, but it can't have helped, your Will in hock to half the county's farmers. When he regains his standing in the community, things will improve, I'm sure."

In June, when Susan came down from Town for her niece's christening, accompanied by James Perry, things took a bizarre turn. The long and the short of it was that he and Mary fell in love.

When he arrived, soberly apparelled beside Susan in pink quilted satin, he flung down his hat and held out his arms, crushing Mary to his breast in brotherly fashion.

"Why, lassie, you found your way home."

From that instant, the sympathy which had taken root at the Lenten masque more than two years ago, burgeoned into bud. Mary could not describe or excuse the sweet madness which swept over her at beholding him. That species of passion created an incandescent sphere of its own, immobilising reason. Nevertheless, it was the soul of sanity after the machinations of Lord Berkeley.

"You were kindness itself," Mary recalled. "When I was in desperate want of a friend, you were there and never looked for a single favour in return."

"Well, I am now come to make a wee claim on your hospitality. Och, but you are tired and lily-pale."

The Scots lawyer saluted Mrs Cole and Ann with jocular warmth. Anxious for something to do, Susannah put on the kettle to boil and brought out the new Coalport teapot which had been bought for a song at a warehouse on the quay dealing in slightly imperfect goods from the Black Country. Mary could not tell what their guest made of it all, but he graciously sat beside her on the horsehair sofa and interested himself in the bundle of rags she had cut into strips ready for knotting on to a canvas backing for a rug, a commonplace craft in households like theirs which did not merit the attention he paid it. Perhaps he would have preferred to see her embroidering a sampler, as the fine ladies did, or submerged in a volume of plangent verse on Ettrick's fair forest and the bloody braes of Yarrow. For him, Mary wished she could boast these refinements. Not that he had never tasted poverty, but he strongly aspired to make a name for himself among the nation's rulers by dint of hard work and a finely-tooled brain.

James Perry put up at The Bell Inn for five days and visited the Coles every day. He filled the compact sitting room in Southgate Street with his exuberance, spreading strongly-veined hands to emphasise a theme. He seemed quite at home among them, though Mary could not think they provided a stimulus for a man of his vigorous intellect. Away from his London chambers, the brusque Scottish accent broadened and was tempered by a blend of roguishness and the lilting sensitivity of the Border poets. He sang *The Flowers of the Forest* in a resonant baritone voice. He made his audience yearn for other times and places. He threw open new landscapes, mountains and moors and silver-blue lochs, that men fought and died for, so that Mary mourned the Jacobites' lost cause, Catholics and Pretenders all. She lived for his smile, for the whimsical eyes that were like cairngorm stones seen through clear water and which occasionally startled hers with a burning tenderness. In her innocence, she longed to express the most wholesome and natural affection towards him which circumstances denied. No thought of disloyalty entered her head.

Breaking with tradition, the smallest Farren was christened at St. Mary de Crypt whose parish boundaries encompassed that part of Southgate Street where they now lived. She was named Susannah Perry after her grandmother and her godfather who generously bought her a silver porringer at Mayer's shop.

It was the hottest Whitsuntide any of them could remember and they took a picnic and spread themselves upon College Green in the lea of the Abbey. Sunlight saturated the chestnut leaves and the sugar-cone blossoms scarcely stirred. Henry and Liam romped with a bobbin and string. The baby rebelled against the heat and nothing would soothe her but that Granny should wheel her in her basket perambulator about the Green. Susan languished in the shade of a parasol and regaled Ann and Will and Billy with her adventures at Bagnigge Wells on May Day. James Perry, meanwhile, strove to elucidate the tangled plot of a Restoration comedy which had amused him in London. Mary was charmed by the hypnotic rhythm of the sentences. He had been watchful of the quartet with their heads together and presently proposed that he and Mary take refuge in the cool of the Abbey.

They walked in silence about the stately tombs decked with painted effigies of the dead, rapt in the transcendent calm of space and time. Upon reaching the Lady Chapel, Perry sought Mary's hand and fastened it in his own. She could feel a strong pulse beating there and a quicksilver shock flowed through her. He was half-smiling, half-grave.

"I've tried my damnedest to be alone with you and have not succeeded until now. Often, while I have been sporting the oak, you have entered my thoughts and sometimes I have been tormented by the conviction that you were unhappy. Thankfully, I see it is not so...."

"Oh!" exclaimed Mary in dismay. "You must not think...."

Before she had done faltering, he stifled her mouth with a most unbrotherly kiss. Her blood fizzed as though from potent cider fumes and she found herself incapable of resistance. He was too honest, when it was done, to apologise for the liberty and she was distressed to have responded as she did.

"We must not. I....I can never care for you....only as an acquaintance."

At that, he burst into laughter. "Then I shall earnestly hope to be here when you have a change of heart! I'm persuaded I have not imagined those pensive glances, the tender affinity...."

In panic, Mary gabbled a swarm of objections.

"You're too honourable a man to be dallying," she said, "and there can be no proper connection between the likes of you and me. You have a promising career ahead of you and one day you'll be rich and much talked of in high places. I should be the most miserable of beings when you learned to despise me for my want of education."

He sat down in a pew and patiently drew her down beside him.

"You will always be beautiful. When you are old and the smiling and suffering have etched themselves upon your countenance, your spirit will shine through. Any man must pay homage to that. Don't you think I have wrestled with doubts – yes, I must be frank – but, lassie, I love you sore. There is no other woman I want for my wife. You are the inspiration of all my endeavours."

Oh James, my dearest, my truest friend, Mary thought wildly, if only I could pour out the whole sorry tale to you. If only I were free! Had you been silent, I could have woven you into the texture of my life, seen you, heard you, touched the quick of you, watched you come and go. God knows I would willingly have conquered that other drive for togetherness. Now it is impossible. You will hate me for rejecting you so cruelly.

The saints in the gem-bright windows did not stir. The brass cross on the altar gleamed. "Sir, I cannot marry you," she told him, jumping up. "It is written in the stars. I do not....*cannot* love you."

She hadn't gone more than two paces when he caught her wrist and swung her round, his fine eyes brilliant with pained indignation. "You lie! Why are you lying when you were born so honest?"

In a forced whisper, she urged him to desist lest this unseemly scene be remarked.

"You owe me an answer."

"Oh, sir, let me go," she implored him. "I mustn't see you again. Ever!"

She ran out through the cloisters, into the blinding sunshine, across the daisy-flecked green, not stopping to look for the others. Hardly caring where her feet led, she hurried up Westgate, turned the corner and, gaining Ann's door, sought the key under the pelargonium pot. Shaking uncontrollably, she stabbed it into the keyhole and, in the refuge of the cottage, wept and wept and inveighed against God for denying her the love of a good man and her one chance of contentment. She had tried to do what was right, and not out of piety, but because she trusted that all would turn out for the best if she stuck to the faith. Her reward had been humiliation and heartache and a forbidden taste of heaven. To preserve truth and virtue, she had had to lie.

When her mother and sisters returned with the children, sticky and begrimed from twists of barley sugar, she told them she had a bad headache. It was a relief to see no gentleman, except Will, step into the room.

"Youm a touch of the sun, my girl," Mrs Cole pronounced. "It's hot as mustard out there, spoiling for a storm an' no mistake.

The poor bairn's been bawling all the way home. She's a good pair of lungs, I'll say that."

"James was put about by your abrupt departure and hopes he has not offended you," said Susan in a quizzical way. "Indeed, I do not know why he should think so, for a more sweet-mannered fellow you could not wish to meet."

Mrs Cole sent her youngest daughter to bed with a powder. The noise outside and below drummed in her skull and Mary's thoughts charged about like a frenzied stallion. Not one of Adam's race was worth this anguish, she told herself, but her heart would not assent to the proposition.

At cock crow, she set to and made the cottage ship-shape, swept out the cobwebs and polished the brasses, took a vinegar solution and a patch of soft hide and made the windows gleam, pegged out the linen and baked a fresh loaf, driving herself as hard as she might towards exhaustion. Mrs Cole said: "You're brainsick. You'll have a relapse. Come, put your feet up and drink this sweet tea." When the rap came on the door and a tall shadow fell across the sunlit aperture, she was half-way upstairs and scrambled to the top in a jiffy, holding her breath. Her mother came bustling up the lower steps after her, accosting her through the banister rail in an urgent whisper.

"Mary, come down. There's that *likely* Mr Perry enquiring for you."

Her beleaguered offspring was so stiff with apprehension she could hardly stammer a reply. What did it mean? What did they want of her? Surely they knew she could not possibly entertain his advances.

"No, mother, I cannot. Give him my respects....make some apology."

Mary heard her address him in fawning tones: she could not make out his reply. It must have been his accessible character and professional standing that made her mother so anxious not to displease him. Sneaking a glance into Bell Lane, Mary spied the crown of Susan's Leghorn hat bobbing up and down beside his tall silk one and the sight smote her with jealousy. Inhaling deeply, she sank against the wall and thanked Heaven for deliverance when the baby set up a wail and brought her very material needs to the attention of the household.

The Widow Cole's prognostics proved ill-founded and the fair weather continued to hold. At eventide, Mary escaped from the buzz and strife of Southgate and went down to the meadows where Hathaway's sheep were grazing. They were fertile pastures on the banks of the Severn, flooded once or twice a year which deposited a silt that kept the soil rich. She'd heard Hathaway say that come hay-making, he could crop near two tons an acre and make a tidy fortune selling it to the bargees going up to the mines and the ironworks of Shropshire where teams of horses were employed day and night in so great a number that the local farms could not keep them supplied with fodder. The lambs were long-weaned and, far from being the frisky sprigs they'd been in the spring, would soon be ready for their first shearing. Their throats were daubed with a band of reddle which Hathaway swore kept foxes at bay.

Solitude. Breezes swelled the surface of Mary's white dimity frock and carried wispy seeds to new ground. She picked a nosegay of campions, ox-eye daisies and coltsfoot and knelt and bound them with plaited stalks. Across the fields, the church clocks chimed seven in happy disunion.

Just then, she jumped. The dandelions' silky spheres were breaking all around her and a long shadow fell across the grass. Turning, she gasped to see James standing there, his back to the sun, a cravatless shirt pulling loose from his nankeen breeches in Bohemian disarray.

"How you startled me!"

"If I'd not taken you unawares, you'd have run away." He squatted down on his haunches beside her. "Hinny, I'm away to the smoke in the morn."

"Oh." Her numb fingers could work the grasses no more. They were slipping undone.

"Shall you wish me Godspeed, then?"

He was leaving. Their paths were unlikely to converge again since Mary was forbidden to socialise with Susan in Town. She did not want to remain unforgiven.

"I shall be sad without you."

"Shall you?" he said hopefully. "Oh Mary, let me not go without hope we'll be wed."

Her heart lurched; her tongue prevaricated. "I'll love you for ever and ever," she breathed. And if lying was subversive, so was speaking the truth. She melted into his embrace, oxtering, he called it in his quaint Scottish way, and drowned in the elemental rightness of loving. How pale and trite were Lord Berkeley's effusions, how powerless to induce the vanquishing ecstasy which dissolved bone and tissue, reason and caution. Nature had plotted the sweetest of ironies to make Mary the fool of her own lofty ideals.

But she did not care. She could no longer distinguish between truth and falsehood. *Let me,* she thought helplessly, *have one memory of pure love as a keepsake against the disgrace of treating with Berkeley.*

"Love me. Show me what it is like to be loved."

"Nay, hinny," Perry said thickly, "I'll not tumble you here among the weeds like some quean from a byre. You are roses and lilies and all things fair."

"And a butcher's daughter," she reminded him, for that was the only weapon to hand against his romanticism, the catches of airs that had spun a mystique around maidenhood and those echoes of Calvin from which no true Scot could find permanent sanctuary. Could he have loved anyone as humble as Mary had he not made her epitomise all the virtues?

"I care nought for that. You shall be the chiefest jewel in my crown. Always wear white as you are doing today."

Shamelessly, there on the towpath, under the pendent willows, she kissed him with an ardour no innocent should have dared to demonstrate. Her racing blood matched the sweep of the tide, bringing cutters upstream into port from all points of the compass, and fishing smacks attended by flurries of excitable gulls. Limpet-like, she clung to him, and then it was he who would not release her. She was conscious of the smell of his maleness beneath the starched shirt, and the pulse's fluttering beat beneath the Adam's apple.

"Come, then," he relented, "and we'll plight our troth as soon as maybe."

Glancing over his shoulder, he took Mary by the hand and led her to a ramshackle boathouse in the curve of the river which, unexpectedly, sheltered a clinker-built wherry such as she'd seen used on the Thames to ferry passengers from one bank to the other. The door had a bolt, but no padlock and chain and needed no forcing to let them inside. There, in the gloom, they were close and secure, cradled in the bobbing boat on a bed of tarpaulins covered by Mary's shawl, a soft lapping noise in the background. She whimpered and wept and the splintered fire of a ripening sunset came through a crack in the warped timbers, flooded the earth-coloured water and limned darting reflections on the cobwebbed rafters above.

James wiped her wet temples on the ruff of his sleeve. "Wisht, hinny, it'll nae pain you so next time."

But it wasn't physical pain that brought tears to the surface, it was the other kind, the having and not having, the saying goodbye and turning one's back on the prospect of happiness.

"Come to London with me tomorrow," he urged. "We'll bribe a bishop for a special licence and be married at once! I'm thinking your mother wouldn't object to a swack lawyer for a son-in-law, and Farren will tell you you could do a deal worse."

Choking, Mary shook her head. "You must go back to your books and I to my lambs."

"But what nonsense is this?" he asked in alarm, guiding her by the chin to look into his eyes. "Dare to say you don't love me now. I defy you to do it."

"I love you," she sobbed, "but you must take silk and become a great man. You cannot support a wife and children at this stage without spoiling your career."

"I'm a dab hand with my pen, I'll have you know, Mary. With you at my side, I'll soar to the gods!"

"I won't marry you. Don't entreat me so."

"Shall you wait for me, then, till I'm through with my studies?"

"You do not know what you ask. Let this be a special memory to keep in your heart."

"A memory! Faith, what is it you want?"

"James, I can never be your wife!" she cried. And she blurted out the story of her commitment to Berkeley who had saved her sister from the spunging-house, then buried her head in her knees. She did not tell him of Susan's part in the plot, she was so ashamed. Whatever he might have suspected of her sister, Perry infrequently attended the *levées* at Charles Street and was unaware that Mr Turnour was a fiction.

Now he was wild with anger; the grip of his hands upon her shoulders was like scorching bruises.

"You peddled your virtue, you who were so fine and chaste when your sister went astray?"

"But he ruined poor Will and the babes needed food."

"By God, let me get my hands on the blackguard! I'll horsewhip him within an inch of his life! Mary, you must leave him, and at once, and be damned to his threats! He's taken his joy of you, what more can he demand?"

"I tell you I cannot!"

Beneath the fury with Berkeley, Mary was sure that Perry despised her for being weak and spineless. He could not be expected to understand just how dependent and circumscribed was the lot of women, how there was her family to consider.

Maybe she was beginning to despise herself for clinging to those principles which were forcing her to reject and disappoint the love of a lifetime.

"Why can you not? What is it you fear?"

Weeping desperately now, she hoisted the chain beneath her modest bodice and showed him the ring where the crucifix should have been.

"Because," she said softly, "he is my husband."

Neap tides. The ebbing of summer. The river awash with frangible reflections. Way out on the estuary, the kittiwakes mewed and the migrant swallow formations diminished to nothing over the horizon. The days fell away like leaves from an oak in the harvest storms.

Soon, it became obvious that Will's business was failing. He'd no credit, no credibility, left. That was a commodity the Earl could not supply. He spoke of tenanting a farm down in Devon or Cornwall where labour was cheap, or else of going up to Scotland where his uncle had the ear of the Laird of Culzean. Ann wanted to go to Susan in London and lead a gay life. As for Mrs Cole, she quite lost the knack of her contacts in Gloucester, being cumbered with the needs of her grandchildren, and the Widow Medlicott, her particular friend, having remarried an upstanding soul from the Southgate Meeting, a Welshman by the name of Williams and a carrier by trade.

When Lord Berkeley learned of these developments, he sent for Mary and booked a place on the London coach. By Michaelmas, she was installed in a cosy house with bow windows, just off the Brompton Road, where some form of domesticity was sufficiently established for the Earl to invite Captain Prescott to take tea. There had been talk of taking up residence in Park Street, but it was rumoured that the lady who leased the house had grown weary of flitting from one Continental hideout to the next, pursued by couriers with long epistles from her royal paramour. She evinced every sign of packing her trunks and returning to England.

"Time's wingèd chariot is bringing Maria back to my door! How sweetly she has capitulated, Fred."

It was November, a month of thickening fog. The Prince of Wales had received the Earl of Berkeley in his silk-panelled bedchamber, attired in a Chinese kimono figured with bamboo. The remains of an epicurean breakfast were spread on the lacquered table by the window. He was as gleeful as a child who had been granted a coveted toy.

"I take it the lady has undergone a Lutheran conversion in her absence."

"Good Lord, no! Catholics don't change. It is our beastly laws which must. The moment I am holding the reins, I promise you I shall see this Marriage Act repealed with a stroke of the pen. A piece of mischief devised by my father to keep the whip hand!"

"Then you are no further forward as far as I can see."

"The separation has confirmed the strength of our ardour. The hurdles must be surmounted. Tell me, Fred," said the Prince in a pointed digression, "how is your enchanting shepherdess, Miss Tudor? I was vastly taken with her at Hampton Court."

"Unfortunately, sir, she has suffered one malady after another throughout the summer, but now appears to be mending, I thank you."

"Another Jacobite white rose. Mary Tudor! What could be more resonant of the Papist faith? And you a confirmed heathen!"

Berkeley grinned in a bashful fashion. The blood rose around his gills. "I believe I mentioned that I am not altogether unacquainted with the cast of your mind."

"Am I right in supposing you have come to some resolution?"

"The nature of the attachment has changed," the Earl dissembled. "For the present, circumspection is of the essence."

"Your secret shall go no further, you may rely. But what a fine example of triumph you are! Where there's a will, there's a way!"

"Forgive me, but your situation bears only the palest comparison to mine. Your Highness has the nation's welfare upon his shoulders."

"Ha! The Hanoverian yoked to the Catholic! There will be insurrection! There will be disputes over the Succession. The marriage itself will be a criminal act at which no upright cleric can officiate," catalogued the Prince. "Well, I'll tell you in the strictest confidence, Fred, since you have honoured me with yours, that I mean to marry Maria. It will be a morganatic marriage, a contract before God, and one, like yours, not to be openly avowed. Society can make of it what it will. Frederick is welcome to the Throne. He has some German Princess in tow which suits the Monarchy down to the ground...."

"If," suggested Lord Berkeley guardedly, "if you could bring yourself to wait until you are five and twenty, Your Highness might conceivably win the consent of Parliament, even against His Majesty. There would be nothing illegal about that."

"But, Fred, that is two years away!"

"Virtuous women! They're a deuced strain on the vitals, it must be said!"

"It would need the downfall of Pitt, for one thing. He's a pawn of the King. I doubt Fox, my staunchest defender, would support me in this. In fact, I don't intend he shall know!"

"Then I must wish you the devil's own luck. There's no knowing what the outcome will be."

"Maria is my *raison d'être*," pleaded the Prince.

"Have you thought, sir," said his lordship, affected by unwonted percipience and treading on regal eggshells, "that if there are issue of this union and it is deemed invalid, they will be illegitimate? Even if Parliament should later consent to an authorised ceremony, that will not help *them*. Only children born the right side of a legal knot would be your heirs. There would be sibling rivalry and odium towards you."

"All these 'ifs' and 'buts'! What I am doing, I am doing in good faith, Berkeley, as God is my witness. Let that be the alpha and omega of it."

"Yes, indeed," agreed his lordship, though he was dubious about the goodwill of the Deity.

When the Earl left Carlton House, he was depressed. Affairs of the heart were lumbered with all manner of responsibility.

Secrecy remained the byword. After residing briefly at several Mayfair addresses, Berkeley commissioned Captain Prescott to take a short lease on the property in Park Street which Maria Fitzherbert had occupied. In fashionable circles, the lady was now treated as the consort of the Prince of Wales. She enjoyed sumptuous living at Carlton House and its environs and maintained some independence by retreating to Marble Hill, Richmond, whenever she desired, or when the parliamentary temperature was raised. There was ongoing speculation about whether they *were* actually married. Well-connected hostesses bowed to the Prince's wishes that they be invited as a couple. The Queen, however, could not upon any showing receive Maria at her Drawing Rooms, but the rival camp of Cumberland House, where the wit was sparkling and the society invigorating, was ready to exploit the rupture. Mary was not aware of any of this, or that the illicit contract between the Royal Heir and his troubled muse had taken place in the drawing room one night before Christmas.

By early summer, when the hedgerows were curded with blossoms, it was clear to Mary that a child was coming and her feet were firmly planted on a new path. Living alongside Lord Berkeley was now the established mode. She determined, the more earnestly for her transgression, to be a good and faithful wife to him and was not unduly distressed by the advent of motherhood. In fact, truth to tell, she looked upon that germ of life within as an extension of her own flesh and blood that would not play her false.

Lord Berkeley took Mary for regular airings in the Parks in an open landau sporting the Berkeley pompadour, though he did not introduce her when accosted by passing friends. These outings taught her to care only for the dictates of her conscience. There was an intrinsic rightness in procreation, a kind of expiation. But as the months passed, she grew uneasy on account of the child. Surely, their wedded state must soon be revealed. What loving spouse could compromise his wife and offspring so?

"It cannot be announced, I tell you, not yet," the Earl insisted.

"My lord, why, when we've been married these eighteen months? People will say our child is....baseborn."

"Then let them! We shall know better!" How disdainful he seemed of the reputation he had suffered to protect.

"I don't understand you," Mary wailed. "You would prejudice the good name of your wife and child sooner than admit you've married outside your class?"

"You must see," he rounded upon her angrily, "the irregular conduct of your sister, Susan...."

"But I have obeyed your wishes and ceased all communication with her."

"And if that were not enough," he went on with great warmth, "your sister Farren shamelessly holds court in Old Burlington Street with a posse of Colonial officers under the same roof as she rears her children."

It was not clear whether Ann had forsaken Will or Will, Ann. Had they parted by mutual agreement, or did they still see one another on occasion as Billy had once implied? Whatever the truth, the upshot was that Will was tenanting a farm on the Cornish coast where the unchecked Atlantic breakers rolled in day and night and new worlds impinged. Ann had come up to

Town to ape her betters and had borrowed Lydia Sharpe, Susan's servant, to supervise her household. The eldest of a large brood herself, Lydia was not unconversant with the whims and demands of toddlers and proved a capable handler of them. Mrs Cole was in lodgings in the same street, paid for out of Mary's allowance. Mary grieved for her that her daughters had turned into strangers, pursuing unforeseen lives. Billy remained in the good apothecary's employ, but was unsettled and wrote of following the pack to London.

Autumn advanced and Mary's condition called a halt on their fugitive lifestyle. Berkeley's concerns took him away much of the time and his official address was still in Grafton Street with his naval crony. Mary was totally taken up with the practicalities of her confinement. When the house was equipped with a nursery, it seemed appropriate that Mrs Cole be invited to come and live in Park Street. Mary broached the idea and his lordship praised it at once for its sound sense and economy. She could not wait to rush off to Old Burlington Street and tell her mother the news. Mary found her in disgruntled mood.

"You should be putting your feet up, my girl, not running loose in the streets. You should have the use of his lordship's carriage."

Mary took off her cloak. She appeared in the rudest health. Pregnancy suited her. "The exercise has done me good. I can't sit indoors all day."

"Tis a queer life, everything at sixes and sevens. I rattle round this place like a marble in a coffin. And there's no knowing what your sisters are up to. I can't make them out."

"Never mind them. I have come to offer you gainful employment as your grandchild's nurse. You shall take full charge of the maids."

"What come and attend you in that grand house while you lie in? No, Mary, I will not."

Mary shrank in dismay. "But why, when you are all alone and in need of company as much as I?"

"And where is your husband, pray? I bain't a hard woman, but I'll not encourage vice. Mary, I think you've been pulling the wool over my eyes, in season and out."

"What are you saying? I don't understand."

"Making out you was wed, right and tight, only not speaking plain."

Mary jumped up from her chair in indignation. "I am married, Ma! There! Now it is out and you must keep it a secret. I am forbidden to own it without Berkeley's leave."

"I don't believe it no more. How can you keep quiet with a kiddy on the way?"

"Billy was there! He saw us take our oath and signed his name to it. He saw the parson bless us. Don't you believe him, either?" Mary fumbled to unbutton her bodice and dangled the ring on its chain that had been unchronologically entered in Walter Mayer's accounts as a 'golden seal'. "See!"

Mrs Cole's harsh frown slackened and she studied her daughter for a moment as if she had fallen to the conclusion that Mary was a simpleton.

"Listen, Mother, tomorrow is Sunday," Mary said. "To satisfy you, we will go and take Holy Communion together, and I hope you will think that I could not do such a thing without I am an honest woman."

"Very well, we'll go to church and I shall be content. Oh Mary, my poor lamb," wept her mother, hugging her remorsefully. "You should have told me afore."

After that, the widow went to live in Park Street and they were snug and companionable together. An extra maid was found, named Dorcas, for the new house was commodious.

There, on Christmas night, when all was still, the pains came, sharp and lacerating. Two ways wrestled within Mary, the past and the future, the old and the new. Mrs Cole sent for the doctor and anchored a sheet around the bedpost like a twisted spill so that Mary had something to cling to, behind and above. She'd not an atom of strength to scream against nature's tyranny when the next generation drained her of every resource and the grave and the cradle were comrades-in-arms. Mrs Cole laved her daughter's brow and murmured words of comfort and Mary could have sworn, in that hoary, shadow-crowded candlelight that she had a dim remembrance of her own birthing, the same dual campaign that banished the naked and unprotected into a cold, harsh world from a place of warmth and peace. Susannah helped her to sips of water, ran about after Dr Keate with hot water and towels and kept the fire going through the night until St. Stephen's Day broke over the roofs and spires of the city and Mary was delivered of a son, as handsome and lusty an infant as any mother could wish.

They named the child William, in memory of Mary's Pa, and Fitzhardinge, the ancestral name of the Berkeleys after the Bristol merchant who had been the financier of Henry II and had gained honour and lands in return. In William, the butcher's marrow was united with that of counsellors and kings, and, gazing into his sleepy countenance, Mary's mind could not compass it.

From the early days, Mary perceived two sides to his personality. Strange humours came over him, clouding his brow. He was by turns happy and petulant, not in the general way of young children with their whims and wants, but as if the spontaneous charm and the spleen which made Mary his slave sprang from having entered the world to settle some score. His mother loved him with a passion she could not describe, the firstborn who had given her a true reason for the course she had essayed with Berkeley. Even Berkeley discovered a new fund of affection.

Berobed in guipure lace, William was baptised on a crisp day in January at St. George's, Hanover Square. Despite the occasion, his father would not hear of going to the church and refused any part in the rite. He sent his long-standing friend from Cranford, John Chapeau, a Reverend no less, to conduct the proceedings and the brave sea-dog, Captain Prescott, to be godfather and stand at Mary's elbow. The baby behaved in an exemplary manner and her heart was bursting with pride. She wished the Earl could have been there. Executing a gallant bow, the Captain presented Mrs Cole with a golden guinea as was the custom, she being the child's nurse, and made to lead the party out from the font to the vestibule where a weak sun shafted through the pillared portico. At the doorway, he hesitated.

"Do you go ahead and settle yourselves into the carriage. I will follow directly, but must first furnish details for the registry."

"Captain, do let me come with you. I should like of all things to see the entry," Mary pressed.

"Tis but a formality, ma'am. You are best occupied with the little one. Pray excuse me," he said and marched off to the vestry, calling over his shoulder in the cheerfullest tone: "Five minutes and I will come and drink a toast with you."

But Mary wanted to see the magic words scribed in the annals of time. When, Nathan, the coachdriver, had seen Mrs Cole into the barouche and the precious burden was vouchsafed to her care, Mary hastened back up the steps into the church.

The organ-master had just begun a practice session and sprightly Handelian music echoed around the stonework. (The church was proud to have been the composer's spiritual home.) The vestry door stood ajar. Mr Chapeau was seated at a table with his back to the entrance, driving his quill over the Register of Baptisms. Isaac Prescott stood at the adjacent window, legs apart as if he were on the hurricane deck, pondering the wintry wild cherry boughs overhanging the tombstones.

Neither heard Mary's approach. The swelling chords built up to a reverberant crescendo and drowned out other sound. Her gaze fell on the page, the ink still glistening wet:

January 23rd, 1787

William Fitzhardinge, son of the Earl of Berkeley by
Mary Cole

Hastily, she turned away into the musty shadows, sick with shock, and clapped her hands over her ears to shut out the tumult of the playing. It seemed that all the organ-stops were out at once. Anguished, she thought of the child outside the door, and of James, the love lost forever on account of that charade in St. Mary's Minster at Berkeley. What a fool she had been! How ripe to believe in the course of action which was right and proper after Berkeley had seduced her. Soon everyone would be sure of her shame, but worse, far worse than that, was the stigma of bastardy for William whose rights could never be asserted and who might be condemned to beggary and vice if she did not please his father well. Gone was the hope of holding up her head. Gone was the vision of innocence, a humble hearth, a patch of land, a husbandman with a labourer's pride, toiling in his vineyard and coming home at sundown to sit at the head of his table.

The clergyman touched her shoulder and she nearly jumped out of her wits. Until that moment, it had not occurred to him that she might have been in ignorance. The music subsided, mimicking itself in softer harmonies. "My dear...."

"You have christened a natural child, Mr Chapeau."

"Every child is a child of God, born in sin and redeemed by the blood of Christ. The Kingdom is as much for outsiders as for those in the fold."

"Nevertheless, the practice is frowned upon...."

"Special dispensation was obtained from the Bishop by his lordship."

"I see."

Of course, they would always be at the mercy, William and she, of his noble father, who had duped her not once, but twice, and whose word, despite his proclaimed atheism and readiness to flout the Almighty, ruled even the spiritual powers of the realm.

At noon, they arrived back at Park Street where Lord Berkeley was waiting with a sparkling libation to wet the baby's head.

"Well," he said blithely, "have you made the lad a Christian?"

"I have so, my lord, just as you contrived it, to bring down a second curse upon us."

Their gaze levelled and Mary saw the flinty resistance in him when every vestige of humour was gone. At the same time, she felt and kick and thrust of the infant submerged in his shawl and cradled in her arms, as benign and sinewy as a lamb entangled in briars. For his sake, she must seek justice.

"When Hagar bore Ishmael, she fled into the desert," Mary observed, "but I shall not do so."

"Ah," Berkeley replied, catching her drift, and there was respect in his eyes, "but Abraham had a wife already, that I do know. You need have no fear upon that score. I have told you, I shall never marry. My resolution is firm."

Seven

In the summer of 1786, the Prince of Wales shut up Carlton House, dismissed most of his staff, and went trotting down to Brighton in a hired carriage with his new bride. He wished to emphasize his niggardly income to the King who had repulsed his appeals for help and demanded an exhaustive account of his arrears.

"Damned if I'll indemnify another folly with a mistress!" shouted the King. He had developed the habit of raising his voice as if he feared he might be misunderstood. The eyes and nostrils would flare like a spooked mount. Whatever tittle-tattle reached him concerning the Prince's liaison, he dismissed. Whispers of cloak-and-dagger covenants must not be entertained. Britain's first family could not live outside the law, especially when they had conceived it!

"He says he vill not part viz her," ventured the Queen.

She dared not repeat her conversation with her eldest son. He had told her outright that he had wed Maria Fitzherbert, that she had a bearing more majestic than any porcine German princess, and that man-made laws would not sever them in the eyes of God. Could his mother find it in her heart to admit her new daughter-in-law to her Drawing Rooms? The Queen had had no compunction in roundly refusing. To which the Prince responded that her gatherings were as dull as ditchwater, anyway, and patronised only by those with superannuated ideals. It had been distasteful to a degree, just when the King needed serenity. These days he was inclined to fly into a passion about the most trivial things and to revisit his grievances by the hour.

"It will blow over, nothing surer," opined His Majesty. "Pockets to let, what! Nothing like it to focus the mind!"

"Oh, I have made representations to him," sobbed the Queen. "Zis is the beginnings of anarchy. I fear for zhese stirrings across the Channel vot come to my ears."

"To say the truth, Madam, I fear more for Frederick. He will be home from Hanover soon. Think what a corrupt climate he will be exposed to. Eh?"

"Vot of the company George himself keeps? Some is not goot. He is young, easily engaged."

"Y'mean Fox and his crew. We shall make short work of that."

"I sink not so much of zhese Vhigs. I sink of my lord Berkeley, for instance. He has not an unsullied reputation and is of an age viz Your Majesty and likely to impress vhere, perhaps, Your Majesty, being next of kin, fails."

"Ah, Fred Berkeley. There's a man who knows how to run with the fox and hunt with the hounds!"

"Lady Jersey tells me zis rumour...."

"The Countess has a streak of mischievous wickedness. She is a confidante of George's. Season well with a pinch of salt, Madam."

"Her ladyship has reason to believe Lord Berkeley himself is secretly married zhese two years. Zhey have a child. She has met the lady in question, a Mary Tudor."

"Good God! A Catholic, I'll be bound."

"I sink, yah!"

At this the King rolled with laughter till the tears began to spill from the corners of his eyes. "Fred Berkeley has his neck in the noose! Oh, by all that's wonderful, did you ever hear such a thing? With a woman of strong religious persuasion! He's in for a rough ride, Madam, that I prophesy!"

"Lady Jersey supposes that Miss Tudor vould not consent to be Berkeley's mistress, so he married her. I hear she is blessed viz charm and beauty, but favours a modest style of attire and has somesing of the *ingénue* about her."

For a brief moment, the King was reminded of his own youth and his *angst*-ridden love affair with an eye-catching Quakeress, Hannah Lightfoot, before he was recalled to the solemn subject of duty. He knew this blend, cited by the Queen, to be remarkably potent. "Desperate fellow! Oh, this is beyond anything! And do we adduce that the secrecy is on account of Berkeley's not wishing to offend us during our own ecumenical crisis?"

The Queen shook her head. "I do not know ze reason, Your Majesty. I only vish George had not taken a leaf out of his book."

When Lord Berkeley delivered his bald assertion to Mary, having become a father, that he would never marry, he had meant – what had he meant? That it should be tempered by an understanding that no one else would have exclusive rights over him, either? That no one, certainly not a woman and a common citizen of the provinces, should rule his decisions? Mary did not seem to understand what a concession he had made in having the child baptised to please her, and having the event recorded for posterity in the parish register. And yes, he had actually *wanted* it recorded. When she had fixed his eye and declared that she would not run away, his spine had prickled. He could not exorcise the spectre of Mary's wounded innocence. She had trusted him.

"You may choose to think yourself a free man," she told him bitterly, "but God knows otherwise. A pledge was made in Berkeley Church which nothing can change."

Fred did not reason that for a moment. It was the least of his worries. And he did have some nagging worries. There was a matter he dare not breathe to a soul, nor write down on paper. His Royal Highness he deemed to be fiercely loyal to intimate friends and above disclosing their confidences. Yet when he considered the risk of excommunication from the Prince's clique, he flushed hot and cold. At the back of his mind, some instinct nudged him to find a safe repository for the information. It helped to explain his silence about the marriage the Prince had just cause to believe in. Who better to vouch for Berkeley's integrity, should it ever be questioned?

During June, five months after William Fitzhardinge's christening, Carlton House was re-opened. Pressure from the Foxites in Parliament, and his own growing unpopularity, had forced the King to relax his tight fist.

Having been granted an audience, the Earl was announced in the gilded saloon decked with many Oriental artefacts and novelty *bonsai*, where the Prince offered him madeira. Much had passed since they had last spoken and the Prince was eager to show off the new phase of transformation at Carlton House. It was mid-afternoon and the sun inclined to the west, soaking the peacock lawns with a blinding viridity. In the far wing, the painters, polishers, carpenters and masons were busily plying their skills to finish the work. The rising generation of royalty was back in business.

"It gladdens my heart to see you, Fred!"

"And mine to see you sprung from exile, Your Highness."

"The King has had to eat humble pie. My fiscal arrangements are on a new footing."

"So I understand, thanks to Fox."

"Mm," said the Prince dubiously. "I am not on the best of terms with that fellow. Behind the scenes, the speech he made in Parliament has brewed some mischief. It could well precipitate a crisis."

The Earl hesitated. He could not be sure that the Prince had actually gone ahead with his defiant plan and married Maria. Was it merely clever semantics, a diplomatic mind-game to satisfy irreconcilable forces? That was an expedient Fred could well understand.

"That is to be avoided now that you are mending bridges with His Majesty."

"To be perfectly honest, Fred, I am more than a little concerned about his mental health. It's as if he has one foot in reality and one in delusion.... But enough! Here I am, come from Brighton and scenes of domestic bliss.... You must see Grove House for yourself. Bring her ladyship and sample the salubrious air."

"Your Highness is most gracious...."

The Prince slapped his forehead with his palm. "Damme, Fred, I nearly forgot. Congratulations are in order! And how is young Viscount Dursley?"

Fred hedged a little. The courtesy title of the firstborn son would never be conferred on the child lying in the cot at Park Street.

"Thriving, I'm pleased to say. We call him 'Fitz.'"

"I take it I am not yet at liberty to mention your nuptials?"

Berkeley sipped the sticky wine and took a ratafia biscuit from the dish. "I...I find myself in the most devilish predicament...."

"How's that?"

"I scarcely know where to begin....how to express...." He wriggled the shirtsleeve inside his coat. "Mary's sisters live in a manner such as to render it absolute ruin for my connection with them to be known. Since coming to London, they have sought out the flesh-pots. Mary has made representations to them to desist. She is of an utterly different mould...."

"That's Catholic influence for you. It goes hell-for-leather one way or t'other!"

"Mary has no choice but to cut them."

"Will gaining their silence prove an embarrassment?" asked the Prince astutely.

"That is not the primary issue at this juncture."

"If they claim kin with Lady Berkeley, will they be believed, do you suppose?"

"They are bidding to move in powerful circles, particularly the younger of the two. She has taken one nomenclature after another and has been living under the protection of a member of the Bar in rank and splendour."

"A Member of the House?"

"It is our desire to see her respectably settled. She is on a campaign to exploit the male sex and will not readily be confined."

"And what of the elder sister?"

"A lady with a penchant for officers of His Majesty's Services, to say nothing of those from America. She has abandoned her husband and has three children to support."

"A ticklish coil. You must adopt a philosophical turn of mind, Fred, and see that were they not so provided, they could be a serious drain upon your personal exchequer."

"Yet there is worse," said his lordship. In some surprise, the Prince watched his once-feckless friend wilt with his head in his hands. Berkeley stared at the dizzying convolutions worked into the Brussels carpet. "It puts me in mind of that ghastly business at Berkeley concerning Edward II."

His Royal Highness cast about his memory for the correct history tutorial. "Banished to the dungeon for months among the rotting carcases of animals and then most foully murdered, I recall. That was in the Dark Ages! I don't follow...."

"He was a cruel and ineffectual ruler....but his crimes against nature...."

A ray of enlightenment dawned upon the Prince. "The catamite, Piers Gaveston. The scapegrace to whom Edward gave his jewels and his kingdom?" He did not add that it was judged fitting that the said monarch should meet his doom by having his innards scorched with a red-hot poker.

"It is the same abomination today as it was then. Trials at the Old Bailey. The scaffold. Transportation for accessories now this new law is coming into force. What I mean, sir," concluded Berkeley forlornly, "is that I understand Mrs Wright, as I believe she styles herself at present, enjoys a princely income from keeping lodgings as a place of assignation *between men*."

The Prince's hand came down upon the Earl's shoulder. "Oh, my dear fellow! I do see how excruciating this must be...."

"Many turn a blind eye to such things but the law holds it a crime for which the forfeiture of life is a just price. I cannot have the Berkeley name dragged through the mire, nor for it to reflect upon Mary's unblemished character."

"Yes, dear Lady Berkeley...." reminisced the Prince with a mawkish watering of the eye. "There is a halo of goodness about her that the world cannot breach."

"There is?"

"Most unusual. I rather fancy myself a *connoisseur* of the Fine Arts, you know. Upon my honour, Fred, your disclosure shall not go beyond these walls."

"I am indebted to you, sir," said the Earl. "It is good to know I have so unswerving a friend."

Berkeley's departure from Carlton House was accompanied by huge relief. His refusal to marry Mary was now dignified by a sound rationale. In the Prince's sight, Berkeley had bought an indefinite stay of execution regarding a public announcement. In his own, it was limpidly clear *why* marriage was out of the question. Further, he had logged a respectable relationship with Mary at the highest level, should it ever need confirmation. Who would gainsay the future King of England?

In Park Street, spring had inched its way past the windows. Sparrows searched under the eaves for hidden crevices where they might build.

The Widow Cole had said her piece, but that was before the child was born. Now her tongue was silent. It was as she had feared: Mary had been cruelly deceived. It was a mother's duty to stick by her daughter and grandson. She was sure that if Mary had not achieved marriage in London society, then neither had Susan. As to Nan, well, at least she didn't *pretend*.

Billy was bored with keeping Parker's accounts and cleansing his instruments. He thought if he could go to London and be with his family, new avenues would open up. Besides, he wanted to see his mother and sisters, to say nothing of the new arrival who was already five or six months old. Learning of Berkeley's duplicity, he reported it to Susan in accents of dismay.

"Did the silly piece really expect him to fall at her feet and vow eternal fidelity? I think not!" she scorned.

"But it was a proper service, with a parson."

"Mary was stupid to push him to that. How unfair life is! She, languishing in luxury in a pucker about lost virtue, and half the females of St. Giles compelled to hawk their bodies in the street to keep their families in crusts."

"But she's got a baby, Sue. She could be turned out any minute."

"Then she'll have to learn to please him, won't she?"

"I was banking on him finding me a decent post. I hope your husband's plump in the pocket!"

His sister was wafting a voluptuous scent. She had acquired the nonchalant poise of the accomplished *demi-mondaine* and twisted before the mirror to admire the saucy masculine cut of her jacket.

"You had better try Berkeley first, Billy. Recollect, he has a lot to hide!"

"You haven't got one, have you, Sue?" Billy said presently.

"What?"

"A husband."

"I've a noteworthy lawyer in tow," she boasted. "The profession is dull but can least afford a scandal. I've grown quite fond of the Law. You see, Billy, I'm honest enough to accept human nature for what it's worth. I don't go in for altruism, but I don't blame my misfortunes on others, either."

"Mary would rather live in a shepherd's hut with a curtain ring on her finger than in a mansion with none."

"Then she's a little fool! I hope she might come to her senses and start running up accounts at the milliner's and the mantuamaker's. Rather spend Berkeley's loot where it can be admired than let him fritter it away in the nearest gaming hell. She still has an ace or two to play, if only she could see it."

"Maybe I have, too," Billy pondered.

That evening, the Earl called at Park Street to dine with Mary. He was falling into the habit of forsaking the Captain and had begun to think that a *single* household would not only be more economic, but also convenient. To Berkeley's surprise, Billy was in the drawing room when he arrived.

"Up in Town to visit your sisters, are you? What does Parker have to say about that, sir?"

"I ain't likely to know. I've given him notice."

"Notice, sir! But you are an apprentice, are you not? That is a deed of covenant. He can take you to court, if he chooses."

"He'd not do such a thing," said Billy, agog.

"My lord! 'He'd not do such a thing, *my lord.*' You forget yourself, sir!"

"I kept his books square....my lord," contended Billy with a touch of resentment.

"William, you are qualified for nothing. You are poorly educated. How can you hope to advance if you are not set upon acquiring skills?"

Billy stared miserably at the carpet. There was a hint of insolence in his bearing which did not escape the Earl. "I'm not cut out to be a sawbones. It fair makes me queasy."

"The hell it does! Shavers near half your age are beating the drum for their country and you dare to play the lily-livered runt at the sight of a lopped limb?"

"I thought you might be well-placed to find me something more congenial, my lord. Now that you're my brother-in-law."

Berkeley ceased pacing the floor with his hands behind his back and turned to meet Billy's bold stare. He nodded slowly. "So, that is the size of it. Well, sir, I might see *you* well-placed out on your ear! But I'll tell you what I will do, because I like to think I am a charitable fellow: I'll see you 'well-placed' in an academic institution abroad. Paris, I fancy. When you have absorbed some Greek and Latin and have acquired the manners of a gentleman, you might be fit to sit at your sister's dining table!"

Mary had been concentrating hard on her sampler. There was a certain patronage in Billy's approach to his betters. She could tell he had been talking to Susan and couldn't help feeling a smidgeon of sympathy for her 'husband'. (She was determined to think of his lordship in no other terms.) Her heart fluttered when she remembered her secret; the new seed already sown.

Billy took his supper in the nursery with his mother and told her of Berkeley's plan, complaining of the rich who ordered society as they pleased and didn't give a button for the peasants who ran about after them. He stared with horrified fixity into the cradle, overcome by an extraneous sense of the blood of peers mingled with his own in the veins of his namesake. There was something fiendish in the knowing grin with which his thriving nephew stared back.

The Widow Cole's crochet hook did not falter. "Best do as his lordship bids. Only fancy! When you're become a fine fellow with a head full of *edificated* topics, you'll be in a way to catch a real match for yourself."

"Lydia's left our Susan's," reported Billy glumly, ignoring his mother.

"Lydia Sharpe? She's only gone up the street to Nan's to help with the little uns. They're a real handful."

"Sue never said. I think I'll call on Nan tomorrow."

"Fine feathers make fine birds," declared the Widow Cole in an oracular tone, content that she had summed up the situation.

Berkeley had been mulling over the question of Billy's future for some time. There'd be plenty to occupy him at Vincennes: fencing, boar-hunting, the heroes of literature, the luminaries of science and philosophy. His lordship did not bend his mind so far as to speculate upon the anarchic influences the gullible youth might be exposed to in France. The aristocracy *must* have the upper hand. The mob must know its place. The government of Europe was down to ancient families such as his own. Paris would make a man of William and remove him from his sisters.

"He'll be rubbing shoulders with Continental nobility," Berkeley said to Mary. "He can cut a figure to his heart's content and few will be the wiser."

The wastrel soon became used to the idea of foreign soil. Privately, Billy reckoned that young Fitz and the prospective sibling were the best things to happen. Berkeley would be forced to take stock of his responsibilities and make an honest woman of Mary. Billy went down to Cranford to take his leave of them. The Earl put away his vintage port, got out the ratafia and wished him a pleasant voyage, then buried his nose in the *Racing Calendar* in a search of a better return for his outlay. Billy was smartly turned out in a high-collared coat, striped hose and doeskins. Already he had the air of one with his sights above domestic trifles, shoving off the chirruping baby who made sport with his bootstraps. He crossed the park and diminished to a speck in the autumn mists, dry leaves fluttering down about him, striding into an unknown for which Barnwood had not schooled him. Watching him, Mary's calm forsook her. Oh, she would have given anything to run wild and free, to have been a man with a chance to roam and find her true course. Her overladen frame rooted her to the earth. With two children playing 'peep-bo' around her skirts, there wasn't a ray of hope that she would ever escape. She could not accuse her husband of mistreatment, but there lurked at the back of her mind the dread that he would take a new mistress, or submit to a more lasting connection to salvage the line, and turn her and her children into the streets with neither name nor nest-egg. She could be sure of nothing when he had abysmally deceived her.

One morning at breakfast, the Earl reported newspaper comment of the new United States Constitution, recently announced in *The Pennsylvania Packet*.

"So our colonies have become the land of liberty. I see Mr Perry waxes eloquent on the subject."

Mary's heart did a violent somersault beneath her bodice. "We saw him in Hyde Park a while ago, mother and I, when we were walking Fitz. He gave us no greeting."

The Earl raised his eyes abruptly. "You sound disappointed, nay, aggrieved."

"Well, but..." Mary floundered, "he is godfather to my niece. It brought home to me my doubtful position as nothing else has done."

"Next week, when Prescott joins his ship, we shall leave to winter at Berkeley. There you will be lady of the castle."

"I hope I may prove a worthy châtelaine, my lord."

"I anticipate a visit from my mother," he told her. "If you pass muster with her, you do well!"

The foray into the country demanded strenuous forethought. Mary gave instructions that bedlinen was to be packed, warming pans and chafing dishes for the baby's food, candles and preserves, lest at any moment her children's expectations be amputated and she alone was left to provide for them. Even some of the family jewels and plate were to travel. The servants shook their heads. It seemed that the new mistress was a novice at running a household. "Tis plain she'll not be long in the saddle, Mrs Crouch," said John Croome, the Under Butler. "Why, she's a mere slip of a thing with no idea how to contrive. She'll go the way of Mrs Bayly faster than you can skin a rabbit."

Mrs Crouch, the housekeeper, glanced sideways. "I have heard tell," she whispered, "that they're married on the sly, with proper lines an' all."

"Never!"

"Make of it what you will, Mr Croome. "Kezzy Trotman says she remembers Miss Tudor coming to the Castle at Berkeley a year or two back with her brother, and his lordship ordering champagne as if he had something to celebrate. Kezzy'd been on an errand in the town and she saw Parson follow them out of the church looking as white as chalk. Lententide, it was, she says. The season fixed in her mind on account of having visited her mother the Sunday before."

"Then why in heaven's name...?"

"Miss Tudor might have the looks of the Quality, but she's a down-to-earth girl. She needs lessons in the ways of a ladyship."

"A little gilding of the lily, you think, before she's fit for society? To be sure, that does put another complexion on things. The Dowager must be in quite a taking!"

"Brandy and smelling-salts together, I should think. That's if she knows they be hitched, Mr Croome, which I daresay she don't!"

Whatever fears Mary had about her unsettled life, the pitching scenes of Cotswold pastures and ochre stone villages, the scent of the resting earth, brought her into harmony with herself. After a night spent at The White Hart at Benson and a delay at Nettlebed while the Earl inspected his hunting kennels, they crossed the Gloucestershire border. Mary listened to the horses' hooves pounding home soil, her eyes moistening with emotions she could not have begun to explain. She was seven months pregnant. The Widow Cole clutched her grandson, lulled by the motion of the carriage. She was content to ride every rut and pothole while her needs were taken care of. These days she felt battered and bewildered by the endless twists of fate. "Tis all a lottery," she mused. "We women must shift as best we can."

A castellated mound from some bygone age loomed through dripping November mists. When at length they drew into the courtyard, the servants had assembled either side of the entrance to meet them, an outrider having been sent ahead to announce their approach.

Mary straightened her posture. All eyes were upon her. The Earl greeted his household with his usual blithe curtness and offered her his arm. "This lady is your new mistress. I know you will respect her instructions as they were my own." There were bows and curtsies as the pair swept in, Mary smiling nervously. Boniface, the Head Butler, grimaced when they were safely past, noting the Old Nurse in tow pacifying a peevish baby and the young woman's ballooning form. A stern Baptist, he was ever fretful of the waywardness of mankind and knew his master to be a committed bachelor. Croome's opinion did not change his own one wit. "Miss Tudor, eh?" he said in clipped, catarrhal accents. "She won't be the first of that ilk to confound history. No good can come of it, mark my words."

Paradoxically, the Dowager, whose opinion Berkeley had taught Mary to fear, turned out to be her advocate She was a dissipated beauty with a taste for effete men, perhaps because they couldn't injure her. She praised Mary's handling of the child and wished she might discipline Fred half so well. She owned she had made a bad job of it, but that was no wonder when his father had succumbed to every ailment in Culpeper's and had died of an overdose of mercury when Fred was a boy. Nugent, her second husband, a ribald Irish peer, whom she'd discarded after a very few years, had not been able to make anything of him either. But then, Nugent had been too busy chasing rich widows and licking the boots of the young king to care. He scarcely knew his *own* offspring and had flatly denied fatherhood of the last daughter she had borne under his roof. Poor Fred was doubly neglected and had learned not to care. The trouble was that his 'not caring' ran to disowning his duties and that, as well as affecting the lives of his tenants, reduced his income.

"Child, child, you have a way with him," the matron declared. "Indent for more housekeeping and rethatch the barns with it!"

"Would that I dare, my lady. When I see the way the poor cottagers toil and barely scrape a living from the earth, it breaks my heart."

The Dowager smiled at her thoughts, bent over her *petit-point* frame. Towards the end of her life she was industrious in the extreme, as if to retrench on her feckless past. She upholstered whole suites with her tapestry work, weaving in the family arms. The lustrous vegetable dyes would remain fresh down the centuries to come. God bless her for her eccentricities, Mary thought. She could have been my bitterest opponent. What she made of the situation, what she had been told by her son, was not revealed, but the Dowager Countess of Berkeley could not have been kinder.

"I worry about Fred more than I care to admit," she confided.

"I can well understand, ma'am, the tug of the firstborn on a mother's heartstrings."

"He needs a steady, caring hand. Young you may be, but I perceive you are wise." As she spoke, she was lacing her tea with brandy and absent-mindedly using the back of the spoon in a most genteel fashion, the better to obtain a stronger brew. "Fie! How clumsy I am! This is the best specific known to man for easing the palpitations."

"I am sorry you are plagued by such symptoms."

"My dear, don't bother your head about it," said the Dowager cheerfully. "I am not long for this world, but I should rest easier if Fred were content. He has danced a footloose jig too long. I own I have been no example."

"Widowhood cannot have been easy."

"Bless you, no!" said the Dowager, delighted with the notion. "Elizabeth, my daughter, has fared little better. Depend upon it, marrying Craven was the grossest thing she ever did. She is such a bright spirit and he a colourless dolt. He squanders his days among his fossil collection of which he is the dullest specimen!"

"I hear Lady Craven is fond of travelling."

"Paris! Vienna! St. Petersburg! Constantinople! She sat down with a Pasha who kept a tame lion instead of a spaniel. Intrepid to the core! I vow she is quite at home amidst a little *civil unrest*. The Royal Courts of the Continent fling wide their doors to her and many a Prince has surrendered to her charm. But she dotes only upon the Margrave of Anspach, a nephew of the Queen. They have set up house at Versailles and the Margravine is obliged to turn away her gaze. So, too, Craven, but he is accustomed to it."

"That must be very uncomfortable," offered Mary.

"Craven and Elizabeth have an understanding. The Church's view of matrimony, you must allow, is too confining. What are marriage lines when the heart is not engaged? A mere document for the benefit of heirs."

Unconsciously, Mary laid a hand upon the curve below her breast. She was less perturbed to realise that Fred's mother set no store by the invitation of God's blessing than the reminder of Fitz's shaky rank. "I must hope his lordship will not choose to stray."

"Child, child, he plainly adores you. He will never forsake what is in his own best interest and he is not so feeble a judge of that. He may be Colonel-in-Chief of his Regiment and Lord Lieutenant of the County, but he has had nothing to fight for. If he had, it would be for you and the children."

"How glad I am, ma'am, to hear you say so!"

"It is Cranfield who goes to sea to defend our shores. There is nothing so calculated as boredom to drive eldest sons to run through their wealth."

"His Royal Highness is no exception."

"Indeed! He punts on tick with the best of 'em. Would you believe it, Lady Jersey says Maria was obliged to borrow five pounds from a postilion at Newmarket to cover the Prince's bets! Now Fred is not so dipped in the pocket as *that*."

No, thought Mary, but what is there to caulk the leak upon his funds? The future King will survive: Parliament will see to that. But shall we?

A Gordian Knot

Eight

Augustus Thomas Hupsman was a troubled man. To begin with, he had never quite dovetailed into English society. He was born of devout and self-respecting Ashkenazim from the Low Countries and the Rhineland. They themselves had been brought up in London when their parents migrated to Britain at the time Queen Anne died and the Jacobites were causing a stir.

Augustus' far-off antecedents had been vineyard keepers, diamond cutters and silversmiths, but had prospered in more recent generations to become managers of palatial estates, merchants, hated tax-collectors and moneylenders. His grandfather had made his mark as a land agent to a Hanoverian Princeling who had transferred to England with the Court of George I. Likewise, his father, Anthony, who had inherited the same office and privileges.

Augustus had no mind for the counting-house. He could not handle money without it melted like ice in his grasp. He was not a negotiator and was blessed with no particular vision. At an early age, he had drawn from life a conviction that the art of ingratiating oneself with one's betters was the first rule of advancement. His maternal grandfather had been a fervid scholar, an interpreter of the Scriptures. Daniel Jacob lived perpetually on the brink of poverty and had been thankful when his plain though lively daughter, Esther, had snagged the attention of Anthony Hupsman at a music *soirée* at which, as an accomplished spinetist, she had been invited to perform.

"The legal mind, the talent for harmony, my dear, these are the supreme gifts of Jewry. Hupsman, that is a fine name. It is a corruption of Hauptmann, meaning Captain or Leader. We shall see what we shall see."

"Papa, do desist from your match-making. I have known Mr Hupsman these seven days, no more!"

"Though her dowry be modest, my daughter herself is fairer than rubies. The right man will judge wisely."

The Hupsmans were not forgetful of their genesis, but by now, the ethos and traditions of the English aristocracy had overlaid it. It was not without a pang of sadness that Daniel, watching the fates of the two young people intertwine, saw that Jewish lore and customs did not take first place in the courtier's life. But it would be a splendid match! No Aldgate Synagogue for them.

When Anthony Hupsman and Susanna Esther Jacob were married, it was in St. James, Westminster, according to the rites of the Anglican Church, followed by all the trappings of a Hebrew celebration. The date was February the twenty-third, 1743, the year George II (the last British monarch to command his troops) defeated the French at the Battle of Dettingen and prompted the exiled Charles Edward Stuart to attempt the English Throne. By the time the Jacobite cause had bloodily expired at Culloden, the couple had produced a healthy son, Augustus, whom they hoped foretokened a large family.

There was no telltale sign of what the future had in store. Within a year, Hupsman, the father, fell victim to a palsy which threatened mobility and left him with the co-ordination of a stringless marionette. His mind was as nimble as ever and refused to grasp the insubordination of his limbs. He was quick to anger, slow to meet the responsibilities of paterfamilias. There were remissions, and he rejoiced in them, but they served to sharpen awareness of what he was losing. It would mean retirement from his post. The Privy Purse might dole out a meagre pension, but it would not be enough to maintain their standard of living and educate Augustus. They might be obliged to vacate their grace-and-favour residence. Hupsman senior looked for no man's charity.

It was then that one of Princess Augusta's ladies-in-waiting who had once served alongside Elizabeth Drax, now the Countess of Berkeley, informed them that her ladyship was seeking a governess. The opening was a godsend. There would be a cottage at Cranford and rooms at Berkeley Castle with all their wants catered for. The Countess was fulsome with her generosity and glad to come to the aid of such deserving subjects.

Hupsman, the son, grew up contemporaneously with the Berkeley children, sharing many of their adventures, knowing his place, but enjoying ample freedom. He ambled half-heartedly through his education and scraped by with the lowliest laurels, albeit at Brasenose College, Oxford. He had no interest in his Hebrew roots and considered himself best suited to the sedentary life of a country vicar where demands upon his intellect and his social acumen would be few. His link with the Berkeley family made it a foregone conclusion that he would seek an incumbency with them as soon as one became vacant.

Lord Berkeley's injunction to destroy the 'marriage' record had been made upon a presumption, not only of rank, but of many years of bonded familiarity. Hupsman's conscience had been uneasy about it. In the eyes of God, Lord Berkeley and Mary *were* married! Moreover, Lord Hardwicke's marriage bill in the fifties ordered a strict account of births, marriages and deaths. The punishment for tampering with them was death.

As if this were not enough, there were some matters of a fiduciary nature which were worrying him. Hupsman's daughter, Lizzie, barely out of the schoolroom, had married in 1786, one, Thomas Hickes, a lawyer with a moderate competence. He was of a prolific local family descended from a renowned silk merchant and benefactor of the city of London during the reign of Henry VIII. (Lady Craven, the Earl's sister, who had been educated at Esther Hupsman's knee, had a mother-in-law who was a Hickes.) Lizzie had no pretensions to beauty and was not particularly bright, though she was keen to do 'the right thing'. It had behoved Hupsman to scrape together a befitting dowry which had crippled the household finances. Then there had been his mother's lengthy tallies with the apothecary.

Esther Hupsman's death, only two months after Lizzie's wedding, had brought yet another issue to a head: what he should do about Mrs Wilmot.

Fanny Wilmot, the estranged wife of a notable MP and Master in Chancery, had become his widowed mother's constant companion during her frailer years. They had been introduced at Benham Park, Lord Craven's seat near Newbury, and had quickly formed an attachment. Mrs Wilmot was dependent on the charity of a disaffected husband. For John Wilmot to divorce his wife, an Act of Parliament was required which would arouse opprobrium.

When Esther Hupsman died, she left the lease of her last abode in Salt Hill, Windsor, to the devoted friend and nurse she had sheltered for nearly three years. She had become awakened to the inequitable deal between the sexes and told Augustus that she wished to see Fanny 'looked after'.

Hupsman needed no encouragement to take care of Mrs Wilmot. He had silently admired her and recognised that his dutiful visits to Salt Hill owed much to her being there. The lady would not have noticed him had she not been penniless and he his mother's son. He knew himself to be unprepossessing. His false eye bulged with an imperturbable blankness and made the socket ache. These things notwithstanding, certain sympathies between himself and Mrs Wilmot were aroused, causing a secret and delicious tension which he unctuously recalled upon his return to the Old Vicarage at Berkeley. His wife did not take him seriously, never had. During the courtship and honeymoon period, he had been fond of her, but was disappointed that throwing in their lot together had not engendered the kind of ardent devotion he longed to give and receive. Miss Lambe, a cleric's daughter from Newton Bromswold in Northamptonshire and a frequent guest at Coombe Abbey, one of the Craven estates, was esteemed a suitable bride, but had turned out to have none of the meekness and mildness her maiden name suggested. Hupsman thought that Lizzie's premature desire to marry and leave home was fuelled by her mother's acid mockery.

Fanny Wilmot was quite the opposite. A patient listener, with a melodic voice, he wondered how she had clung to her good nature when life had ill-used her. He saw her as defenceless, a casualty of circumstance. He would have liked to pass his days in the embrace of her companionship, here in his mother's house in Harris Gardens, Salt Hill. It was a daydream made more vibrant by the dullness of his circumscribed life in Berkeley where promissory notes were scattered about the parish like wedding petals and he was expected to be a paragon of rectitude.

After the funeral at Cranford, when the mourners had dispersed, Hupsman travelled in the coach to Salt Hill with Mrs Wilmot where she bade him take a dish of tea and a slice of angel cake. He had dared to presume that she would not discharge him hastily.

"Is it not a miserable thing to lose a dear friend and mother?" she asked, fastidiously dabbing a lace handkerchief to her eyes and the tip of her nose. "Esther was my champion in distress. A wise counsellor."

"I hope that I, too, may prove the same," Hupsman heard himself say.

"You are a man of principle, Mr Hupsman, content to walk the humble path. If our statesmen had your qualities, the country wouldn't be going to rack and ruin."

Hupsman dissembled foolishly, well pleased with the comment. The drowsy housefly aroused from hibernation and alighting that moment on the gâteau St. Honoré varnished with syrup was not more delighted. "Alas, the sons of Israel are not openly welcome in the chambers of government."

"Unless, they are as foully rich as my brother-in-law," Fanny said wearily.

"I take it you refer to Sir Sampson Gideon, or Baron Eardley as he has become?" Hupsman recalled that his own family's naturalised status had been purchased by a private act of George

II and defection to the English Church. (Mrs Wilmot's crucifix nestled beguilingly between the frothy folds of her fichu.) "I have attained the view that Christianity is the ripe fruit of my Jewish stock." He was astonished by his own florid metaphor. As he spoke, a plump, garnet-coloured cherry, hothouse grown, slipped between Fanny's lips. "I have not forsaken it: it has been *subsumed*."

"Now, the new Constitution of America, that manages to combine religion and politics. Mr Wilmot speaks of it with admiration whilst he works hard to see the Loyalists recompensed for their losses in the war."

"Your....your husband is a man of vision, madam," remarked the clergyman in hopes of eliciting a tasty morsel of personal information.

Fanny sighed heavily and touched her forehead as though she were about to faint. "What is so vexing.... I fear I must speak plainly here.... What it pains me to express is that sometimes people aren't all of a piece, you know. Mr Wilmot is revered by his colleagues. He is occupied by many humanitarian endeavours...."

"And an antiquarian, a patron of the Fine Arts, I understand."

"That is well and good, but he does not always keep the best company. They may be politicians, Admirals, men of stature....but they engage in sacrilegious practices."

Hupsman's cup clattered on to its saucer a little too noisily. "You don't say so."

"Unspeakable things. I refer to Medmenham, Mr Hupsman, a short distance from here. The West Wycombe Caves. I take it you have some idea what goes on there?"

"It is the headquarters of the Hell Fire Club, that I know. My dear Mrs Wilmot...."

She held up her hand as if to stem a protest. "It is immodest in me to mention such topics, but Oh! I have longed to talk to someone who will not bid me shrug off the follies of husbands and stop being a silly goose."

"I find that London society is overweeningly censorious in many ways, and lamentably lax in others."

"I cannot imagine what the children will think," she went on, referring to her daughters and small son from whom economics had forced her to separate. "These are vile perversions! At Medmenham, people of import, overseas dignitaries, are entertained! Why even Benjamin Franklin has visited! Mr

Wilmot and his friends, Sir George Warren and William Cokayne, were trustees of the Danesfield Estate in the neighbourhood. It belonged to Sir John Borlase Warren and was used for the very purpose of playing host."

"My wife is from Northamptonshire and knew the Cokayne family," interjected Hupsman, feeling a diversion might serve to defuse matters.

"I may be a mere female without independent means, but I can't bear to live with a spouse who condones such goings-on," declared Fanny.

"No lady should have to endure it."

Fanny wore her probity like armour. The mother of six children, she had reached a comfortable plateau of self-assurance at thirty. John Wilmot was ten years her senior and had taken her to wife when she was sixteen, the age Lizzie Hupsman had fled the nest for Tom Hickes. Fanny Sainthill came from Osmaston in Derbyshire, on the Wilmot estates, and had lived in supernal ignorance of the world and its ways. She had idealised Wilmot, her paladin with a zeal for justice. He sought to be a worthy protector and had feasted upon the marrow of her adoration, until, one by one, his failings in her sight were enlarged by disillusion and he came to think of her as a harpy.

"It is in Mr Wilmot's nature to be distrustful of women. He believes an aunt has cheated the family of justifiable expectations."

"How so?"

"Sir Robert, Mr Wilmot's uncle, bequeathed the baronetcy and Osmaston estates in Derbyshire to his eldest natural child, also Robert. When his wife died, he flew to the altar with his mistress, Elizabeth Foote, a doctor's daughter from Connecticut. All his children had already been born out of wedlock to her. Imagine how insupportable that must have been for the first Lady Wilmot who was a martyr to sickness. She had my husband's abiding sympathy. Sir Robert died only a couple of years afterwards, having readjusted his will and covered the monstrous truth. Details of the first marriage have been suppressed, dare I say 'lost'. Posterity will be none the wiser."

"I see," said Hupsman, his mind elsewhere. His upright collar glowed like a furnace.

"It meant that Sir John, my father-in-law, did not inherit. Robert and John were as good as twins. They were born as closely together as nature singly allows. They even married around the same period."

"What is remarkable," said Hupsman, "is that the son was able to succeed. These things are cumbered with rigorous rules."

"They are respected servants of the nation, the Wilmots. The offices they hold wield more power than the Throne. The trouble with Mr Wilmot is that he is a man of dual standards. Do you not think, Mr Hupsman, that I did the right thing in deserting him?"

"You have no cause to admonish yourself," Hupsman consoled. "Marriage should be more than a legal bond in Christian civilisation. It is a union of souls."

He thought of poker-faced Elizabeth and how she seldom deferred to him. What a repressed organism his own marriage was! His twin sons regarded him with barely concealed loathing for his corrections of syntax and disparagement of their iconoclastic views. But Fanny was a woman of sophistication and intellect. She valued his worth.

Outdoors, the air was dank and listless; a dim February afternoon was beginning to garner the shadows of evening. He pictured his mother's coffin, interred in the silent earth, and shivered. Indoors, the coals in the hearth had long taken fire and the phosphorescent warmth seemed to Hupsman to correspond with his own inner glow. He was caught up in a kind of suspenseful elation. Nothing had meaning beyond the shared warmth of this cell. "Fanny," he said involuntarily. "May I call you Fanny?"

"Oh, please do. Esther would have wished it, I am sure."

"And you must call me *Huppy*. Tis a foolish nickname, but my lord has fallen into the way of it, you know."

Fanny Wilmot smiled beguilingly and owned it a privilege. "Won't you stay and partake of a pheasant supper? You cannot set out at this hour. Esther's room is well-aired."

And steeped in the mystery of death, he thought. The Grim Reaper overshadowed every aspect of his life. He must snatch what brightness he could while he may.

He had intended to take a chaise to High Wycombe and catch *The Regulator* which would convey him to Gloucester overnight, but Fanny's offer was tempting. The longcase clock chimed a portentous half hour and he saw that it was already too late: he would miss his connection. Elizabeth would guess he had been delayed. That she had chosen not to accompany him, making her excuse their straitened circumstances, irritated him as much as it relieved him. Neither was the boys' education to be interrupted. As for Lizzie, she had pleaded some feminine indisposition. His children had not been close to their grandmother. She was too remote, smelling of stale Hungary Water and archaic gentility. The sentimental Dutch masters about her rooms spoke of a vanished homeland, a felicity and order more wistful than remembered.

While they were dining, Fanny said: "And how does my lord Berkeley these days?"

"Tolerably well. He is in the rudest health. The same cannot be said for the Dowager, I fear."

"So matrimony suits him? Contrary, is it not?"

Augustus Thomas Hupsman stuttered, turned a mulberry colour and wiped his mouth on his napkin. "He....I.... Where can you have heard that?"

"From a most disagreeable source and I daresay it is indecorous of me to mention it, but thus it was: William Cokayne attended a *levée* in Holborn given by a Mrs Wright who is alleged to have enjoyed liaisons with at least two Members of Parliament. Both are lawyers and friends of Mr Wilmot. This unknown female appears to be all the rage in Town. She asserts, would you believe, that the Earl of Berkeley is her brother-in-law!"

"Dear me," said Hupsman, visibly flustered. In an awkward reflex, he put up his hand to mop his brow and the quavering candleflames all but guaranteed darkness. "Dear me, this will never do. It cannot *be*."

"Then it is a falsehood? I knew it must be!"

"I....I am not at liberty....to divulge his lordship's affairs. Not even to you, Fanny."

"Forgive me. I see I have spoken out of turn," said Fanny, finding this reply supremely unsatisfactory. What she didn't tell him was that she had reason to believe her husband had had an amourette with this *femme fatale* and was curious to know what manner of woman Lord Berkeley had chosen to reproduce heirs if Mrs Wright were her sister. She deduced from Hupsman's reaction that there was something in it.

"This is a most toothsome Burgundy," said Hupsman, having recovered himself. "Mama, God rest her, was fond of her wine. It is to be hoped that we do not cross swords with our French cousins."

Hupsman retired for the night in a restless mood. The rich, gamey meat consumed at supper had been riddled with shot and argued with his digestion in the small hours. His head was milling with fear and fantasy. Next morning, he took his leave of Fanny, planting a well-considered kiss upon her hand, and set out for Berkeley. "Goodbye, Huppy," she said and her kittenish amber eyes came to rest upon him. "You have illumined a dark night."

How he wished he dare flee from the gloomy Vicarage, his responsibilities and his joyless family! Executor duties might afford an excuse, but the cost of regular expeditions to Berkshire was prohibitive at present. He had years of educating his sons ahead. To bring disgrace upon his household was unthinkable. Besides, he was sure Fanny's conscience would not allow any but a full observance of the proprieties. Imagination was running away with him!

As the chaise battled through driving rain, he started to think about 'Mrs Wright'. When the Earl had confided in him that Miss Cole had sisters whose mode of living was open to question, Hupsman had no clue that they moved in such astral spheres. The secrecy was not to be wondered at. If the sisters were aiming to foment scandal as a means of assuring their futures, it could bring down not only the Earl, but himself.

At last, as the charcoaled lineaments of Cheltenham came into view and the coachman sprang the team at an incline, Hupsman recollected that he had one ace card. Yes, he had set light to the wedding certificate and had been instantly overwhelmed by fear. Compunction and wit had been a two-edged razor. Belatedly, he had set about creating Banns to corroborate what had taken place, should he ever be called upon to defend his corner. (There had been a lot of to-ing and fro-ing at the Castle in the early months of 1785. Berkeley was absent in London a good deal and Hupsman had filled in dates during the Advent season, within the specified legal time frame, when his patron had been in residence.)

The irony was that that scrap of paper, a blatant sham, testified to what Lord Berkeley's chaplain was convinced was the truth.

"Don't speak of that woman, Lizzie! Don't sully your tongue!"

Elizabeth Hupsman ceased harrowing gossamer-thin lawn with her dart of a needle and stared over her lunettes. The weasel features were deeply pinched with disapproval.

"But, Mama, Tom says there is nothing unseemly. Lord Berkeley and Miss Tudor are joined in wedlock."

"Then your husband is stupider than I gave credit for!"

"His lordship does not choose to announce it yet."

"For the simple reason, Lizzie, that it is a figment of supposition. Regrettably, Lord Berkeley is a father, but it does not make him a husband. Why, no lady in this county will risk her good name by calling on *that woman*."

"Mrs Black does."

"Ha! Edward Jenner's sister. Well, she is a lone widow and soft in the head about charitable works."

"Mrs Purnell visits, too," pursued Lizzie in a solicitous tone, striving as ever not to sink under the weight of her mother's sarcasm. "She is fond of Miss Tudor and reports that *Mary* is a very good sort of person and a devoted mother."

"Mrs Purnell! That rackety hussy!"

"She has dined with the Prince of Wales at the Castle. They say he finds her amusing."

"Lizzie, I shudder to think of his like ruling us if the King continues to sicken."

"Mrs Purnell has a heart of gold."

"But certainly no silvered tongue!"

Elizabeth Hupsman gave a peevish sigh. Here was her daughter, seventeen summers old, head full of romantic beneficence, already shackled to a man as dull as Augustus, and on the threshold of becoming a mother herself. Lizzie buttressed her aching back with her arm while she eased herself on to the couch and surveyed still and silent snowdrifts, bluish, in the Advent light.

"Anyway, Mama, Miss Tudor is in the best of company," she said mischievously. "Her own confinement is due soon."

"How can you know such a thing? I did not think her cloak was falling straight!"

"Papa told me," Lizzie announced in muted triumph. "He stands firm in his opinion that Berkeley is married."

"Your father does? He never said so in my hearing!"

"Then, of course, he must be joshing. How disappointing! Papa finds Miss Tudor engaging," offered Lizzie experimentally. "His manner towards her is most chivalrous when he escorts her to church. He treats her in every way like a ladyship. Have you not observed it yourself?"

"*I turn away from sin. I turn to Christ,*" incanted the clergy spouse.

Lizzie wisely ignored this specious reply. In fact, in less public moments, Lizzie's Reverend father was inclined to treat Miss Tudor with undue familiarity, as a man might treat a lady whose reputation is not altogether sound, but whom he finds immoderately attractive. Mary returned a stony face, refusing to make an issue out of something which could be construed as subjective. She was in no position to argue against this representative of the Holy Church and longstanding dependant upon Lord Berkeley

"You don't suppose, Mama, that Papa actually performed the ceremony? That he is under oath to preserve the secret?"

"Don't be absurd! You read too many sensational novels from the circulating library. The Minerva Press has much to answer for and has driven many a silly butterfly to flights of folly. I tell you, Lizzie, there is no marriage. Never was. Never will be."

"Well, I do not think his lordship would live in quite such an *established* way if the union were irregular. He would not be so brazen."

"Lord Berkeley may do exactly as he pleases without consulting us," sniffed Elizabeth Hupsman. "We are not deemed to have an opinion. He cares only for tribute among his peers and they will find nothing amiss. If one were to try and set the upper classes on the straight and narrow, the royal family would be one's first port of call!"

Several days later, at the time of Hanukkah, Lizzie gave birth to the Hupsmans' first grandchild in the village of Stone. He was named Frederick in tribute to my lord Berkeley and on December 19th, Lizzie and Tom's first wedding anniversary, his grandfather had the pleasure of baptising him in All Saints Church, a chapelry of Berkeley Minster. Festivity ensued with half the parish enjoying hot rum punch, mince pies made with spiced beef, and plum cake. It was a community meshed by its reliance upon the land and it was common for its members to have more than one job. Tom Hickes was a novice attorney, but also acted as a cheese factor to the local dairies.

Other representatives of the Hickes clan were his cousins, confusingly, the Reverend Thomas Hickes, and Nicholas Hickes. The latter, a wearer of many hats, found his work as a lawyer neatly compatible with that of a money scrivener, that is to say, a lender of money at gratifying rates of interest. He was also a property speculator and would dabble in just about anything that promised to turn a shilling or two in double quick time.

A happy hum came from the drawing room when they arrived at the house. Elizabeth Hupsman excitedly bore off Margaret, the Reverend's wife, to marvel at the comeliness of her grandson, leaving the brothers to make a beeline for the punchbowl. Passing the library door, Nicholas caught sight of his host in deep conversation with Hupsman who stood guardian of a roaring fire.

"Ah, Hupsman. How fortuitous. A word with you, sir."

"Cousin Nick. Thomas," Tom looked toward them in bemused surprise, saluting both with a manly slap on the back. Hupsman's eye went blank to be thus buttonholed by the notary.

"If you'll excuse us, Tom, there is a matter to be settled with this good fellow."

"Then I'll make myself scarce. Keep wassailing, mind!"

Hupsman heard the word 'settled' in some alarm. 'Settled' was not what he was about. It generated a granite resistance in his mind. "You have the advantage of me, sir."

"You might say so. There are vowels to be redeemed which are now overdue."

"All in good time. The matter is in hand."

"As I hope is the matter concerning your son and the frenzy of destruction caused by his mount when he ran wild across Wetmore's farmstead a few days ago."

"What! I have no intelligence of this. Which son?" It would be Gus, he knew, the elder twin, who referred to him as 'the old goat' behind his back. Had he not complained of bruises from sparring? It was a week since the boys had returned from school for Christmas.

"Augustus, I believe, though it requires some acuity to tell him apart from the other. Wetmore is claiming damages to his property against my brother here, whose stallion it was."

"Your son persuaded me," explained Thomas Hickes, "to allow him to put the beast through his paces. He gave assurances that he had often ridden to hounds. Indeed he said he was shortly to own a filly himself...."

"A regular flat, sir. He was seen to spur the creature, give him his head, and couldn't bridle him. Wetmore's Collie scented danger and tore out of the yard, barking ferociously, causing the charger to stampede through a paling fence, barns, outhouses, and run amok in a field of kale. The horse could have been killed!"

"Put plainly, Hupsman," summed up the cleric in an a more anodyne tone, "I am newly graduated and have no means to compensate him. And I'm jiggered if I can see why I should. I loaned your son my horse, not without misgiving, I admit, but 'twas *his* doing."

"The young dolt was trying to cut a swell," added Nicholas. "He wants the whip for treating a sensitive animal in that fashion."

Hupsman's viscera felt raw. A most fearful exhilaration gripped him. He could see it all, the steed with its rippling muscle, the ungelded power of him, urged to gallop like the wind, rearing up and crashing through barriers without a care for tomorrow. Harness strained to breaking. Release!

"I will tax Augustus with it," he promised thickly. "His side of the story must be heard."

"Let us understand one another, sir! Wetmore must have satisfaction out of court! Thomas don't have the rag and, frankly, neither do I until some debts have been called in, if you take my meaning, Hupsman. Responsibilities must be shouldered all round."

"Ah yes," agreed Hupsman, "fences must be mended. Every man will do his duty, Hickes."

There was no getting the measure of the parson. Hupsman dwelt in the realms of allegory at the best of times, but, today, he appeared strangely aloof.

In the drawing room, the medley of voices swelled and ebbed like a flight of drones, interspersed with bellows of laughter and strident opinion.

"Tis plain as the nose on your face, she's no upper customer," declared John Jenkins, a yeoman farmer.

"Be that as it may," Mrs Purnell told him, "twould be a mistake to underrate her. Miss Tudor's no frivolous girl. James Simmonds says she pays metic'lous heed to the day books and wants only a quizzin'-glass for finer detail!"

"I've heard," offered Joseph Cullimore, freeholder of the parish, "that Bloxsome comes, hat in hand, when she summons him for advice about Lord Berkeley's affairs."

"The attorney at Dursley? Well, he's not one to be trifled with," averred Mrs Purnell.

"Tan't nat'rel," opined William Vizard, tenant farmer. His slack jaw and open stare gave him an appearance of permanent incredulity. "A female's place is by the range, else diggin' tatties."

"Plucking fowl and skinning hares," agreed Sam Pye, cramming his mouth with pastry.

"Swapping receipts for punch like this!" concurred John Jenkins. "Though a tad more brandy wouldn't go amiss!"

"You can all barrack," said Mrs Purnell, "but Berkeley's a lazy fellow with no head for the debit columns. He's let things slide. He may be well-breeched, but his estates will be done up in no time for want of a firm hand. His only enthusiasm's getting his blood up in the sports field!"

"Beggin' your pardon, Mrs Purnell," said Joseph Cullimore politely, "but you must own it topsy-turvy. Adam's rib was made for a helpmeet."

"For breedin' stock," affirmed Pye.

"Well, gentlemen," huffed the good lady, "I can tell you Miss Tudor has not neglected her duties in that department. There's to be another child this very Yuletide."

Vizard struggled with this information. "She be a real goer, then, this Miss Tudor. Come to think on't, I had a fetching saddleback sow knew how to get served first. Knew how to get her grub as well! Little charmer, she was...."

"For pity's sake, Vizard, hold your tongue! Do we ask your pearls of farmyard cant in the drawing room?"

"Bloodsports, be hanged!" the farmer burst out. "You can't fool Bill Vizard. Tis bedsport his lordship favours, either side o' the blanket!"

Hearty guffaws ensued. Unfortunately, the Earl chose that precise moment to enter the room. He had ridden over from Berkeley as a gesture of goodwill, having eschewed a further brush with religion by absence from the christening. A startled hush fell upon the gathering.

"I'd be a churl to call out an old chaw-bacon like you, Vizard, but I'll thank you to keep your cloddish wit for the byre. And know this," he said, with a forbidding glance around his audience, "if anyone fails to accord my lady the respect she deserves and full compliance with her wishes, I will see him evicted from his hearth and he will never prosper is this Vale again. I don't think I need add anything further. Now, Tom, Elizabeth, I trust I am permitted a peek at the young Christian."

The Earl of Berkeley had said it. It came from his own lips. *My lady.* The news would catch fire around every parish in the county in less time than it took to say 'Double Berkeley'.

The ire had festered beneath his good manners for the rest of that afternoon. When he returned, Mary was with her mother in the nursery, embroidering the letter 'T' upon new underlinen for identification by the laundry-maids. The boy was romping around her feet, absorbed in the noisy, unfocused activities through which infants explore their environment. The sight caused unreasonable anger. Mary's simple-minded morals had driven him to share his intimate life with a peasant widow and daughter and was punishing him with a brace of bastards as monumental evidence of his stupidity.

"I am made the laughing-stock!" he shouted from the doorway, having wasted no words of greeting. Mrs Cole looked terrified.

"My lord?" Mary got up from her knees in concern, not without effort. Her bloated waistline strained under a loosened stomacher. "Fitz! Hush!"

"Our tenants make sport over at Stone at our expense. We are compared to livestock!"

"I can see how shocking that is...."

"Shocking!"

"...but if we live in such a way as to invite slander, it is to be expected."

"You suffer me to tolerate it, madam?"

"Indeed, no, for it is not becoming in them to disrespect their lord. But we should be setting an example."

"I was never exemplary in my life!"

"Well, lesser mortals do have regard for decency. Men's eyes search, and tongues chatter."

"Is it not enough that I have raised you to a life of privilege from the gutter?"

Mary's locks were falling down about her shoulders beneath an oversized mob-cap. The eyes, vital with the promise of a smile, were the hue of tourmaline and smouldered with reproach. It startled Berkeley, as though out of a dream. What was he doing with this filly, easily young enough to be his daughter? Everything about her was *recherché* and indicated that she was unfitted for such a role.

"It be no more'n the truth, Mary," said Mrs Cole quietly into the void, concerned for the outcome. She picked up the wriggling Fitz who had started to whimper and trundled into her bedchamber.

"If we were married...."

"You maintain that we are!"

"Before Heaven, yes. But tis more than two people plighting their troth. Marriage is a public promise, for the benefit of the whole community, else no one knows where they've come from, or where they're going, or who they are."

There was no point in trying to humour her. He must be blunt. "I cannot marry you," he said gruffly with a catch in his voice.

"My lord, you have a child. Two! What will you tell them? Are they to be cheated of their birthright?"

By God, he thought, there is more than a child in her belly: there is fire! It was the protection of a tigress for her cubs. "Am I such an ogre that I would forsake my own flesh and blood?"

"I don't know! I don't know!" cried Mary, now distraught. "You will marry a wife and have proper heirs and make our babies the enemies of hers, and of me!" Tears were beginning to run down her cheeks. She was too distressed to curb her tongue. "You have no notion how unendurable my life is here. The servants gossip. Boniface does not care to wait on me at all. He says Mrs Bayly went her ways as discreet as a mouse and did not seek chapter and verse how the castle is run and...."

"How dare he!" raged the Earl. "I shall reprimand him. He shall understand who is master here." (That the butler was a good and faithful retainer of fourteen years standing only complicated the pucker.)

"Oh, he does! When you are here."

"Am I to understand that the whole world is poking fun at us? That my authority is undermined by installing a....whom I choose?"

"If we were married, it wouldn't signify. Oh, you can do as you please, keep a mistress. I shall look the other way, but set the thing to rights, I beg you."

"I cannot marry you, I tell you!"

A slammed door reverberated several rooms away. The heavy oak sent a draught gusting up the stairwell so that even the Oudenarde tapestries lifted away from the cold stone they had clad for centuries. (They told the story of the beautiful Jewess, Esther, who supplanted Queen Vashti in King Ahasuerus' affections and won a reprieve for her people.)

Berkeley turned away and headed for his study. "I will never marry you! My decision is unshakeable!" She could hear his angry tread receding down the staircase. Not for a moment did she guess that she had inflicted real pain. She might as well have driven a stake through his heart. "*You can do as you please, keep a mistress....*" Was preserving appearances all she cared about? When he had calmed down, he saw that he could not reasonably hope that she felt more kindly disposed towards him, but that did not stop the wound from smarting. Because she had tried so assiduously to please him, he had dared to fancy that she was growing fond of him. At least she would not abscond: he had her at his mercy.

The birthing of Maurice was a gentler affair than Fitz's had been. Fitz had kicked and protested and taken his aboriginal breath with a roar, as if he knew something of the injustice of the world.

On the second day of the New Year, 1788, the waters broke. In the early hours of the next morning Maurice Fitzhardinge Berkeley arrived. Mary gazed in awe at her two hopeful babies, only a year between them, and her heart swelled with pride and a fierce desire to provide for them.

No sooner was her confinement over, than, looking about her, she felt mounting frustration at the badly appointed farmsteads and the ramshackle granaries. It offended her finely wrought notions of thrift and efficiency. Berkeley might have been on a different scale from Barnwood and Butcher's Row, but the rules of economy were the same. Bridling her mare, she rode about the estate and listened to the peasants, got to know their tone of mind. Then she called for the House Steward, James Simmonds, to bring the account books so that she could study them in earnest. There was nothing like parenthood and the threat of beggary to sharpen the wits!

Boniface looked askance when he heard about this and opined that women ought to know their place (which was in the nursery and drawing room). He did not care to entertain thoughts of the bedchamber. What was the Earl thinking of to let a giddy young trollop loose among his ledgers? Even had the pair been bound in wedlock, which he did not believe for a second, it was insane to surrender the reins to a country wench whose courtly bearing and quick brain did not belie a lack of refined education.

"The devil of it is," reported Croome to his sweetheart, Miss Esther Longden, "that we misjudged her. Her talents are to some purpose. She's no time to go netting purses and writing sonnets and such. She's a woman of business!"

"Tis a rare thing to find a mistress who's as much use as ornament," Esther responded, wide-eyed.

"His lordship don't seem to care one way or t'other. If he's not out with the hounds, it's the gun-dogs, or he's off to the Barracks in Gloucester, or sitting at the Quarter Sessions, or dining with the gentry hereabouts. Miss Tudor is left to her own devices."

"With two chavvies an' all, that must be mortal lonely. But I do think, John, that if they were married, she'd go about with him more. He can't introduce her to the Quality, can he, if she's only his fancy piece?"

"I'm as flummoxed by it as you are. All I know is, she has a genuine care for the staff and tenants. Likely she'll keep mutton on our table. I'll not hear a word said against her!"

Increasingly, the Earl received good reports of 'the lady of the castle'. He could look his tenants in the eye and know that their grievances were being addressed. The smooth running of his household was undeniable, with every comfort and pleasure considered. That an inexperienced girl could wreak such a transformation and foster his children so patiently was remarkable. The battlements of Berkeley Castle, jealously hoarding their premium spaces from enemy infiltration, seemed to possess a rosy glow in the meek snowdrop light of February from the hunting fields below. He looked forward to a dinner of roast beef and claret and Mary's company at table. He thought with regret and longing of the false deed done in Holy Week three years ago. It was something upon which he could never retrench.

There was no doubt about it, he had uncorked a demon genie the day he first tangled with the Coles.

Nine

"Our tiff is forgotten. Fox has been recalled from Bologna. The Exchequer will go to Sheridan," asserted the Prince of Wales to his friend of the South Gloucesters. His Royal Highness was resplendent in robes of chivalry as he sat waiting for news of his Accession. His hunger for acclaim was only superseded by his taste for theatre. The King is dead: Long live the King!

Berkeley found the presumption somewhat distasteful. "His Majesty may yet recover."

The royal dumpling face fell. His appearance savoured of the young character in Zoffany's painting of him as a Roman General and his brother as a Sultan, gazed upon by a doting Queen. Rome and Byzantium had better beware!

"You haven't seen him. Only days ago he was out hunting at Windsor, but he suffered so severe a relapse as to call for Frederick and me to attend him. Do you know - without the slightest provocation, I swear! - he seized me by the throat at dinner and my brother was hard put to tear him away. His nights pass in raving delirium and Sir Lucas Pepys advises that we find our black-bordered stationery!"

"So much for lettuce and lovage!"

"He thinks he's King Lear. He blames himself for the loss of the Colonies. His decline is now such that he is a danger to himself and others and must, perforce, be strapped in his chair. The First Sovereign of the civilised world and he is come to this! Mama is in fits of distress and I can do nothing right."

"Which leaves the Buff and Blues jockeying for position."

"Fox is poised and ready to pounce. My energies have been greatly taxed these eight and forty hours with matters of politics. Most sensitive matters. Should I promote Frederick to Field-Marshal, or retain that distinction myself? I am proposing to have medals struck to mark the new era and wonder what inscription they should bear. Then there is the tricky question of Maria: if I create her a Duchess, what should her title be...?"

Berkeley could sympathise over forms of address since they had caused such mystification on his own turf. If Maria Fitzherbert were anything like Mary, only one title would answer, and that was not in the Prince's gift. Having obtained a grant through Parliament to help soak up his debts and to facilitate expenses as Heir Apparent, he had taken a house for Maria in

Pall Mall, in the vicinity of Carlton House, where they evolved a species of married life concocted for the circumstances.

"Your Royal Highness must await inspiration in season. This wretched malady is not drawn to any conclusion yet."

"Dear Maria is anxious that I seal the rift with the King, lest the chance be lost. But enough! What of you, Fred?"

A slight flicker of unease passed over Berkeley's face. "Our second son, Maurice, went to the font last March and, in February, there is to be a third child."

"Good grief! Paternity does seem to be your forte! At any rate, the pedigree is well supplied!"

The drawing room in Maria Fitzherbert's minor London mansion had been skilfully extended to the eye by vertical lakes of mirrors in the rococo panelling. It was cast in a cheery dandelion hue which lent the illusion of sunlight even on the darkest winter day. When the Prince was announced she sailed into the room, the finest prow of any galleon.

"Fox is a hot-head," he burst out. "He is not so wily after all."

"Why, my dearest, what can have happened?"

"He is making mischief in the House. How can a Whig demand that there be a Regency without Parliamentary debate? He claims it is mine as of right...."

"Isn't that what you want?"

"It is a heinous tactical error! A full-scale rumpus has erupted over my preference for the company of Papists."

"It will die down, my dear, just as it did before."

"We don't want a repeat of Gordon's spleen."

"No," agreed Maria sombrely, for she had lost Mr Fitzherbert as a result of the Riots. "The newspapers will make a meal of it. There will be scurrilous cartoons and all manner of wicked distortions, but we shall ignore it."

"I have asked Sherry to come here this morning. He will confound the gossipmongers as to our precise connection."

"That's masterly," chuckled Maria, "since he is unsure of it himself!"

"I did not ask the up-and-coming Grey since he refused a hand in our ceremony. His conscience is too fine a marksman for his own good."

When the man of letters arrived to drink coffee and discuss strategy, he reminded the Prince what he was inclined to forget in the intoxicating climate of Whiggism, that England was Tory at heart. Pitt would carry the Press. The King was making an amazing recovery and his Prime Minister was quietly cunning in delaying the issue of a Regency. He would yet un-Whig *Princeps Juventutis*, Pitt had declared.

"The vacillations of my father's health leave no room for optimism," the Prince protested.

"Your Highness, perhaps this is the wrong chapter," suggested Sheridan. "You need time to travel and win the hearts of the populace. They will have the benefit of your dynamic person, your coruscating wit, and there will be a sea change."

The Prince was crestfallen. He had gambled upon a Regency and it was to be denied him.

"It is for the best," said Maria. "We shall not be in the limelight."

"Our bond is too sacred for communal scrutiny," said the Prince.

Sheridan's brow lifted. Whatever the promise sealed between the two before him, he was sure it would not stand the test of law. He finished his cup of coffee.

"Oh, I must tell you a most singular thing which will interest Your Highness. Sam Lysons invited me to go with him to a gathering at the home of a Mrs Edge the other evening. The legal fraternity was well represented and there were some mummers, Mrs Siddons and John Kemble and a hack or two. Twas a capital diversion! I confess I'd never heard of the lady, but Lysons told me it is rumoured that the Earl of Berkeley is her brother-in-law. What do you make of that, sir?"

"Make of it?" replied the Prince suavely. "Why, I make nothing of it, Sherry. If Fred Berkeley had a sister-in-law called Mrs Edge, I'm sure I should know. I saw him only recently and he mentioned nothing of a Mrs Edge."

The politician thought this a canny reply. "A Chinese whisper, perhaps."

"Who is her husband, pray?"

"That is a sphinxine riddle and a half! He was not present and no explanation was given. Lysons has reason to believe her the inamorata of James Edge of Bolton. She was even known as 'Mrs Bolton' formerly."

"Another lawyer," muttered the Prince to himself. "A Member of Parliament?" he spoke out loud.

"Not the first, I gather. Wilmot found her alluring."

"John Wilmot, the American Loyalist commissioner? The Master in Chancery?"

"An out-and-out 'chancery suit', I've heard tell," quipped Sheridan.

"But he is one of *us*," said the Prince, failing to hide his dismay. "A Whig."

This woman was Greek Fire! Wright, Edge, Wilmot, men dedicated to preserving and improving the law. All entered at the Inner Temple. Wright and Wilmot's estates marched closely in the Midlands. Edge was no stranger to them, having strong family connections in the area. Evidently, she did not cast her net wide in her quest for kudos, the basis of all incest and treacherous passion. Add to the cocktail her lack of discretion.... And then there was that other profanity Berkeley had spoken of.... Could her canon of vices possibly stretch so far?

"The lady is of light character and, I'd like to think, more opportunist than ambitious."

"If she can inveigle Wilmot...."

"He does strike one as upstanding," interposed Mrs Fitzherbert.

"Everything is being done to underplay his divorce proceedings," Sheridan promised them, while mentally adding: Just as everything is being done to underplay your putative marriage. "Since Mrs Wilmot's desertion appears to be the stated grounds for the rupture, the case will be unsensational. I gather she ran off with her groom."

The banks of the Severn had burst and the spring tides were creeping over the watermeadows towards the foundations of Berkeley Castle. Drifts of wading birds were taking off from the marshes. Mary strolled in the Pleasure Garden beside her mother who was pushing the newborn Augustus Fitzhardinge in his baby carriage, cocooned against a bracing wind.

"Dorcas had a letter this morning from Lydia," said Mrs Cole. "It turns out our Billy writes to her reg'lar. He don't write to us once in a blue moon."

"He's long been sweet on her, Ma. I could wish that she wasn't under Susan's roof. It will do my campaign no good with Berkeley if Billy becomes involved with her."

The Widow Cole surveyed a bank of kneeling daffodils, trampled by last night's gale. "That's a lost cause, Mary. You'd do well to square up and make the best of a ham-handed job."

But her youngest daughter was adamant that she would never give up. "We have to live in hope. It's the only life worth living."

"You always was the clever one. You've learned fast and I can tell that in some ways you ain't out of place. You're winning the respeck of the servants and so forth. Berkeley was as mad as fire when you turned off old Boniface and his Mrs for disobeying orders, but he never interfered over who would fill their shoes."

"John Croome and his bride are hard-working and loyal."

"Tis a thankless task, though. The breedin's taken the roses from your cheeks."

"I shall survive. "

"Youm lucky to have a strong *institution*, Mary. But, you see, I don't feel I'll ever come up to scratch no more. This old pile's draughty and my bones do ache with the lifting and carrying an' dozens of stairs. I get so *disjointed* with all the passages and want d'rections to find my way."

Mary stopped on the sandstone path. "Ma, I had no notion you were so unhappy."

"You've set up your life now, my dear. Billy's in another country. I can't countenance your sisters, so help me. I been thinking I might bide in Lincolnshire for a while with your Grandma and then go back to my friends in Gloucester. I'd be near your Pa's resting place."

"But it's spring! We'll soon be leaving for London. Augustus is to be baptised in St. George's. How can you desert the children?"

"They'll not want to do with the likes o' me when they've gained a few inches. I was never used to fine ways. They'll need a governess, then a tutor. They'll know the names of explorers and how to spell words in the right order and the battles their gran'folks won and lost. They'll not want reminding that your Pa sold tripe and gutted fowls and your Ma gave suck to starvelings."

Inwardly, Mary had to allow this would not sit well beside her own prudent siege of Berkeley. Would he even permit that the children should know that the 'Old Nurse', as she was called by the servants, was their grandmother? It did not enter the heads of Captain Prescott and Colonel West, house-guests for months at a time, or the Dowager, that the nursery supervisor was Miss Tudor's Mama.

"I am tormented of conscience over poor Fitz. A great wrong has been done....to the three of them. Sometimes, I see accusation in his eyes."

"Tis a fume of fancy. He's no bigger'n an emmet."

"I shall miss you, Ma," said Mary with brimming eyes.

The wind blustered across the open spaces and funnelled around the castle walls increasing a sense of isolation and exposure. Respectable families did not visit. There were only the gentlemen who came up from the town in the evening to play cards and a couple of local ladies prepared to run the gauntlet of controversy. Or Berkeley's friends from the country who came to stay overnight but did not bring their wives. Dr Jenner visited the children and he was the kindest of men and a steadfast friend. He could have been a pre-eminent physician or surgeon in London, commanding fees that would have made him a man of substance, but he preferred to return to Chantry Cottage where he had been born. There he could practise among those who were not so privileged. Ever since his apprentice years, he had been obsessed with a mission to conquer that most dreaded of diseases, smallpox, which, if it did not leave its victims hideously disfigured, slew them in the grip of fever. It accounted for one death in ten and had claimed the lives of five European monarchs during that century. Flitting around Jenner's mind was a snippet of folk wisdom imparted by a Sodbury dairymaid. She had presented with symptoms very similar to the early stages of smallpox and, fearing the worst, Jenner had prescribed accordingly. "Oh," replied she, "I cannot take that disease. I have had the cowpox." Since then, he had not ceased to badger the subject and had become convinced that, with enough scientific research, it would be feasible to produce a vaccine.

Mrs Cole said: "You'll get along deedily enough, Mary."

Two days afterwards, Mary drove her mother in a tilbury to Newport to board the coach which would take her to Gloucester where she would find others bound for Stamford and Bourne. The vehicle swayed, leapt into motion and swayed again, its form shrinking as it gained speed along the turnpike.

Mary bit back the tears and snapped the reins. How could she guess that she would not see her mother for another twenty-two years? And when she did, it would be within the walls of the nation's Parliament, the great House of Lords.

It was the time of the equinox. They were to vacate the castle the next day and over dinner that night the talk was of running tides and a new proposal for the Gloucester & Berkeley Canal. For all he had been a pupil of James Brindley, a project based on Robert Whitworth's survey of 1784 had not aroused sufficient interest to raise a share subscription and the drawings lay idle. The lower reaches of the Severn were hazardous to navigate and the plan had been to join the Gloucester and the Stroudwater Canals. Now a further stretch was mooted as a ship canal to join the Severn at Berkeley Pill.

Lord Berkeley ran a capacious wineglass under his nose and swished its contents. "The population of this castle's escalating fast! Further depredations on the coffers come hard at the moment. The government will be looking to this house for investment. Croome, this burgundy is liquid velvet. Pour!"

The Honourable Sir George Cranfield Berkeley, who was soon to return to sea, reddened a shade and he stared at his duck liver pâté. His own nursery at Bosham Manor in Sussex flourished with three animated offspring and, on the present showing, young George looked set to inherit his uncle's title and estates. Captain Prescott and Colonel West glanced at one another but were dutifully silent on the issue of lineage. West's aunt had married Charles Berkeley, deceased brother of the last Lord Berkeley of Stratton, a distant cousin of the 5th Earl.

"Can you afford to be short-sighted, brother? The scheme will regenerate the whole region. Some tokens of prosperity, I am sure, will find their way into your pocket. Won't they compensate you for carving up your land?"

"Cheers!" exclaimed his lordship. "I should hope so, Cran."

"If transport be quick and cheap," said Mary, "corn and coal and potatoes could be better distributed."

"It would ensure the smooth passage of vintages such as this," reasoned Prescott.

"I fear the time is coming when trade between us and our Gallic neighbours must cease," said West. "This unholy revolt across the Channel is getting out of hand."

"Indeed," agreed the Captain. "I myself am bound for King's Lynn and the Impress Service within the month."

"When I was in America and the West Indies, I saw how valuable, nay, essential, our trade routes are in the Pacific. But those damned Frenchies will go for the vitals, begging your pardon, ma'am. We must improve the economics of growing our own food."

"The Corn Laws...." began Prescott.

"Nation can't be expected to draw swords on an empty belly," grunted Berkeley helpfully.

"How glad I am to hear you say so, Colonel," said Mary, "because I have been devoting much time to the study of such things. We are lucky to live in a county which lends itself naturally to cultivation."

West's eyes dilated with interest. This was no run-of-the-mill female were you to search any stratum of society. "You have the Cotswold Hills, the Vale and the Forest of Dean, ma'am. All, I suppose, contribute well to the market-place. Your butter and cheese are the envy of the kingdom."

"Ah, our handsome Gloucestershire cows! And there is nothing to rival our Ryeland and Cotswold sheep, even though Mr Bakewell has developed his Leicestershire breed to yield more meat to bone. They do say ours are uncommon flavoursome. My dear old Pa used to declare....."

The Earl cleared his throat in an ostentatious manner. "....that you have much in common with Cardinal Wolsey, my love," he cautioned obliquely.

Oh dear, I am running on, thought Mary. My tongue is not always my ally when conviction overtakes. "Our wool is especially fine. The weavers of Flanders prize it."

"Wool is the source of the nation's wealth after all," Cranfield said. "Our Chancellor still sits on The Woolsack."

"Fleecing us at every turn!" grumbled his lordship.

"We are also looking to arable land to produce enough food for our citizens. There are new methods of tillage which must make it achievable."

"The Danes taught us everything we know about that," claimed Berkeley. "My ancestors knocked this Vale into shape a thousand years ago."

"My lord, I do not doubt it," said Mary earnestly, "but the population is increasing and we are an island. If we go to war again, we might starve. To replace rye with wheat and barley, for instance, would result in bigger crops. Gone are the days of fishing and fowling for survival: they are mere sport. In some areas, the forest is being cleared for planting."

Colonel West wiped a spot of crab apple jelly from his chin. "I believe I've heard that by sowing certain crops, beneficial minerals in the soil are thereby conserved."

"Oh indeed, Colonel, you may rely that red and white clover do the business. When that is followed by beans and vetches, the effect is multiplied. We are even ploughing up some grazing land and feeding bullocks in their stalls from the fodder crops. Then the manure can be collected to fertilise where it is most needed. Do you not judge that perfect husbandry?"

"Hell's teeth!" swore the Earl. "It is enough to cleave a man from his appetite! Where did you glean this pungent intelligence?"

"In part, from your own library, my lord. There are so many treasures upon its shelves, I could lose myself for a month. But I had a most interesting encounter recently when I called at Mr Bloxsome's rooms in Dursley. There he introduced me to Mr Thomas Rudge...."

"The Bishop's secretary!"

"The same. Mr Rudge is an expert on farming traditions and intends to write a book compassing every aspect. He has visited the castle twice while you have been hunting deer." Mary was flustered by this careless confession and went on apace: "I did not think you would wish to be detained in so tedious a cause, my lord, nor to have to make yourself agreeable to a Bachelor of Divinity...." A corporate bellow resounded around the table. "Scribes and Pharisees, have you not said...? Mr Rudge is of the former school, I do assure you."

"Bless you, ma'am!" cried Cranfield with tears in his eyes. "You have the measure of my brother."

The Earl affected injury. "Some of my best friends are men of the Cloth. There's old Chapeau at Cranford. His Royal Highness, Prince Frederick, is the Bishop of Osnabruck for his sins!"

"To name but two," quipped Captain Prescott.

"I wonder you are not a full-fledged Dissenter, my lord," laughed West.

"Daniel Marklove was one," said Mary informatively, "though he never owns it when he comes here. He used to worship at Newport in the home of Josiah Clowes."

"The engineer on the Thames and Severn?" asked Berkeley.

"When I went into Marklove's today for a length of muslin, Daniel told me that Mr Clowes is to be appointed to survey *our* canal. Mr Hickes was there, Mr *Nicholas* Hickes, that is, and he most particularly emphasised that the proposal deserved robust investment. We should all gain in the future. That was exactly your point, I think, Sir George."

Colonel West was rapt in admiration. He had grown exceedingly fond of Mary in an avuncular way and thought that while his titled friend deferred to her, possibly more than he might a wife, he was in other respects cavalier. The talk at meal-times did not include that freedom customary in the presence of mistresses. It was a curious coupledom. Only yesterday, Mary had intimated that the Reverend Mr Hupsman knew more of the matter than the gentry of Gloucestershire and that everyone would be wiser in due season.

She laid down her napkin upon the table and excused herself to oversee the children's bedtime, leaving the gentlemen to their port and cigars. How empty and dull the room seemed, boorishly crowded with dark Jacobean oak and pregnant with atmospheres from ancient disputes.

"Your lady combines so many talents," remarked Cranfield. "Each time I see her, she is grown in self-assurance and her character unfolds delightfully." Had they been alone, he might have imparted a gnawing feeling of trespass. Nevertheless, the facts were undeniable: his own line would supersede his brother's. Mary played a virtuous role, but subtle hints of matrimony did not sway the naval Knight. He was sure he of all people would have been taken into Frederick's confidence.

"Knows her oats, I can't deny," agreed the Earl. "I have long been put out to pasture!"

"Where you are mightily in your element with your hounds, my lord," grinned the Captain. "Miss Tudor has chosen to take upon herself a burden of responsibility and patently thrives on it."

"We lick the platter clean, Prescott," the Earl told him, leaning back in his chair to blow a controlled smokescreen.

Lord Berkeley was first down to breakfast next morning, closely followed by Colonel West.

"I find I am more disinclined than usual to leave the old place," the Earl sighed. "Many things cry out for attention. The pictures are badly in want of cleaning and the some of the tapestries need repair."

"It would be a shame to lose sight of what your ancestors saw."

"That sentiment struck me only yesterday, confound it! I begin to think I have spent my youth with my eyes closed."

"Miss Tudor was telling me the other day that she would like a portrait of you and Fitz if she can persuade you to sit."

"Would she, by God! I know nothing of it."

"Pray, go easy on her, my lord. No one could be more assiduous in nurturing your interests."

"Do you imagine I don't realise that? I tell you, West, I've no wish to speak ill of the Dowager, but when I remember how we ran wild under the eye of a succession of tutors and nurses, budding insurgents that we were, I am grass-green with envy of my own sprigs."

"Actually, I was wondering....bearing in mind that Miss Tudor deserves to extend her circle of friends....whether you might permit me to introduce her to my cousin, Mrs Bell, when we are at Cranford. To be blunt, my lord, it pains me to have to address her as Miss Tudor...."

"She won't mind if you call her 'Mary'," smirked his lordship, pretending to misunderstand what was implied.

"Obliged, I am sure."

"This is the lady who paints, if memory serves. She is married to a fellow who is something in the city?"

"Thomas is a leather merchant, yes. Catherine is uncommon talented. Her brother is William Hamilton of the Royal Academy, so perhaps that is not very surprising."

"Women have taken up the paintbrush now, have they, West? Not content with penning improving novels and following the drum.... Whatever next? We shall have them doing more than whispering in the ear of our politicians." A repellent image of Susan twined like columbine around John Wilmot's neck accosted the Earl's mind.

"If I may say so, agriculture is an enterprising departure."

"Mary wants to build cottages. Not a gainful investment on the face of it, but she says overcrowding brings disease. This in turn causes low morale and poor returns."

"To say nought of early mortality! I believe it is not hypothesis, my lord. She must see it every day on her travels around your estates."

Berkeley said soberly: "It is as well her mind is occupied." He pushed away his plate of buttered eggs. "I am in no mood for London. Mary does not socialise where she might, and I have no mind to sanction it, though you have my blessing to bring in Mrs Bell. To speak plain, I'm no oil-painting, and no longer in the flush of youth. She'd be swept off her feet by some debonair cavalry officer the minute I'd gone off to Boodle's! *And then what?*"

The Colonel's laughter was polite but dismissive. "Phantoms, my lord. You are sparring with phantoms. Mary's not that sort of female. She is utterly constant."

"I'm a lucky dog, West, but I must never tell her so," admitted his lordship. "Twould turn her head in a trice."

Throughout that winter, His Majesty maundered in a land where he was subject, not ruler; gaoled within the Stygian precincts of his own psyche and immured in his ancestral home at Windsor, or else at The White House, Kew. An endless throng of courtiers loomed and receded about him with visages distorted like Gillray caricatures in this realm of Hieronymus Bosch disorder. They tied and tormented him, forced potions down his throat, whisked away his chamber pot for analysis of the contents, fastened leeches upon him with the routineness of dairymaids milking the buff Jersey cows at his model farm. Stripped of his outer vestments, he cast about for identity, convinced that he was Lear, else Charles I or Edward the Martyr, stabbed to death by a servant in Corfe Castle at his stepmother's behest to make way for Ethelred, his stepbrother. Conspiracy abounded. The Prince of Wales was waiting in the wings: George was certainly The Unready. His perception of politics was that of nursery games. His mind knew no distinction between stage and state. The King must grasp his tether upon the outside world for all he was worth and implore God to spare him for the sake of the nation. In some telepathic way, he sensed encroaching danger from outside. The smell of it wafted across The Channel from an unstable kingdom whose throne disdained the subtle art of using Parliament as its tool. Had not his precious Colonies across the Atlantic Ocean dared to elbow their way to liberty?

Then, one morning, the sun gleamed on the embossed walls of His Majesty's prison. The firmament was azure and the birds were twittering in a different language. The world had not capsized. Peace stole over the King as the green parks beyond the castle slaked his eye. No mistaking the oak trees for the King of Prussia now! They reached up their bare arms to the sky, awaiting the benediction of spring.

Appropriately, on St. George's day, about a month after the christening of Augustus Fitzhardinge Berkeley, a service of Thanksgiving was held in St. Paul's Cathedral. Even Fred Berkeley, who felt duty-bound to re-acquaint himself with the interior of Wren's masterpiece on that occasion, was appalled at the conduct of Wales and his brother, York. They were deeply chagrinned at the turn of events and munched florentines with sublime insouciance throughout the Archbishop's address. "It was a pantomime to take the biscuit, Fred," joked the Prince later with his usual blustering arrogance. "Maria was not invited. Just as well, all that hissing!"

Whereas the King and Queen and Mr Pitt had been rapturously cheered, the Prince and Mr Fox had received the brunt of the people's anger. The Prince drank himself into oblivion at two Ambassadors' Galas put on to commemorate the King's birthday on June 4th because Maria had not been there to steady his hand.

In France, Louis Seize, idling away his days at the Palace of Versailles, wrote in his diary for July 14th: *Nothing*. Meanwhile, the eight towers of the Bastille were scaled by the mob, blitzed and bombarded by rifle and cannon in a riotous confusion that had no obvious side. A mindless beast was unleashed to rampage the streets of Paris, with a single end: to demolish the old regime and bring in a Republic. In one day of scorching heat and detonated passion, the tide had turned for ever.

Billy Cole wrote to his sister, describing some of the macabre sights. He had seen the head of the Marquis de Launay, Commander of the Bastille, mounted on a pole and paraded, along with others, outside the Town Hall. Mary did not know what to make of his letter, whether it was intended for Berkeley's eyes, or hers alone. He had revelled in the oxygen of freedom. His sympathies were not with the aristocrats, that was sure. Bloodshed was a regrettable concomitant of change. His butcher's mettle had surfaced at last! He said that James Perry had bought the *Morning Chronicle*: it was the only English newspaper permitted in Paris, which spoke for itself. There was a stinging reference to the 'baby manufactory' at Berkeley and a warning that it was time she made a stand. It was an abuse of power on the Earl's part to hide her like a *petite dame*.

While Mary was upset by Billy's oafishness, she decided to ignore his letter and secreted it in a compartment of her escritoire. She would not vex the Earl. With three infants, two of them still in breechcloths and Mrs Cole never having been replaced, she needed no further strife. She fretted about what needed to be done in Gloucestershire. Catherine Bell, whom Colonel West had introduced on their short stay at Cranford, visited her on a trip to the Royal Academy. She was a lively, assertive woman, a trifle *outré*, who favoured jewelled Ottoman weaves throughout the winter and angelic whites and creams in the summer to contrast her dark hair.

"When you come to Cranford for the shooting in October, I must begin at once on the painting. I do hope his lordship is agreeable."

"Oh, be sure of it, Catherine. He was a little bemused at first. I told him that I should like to have some memorandum of him with the children.

"And for posterity, dear ma'am! These phases must be captured. They are so transient."

It would be another step, Mary thought, to being more firmly embedded in the Earl's life. Could he honourably discard what had been committed to oil-paint and displayed to the world? It might further strengthen the rumour of marriage.

The following week, the Prince called unexpectedly at Berkeley House to speak with Fred. "Fred, old friend! How good it is to see you!"

Mary was holding Augustus and managed a flustered curtsy, conscious of her mended fichu, although it had been expertly done. "Your Royal Highness."

"My dear Lady Berkeley," he gushed, bending over her hand - how sweet were these words, yet how hollow they rang! "permit me to borrow your husband for a while. There is a pressing concern to discuss. May I say how ravishing you look *en famille* with your cherub. Quite the *bergère*."

The Earl led him into the library and offered him a glass of claret, somewhat disconcerted himself.

"This is a rather sensitive matter, Fred, and is guaranteed to pain you, but I'll come to the point. I don't know how aware you are of your sister-in-law's movements, but she is a spill to a powder-keg and I quite understand your predicament regarding your marriage."

"Susan?" The Earl sounded choked. "Why, what has happened?"

"Mrs Edge, by all that's famous!"

"Mrs *Edge*!"

"Sam Lysons and a handful of others have attended assemblies at her house. She seems to be a honeypot to the legal profession, to say nothing of actors and writers. It is widely conjectured that she is the mistress of James Edge, in the absence of tangible proof. You know that John Wright, his colleague, is also reputed to have fallen prey to her charms and some maintain the Isle of Wight Governor was in her toils."

"The old rebel Harry Powlett, Duke of Bolton?"

"The woman's movements are carefully choreographed. She tantalises and threatens by assuming the names of her lovers. It may be mere vanity, but it wreaks of extortion. Thank God Wilmot saw the light in time. He has been put in quite a spot by having his name linked with hers."

"All trusty supporters of His Majesty's Opposition!" His lordship flushed with a very great warmth beneath his garments when he thought of the manner in which he had enlisted Susan's aid to gain possession of her younger sister.

"At Cumberland House it is constantly spoken of. I cannot stress too keenly, Fred, that no scintilla of scandal must attach to the Whig party. I shall put them in office when I come into my own, which, please God, won't be too long. The King is in a period of remission, but I cannot think it will last."

"A Regency will afford no satisfaction since Pitt's latest Bill."

"It gives me few powers worth having," agreed the Prince, "but we shall change all that."

"It hurts the brain, the Tories so democratic and the Whigs quoting the Royal Prerogative! Small wonder one's ancestors had to duck and weave!"

"Parliament makes strange bedfellows and one of them, you can be sure, is Mrs Edge!"

"Your Highness, I am mortified that the situation is so out-of-hand. I had no idea it had gone so far."

"You have been out of circulation, Fred, not as 'about-town' as you was used. Depend upon it, you will be the last person to be consulted!"

"I must warn her, pay her off. I....I don't know, frankly. What is your wish?"

"I think *we* should pay her off. I will ask an aide to contrive a discreet meeting with her. I might even risk the errand myself!"

The Earl was appalled that the Prince was thinking of going to these unprecedented lengths. "She is elusive to a fault, moving from one address to another as nimble as a cat," he protested. "It would make her the more determined to outwit us!"

"If it does, then we might employ your grandfather's plan to remove mine from these shores. Transportation to the Americas, was it not?"

"Gadzooks, what a capital notion!"

The two friends stared at each other, astonished by the sheer simplicity of the plot. "You may wait a long time for Mrs Edge to become respectably established. Removed from the scene, you can conduct your life openly. Damme, Fred, your cellar is better than mine!"

Was that what he really wanted? When Susan was first given as the prime reason for concealment, it had not been *the* truth. He had imagined his time with Mary would run its course and that it would be the kind of arrangement to be terminated at will. It had not occurred to him that relationships could have a life of their own.

"Do come down to Brighton before the summer is done. I shall certainly take Maria. This wretched business with Withers and his cruel pamphlets against Popery is too vile a slur to be borne. As I said to Lady Salisbury the other day: I believe the Roman Catholic religion the only one fit for a gentleman!"

Upstairs, Augustus broke into a wail. The Earl grinned and could not resist the riposte: "And they say the art of politics is dead!"

Maria Fitzherbert was as tight-lipped about the affairs of the Berkeley household as she was about the details of her 'marriage' to the Prince of Wales.

"Poor Mary," she sympathised when her consort returned from his visit to Spring Gardens. "How intolerable it must be for her. Her dilemma is so like our own. The pamphleteers would tear her to ribbons."

"Delightful woman. She has not your cosmopolitan charm, dearest."

"This Mrs Edge must be silenced." Maria was deep in thought. "Mr Sheridan," she ventured, "might be deemed to owe us a favour. He is acquainted with Mrs Edge. Might he not be the best person for the assignment?"

"I hope Sherry does not need favours to do his duty! But you have a point! You did give them shelter when they were in debt and the duns took their home and carriage. I remember Sherry said it was not in his interest to pay the principal and not his principle to pay the interest!"

"So how best to make her disappear? There will have to be some kind of bond. A woman who has made her way so outrageously thus far will not be readily thwarted."

"Fred Berkeley and I have discussed that. We have a cunning ploy if all else fails. Would the other side of the Herring Pond be far enough?"

Lydia Sharpe, Susan's servant so admired by Billy Cole, had returned to her first mistress. They were living in a house in Half Moon Street, a short distance from the Half Moon tavern. In Susan's boudoir, Lydia was busy removing a tray of cups with chocolate kettle and tidying the surface of the dressing-table in preparation for the elaborate ritual of the morning toilette. A hatpin stand, a hog's bristle hairbrush, silver glove-stretchers and a boxwood glove-powder flask for peppering inside them. Rose-red salve for the lips, burnt cork for the eyebrows and *The Countess of Feversham's Lotion* concocted of borage, irises and gentian root, steeped in white wine and simmered for a day.

"I always feel," said Susan, reviewing every aspect of her countenance in the mirror, "that one owes mankind a vision to gaze upon."

"I vow, Mrs Edge, there's times when you could strut fit to put that Mrs Siddons out of pocket!"

The two women were falling about with laughter because Susan's new stays would not tighten without a great effort and required Lydia to apply a knee to the small of her mistress' back. The petticoats in place, her lutestring gown rippled over them. She was all but fastened when a terse knock echoed on the front door.

"Quick! Hook my bodice. See who it is." Susan ran to the window, but no vehicle was drawn up in the street.

Soubise, now crammed into an expanded frame, appeared in the doorway with an expression of jovial boredom and presented the visitor's card.

"Great heavens, it's Sheridan," hissed Susan. "What can he want at this hour?" It was five and twenty to eleven in the morning and the MP knew that James Edge would be in Chambers. "Show him into the drawing room, Soubise. No! Show him upstairs. (Less neutral territory.) Lydia, you can finish doing my hair while I speak to him."

"Lud, Mr Sheridan, you've caught me on the hop," declared Susan when a stilted greeting had been exchanged and the caller had handed his cape and his quaint buckled hat to Soubise. She gauged he was in no mood to be trifled with. Sheridan's caustic wit could be punishing at the best of times, though it was usually moderated with humour. "Will you take a dish of tea?"

"Thank you, I will not, Mrs Edge. I have come on a matter of some delicacy from His Royal Highness, the Prince of Wales. You might prefer to speak in confidence."

Susan's heart thumped. His Royal Highness! This was beyond her wildest dreams! "Lydia, you may go."

Her euphoria was short-lived. Sheridan did not mince his words and, unsettlingly, refused to be seated. He recalled his own advice to do everything in a mild and agreeable manner. His courage must be keen, but at the same time, as polished as his sword. Oh dear, he thought: my valour is going. It is sneaking off!

"To be concise," he began in his Dublin brogue, "His Highness is dismayed by the gossip you have aroused among the Whigs. Your attachment to certain members of the party has, frankly, become a menace to its stability and...."

"Oh, Mr Sheridan! Always the pineapple of politeness! How sensitive your conscience is!"

"Conscience has no more to do with gallantry than it has with politics, madam."

"And what exactly is the nature of the charge, I'd like to know? Have I jeopardised the reputation of any of our friends? Have I embezzled their fortunes? Have I murmured diplomatic secrets between the silk sheets? No! You have not one shred of evidence to support your claim."

He could not explain that her simply *being* was enough. She had a distracting, mercurial quality that threatened to wreck order. "You seem to thrive," said Sheridan weakly, "upon veiled insinuation. Your tongue is unguarded."

"Oh, but never scurrilous!"

"You adopt the names of your familiars."

"I never had chance to be 'Mrs Wilmot'!" Susan retorted in impish mood. "And have you spied me with them, sir? Have you challenged the good fellows you speak of?"

"The fact and the fiction have may equal weight in government circles, don't you see?"

"I know you to be a spinner of tales yourself and not an attorney, else you'd know there's no law against such. Circumstantial, His Honour would say. The intrigue is in the minds of others. I might as well scream 'slander' as the next person."

"You have a ripe conceit of yourself, madam, if you think you alone can defy the proprieties."

"Be easy, I shan't attempt to breach the coterie at Devonshire House yet awhile!"

"Do I understand you to deny any intimacy with members of the Opposition?"

"Holy Mudder of Gahd an' ahl the saints!" cried Susan in a mimicking accent. "Tis no question for a gentleman to put to a lady! Sure, me affiliation has ahlways been to the Whigs, now. Pitt's face is as long as a poker and the King's Tom o' Bedlam."

Sheridan hooted with laughter. He was tempted to invite her to audition for his next play. "Dorothy Jordan had better watch her step! I perceive you to be a creature through whom the truth is revealed in jest."

"Why, sir, tis a mixed blessing having me on your side. I'm a dangerous alloy!"

The visitor wiped his eyes on his handkerchief and tried to compose himself. "But we digress. I am here to some purpose. The Prince advises that you lose the prominence you at present enjoy."

"Does he now? Can I help it if my head is turned by the cut of a nice buff and blue coat, or the wearer's is turned by my décolletage? Of course," Susan said, raising her hand and shuffling the thumb and forefinger together, her voice assuming a seductive timbre, "it could be turned *away* by a stout draft upon your bankers."

"I have heard you are a woman of commerce. You have a fine ear for timing!"

Sheridan went on to outline the terms of the agreement and the need for a signature in front of legal witnesses upon which she would receive a generous consideration. At least that would restrain her. No one could prevent her from conducting affairs under cover.

"It may be observed," Sheridan said, "that you are not drenched in disappointment, madam."

Susan smiled in angelic mode, for her looks in repose were purged of guile, even of emotion. She was parchment, he realised, to write any character upon, wafted hither and thither by life's vagaries, shifting where she must, catching her reflection in the countenance of others.

"I was wondering what my brother-in-law would make of it," she said.

Sheridan stared at her in silence.

"My Lord Berkeley," she amplified. "He *is* the husband of my sister, Mary. And that is a statement of plain fact."

"Indeed? When did this take place, may I ask?"

"Oh, several years ago. I am an aunt three times over by now to their children! It has been fiercely withheld for reasons," she told him, fluttering her lashes shamelessly, "I am unable to discern."

"Your activities cause a little concern, perhaps?"

"What hypocrites you all are! Cocks crowing on middens!"

"Whereas, your philosophy, madam, is that fertiliser does no good in a heap. A little spread around works miracles! Be good enough to present yourself at this address at eleven of the clock next Tuesday morning." Sheridan passed Susan an address card. "I bid you good day."

"Do present my compliments to the Prince and tell him I am flattered by his offer!"

His Royal Highness was relieved to hear that Mrs Edge had been so compliant and ridiculed her claim of kinship with the Berkeleys. Nevertheless, he was beginning to doubt that they were married in law. Maybe some clandestine vow had been undertaken much as had happened between himself and Maria. The doubt had arisen only days ago when the Countess Dowager had petitioned him to discover whether Miss Tudor was actually the Countess of Berkeley. It was an awkward request and the Prince did not want to break Fred's confidence, so had merely replied that others were asking the same question. Lord Nugent was dead and the old lady was growing feeble: she was possibly considering what revisions to her Will would be necessary if the children of the union were unratified 'heirs of the body'.

It would be interesting to see what news emanated from Berkeley House when the dust had settled.

Ten

In the winter of 1791, cutting winds blew around the brace of gables on the Old Vicarage at Berkeley. Within, there was a disquieting flurry of draughts stirred by people going their separate ways, having no common purpose or shared rhythm to the days. The beams creaked and cracks ran live through the plasterwork. A great fissure appeared in the chimney breast.

The Reverend Mr Hupsman wore a fixed hang-dog expression and his poor attention to duty was noted in the parish. Only his glorious stolen interludes with Fanny made it worth drawing breath. Any filial respect from his sons had dissolved since his rage at the incident with Thomas Hickes' horse, when his face had turned the colour of splitting plums. Damages to Wetmore's property had been paid by Nicholas Hickes on his brother's behalf and, now, Hupsman was being dunned for that amount plus an outstanding debt of his own to Nicholas Hickes at three per cent per week. A pattern of obsequious scrounging was established at Mr Whittard's office in Dursley who collected the profits from his living.

As for Lizzie, she and Tom rarely visited, being taken up with their multiplying family. There were two sons and a daughter already. Mrs Hupsman appeared to derive pleasure from her walks to the village of Stone, but did not request her husband's company or convey any message from their daughter. He liked best to visit when he knew Tom would be at home. The lexicon of child-rearing enthralled the women and had become a device Elizabeth used to diminish him and keep him mindful of his failings as a husband, parent and grandparent.

Oh Fanny! What a woman she was by contrast! All empathy and devotion, in the pink of youth and aglow with a sentience of soul he fancied he managed to compass for an instant in time. She was his! God would vindicate them. Their beings naturally entwined like tendrils of fragrant honeysuckle. Elizabeth was poison ivy, whose choking bonds bore berries of the blackest stain. Fanny's were innocent wounds and Hupsman was convinced he could be Christ to her and heal them. That was what it meant to be a Christian, not the travesty enacted each Sunday inside St. Mary's Minster. She had risked Eternal Life for him. And now they were both earmarked for public disgrace since Wilmot had called unannounced, charging past her servant and had burst in upon them *in flagrante delicto*. It smacked of seeking a scapegoat. Hupsman went by the name of Harris, in respect of Fanny's address in Salt Hill, and was sickened to think that if Wilmot stumbled upon the truth, he might find himself embroiled in a costly case of crim. con.

Then, one morning, out of the blue, Elizabeth received a letter from Barbara Cokayne, regretting how they were losing touch and inviting her to London. Elizabeth, whose opinions on the ways of high society left scant room for negotiation, was surprisingly keen to accept. For, it could not be denied that there was an inconsonant presence in the air which spurred Elizabeth to seek change.

"The only reason I hesitate," she said, "is the cost of the fare."

"His lordship might give you a seat in his carriage next time he heads for Town."

"He has done you so many favours this year, I don't have the gall to approach him. Will these tedious 'loose ends' of your mother's estate never be tied? You have been at the beck and call of her lawyers since she died."

Hupsman clung to a deep-seated sense of justification. "I expect my journeys to Windsor will come to an end ere long," he replied opaquely.

"*That woman* has no right to live in her house."

"She has every right. She looked after mother when we did not."

When Elizabeth returned from her stay in London, the air was stiff with a righteous contempt that tightened her resistance to the truth. Augustus was about as romantic as a hooked trout. What woman would look at him twice?

"We dined with Barbara's relations, Sir John Borlase Warren and Lady Caroline. He and William Cokayne have business dealings with Mr Wilmot. It transpires that Mrs Wilmot, of all things, has an admirer. She entertains a gentleman under our roof!"

Alarm glittered in Hupsman's eye. Elizabeth was drinking Darjeeling tea in the drawing room to revive her flagging energies after the journey. Even then, she was sitting primly on a spoon-back chair as if she dare not let herself go.

"I am not Mrs Wilmot's keeper," he replied calmly, wishing it were different.

"*I* want her evicted!"

"We wouldn't have a leg to stand on. It is not our affair."

"It is yours, Augustus," Elizabeth said. Was there a hint of *double entendre*? "I want you to engage a lawyer tomorrow."

"Madam," he shouted in a blaze of anger, "lawyers cost money! Fanny is entitled to live as she thinks fit without being hounded out of house and home. There will be no witch-hunt!"

Their glances coincided in a flash of understanding. Hupsman realised what he had done. "I see," Elizabeth nodded slowly.

"Mrs Wilmot will be divorced by Deed of Parliament and that's enough!"

"You are very quick to take her part."

"I hope I am a fair man. *Let him who is without sin....*"

Hupsman could not tell whether his wife believed him the guilty party or not. He bent to the opinion that she was merely using the information as a weapon against him and did not think him capable of seduction on technical grounds. She lapsed into a mean-looking daydream for a few seconds, then continued on another tack: "Sir John is a crony of Cranfield Berkeley's, you know, both being in naval service, and he declares what any sane person has deduced all along, that Miss Tudor and the Earl are *not* married. Cranfield's line will inherit the Berkeley estates."

Hupsman managed to curb a smile. Next door, in his study, was a piece of parchment that told another story, not marriage lines, but Banns of marriage. The fact of its existence was as cogent as the instrument itself. To use it must entail the loss of his living, but the beautiful Fanny awaited rescue on the edge of Windsor Forest.

Wilmot's unseemly invasion had given the lovers sterling morale.

"It is not very pretty in him to pursue justice so," said Fanny, tearfully, letting slip the volume she was reading which had done nothing to take her mind off the subject, but rather the reverse. "I am more wronged than he!"

Hupsman relinquished his book to the small pie-crust table, training his seeing eye upon her in a benign and meditative manner. Butler's *Lives of the Saints* was engrossing his mind a good deal of late, particularly those who had fought the torments of the flesh.

"Sadly, the law takes no account of his infidelities, my dear."

"A true gentleman would spare a lady's reputation. We have been discretion itself. Why couldn't he be satisfied with a church divorce?"

"He may wish," conjectured Hupsman, "to remarry. Only an act of Parliament will suffice in that case."

"I begin to think, Huppy, he deserved Mrs Wright very well! Caroline Borlase Warren believes he took the woman down to Dunsford Manor in Devonshire, his new estate, and openly entertained the Barings from Larkbeare."

"That was callous and imprudent, to say the least."

"Flaunting his mistress! How could he be so bereft of decency?" A fresh outbreak of weeping prompted Fanny to grope inside her sleeve for a handkerchief. Hupsman did the gallant thing and supplied his. He kept a spare one these days. "Pray, find my vinaigrette, dearest, I have mislaid it."

His caper down the primrose path of adultery had started to make him nervous. He had not guessed how far it would lead into the barbed thickets of Machiavellian revenge. At first, it had been thrilling to defy his upbringing and what was expected of him. It was deliciously illicit and made him feel daring and *whole*. He could take flight from himself and discover the being he really was, away from Elizabeth and her invasion by stealth of his personality and will. But the fruit hung from a mildewed bough. Fanny seemed to expect Hupsman to compensate for all her disappointments and slights. A militant streak had hardened her character, influenced by the writings of the feminist Mrs Wollstonecraft. The author's soon-to-be-published *A Vindication of the Rights of Woman* was the butt of sensational rumour even before it appeared. None of her views was couched in euphemism and should have brought a crimson blush to the cheek of any modest female.

Having reunited his heart's delight with her smelling salts, Hupsman sank back into his chair with a decrepit sigh.

"You must let go, Fanny. Put away this noxious literature which teaches you to nurse grievance. It is unnatural and against God's order. Who is the woman, anyway?"

"The daughter of a Spitalfields weaver. Oh, but do not discount her. She is articulate and dares to air what we women are feeling. She speaks!"

"I confess," said Hupsman, rubbing his brow, "I find it incomprehensible why the weaker vessel should wish to dispense with a man's protection."

"Because he owns her, don't you see? He demands slavish obedience. She is dependent upon him for her very livelihood. Men are entitled to beat their wives with a stick as thick as a thumb, and rape in marriage is not a crime. That makes us legal harlots."

"Fanny, Fanny, this is unbecoming. To see your tender heart so corrupted...!"

"But I would have nothing if it were not for your mother's charity," Fanny protested. "There never was so mean a miser as Wilmot since he has been denied his rightful inheritance. That's why he seeks restitution for those deprived of lands and connives in Bills to prevent divorced women marrying their lovers!"

Hupsman winced. He had not considered this as part of their agenda. As far as he was concerned, he might leave Elizabeth, but he would always be married to her. Squaring his conscience was a private matter between himself and God, but the laws of the nation, informed by the Mosaic Code, must be upheld.

"Fanny," he said at length, "you need protection. My life in Berkeley is wearisome and has become a sham."

"You mean to leave your wife and living? Oh!" whispered Fanny, aghast, covering her mouth with her fingers. Could she really be responsible for causing such injury to her sex? But Elizabeth was no wife, she persuaded herself. It was God who judged the heart.

"Elizabeth will wear a plaster mask as though nothing has happened."

"But where will she go? How can you support her?"

The ghost of a smile hovered upon Hupsman's countenance and his vitreous eye was never so eloquent.

"His lordship won't constrain her to quit her hearth, I believe. He won't want a stir."

The time had come, as some instinct had told him it one day would. On the journey back to Berkeley, Hupsman reviewed his plan for exacting funds from the Earl. He had long resented the servility that entangled him in Lord Berkeley's iniquity. God was not mocked: the marriage was as sound as any attested by Lord Hardwicke's Act. And, by an ironic quirk of evolution, that was what it had become.

There was tension in the air. The Prince tried to be as attentive and cheerful as usual, but Maria was not taken in. The magic was dwindling.

The campaign for Catholic reforms had culminated in laws which meant that Catholics were no longer stung by a double land tax and could qualify in all aspects of the legal profession.

They were now allowed to live freely in the City of London, and in Westminster, and recusancy was a thing of the past. Maria knew, however, that her association with the Heir Apparent left her no less susceptible to the risk of summons.

The plight of the collapsed French establishment daily impinged upon them. Members of the nobility whom they had reciprocally entertained were beheaded, else butchered by bayonets. Monks and nuns scrambled into anything that would float to seek asylum on British soil. The Prince and Maria joined forces to raise money and see them temporarily accommodated in Brighton, personally welcoming them where they could.

The King was perturbed to find his eldest son giving quarter to the French and denied him any formal office. "Be certain of this, your libertarian deeds may bear the stamp of humanity, but will be mischievously construed," he said. When most of George's brothers were engaged far and wide in the defence of the realm, this riled him. There was widespread unrest over division among the Whigs caused by attitudes to the Revolution. Fox, peeved that he had fallen out of favour, made it clear that he admired the French for their twenty-four carat Republicanism!

"Portland feels that such are the times, a Coalition with Pitt must be sought," advised Lord Malmesbury gravely in his capacity as friend and ambassador.

"The Tories! How dare Fox play fast and loose with the nation's security!"

"I am sure your Royal Highness would be the first to take up the sword if circumstances permitted."

"My hands are tied, Harris. I have borrowed on an Olympian scale to cover my debts. It pains me to concede the pleasures of the turf, so you can see what a coil I am in! He that diggeth a pit falleth into it, eh? I can see I shall have no choice but to prostrate myself before the old man," said the Prince miserably. "How he will relish it!"

Lord Malmesbury gave a slight cough. "I fear His Majesty might require earnest of a proposal to set up, shall we say, a more regular household?"

"Upon my oath, if I didn't know better, I'd say you mean he'll foist on me a nervous filly from some Prussian stable without any form in the bedchamber stakes! Abandon Maria! Execration!"

"Your Royal Highness will do his duty, I know."

The Prince was depressed when Lord Malmesbury went on his way to Devonshire House. His thoughts flew to Fred Berkeley. Mrs Edge appeared to have gone undercover. Nothing had been heard of her since Sheridan had bought her off. Yet Fred had made no move to acknowledge Mary as his wife. It was perplexing to a degree, but did not rank with being driven to contemplate one's royal duty because one was shipwrecked by debt!

It was a trying year for Fred, 1792. When he passed through the King's Gallery at Berkeley, hung with the portraits of monarchs his ancestors had been privileged to serve, the unilateral accusing stare made him shudder as much as the dungeon spiralling below where Edward II had been baited. The Gallery was furnished with items Sir Francis Drake had taken upon his voyages, stout ebony pieces not best calculated to keep the Golden Hind afloat but which, quite apart from their utility, supplied a reminder of home. Queen Elizabeth had played bowls with the hardy adventurer upon the baize turf within the grounds and must have discussed plans for the nation's prosperity.

The Dowager was unwell: the will was ebbing out of her and Fred knew she was disappointed that his affairs were open to debate. He had intimated that his children's future was by no means settled. Poor Craven had gone to his grave last autumn, not that there was much love lost there, but he was the father of legitimate grandchildren and an era seemed to have come to an end. Elizabeth, Lady Craven, had entertained no scruple about plundering his coffers with a budget of wants during her escapades abroad. As Mr Walpole wryly reported: "Lady Craven received the news of her husband's death on a Friday, went into weeds on Saturday, and into white satin and many diamonds on Sunday, and in that vestal train was married to the Margrave of Anspach by my cousin's chaplain."

Berkeley slapped his brother on the back and guffawed: "Demure as a whore at a christening, eh! I tell you, Cran, I'm having nothing to do with that Hun."

The new Margravine and her husband purchased a capacious villa at Hammersmith, naming it Brandenburgh House, and set themselves up in munificent style where their hospitality and hunger for audience were well-indulged. The Dowager had longed for her daughter's return, but all this was too much. She craved singular society in quiet surroundings and did not think that star-struck Elizabeth, with her passion for turning life into romance, would choose to linger in the shadow of death.

"I am of all creatures most miserable, Fred. Your sister and I have become strangers. The children are cutting her. The King will not accept her at Court. Her spouse is a charmless clodhopper, they say."

"Well, if that ain't Elizabeth all over! She'll rewrite the rules and devise her own court and be splendidly disreputable."

"She has a hart's eye and a jackal's heart!"

The Dowager's abiding solace at this time was Mary. She more than half wished that the butcher's maid *was* her daughter-in-law. Anyone could see that she was good for Fred and had the family's welfare at heart.

The strain of serial child-bearing and the tenuousness of her position were telling on Mary. She had worked hard to goad the lumbering dinosaur of the Berkeley estate into the modern world.

Soon after Epiphany, Francis Ducie Fitzhardinge burst upon them a month or so prematurely. The pulsing cord was round his neck and his face cyan blue. Jenner acted with speed to extricate him.

Annie Joyner, a midwife from the town, bathed Mary's brow with a wet flannel. The temporal arteries stood out and her screams stonewalled like the fiery arrows of an invader. "This little soul an't keen to fill mortal shoes, but he'll change his tune when he gets here."

Wax-pale, Berkeley led by an age-old impulse, took refuge in the Tower Room, a haven in times of siege, where he strode back and forth at his wits' end, not understanding why he should be so affected by what was women's business and had to be endured. His guests were left to themselves. Thomas Hickes, Daniel Marklove, Colonel Whatley of the South Gloucesters and Mrs Purnell had come to play cards and enjoy his cellar and pantry. John Clark, a registrar of the parish and building cum timber surveyor to Lord Berkeley, and the Reverend George Hickes, curate, who was standing in for Hupsman, were also present.

"What a taking his lordship be in!" said Mrs Purnell. "If he ain't left a half-hand of wine in that glass! M'dears, did you ever taste macaroons so scrumptious? Do help yourselves while you may."

"The pangs of creation," sighed the Revd Hickes. "We are apt to overlook the anguish of the male at such times."

"Tis the stamp of a good husband to take pity," said the relict.

Tom Hickes, Hupsman's son-in-law, flashed his brother a knowing glance, but made no comment, while Colonel Whatley, who had the ear of the great and the good, lifted a sceptical eyebrow.

"If husband he is, Mrs P. I sense His Royal Highness doubts it, though he'll not be drawn. It is difficult to know what to conclude."

"Oh, to be sure, they are man and wife," said Daniel Marklove, gratified to be able to impart superior information. "I have heard it from their own lips. His lordship was shuffling cards for a rubber of piquet and her ladyship was busy with her crochet hook by the fire when, says he, turning to her of a sudden: 'Do you remember that occasion when so-and-so happened, Mary?' She put down her work and replied: 'Oh dear, I do not have it quite as distinctly as I should like. That was long ago, before you and I were married, peer.' To my mind, that is enough. When I got home I told mother and she said she'd always known they had their own reasons for holding their tongues. People would know the truth by and by."

"I believe Mr Hupsman *suspects* them married," said Tom Hickes, colouring slightly.

"Well, if parson's not certain, then neither am I," John Clark told them. "I was never asked to do duty as witness, no, nor ever heard any Banns, though sometimes my gout plays Hamlet and keeps me from Matins. There's no entry in the registers, else I'd have known, for I keep them at my house in a locked desk and the key in my pocket. Pruett comes to fetch 'em when he deputises. Parson used to send down for the registers if he wanted to write them up himself."

They were interrupted by Lord Berkeley who staggered to the doorway in his waistcoat and leaned on the lintel looking distraught, his eyes filmed with unshed tears. "A son! I am the father of another boy!"

Colonel Whatley struck his thigh, and, rising to his feet, shook Berkeley's limp hand with vigour. "Congratulations, my lord! Capital news! You'll raise a regiment for the county yet! This calls for a toast, what!" he said, turning to the company. "Why, sir, you've gone a ghastly hue."

"Polly has taken a fever. Her life is haemorrhaging away. The burns of Culloden were never so red."

Consternation broke out among the guests. George Hickes took command and sat Berkeley down in a leather chair and plied him with brandy. "Miss Tudor is in the best hands. Jenner is an enlightened physician."

"He needs neither leech nor lancet, Hickes. The child is sickly. There's no fire in his belly."

Upstairs, an unsettling hush had descended. Annie Joyner pressed wet towels upon the patient's febrile brow. The pupils of both eyes were dilated, the irises dead black. Alarmingly, they began to roll under the upper lids. Parched as she was, the sight of water threw her into a frenzy.

"A classic *belladonna* symptom," Jenner muttered. He had been studying the findings of the German homoeopath, Samuel Hahnemann, whose pattern of thinking on the cure of disease had a marked similarity to Jenner's own on inoculation. The doctor worked swiftly to moisten Mary's mouth and drop several grains from his phial upon her tongue. The dose was repeated at intervals during the night until her face and throat had paled to a calm rose. Reason slowly crept back and her breathing evened.

"Where have I been? Some hideous place."

Jenner perched on the bed and patted Mary's hand. "Mrs Cunningham is taking care of your son and has sent for a wet-nurse, since you were in no condition to put him to the breast."

"I sensed a dark presence – I can feel it now. It threatened to cut the cord of life...."

Atropos, thought Jenner. A Greek Fate wielding shears. Atropine was the principal constituent of *belladonna*. The remedy had been well-matched to the sickness. "Tis but a chimera. You are still with us, thank God. And the baby's cord was cut to some purpose!"

The patient's eyes filled with tears. The open wound of new motherhood seemed to express her whole existence. Jenner rolled down his blood-smeared sleeves and, shrugging on his coat, suggested to Berkeley that the children be admitted to cheer their mother and see that all was well.

Fitz was quickly bored and did not know what all the to-do was about. He would rather be aiming pellets at pigeons. Freddy clung to his hand warily and sucked his thumb, while Augustus directed a troubled gaze into the tenanted cot from the dizzy heights of Dorcas' embrace. The baby slept, unheeding.

"My rosary of children," sighed Mary. "Are they not the most beautiful ever created?"

"Polly, how frail you look," said Berkeley when they were alone. He was unkempt and unshaven, wearing riding boots from yesterday and had slept in a chair.

"I hope you aren't treading mud over the Spanish carpet, Fred, or the housemaids will have something to say," she chivvied. She was watching him through narrowed lashes, her mouth quirked with humour. "We must all know our place since the Bastille fell, though I fancy mine is none too clear," she broke off, suddenly choked with tears. That emotional syncope in the voice was what his lordship dreaded most. "If it were not for the little ones, I should not stay with you a moment longer on the present footing. They are the ties."

"Then I am doubly thankful for them," he said with solemn grace.

"To have such innocent creatures tarred with bastardy.... What they will make of their mother, I dread to think. Mrs Wollstonecraft is right: *A woman who has lost her honour imagines that she cannot fall lower; no exertion can wash away this stain.*"

"My dear, I will continue this conversation no further. You are overwrought."

"Yes, go away, for I am become carping and womanish and will vex you with the subject!"

Mary's limber young body made a quick recovery, but Francis Ducie Fitzhardinge hardly stirred and demanded little sustenance. He was engulfed in an 'otherness' from his earliest breath and fled the earth within a very short space. They buried his tiny body in the baronial vault at Cranford and his mother was convinced that this was Divine Reckoning. Berkeley failed miserably to reason with her. She stood by the tomb, valiantly stemming a tremor of the shoulders and he could not take his eyes off her. She was veiled from prying glances, her slight but resolute figure cloaked in black velvet. In a moment of smiting agony, gone like lightning, he realised he loved her with a passion he could not express and that his love for his children was incremental in this overwhelming grace. How laggardly, dull-witted, leaden-hearted, ironical, he had been towards the fair sex in the past, cosseting them only to embellish the hour. It was the first funeral since the day of their infamous wedding.

In June, they were summoned to Berkeley. The Dowager's life was at its close. On the 29th, she was given the last rites and stole away soon after. It was the festival of St. Peter and St. Paul, the day of the sword and the keys. She passed away with the briefest sigh, having made no acknowledgement of her eldest son's children. Under the terms of her Will, the education of his nephew and nieces of the male line was provided. They were piquantly referred to in the document as 'lawfully begotten'. One or two long-serving retainers were singled out for appreciation.

Her eldest son could not expect otherwise, but the fact of it was a sledgehammer blow.

Hupsman was duty-bound to assist in the liturgy. It was a stressful obligation, with townsfolk and country folk, including his wife and children, saying their last farewells to her ladyship. The only consolation was that it offered the renegade cleric a chance to convey critical news at the Castle.

Lord Berkeley feared that it boded no good when his chaplain respectfully turned down his hospitality and chose to put up in Newport, where he might enjoy anonymity and avoid imposing upon his relatives.

On July 2nd, Hupsman took the field footpath to Berkeley, just as his patron's ingenuous 'bride' had done seven years ago, and, knocking on the door of the Castle Keep, requested the favour of an audience with his lordship.

Berkeley's greeting was cordial enough. He came out, showed Hupsman into the library himself and pulled the bell-rope to arrange some refreshments. Hupsman looked overheated and done in.

"I can see there's something biting you, Huppy. Spit it out, fellow."

"First, I must commiserate with your lordship on the death of the Countess Dowager. Tis a melancholy business. Life offers no easy exit for most of us."

Berkeley bowed his head in polite acknowledgement. "Ride it we must. She had a good innings."

The Reverend was inclined to think the use of cricketing parlance inapt, but was well-used to his lordship's graceless cant. That he took nothing very seriously was the cause of Hupsman's being there.

"My lord, I am not come to crave your blessing, nor even your understanding of my desertion, but in consideration of that esteem in which my family has ever held yours, I wonder whether your charity might extend to a little material support.... The scrivener Hickes is pursuing me for damages and for loans that are owing.... I confess....I find myself encumbered. The path I am forced along...." Hupsman had been fingering a loose button on his coat as he spoke. His eyes were downcast in a parody of penitence.

"Reduced straits, eh?" the Earl barked with a sarcastic laugh. "The answer to that is a provident wife!"

180

Hupsman was appalled at the thought of putting Elizabeth and his family through the ignominy of divorce. The people of Berkeley would likely assume his disappearance was on grounds of debt and constitutional delicacy. He was about to reply to this effect, when he stalled. "A provident wife, my lord? Ah, you mean like your own?"

The peer covered his unease well. He said levelly: "The reasons may differ, but we recognise that conjugal felicity is denied both of us."

"I seem to remember that you, however, plighted your troth in the Minster...."

"Damn your eyes, man, I did! You well know what it was worth!"

"I know that it was made in the House of God."

"You know where I stand on the Deity issue, Hupsman. Since I don't believe, any pledge must be meaningless, so there's an end of it."

Hupsman, having confirmed the ground beneath his feet, grew bolder. He was on an extraordinary errand of mixed motives. "As your Chaplain, I have to tell you it is quite the reverse. The fact of God's being is not subject to your belief in Him, nor His laws cancelled. I am obliged to refer you to the motto underpinning the Berkeley crest, heroically sported down the ages by your ancestors. *Dieu Avec Nous.*"

"It may have spoken for *them*; it does not speak for me. Now...."

The cleric raised his hand to indicate that he had not finished. "Forgive me, my lord. It was with these factors in mind, fearing an even higher authority than your own, that I found myself unable to comply wholly with your request to destroy the entry...."

For one time-stopping moment, Berkeley was stultified. "You assured me...! How dare you disregard my orders!"

"I assured you that the registry of the marriage had been destroyed. That is true. The Banns are still in my possession."

"You mean you chose to preserve the fiction, rather than the fact?"

This was a rather curious quibble when the Earl might have questioned why it had been necessary to prepare them, but Hupsman let it pass. "You do not comprehend my frame of mind at the time. I was in the shadow of the gallows," he protested, "between Scylla and Charybdis. My very soul was at risk. Should your lordship wish me to *resurrect* the missing document...."

"A forgery! That is unthinkable!"

"Hardly a forgery, my lord. Only the mark of the vagabond, Barns, would be false. How could it be wrong when it would verify what actually existed....*still exists?*"

Berkeley's eyes were sharp as flint. His heart battered his ribcage as it had rarely done during his phlegmatic life, unless the occurrence were linked to Mary Cole. He fancied the quadrant logs stacked in the grate started to smoulder. Even the dark China tea Croome had left on the pier-table had a smoky aroma.

"Fire and brimstone! How conscience puts the cat among the pigeons and interrupts the smooth flow of our days!" Hupsman had thought it through carefully, Berkeley realised. One way or another, he was going to have his pound of flesh. "Blackmail is an ugly business, fellow."

"Your lordship knows I have been sorely compromised. I might observe that it was an abuse of privilege to co-opt me. Of course, if you do not wish to avail yourself of my offer...."

"While the registry is mislaid, you have the certificate of Banns," Berkeley finished. "They are a statement of intent, nothing more."

"Sight of them – a copy of them – would do much to still the controversy in prominent minds, which you yourself have sometimes fanned into flame when it suited. It is doubtful the loss of the counterpart would be held to my charge."

"A theory it would be unwise to put to the test," Berkeley warned. "You are treading a perilous tightrope. God's blood! You know how awkwardly circumstanced I am with regard to Miss Tudor's connections!"

"I do indeed, my lord. I may even know it better than you!"

"What the deuce do you mean?"

"Mrs Edge...."

"Has retreated into the underworld where she belongs."

"I think your information stale. Mrs Edge is no longer sheltered by her distinguished brief. She lives under the aegis of *two* Corinthians in Grafton Street, in fulsome style, I gather."

"The strumpet!"

"Clearly the lady has repented of her dissolute habits...."

"Now that don't sound like Susan!" declared the Earl in some relief. "A barrel of starch, I'll wager."

"I think not. Oh dear, this is a most distasteful task.... How shall I put it? The vile fellows in question are not noted for their preference for the fair sex. Mrs Edge's lodging, one infers, is a 'safe house' for gentlemen."

The blood drained from the Earl's countenance. "As near as damn to a Molly House! Up to her old tricks, is she?" he muttered. "You don't feather-edge it, do you, Huppy?"

"I am told they give a very good account of themselves in society."

"How came you by all this?"

Augustus Thomas Hupsman bowed his seditious head again. "It was the Margravine...."

"Lilibet!"

"You know how fond she was of my mother and is of my daughter, Lizzie. It was at Benham Park that Fanny....Mrs Wilmot....was first introduced to Mama, being mutual acquaintances of the late Lord Craven and your sister. The Margravine never forgets her old friends and condescends to pay the occasional visit."

"How she revels in sensation! Admires anyone who cocks a snook at form and carries it off."

"She understands," the clergyman went on, "that certain persons are briefed to keep Mrs Edge under surveillance."

"Mm," said Berkeley. "That could go either way. It's high time she was induced to marry."

"If I may say so, that might prove difficult. Make no mistake, Mrs Edge is a dedicated social climber. Her chances of landing a brilliant catch would be vastly enhanced by her sister's rise to the peerage. So you see, my lord, how one thing hinges upon another."

The Earl was aghast. "You mean the hellcat seriously cherishes hopes of becoming my sister!"

"Her appearance is most agreeable, I understand, and that alone might snare a man of high fortune and standing. But add noble connections...."

Berkeley threw up his hands in horror. "Go no further! Desist, I say! Where are they now, the Banns?"

"Why, in the Parish chest at the Vicarage, under lock and key, as the law dictates."

"You mean they are available to any clergyman who fills your shoes, or anyone with licence to examine them?"

"Just so."

"Then you had best retrieve them as soon as maybe and we will discuss terms!"

"A judicious move, my lord, if I may so observe," said Hupsman with a restrained smile that disguised boundless joy. He rose to his feet with a slight movement of the head which

183

suggested the room had a low ceiling. "Excuse me, I must be on my way."

"Yes, go speedily and make sure you return with the Banns before dinner."

The minute he had gone, Berkeley raided his cabinet for liquid fortification. His mind was congested with images of doom. Prurient whispering behind his back. Lewd cartoons reducing it all to schoolboy humour. Courtroom scenes where the debate was dressed in squalid circumlocution and to which he might be summoned. Even the hangman's noose. The Berkeley name, the whole of his heritage, in shreds. And, finally, the contempt of his children. Through it all, loomed Susan's beautiful face, cosmeticised with the native skill of a Venus fly-trap. He had underestimated her. She was biding her time, gently pervading menace through the medium of gossip, without speaking a word.

Eleven

Even before Francis Ducie Fitzhardinge had taken flight for paradise, Mary fell pregnant. It was as if there was a vying of souls for destiny upon earth. The many roles she filled were becoming a burden and Berkeley agreed it was high time the children's active minds were schooled. An air of rebellion hung over the noisy coop and Fitz seemed to be the ringleader. To this end, advertisements were placed in the London journals for the post of governess. Mr Bloxsome vetted the applicants in the first instance and then discussed a short list with Mary.

"Six or seven persons have been interviewed, Miss Tudor. There is only one, perchance two, who stand out from the rest."

"I depend upon your good advice, Mr Bloxsome. The lady should be neither too young, for she must command a proper respect, nor old enough to frighten the little ones out of their wits."

"I take your meaning, yes, indeed," said the asthmatic man of business. "Those were my criteria, rest assured. Discretion, also, was my watchword. This personage will be living under your roof, sharing your domestic arrangements, your dining table...."

"Her character must be unexceptionable."

"She must be able....forgive me....to deflect curiosity. She must be broad-minded in her acceptance of what she may perceive as irregularity."

"Oh, it must stretch from ear to ear, Mr Bloxsome! Never doubt it!" Mary exclaimed, tempted to laugh outright. Would he have dared make such a remark to Fred? "Our children are reared in an atmosphere of temperance and the nicest regard for Christian standards. There is no scandal here. In short, we are dull, sir. Pray, employ none likely to be discontented with it."

The shaggy Bloxsome brows shot high with all manner of disbelief and the skirl of his breathing increased in tempo. He feared that there were those who, learning of the indeterminate relationship between Lord Berkeley and his consort, would shrink from residence in the household.

"Well, I think we have a suitable applicant. Her name is Mrs Price. Her husband is a master mariner who, I suspect, seldom returns. Finding herself in reduced circumstances and having no children of her own, she seeks employment promoting the welfare of others'."

"And has she experience of them?"

"As much as a dozen terms in a young ladies' academy can give. She has lived in Bristol these five years and has put up at the Berkeley Arms."

"And do you feel she will adapt to the nursery?"

"She has many young relations, I understand, who profit from her instruction. May I suggest, ma'am, that you speak with her yourself at some convenient time?"

"Be good enough to send her on Wednesday at three."

Mary Jane Price, a lady who had not long entered her fifth decade, resembled nothing so much as a small, bright-eyed ferret. It was apparent from the start that she was laser-witted and possessed a refined sense of self-importance. She cared not a farthing for her own popularity, but knew to a fault what was her due, as might be expected of the daughter of a Plymouth excise officer. Beneath her stiff modesty, there was a seething elation at obtaining a post which she considered quite a feather in her cap. Her darting gaze was noting every detail of her surroundings and storing it for future use.

"How pleasing to see that you have a pianoforte, ma'am. A Broadwood, too!"

"His lordship has been known to play when the fancy strikes," said Mary, "but he prefers the violincello."

"I have heard his regimental band highly esteems his playing."

If Mary was slightly taken aback, Mrs Price did not notice.

"There is a spinet at Cranford, and a harpsichord of great repute. A Shudi, I believe. I should like the children to receive some instruction in music."

"Such an appreciation is what I most desire to impart, ma'am. The education of any young gentleman cannot be complete without it, whatever his status."

The watchful governess commenced her duties late that August and was cloistered with the children for hours at a stretch, causing hackles to rise among Mary Cunningham's nursery staff with her despotic rule. The wheat turned the colour of old thatch and the bevelled air popped with dehiscent grain. Unable to ride, Mary took to her couch in the afternoons.

Her fifth child, a daughter, was bent on outwitting all natural calculation and rushed to make her entrance. Mary cuddled the infant close, delighted that it was one of her own sex. How much she missed her mother and sisters! "What do you think, Fred? Shall we call her Maria? Tis a little more aristocratic than Mary."

"Maria Fitzhardinge." His lordship appraised.

"That is so like Maria Fitzherbert, do you not think?"

"A lady who has long interested you."

"Let's say I share her frustrations. I'm sure she will be unacquainted with mine."

"Confound you, Polly! You know nothing!"

Maria Fitzhardinge was three days old when news reached England that radical factions had overrun the Tuileries Palace. The King and Queen had been seized and imprisoned in the Temple where they awaited trial.

"Don't ask me what it portends," snapped a harassed Berkeley at supper one night in the presence of Mrs Price. "The overthrow of civilisation, no doubt. I do know this: democracy is for blithering fools who fancy *noblesse* is born of enlightenment."

"Then you'll not allow that Rousseau has a point?" said Mary.

"Damn it, woman, he is against private property!"

"Our enclosures have caused some distress to the poor commoners."

"Philosophers! The wholly bally parcel of 'em should be put up for sport!"

"Dr Johnson," mused Mary, "insists that all property depends upon the chastity of women. Don't you think that an interesting idea?"

"Where's Croome?" roared his lordship. "The first shoot of the season and this bird is tough! Mary, your head is too much in the pamphlets. Beats me how you find the time. Females should refine the domestic arts and defer to their *husbands* in all other things. They'd have penetrated our academic institutions long ago if they were meant for learning."

"What do you say to that, Price?"

Mrs Price's eyes were like live coals. There was more animation in them than her tongue permitted. Unconditioned to wine, she could feel her cheeks glowing stupidly. "Oh, I think I know my place, ma'am." She dabbed a napkin to her mouth in a self-effacing gesture.

"Tis time we made tracks for Cranford, lady, or we shall miss the best of the shooting," declared Berkeley.

"Mr Chapeau will say 'amen' to that!"

One of the chief delights of the Revd Mr Chapeau, Lord Berkeley's long-standing friend who had christened their first child, was to join the select shooting parties arranged by his lordship during the autumn retreat to Cranford. He lived in the neighbourhood and a cover was daily laid for him at the Berkeleys' dining-table, to the chagrin of his straitlaced wife who did not want him associating casually with their like. Elizabeth Martha Chichele Chapeau never let her husband lose sight of the fact that one of her forebears had been a distinguished Archbishop of Canterbury. She could not be seen to be condoning the unyoked Earl and his partner. The good name of her whole family was at stake and she impressed upon her husband that his eternal destiny must be imperilled, and those whose souls he might cure, if he was set on maintaining his friendship. When the carriage with the ochre and black livery drew up at their door, only the Earl was invited to step into the parlour. Miss Tudor had to grit her teeth, raise her chin and wait with forbearance whilst he drank sherry and discussed the coverts, what was rotten in the state of Gaul and Thomas Bell's ominous tender for cavalry saddles. That Thomas and Catherine Bell shared no such misgivings did not ease matters, for Martha Chapeau regarded them as morally slipshod. Artists were a decadent species with their own Bohemian values.

Things came to a head that October. One morning, Mary looked into the schoolroom upon her two elder sons, Fitz and Freddy (Maurice Frederick), to enquire of Mrs Price how they were getting on. Fitz was then rising six, a big boy for his age and smart at sensing undercurrents. Something jarred. He couldn't work out why it was, but he knew all wasn't as it should be. Rage boiled under his skin and distorted his immature features, so dreamy and complaisant in the portrait Mrs Bell had painted of him with Freddy and his horse. After a whispered confabulation, their mother took her leave, the door closing behind her with a cocked pistol click. Fitz's pencil came down, dagger-mode, upon his drawing-book.

"Manners, Price! You should curtsy to Mama!"

"I'll thank you to hold your tongue, Master Fitz!" the dame snapped. "That is the outside of enough! Get on with your drawing or it will be the worse for you."

The child could not contain himself. The Atlantic eyes, so much resembling his mother's, were pellucid with tears. "Why don't you call her 'milady'? Why don't *they*...! Mama is a lady. Why? Why? Why? Why? *Why?*" The pencil cracked.

"Silence! Go, stand in the corner with your face to the wall." Freddy began to whimper. "Now, see what you have done. You're frightening your brother with this carry-on."

Ten minutes later, the atmosphere was becalmed and the governess explained to her unhappy charge that his mother did not wish to be curtsied to by upper staff. As for addressing her as a ladyship, that was a title reserved, she said testily, for his father's wife."

"But Mama is his wife!" wailed poor Fitz. He was clutching his hair in clownish bafflement. "She's our Mama!"

Price grunted, girded her bosom and swiftly guided her pupils' attention towards the equally mystifying business of sky meeting the horizon in pictorial composition instead of sitting overhead like a canopy.

That afternoon, when Mary chastised him for speaking rudely of Mrs Price, Fitz started to prance about the nursery with his hands over his ears, shouting: "I won't listen! I won't listen! She don't have to curtsy! Lily Tudor reckons you're a kept woman and Papa's not your husband!"

Flabbergasted and pinched with anger, Mary took hold of her squealing son and steered him by the ear into the nearest broom cupboard, dropping the latch with a shudder of triumph. "There! When you are ready to apologize and can conduct yourself like a young gentleman, you shall come out. Not a moment before! As for Lily, I shall have words with her!"

The new nursemaid had let her guard slip. She was bent on giving notice and taking the stage-coach up to Town to better her fortune. The household had run berserk and she could not cope with hot-headed 'younkers' as she called them. Before Mary in the Day Room, she was respectful, but there was something unbiddable in her deportment.

"I don't mean to scold you so much as to advise against leaving," Mary told her. "I am deeply concerned to hear of your plan."

"I'm a full sixteen, mum."

Nine years younger than Mary herself and a chasm of difference in the quantity of experience! "What does your mother have to say?"

"She's dead, mum," Lily said with a hardness that might have come from undealt with grief. "She drowned at Sharpness last Michaelmas when the tide washed up too quick."

"That is most unfortunate," Mary condoled, "but please think again. You are unversed in worldly cunning and comely into the bargain. In London, rogues abound who exploit girls such as you. *In this situation, I was once myself....*"

Mary broke off and bit her lip. She averted her gaze from the fascinated maid, trying to staunch a wave of embarrassment. That the girl's name was really Tudor gave the situation a compelling twist! "I entreat you to stay in Gloucestershire among those who care for you."

That minute, the front door bell jangled. Fitz resumed his howl of protest and thumped on his prison door. A visitor was duly announced by the butler. "Mr Chapeau presents his compliments, ma'am."

"Oh dear! You had better show him in. Fitz! Be quiet! Lily, you may go. Do mind my warning, child."

Mr Chapeau swept off his clerical hat, more, one felt, out of reverence for the hallowed territory where Dean Swift and Thomas Fuller cast a venerable eye upon the comings and goings, than protocol. "What, in the name of God, is all that hollering!"

"Pray don't mind Fitz, Mr Chapeau. I have relegated him to the cupboard for insurrection!"

"Do, I beg you, dear lady, release him forthwith! He will die of suffocation!"

"I doubt that," responded Mary wryly and rapped on the cupboard door with a stick. "To prove I am not totally without mercy, I'll do as you request."

Hardly had the door opened, than Fitz darted out, dodging a clipped ear. "There! You little dog! *I may not be your father's wife, but I will make you know through life that I am your mother!* Go and thank Mr Chapeau for your release, then go to your room!"

The sentiment was more prophetic than either of them could have imagined. Mr Chapeau, within earshot, shook his head, tut-tutted and made himself at home on the jacquard sofa while Mary flounced down in a chair under an expiring breath. She was in the early stages of her sixth pregnancy and slow to regain her equilibrium.

"What, in heaven's name, can have put you in such a taking?"

"Gossip! Fitz picked up some mischief from one of the servants and was haranguing me with it. That servant tells me her fortune will be improved in Town and she means to leave tomorrow. I could not impress upon her how headstrong the plan is. Only conceive! She is just sixteen and has no one to take her under the wing. I told her: *In this situation, I once was myself....* It was ill-advised of me, I know. Do you not think her extremely obstinate, Mr Chapeau?"

"I think," said the cleric, "that you are a very good-hearted young woman who must not take upon herself the cares of mankind."

"But such a course must blight her whole existence!" insisted Mary. "Oh, if only you knew the calamity that once befell me!" Then, between sniffs and sobs, she poured out the tale of her abduction by Berkeley while she sat at meat with her sister, how she was purchased for one hundred guineas. "*Mr Chapeau, I have been as much sold as any lamb that goes to the shambles.*"

The clergyman listened agog. The reputation of his friend was not untarnished, but he would not have expected the Earl to act in that farcical manner. Miss Tudor had not impressed him as prone to false exaggeration and her confidence had bubbled forth so naturally, he could do no other than believe her account.

"I do not think I shall see his lordship in quite the same light in future," said Chapeau sombrely as he tried to digest the information. "Where is he, by the way? I take it he is not at home."

"Goodness me! How remiss!" exclaimed Mary. "I have been so taken up with my own misery! I did not tell you he has gone up to Town to dine with his sister, Mary, and the Marquess. May we look forward to seeing you tomorrow evening for a game of cards?"

Chapeau resolved to keep silent about what he had heard. Martha must not learn of it. There was no question of cutting Lord Berkeley. How could he affront one of the leading peers of the realm who had shown him kindness and hospitality for a period of more than twenty years and whose mistress had reposed in him a touching trust? He would not have wanted to be the author of trouble between the two of them when there were children in the equation. The younger ones were outside on the lawns at this very moment, trundling their little wooden barrows painted in primary colours. They were all wrapped up against a subtle nip, the faded grass beneath their feet glistening with illusory diamonds.

Next morning Chapeau went shooting with Lord Berkeley who displayed none of his usual ebullience. Sunlight dazzled the woods rich with the Renaissance tints of autumn and pungent with damp bracken and outcrops of fungi. Riding through a coppice, the pointers sniffing scents in the undergrowth, his companion remarked: "You are not in spirits today, I think, my lord."

"In truth, I have much on my mind."

"Then a good day's sport is the best restorative."

"There is none for my problem, Chapeau. I'm always depressed when I think of an old schoolfellow nicknamed 'Smith'. He was the son of the Duke of Dorset, born out of wedlock, and I loved him exceedingly. He drank himself to death because he was disappointed in the title. I attended him all through his illness. Believe me, my children shall never experience such villainy through my means."

Charles Sackville was the natural son of the 2nd Duke of Dorset, a family which had intermarried with the Berkeleys. He was enshrined in Berkeley's memory both for the love he had borne him and for the cause of his affliction. When the Duke of Dorset died without legitimate heirs, though he was later married to the mother of his son, the dukedom went to his nephew, John.

Chapeau listened intently. "I take it you mean to imply an affinity with your own position," he said cautiously. Was the Earl repenting of his prodigal ways? Did he mean to rectify the situation with Miss Tudor at last?

"It's a cursed tight fix. The notion plagues me incessantly that when I die, the Castle and Honour of Berkeley will be split asunder."

"Did you not say you had come to an arrangement with Sir George Cranfield Berkeley?"

"That was long ago, before the children were born. I confess I am loath to carve up their inheritance now. Tis a monstrous betrayal, Chapeau, you can't say it ain't. Ghastly thing for a father to do. But I have an ingenious plan."

"You have?"

"It occurred to me, now I've a daughter, that there is a female barony at my disposal. If Maria were to be united with my nephew, George, Cranfield's eldest child, I could bequeath the Castle with some distinction to them."

"A courageous solution, if I may say so," frowned Chapeau, his mind swarming with doubts. "But the young lady in question is only lately christened and Captain Berkeley's son still in the schoolroom."

The Earl did not appear to hear and reined in his horse to keep abreast of Chapeau whilst he enlarged on his stratagem. "Visited my sister, Nugent, and Buckingham yesterday. The children are growing apace. They're a fine-looking crew and enviably settled. I wanted to discuss the plan with the Marquess, to see if he did not think it shrewd."

"And did he?"

"Disappointingly, he did not. I hoped he would agree to act as go-between in such delicate negotiations, but he was starchy to say the least, put up all sorts of objections. No spine!"

"Well, if I may speak plain, my lord, I should think Sir George and Lady Emily must view the proposition with alarm, the bride having been under the jurisdiction of a mother who was not your wife and had no rights in the matter."

"That's what Buckingham said, damn it!"

"Miss Tudor is an excellent woman and an exemplar of motherhood, but...."

"Buckingham has not met her and believed her unrefined, since she ain't gilt-edged. I told him she'd received some education in Gloucester and had a very fine wit and many accomplishments."

"None could dispute it."

"I also stated that if that was his only complaint, Lady Emily should take charge of the infant right away and oversee her upbringing and education...."

Chapeau practically choked on this absurdity. "But, my lord, might not Miss Tudor be expected to have an opinion? Might not Sir George and Lady Emily wish to give their son the choice of a bride when his time comes? There's no telling whether the young people would take to each other."

"Simple fellow! Love don't enter the case. It's for the Honour of Berkeley and the salvation of the line. They may do as they please when they're safely married."

"Such a union.... I cannot think.... Marriage is an institution ordained of God."

Terrified squawks erupted in a nearby thicket. There was a flap and flurry of wings. A portly pheasant propelled himself into the upper air and freedom. Almost as a reflex and without thought, the Earl steadied his mare and, squinting down the barrel of his rifle, took aim, the report clattering around the beech and maple trunks. With a flash of turquoise and blood red, the bird fell limply to the ground while excited dogs competed for retrieval.

"Oh, well done! Capital shot!"

"The truth ain't in the nuptials, Chapeau," Berkeley said.

France had pronounced itself a Republic and guillotined its King. In February, war was declared on Britain which threw everyone except the Prince of Wales into a state of turbulent consternation. That gentleman, arrayed in the scarlet of the Tenth Light Dragoons and accoutred to the hilt, paraded the Drawing Room at Carlton House flourishing a glass of champagne. The King had relented and given him a Commission, but his joy was modified by an embargo on active service. His only pleasure, though it was no mean one, was to inspect at the Horse Guards a detachment of troops about to leave for Holland.

"*We* shall put up a good fight and put Frog in his place," the Prince told Berkeley. "I offered to serve under Frederick, if His Majesty would allow, and got nothing but a flea in the ear!"

"No telling where this feud is going," said Fred gloomily.

"It is no time for dividing the House, or indulging in squabbles with my father. I've lost my head to a temptress or two in my time, but damned if I'll lose it to those rascally barbarians."

"Flexibility is a wonderful thing for keeping the head and the heart united," opined Fred.

"The Countess of Jersey is persuaded that my best response to those snivelling republicans is to expand my establishment, show them the English aristocracy is undaunted. We won't be licked, Fred."

Lady Jersey, conniving, corrupt and utterly captivating, gamine where Maria was Juno-esque, had lately beguiled the Prince's flea-bitten ear with her well-informed gossip. The Margravine of Anspach had divulged to her brother with salacious glee how when HRH called upon her ladyship, the linen blinds went down. She supposed it was either to protect against scandal or create a report of it! "Husband may be Master of the Horse," Lord Berkeley had jeered, "but he can't keep the Jersey in check!"

The Earl did not ask where poor Maria figured in all this intrigue. His brain ached in contemplation of it. What had become of the Prince's 'marriage' before Heaven, even if it had no ratification on earth? George still signed himself '*Unalterably Thine*' in his letters to Maria, but made no attempt to hide his dalliance with the youthful grandmother, Frances Jersey. Everyone knew his passion for 'Princess Fitz' had been going downhill for some time. The expedient of marrying for the Monarchy and looking his creditors in the eye was becoming increasingly attractive.

By now, George was so absorbed in his own affairs and weary of the Berkeley fiasco that he, likewise, ceased to enquire after Mary and the children. There was a kind of tacit collusion between the two men to circumvent these quicksands, as if each suspected the other's dealings were dubious.

"I am resigned to my fate: the King shall have his way," sighed the Prince. "Duck and weave, Fred. I've taken your advice! The ship of state is threatened. Fox is being won over by the Radicals and the Whigs are so fragmented, they can't hope to scramble into office for years."

"How life has a way of ambushing the hapless pilgrim!"

His Royal Highness took a pinch of snuff with elegant precision. "The art of living, that is what I mean to pursue. If I cannot make my mark in the theatre of battle, I will foster our English culture. It must be defended every jot as fiercely as our boundaries. These islands have been unmolested for nearly a thousand years."

"At least the Normans didn't mug us with mob rule!"

"Our children deserve to live peacefully on 'this sceptr'd isle set in a silver sea....'"

The Prince was speaking of children! He was thinking of heirs! What a potent mix was the scent of war and the *ascent* of debt at a growing rate of interest! So, the human race must replenish itself of fighting sons and acquire prosperity through the upholding of traditional values!

Berkeley was poignantly reminded that only yesterday he had called upon a trusted friend of the family in Highgate, Maria Lumley. Her brother was in the South Gloucesters and on intimate terms with Fred. She mentioned attending a portrait exhibition at the Royal Academy and spoke in glowing terms of a picture of his lordship and two eldest sons.

"Such angelic features," she said, "such bright eyes full of expectation...."

"They are indeed lovely children," the Earl replied and his hand flew to his forehead with a noise remarkably like a sob. "Would to God they were legitimate!"

"It is a thousand pities," sympathised the lady. "Unfortunately, that cannot be remedied."

Billy had come back from France sporting sansculottes and a raffish red necktie. It was dangerous to dress elegantly there. His head was stuffed with egalitarian notions and his muscle braced for contest. The air of Paris was charged with electrifying triumph, stronger than mourning for the loss of perennial nobility.

Discretion being the better part of valour, he chose to cut loose, with the onset of war, and make a bid for his homeland. Hardly had the vessel docked, than he sped, post-haste, to Mayfair where he found Susan and Lydia Sharpe in her new incarnation as 'Miss Walton', his sister's companion. He had never forgotten Lydia and was as startled by her metamorphosis as she was by his. Susan was a more frequent correspondent than Mary and had kept him informed of family news during his exile. Grinning broadly at the surprise he had sprung upon them, he swaggered half-bashfully into the room to kiss them on both cheeks in French fashion.

"Well, you are become quite the maverick! Do you not think so, Lydia?"

Lydia lowered her lashes demurely. "He is six inches taller, I'd swear."

"You have grown into yourself," pronounced Susan. "I daresay we should call you William now! But divest yourself of that garb if you want to recommend yourself to Berkeley."

"Do I want to?"

"Of course you do, you great ninny! Is it not our life's work? If Mary were openly acknowledged as Lady Berkeley, we'd all be in clover!"

Billy admired the plush decor and noted that his sister had gained a dash of *sangfroid* and was attired in the latest *Directoire* vogue. He was of the opinion that she was surviving splendidly without Berkeley and said so. She told him that was all very well, but she had no status. Her empire needed a solid foundation.

"It's high time Berkeley declared his hand. I've been absent these five years and my sister is still in *purdah* with a host of small fry. It's slavery, no less! How dare he call himself a nobleman when he behaves like a cad?"

Susan chortled melodiously. "Oh, spare us the apoplexy, do! You know how offended he is by my free spirit. Even if I made a grand match, there's Ann to consider. She may pass as Mrs Claiborne and the Major may be eminently respectable, but she can hardly marry him when Farren might turn up like a bad penny and sue for bigamy or desertion."

"He wouldn't dare!"

"Well, he could be dead for all we know," Susan admitted. "We've not heard a whisper since he vanished in a Cornish mist!"

"By God, it's good to be home! It's good to see you, both of you. A feast for the eyes. Speaking of which, I've been starved of good English victuals too long. Is there roast beef for supper?"

When Billy had gone to his room to wash and change his linen, Susan commented in a tone more resigned than rejoicing: "He has lost his gaucheness and gained in self-assurance, but how little France has changed him. His grudge against the aristocracy won't do in England."

"He sides with the redcaps, Mrs Edge. I think that's brave and just."

Susan turned to her companion, simmering with amusement. "Do you indeed? If I didn't know better, I'd lay odds you were love-struck."

"The Welsh dragon's in Billy's blood."

"Fighting talk! Billy won't go looking for trouble."

That her hero might opt for an easier life than his views allowed did nothing to extinguish Lydia's admiration of him. As the radiance of summer faded under the milky blue skies of September, her idol began to see himself in a new light, so exalting to the ego. While his sister supped with a mysterious lawyer in the Pavilion at Vauxhall Gardens, Billy conducted his own siege of the fair Lydia which ran aground in her bed and ended in tiresome floods of tears at virginity lost outside wedlock.

"I'm a good girl, I am. God forgive me, I'd never have let you if I wasn't so powerful fond of you, Billy."

Billy sensed that he was in danger of slipping from the gods. It had imbued these latest weeks with so much sweetness. "We have done no wrong, Lydia. Tis no crime to love. I'm an honest fellow and don't shirk responsibility. I'll get a licence and we'll tie the knot as soon as blink."

Lydia was overjoyed. She felt safe binding in her destiny with Billy's. The fortune of the Coles was charmed. They'd never beg for bread. As for Billy, he took it all in his stride, neither with trepidation nor especial pleasure. For all his muscular pronouncements, he was wrapped in an air of passivity. He habitually blinked like a bewildered fledgling, as if he could not hope to digest the fare before him.

When Susan learned of the wedding plans, she groaned behind her mask of delight. Life would always take Billy by default and he would stumble on making the best of it. To that extent, he had much in common with his mentor, the Earl of Berkeley.

"You can be proud of yourself," said Susan, instantly seeing how the situation might be used to advantage. "You can hold up your head where Berkeley cannot."

"You think so?"

"You're marrying to protect innocence and virtue, which Mary's rogue of Quality has failed to do. You should tell her the news."

"It might shame Berkeley into action."

"What is my want of morals compared to his! They had four children at the last count!"

"I'll write," Billy decided. "I'll write setting forth what you have said. That was a capital phrase, Sue, 'rogue of Quality'."

"It will goad Mary to use her arts of persuasion."

But, however quick her intellect, Mary was not possessed of her sister's guile. One morning, in the middle of October, when the post was brought to her dressing-room at Cranford, her pulse quickened at the sight of her brother's hand. It was from London, not Paris. It was over a year since she had heard from him. He had married Miss Sharpe on October 12th in St. James's Church, Westminster. When Mary had read the whole of it, she was cut to the heart. How dare he!

Mrs Price, who occupied the next bedroom, heard the strains of misery and bent her ear to the wall. Ought she to intervene? She paused in the doorway when Mary rushed out on the landing, clutching the treacherous missive, and collided with her.

"Dear Miss Tudor! Whatever's amiss? Come and sit by the fire."

Mary stifled her weeping and blew her nose with a snort which well advertised her disgust. "My brother is lately married and thinks to chide me because I am not. He says he has done what my 'rogue of Quality' has not dared to do. But he has, Jane. Oh, it is a long story!"

And a tall one, thought Price.

"Is your lot so very bad? You have as much authority as a wife, nay, more!"

"I have no reputation but what can be earned against the odds."

Price decided that her employer was either eaten up by overbearing conceit or by abject humility and that the effects were the same. Did she really expect the world to co-operate in her myth?

"I... I understand your forerunner, Mrs Bayly, a lady of some standing, was turned out to make way for *you*. Oh, paid handsomely, I am sure.... It is the way of the world, Miss Tudor."

This was not a sentiment designed to soothe a mother of disenfranchised children, but at that moment, Berkeley's call cut through the conversation. She fled from the governess back to her dressing-room.

"Mary! Tell cook Cranfield and two of his colleagues will be joining us for dinner!"

"Cranfield!"

"Great heavens, woman! What's wrong? You are a study in anguish!"

Mary made no reply, but thrust Billy's letter under Berkeley's nose. He scanned its contents with an impatient frown and handed it back in a detached manner. "I have not seen this letter. If I am acknowledged to have seen it, I must call your brother out. Frankly, he is not worth the powder. I can see I must find him work to do if he is to make a stab at independence."

Evidently, Berkeley had read a subtext which Mary had not. "Why, will you not marry me, my lord?" she pleaded.

"Polly, I can't!" The portcullis came down: the drawbridge came up.

"With this war about to be waged against us, the Militia will be summoned to the coast and you will meet a refined lady and forget all about me and the children."

"Nothing is more unlikely. Now dry up those tears and come downstairs."

During the spring of 1793, British troops were deployed upon the Continent and camps set up the length of the south coast of England. The South Gloucestershire Militia was duly called out to Plymouth. The Regiment had been posted there some years previously.

"It could be a lengthy stint," his lordship told Mary, "but I shall not be in attendance without some relief."

Mary was in no position to cavil and would not have wanted to stay him from his duties. This would be a way of life until the truculent French had been defeated.

"Ah, Plymouth! My native town," exclaimed Price in nostalgic accents. "His lordship is uncommonly familiar with Plymouth, as I recall."

"You saw him there?" asked Mary.

"Oh no! I did not see him, but his movements were well chronicled upon one particular visit."

"And why was that?"

Price spun the terraqueous globe which reduced to a nugget the concept of the planet for tender minds. She had overheard and savoured a quarrel some months ago between his lordship and Miss Tudor concerning the Militia being called into the country where Berkeley might be introduced to eligible contenders for his hand.

"It seemed for a while that a local *belle* had him eating from her palm. She was all the rage, Miss Caroline Treby Ourry. The Dockyard Commissioner's daughter, you know. Everyone expected they would make a match of it."

"Miss Ourry must have been exceptionally lovely to set Fred thinking of betrothal," Mary said ruefully. "Why didn't they marry?"

"It fizzled out like a damp squib, the way these things sometimes do. Lady Craven considered it unsuitable and did not hesitate to make her feelings known, as only she can!"

"And did Miss Ourry find consolation elsewhere?"

"I really could not take it upon me to say, Miss Tudor."

Price was aware that the lady in question had three years later become the bride of Sir William Molesworth, Bt. Neither did she explain that water had flowed fast and freely under that bridge for a decade. She saw that she had succeeded in planting in Miss Tudor's mind a notion that the Earl might have regretted his cowardice and was returning upon an exploratory mission.

It was spiteful, to say the least. Price was that sort of woman. Besides, she could be said to have had something resembling a private vendetta against Miss Tudor. Elizabeth Bayly was a Lady of Quality who might even have made the grade as the Countess in Price's view. She was cognate with the family of Henry Paget, Earl of Uxbridge, Lord Berkeley's stalwart friend. Price knew this, for she was none other than the cousin of the lady whom the Earl had so brutishly ousted in favour of the butcher's daughter.

Jane Price experienced a sensuous thrill in pacing the floors once dusted by Elizabeth's gowns.

"These instructions to pack like an expeditionary force are absurd! It makes a great labour of moving from one place to another," Price complained to Mary Cunningham.

"Well, they do say, ma'am," confided the nurse, "Miss Tudor fears that if misfortune befall the Earl, his brother, Lieutenant Berkeley, would come and seize the Castle and not let anyone belonging to her near it. She'd have to start again in the world, and so many mouths to feed, poor thing."

"Presumably she consented to be his mistress at some point," replied Price primly. "I daresay she thought she could persuade him to marry her and share the dividends of privilege."

"There are others as do whisper that they're actually married," Cunningham said knowingly.

"Nonsense, my good woman! I can tell you, and with some authority, that nothing could be further from the truth."

The knowledge that the Honourable Sir George Cranfield Berkeley would come into his own upon the Earl's demise was a cloud under which Mary had toiled for several years. It was not helped by a frightful discovery one morning in the Earl's Gun Room.

In search of his lordship, she had gone to the library, the stables, the terrace, and finally to the Gun Room where he made periodic surveys of the account books and received his tenants. Arms from long before the Civil Wars were displayed on the walls; bastard swords and bodkins, mattocks, pikes and halberds. The room was forsaken, but a cutter and goosequill laid down by a sheet of headed and dated parchment suggested recent occupancy. Beside it was a letter with open folds to which he had been about to dash off a reply. Mary sensed danger that he had chosen where he was least likely to be disturbed. Stealing closer, she saw that the letter had come from Berkeley's brother-in-law, the Marquess of Buckingham. The name Maria Fitzhardinge leapt out at her within the first paragraph. She read on, shaken, power leaching from her limbs, her pupils widening in horror. The plan for keeping the Castle and lands bonded with the female title in the Earl's own gift was still under consideration. Fred had disclosed it to his friend, Mr Chapeau, but he had not told the child's mother what was in his mind.

Reluctantly, the Marquess had played go-between. Cranfield was away at sea. Lady Emily's only reaction was one of cool politeness. Wisely hedging, she thanked Lord Berkeley for his kind offer and agreed to inform her husband of the proposal upon his return. With the outbreak of war, no one knew when that would be.

Mary wanted to bolt to the nursery and gather up the infant from her cradle and rock her and weep. "No one shall have you! I will not let you go!" And she could not tell where she ended and the baby began.

When Berkeley returned, she admonished him and railed at him, not caring that she admitted invading his privacy. The tirade was so shocking, that this hardly entered his head.

"How could you do it? How could you conceive such a thing! Our daughter is not stock to be bartered in the market-place! I tell you this, Fred, you may turn me out into the gutter tomorrow, but if you do, as God is my witness, I will take your children with me! I will fight for justice through every avenue open to me. There are some in high places who would take my part!"

For all Mary's impotence, the Earl knew the latter to be true, for she owned rare qualities which drew people, often against expectation, towards her. His own reputation, as opposed to the honour of his rank, was not one of unmixed merit. "I can see that your sisters are not the only thorn in my flesh."

"How can you equate me with them? I beg you to look back and see what my conduct has been as a faithful *wife* and mother to your children. I have never run you into twenty pounds expense that was not for the comfort, interest or health, of you, or your offspring; or spent in any one year, on my own person, more than your common steward costs you. I have fulfilled the role long enough for you, and everybody who knows me, to feel how capable I am."

There was no arguing with this. His vitals were churned up with pity and remorse. He wanted to take her into his arms and tell her he had the very solution; he was going to make everything right as a protector ought to do.

"This cannot be good for you or the child," he said gently. "I recommend some rest. We'll talk later."

"Only promise me you won't pursue this monstrous plan," she importuned him as he made to go.

"You are right," he said, turning back, "I should have discussed it with you, but I can make no promises."

That midsummer eve, Henrietta was born at Spring Gardens without any preface of overwhelming pain. From the earliest days, Mary was uneasy about the little girl. Her responses to stimuli were not what her mother had come to expect. In some ways, Henrietta reminded her of Francis Ducie. The main difference was that she screamed with fits of frustration and appeared to view her habitat as from a bubble. Dr Denman tried to allay Mary's anxieties by saying that babies were individuals and tended to develop at their own pace.

"In her own good time, ma'am. Leave it to nature." He was drying his hands on a towel as he spoke and gave no indication that she might not last out the year.

Mary wished she were at Berkeley with Dr Jenner in attendance. She sensed in her bones the turning of the solstice and longed to be back there. William had set up home with Lydia in Lambeth on the other side of the Thames, courtesy of his lordship, and pursued a dilettante existence pending a suitable post procured under Berkeley's influence. His sisters had both chosen to live in the purlieus of Berkeley House which was in itself intimidating for its occupants.

Susan was still Berkeley's chief worry. Deuced if he didn't think his grandfather's plan for ridding George II of the troublesome Frederick, Prince of Wales, had some merit! The Lost Colonies! Untold leagues of tempestuous sea between them and the shores of England.

What he did not guess was that fate was about to play right into his hands.

One frosty morning he ran into Samuel Lysons in Chancery Lane, a bright young antiquary and son of the Vale, who was studying for the Bar at the Inner Temple. The Berkeleys and Lysons had been neighbours for generations. The Lysons family owned extensive acres at Hempstead through which the projected new Gloucester and Berkeley Canal would pass. An Act of Parliament had recently promoted the work and Lysons mentioned it to the Earl.

"I'd esteem it a favour, my lord, if you could spare time for a little refreshment at The Grecian. We can talk in comfort there."

The Grecian Coffee House, noted for the erudition of its patrons, was a haunt beloved of scientists, collectors of ancient artefacts, aesthetes and law reformers who shaped current wisdom. Its proximity to the Inns of Court made it a magnet for the legal profession. They would owlishly convene in their perukes, gowns and spectacles, looking comical against the monochrome studies of the immortal Plato, Socrates and Pliny. Berkeley was more at home among a company rejoicing in the skills of Gentleman John Jackson, or at Manton's Shooting Gallery, or Boodle's which offered games of hazard. He stared moodily at the thimbleful of Turkish coffee and the pastries encrusted with honey and almonds, regretting that he hadn't made some excuse to be elsewhere.

"As you are no doubt aware, my lord, a new survey has been done since Mr Clowes'," said Lysons. "There has been some disagreement about the line of the canal and tis felt that the advice of the maestro Mylne should be sought."

"Who commands astronomical fees, I don't doubt."

"When the good folk of Gloucestershire understand what benefits the new stretch of canal will bring, we shall drum up support in a jiffy. As Lord Lieutenant of the County, might we count on your good self to widen the appeal and...." Lysons broke off, his plea losing inflexion where it was most needed. He was gazing abstractedly between the bullioned panes at a couple who hesitated on the pavement. "Er, as I was saying, my lord, a most worthy investment."

Berkeley followed the line of Lysons' errant gaze and to his astonishment beheld Susan on the arm of a tall, good-looking buck, exquisitely turned out and sporting a striped yellow waistcoat. The fellow had the swagger of established wealth.

"Ah, the Incomparable Mrs Edge," swooned Lysons, seeing that Berkeley had recognised her and knowing that the lady asserted kinship with him. It was fashionable to languish in admiration of Mrs Edge. Lysons himself, who had the brow of a poet and was locked in an esoteric air, was not tempted to fritter his finer feelings on an archetype of human beauty when there were Roman pavements to be disinterred in Cirencester!

"Handsome is as handsome does, Lysons. Who is that fellow on her arm?"

"No passing fancy! Half the gentlemen of London are in mourning now that she is betrothed."

"Betrothed, you say!" She is up to her old tricks, thought the Earl.

"Indeed, my lord. I wonder you have not heard. James Heyward is an uptown planter from South Carolina. Nay, that is selling him short. He is the dripping rich half-brother of the celebrated Thomas Heyward."

"Judge Thomas Heyward! Who underwrote the Declaration of Independence? Member of the Continental Congress and the South Carolina Assembly? Who learned the arts of law here at the Middle Temple?"

"You have it, sir! I do not think Mrs Edge will want for diamond trinkets!"

Berkeley tossed off the bitter coffee and took a draught of iced water. To his relief, Mrs Edge and her escort turned away and walked off down the Strand, huddled in a *tête-à-tête*. Ye gods! Susan had hooked a bruiser from a family of rank! The fact that he was American meant her reputation was spiced with the exotic and tended to support her claims of links with high estate.

"I take it," Berkeley submitted casually, "all the young blades are displeased that she will be swept off to the Southern States."

Lysons mimed the mask of tragedy. "I believe the pair are to marry in the New Year."

Berkeley was speechless. What a prize booby the Coles must think him to have stooped to such antics to win Mary when Susan had the nous to get what she wanted at the crook of her little finger.

Billy, who had made no contact with Mary after the impudent letter berating Berkeley, was still keen to put the Earl to shame. Eager that his youngest sister should be apprised of Susan's conquest, he wrote accordingly. Susan was to make her home in South Carolina and Ann was to leave for New Orleans with Brigade-Major Richard Claiborne (who had been an aide to General Green of the Virginia Line in the war) and was to take up duty as a Judge in due course. Mary knew that Ann and her soldier had two sons named Richard and James. The Farren children were to remain in England in the care of their grandmother and uncle.

In astonishment, Mary's vision tripped and fell over the gloating sentences her brain could scarcely absorb.

"Don't you see what this means?" she cried. "We can be married!"

Berkeley said wearily: "We have visited this pass so many times, Polly. If we let go all predication of the first marriage, we forsake the children."

"Then," said Mary, "there is only one conclusion to be drawn. *We must make the first marriage hold fast.*"

Susan and her American *beau* sealed the knot in St. Marylebone Church on the fourth day of February, 1794, the bride describing herself as a widow. Since she would be leaving England, the risk was negligible. Lord Hardwicke's act was into its fifth decade and still suffered from parochial incoherence. Certainly, Mr James

Edge, the respected lawyer from Bolton who was making a name for himself, would be pursuing no claim. The witnesses were Billy, Mr John Brown Cutting of her own address, and Mr John Harriott Roe, another quasar of the courtroom. The officiating cleric, Mr William Collier, Rector of Orwell, was a Fellow of Trinity College, Cambridge and a friend of Roe who went the Cambridge Circuit. Roe was of that same band of lawyers who provided a sound portal for Susan's enterprises, amorous or otherwise.

The Candlemas lights burned brightly while they made their vows and presently descended the church steps to drink champagne at Grillon's Hotel where Mr Heyward had been staying. That week they would embark on the long passage to the New World. Ann was already settled in New Orleans and looking forward to Susan's arrival in South Carolina.

Billy could not help an unmanly blub when he said his final goodbyes. He knew he might never again see his two elder sisters, those who breathed success and had infused his life with colour. Susan was deeply content the last day Billy saw her, half-turning on the gangway beside her husband to give him a little wave and a knowing smile that seemed to say: *You see, I made it!*

Yet within a year of taking up residence together on the Beaufort Plains, James Heyward died, leaving the second daughter of William Cole, bankrupt butcher of Barnwood, Gloucester, his entire fortune. Susan was now a wealthy widow at large on a vast continent of pioneers and speculators.

The icicle jaws of winter had lost their hold. The Berkeley fields were lustrous with pea-green blades of wheat. Goat willows burst their furry buds and crab apples blinked awake their rose-and-cream blossoms. Cattle went shambling into the meadows; lambs skipped under the sapling hedges. Mary was caught up in a lightness of being. She went about her work singing under her breath. Susan was married! Susan was in the wide blue yonder! Nemesis was giving up the ghost!

But while the tide of regeneration flowed, the health of her surviving daughter, Maria, subject of Berkeley's proposed pact with Cranfield, conversely began to fail with sharp spasms of coughing and bright, doll-like patches in her cheeks. The May pollens inflamed the child's lungs and hindered respiration. She wheezed and puffed bravely, but by the end of the month had given up the fight. On June 2nd, they laid her to rest at Cranford, Mary's third consecutive child to join her siblings in eternity.

The mother's lament was loud and long. She rocked herself to and fro and Berkeley was at a loss to know how to comfort her.

"My poor little girl is no more," he uttered in forlorn disbelief. Maria had been his favourite child.

"She should have been given her medicine sooner. Tis our cursed situation that killed her!"

"Now how can that be so?"

Mary turned up her face to the Earl, the eyes red-rimmed with weeping. "After I'd spoken with Dr Denman, I went away to the laundry to settle a dispute between two of the maids. When he'd made up the potion, he labelled the phial for 'Miss Tudor'. Price said she dare not administer it without my permission, and so waited, and it was too late, Fred. Too late!"

"Why your name on the phial?"

"It wasn't *my* name. The doctor did not think it fit to write 'Miss Berkeley'!"

"Mightn't he simply have thought you would not wish to relax your scrupulous charge of the children?"

Mary gave this some anxious thought. "I think Price was making dangerous mischief. She tries to undermine me in subtle ways. Shouldn't we dismiss her?"

"No!"

"She's not up to the mark. The boys are growing fast and need a master."

"I think it ill-advised to release Price at this stage," insisted the Earl, recalling the quantity of information the lady had absorbed in her two years of service and her personal disposition towards the family.

That September, the Prime Minister, on behalf of the Crown, presented Hupsman to the benefice of Beverstone a few miles from the Castle. Berkeley had besought the Prince to intervene with Mr Pitt concerning any living which might become vacant in the Gloucester Diocese. It would enable the delinquent vicar to keep his distance and would yield much-needed revenue. (Fanny was now a free woman. The outbreak of War had guaranteed a quick evaporation of Wilmot's Divorce Bill and she was mortified to learn that her former husband had wasted no time in marrying Sarah Haslam, daughter of a Colonel.) Hupsman was still the nominal vicar of Berkeley and the Revd William Davis, a nephew of Edward Jenner's, was appointed curate to breach what was, in effect, a long interregnum. The young man was finding his feet and was unnervingly *local*. The Earl hesitated to add to his duties those of house chaplain and tutor to the boys. Thus, another candidate was sought in a neighbouring Diocese.

"I am to interview a Revd Mr Carrington on Friday," Berkeley told Mary. "He is a carpenter's son, a detail he feels has a *bona fide* precedent. He hails from Lambeth, not Nazareth!"

That same month, Lydia Cole discovered she was expecting and Billy was found a post as Assistant Commissary at Maidstone. It meant he would be travelling the Continent with the British Army, keeping a careful record of the ordering and dispensation of supplies. It seemed apposite that he would be taking up the pen rather than the sword.

A year and a day after his youngest sister had been buried, and six months after the elder one, Francis Henry Fitzhardinge was born at Berkeley one December night. He joined humanity, bawling with gusto, and his mother knew that here was a fellow survivor. The principle of life was in him.

Twelve

Before the Berkeleys left to spend the winter in Gloucestershire, the Earl encountered Lord Malmesbury at Brooks's Club. The diplomat was enjoying a solitary supper in the olive, gilt and crimson Subscription Room and requested Fred to join him, instructing a waiter to fetch another bottle of wine. The Earl parted his coat-tails and sat down in the opposite chair.

"So how goes it with you, Harris?"

"My dear fellow, I am bound on the most thankless errand imaginable."

"How so?"

"I am to play marriage-broker to His Royal Highness. Tomorrow, I leave for the Court of Brunswick to accompany Caroline, his cousin, back to England."

Berkeley's hackles twitched in alarm. The journals had bristled with speculation. "You mean it is all arranged?"

"Bar dotting the Is and crossing the Ts. Penury has brought him to it. Whether you are prince or pauper, debt is not a pretty corner."

"The Prince sees himself as a curator of the Arts on England's behalf. Can't be done on a shoestring."

"There is also the matter of the Succession."

"He had settled that with York."

"Frederick seems in no haste to comply."

"No shot in his locker, I'll be bound!"

"I believe he and the Duchess are estranged. In any case, the plan butters no parsnips with the King! Frederick has written from Germany lauding his reception at the House of Brunswick."

"I'll be hanged!"

"To be frank, Berkeley, it is a matter of Hobson's Choice," said Harris under his breath. "The Houses of Europe are greatly depleted of Protestant brides. If the Prince had not been so frowardly, he could have had his charming cousin, Louise, on his mother's side. She is now Crown Princess of Prussia."

"And what are His Highness' feelings towards the Princess Caroline?"

"Oh, they've never met! The lady is not, shall we say, noted for her pulchritude."

"A ghastly prospect, Harris!"

"He has given Mrs Fitzherbert her *congé* and hopes to remain on friendly terms. She has a high temper, but has occupied a confusing position with estimable grace. This was always on the cards, say what you will. The facts have to be faced; duty to be executed. That is what makes for a stable society. Or we might find ourselves in the teeth of Revolution like our Gallic cousins!" Lord Malmesbury put down his knife and fork and blotted his jaws. "The condemned man ate a hearty dinner, eh! The woodcock is excellent with the port and cranberries. Why don't you try it?"

The Princess Caroline of Brunswick was a regular hoyden, but the Ambassador gave no inkling of what to expect. His instructions were to bring her back safely, skirting war-torn France. This took the best part of four months and allowed rumour to precede the entourage. When it filtered through to the Prince of Wales, he subsided into despair. She was as coarse-minded as a farmhand and swore like a Thames bargee. She spent no time in ablution and dressed with little forethought, her overblown bosom straining at the seams of her gown like grapefruits tumbling from a Covent Garden pannier. Her figure was dumpy and her countenance fresh and rubicund, as though she were bursting in upon one of Queen Charlotte's sedate tea parties from a high-speed gallop across mountain and moor.

"No wonder Frederick sings the praises of the Brunswick Court," said the Prince. "To dilate upon my cousin's assets would be perjury!"

He was in a lather about his forthcoming ordeal. Instead of greeting his bride at Greenwich where she landed, inauspiciously, on All Fools' Day, he sent a detachment of the Light Dragoons to usher her to St. James's Palace and confronted her in the Red Saloon with Lord Malmesbury at her elbow. It was the most desultory greeting the envoy had ever witnessed. His Royal Highness was visibly nauseated and took no steps to meet the Princess halfway. "Harris, I am not well. Pray get me a glass of brandy," he ordered and fled the room.

The Ambassador fielded the repulse with professional aplomb, sure that conciliation would follow. The Princess had attempted to kneel in accordance with English etiquette, but the Prince swiftly raised her up in a manner that suggested she had put a foot wrong. Peeved by her reception, she complained to Malmesbury: *"Je le trouve très gros, et nullement aussi beau que son portrait.*" The criticism sounded less devastating in the diplomatic tongue.

Just seven days later, their wedding took place in the Chapel Royal with heralds trumpeting and all the ritual of sacred ceremony. A contagion of church bells broke out across England to inform all her subjects, from Count to commoner, that the Heir Apparent had a wife.

How the bridegroom managed to consummate the union on his wedding night when, as the Duke of Norfolk observed, he had 'shot the cat' was anybody's guess. Caroline told one of her ladies-in-waiting that he had fallen into a drunken stupor and spent the chief of the night in the hearth. That none should be in doubt he had done his duty, there was soon compelling evidence of his prowess. Exactly nine months later, a daughter was born. They called her Charlotte after the Queen.

The bells of St. Dunstan, Cranford, swung into motion and cascaded into a sonorous peal while the fragrance of bluebells and violets clung to the damp of evening.

"Hark!" said Mary to the children. "That is to tell us the Prince of Wales is married."

Freddy listened, starry-eyed. "Did you have bells, Mama, when you were married?"

"Goodness me, no," replied his mother. "It was a very quiet affair. You see, I was not a Princess. I was poor as a church mouse and along came your Papa upon his white charger and carried me off."

"The poor sap's gone to his doom," said Berkeley in elegiac tones.

"*You* would not marry to save your bacon," Mary chuckled wryly. "Children, it is dusk. Time for bed. Price is waiting to take you up."

By the time the Princess of Wales was delivered of an heir in January, 1796, Berkeley had an unwelcome feeling that he was lagging behind.

That same winter at Berkeley, Fitz fell ill. Initially, it was feared he had contracted smallpox, but the symptoms presently revealed themselves consistent with scarlet fever. Mary spent hours upon her knees in the Minster under the watchful eye of

Mr Davis, pleading that God would stay his hand. Under Dr Jenner's care, the crisis passed. The parents breathed again.

"Thank God it wasn't smallpox," said the doctor. "It leaves a legacy for life if the patient is lucky enough to survive."

"And how do your experiments progress?" asked his lordship.

"After many trials, my lord, I have concluded there is an optimal stage in the cowpox disease when the lymph can be relied upon to bestow full protection against smallpox. It is a delicate balance, as so much of nature."

"Most interesting."

"I have spent half my life puzzling over this terrible affliction and shall publish my enquiry if tests prove efficacious."

"Won't it be necessary to inoculate some poor chub?" asked Berkeley.

"Oh yes, indeed. It cannot be avoided. First with the cow vaccine, then with smallpox itself!"

"And who's going to volunteer for that?"

An offer had already been made by a town family, named Phipps, of their eight year old son, James. They appeared to have every faith in the doctor and his painstaking research. On May 14th, 1796, the child was injected with lymph from the hands of an infected dairymaid, Sarah Knight Nelmes. He developed mild signs of cowpox which soon disappeared. Six weeks later, Jenner, with burning anxiety and fervent prayer, gave the boy a shot of the deadly disease. Wildly exultant, he recorded that the subject remained in the rudest of health.

James Phipps grew up to be a vigorous labourer in the Cotswolds, marrying a youthful widow and becoming father to a generation who succeeded in bettering their lot. He lived for sixty-six years.

The appointment of the Revd Caleb Carrington within the household set Price on edge and sharpened her competitive instincts.

"Of course," she had explained at the outset when she and Carrington were drinking tea in her sitting room, "they have no daughters. Sadly, the little girls were taken. A son, too. But while there are infants of either sex, I can safely expect to prove of use."

"Hard to divine the workings of the Almighty. If there is one," Carrington mused beneath his marmalade whiskers. He leaned back in his armchair with an air of one who knew his tenant's rights.

"Miss Tudor maintains that she and his lordship are man and wife, but I think it a deluded fancy. She is not aware what I overhear," said Price darkly. "I cannot help it. Voices carry!"

Mr Carrington was newly-married and on the way to parenthood. Except at Spring Gardens, he did not live under Berkeley's roof but was accustomed to dine alongside Price at his lordship's table when in Town. One morning, the governess took delight in retailing the news that Admiral Prescott was home from the mighty main and would be joining them. His thirteen year old son, Henry, was entering the Royal Navy aboard the ninety-eight gun Frigate, *Formidable*, and his father was keen to see him off. She gave the unmistakable impression that she herself was well acquainted with the seafarer, painting him in the colours of celebrity. In fact, he had not been present at any period during her 'reign'.

The Admiral did not stay in Spring Gardens. Berkeley House was the eye of a tornado these days and rather cramped. Besides, he had interests of his own to tend. When he arrived, around three in the afternoon, the Earl alone greeted him.

"Does the cockles good to see you, Prescott. Upon my word, you have weathered well in the West Indies! Reynolds, splice the mainbrace for our guest!"

Prescott, an undemonstrative man, received these overtures amiably and handed over his braided bicorne and cape. "A little whisky and water should do the trick. ....A new butler, I see."

"Mary's domain! We've passed through many vicissitudes since you were last here."

"You have my heartfelt condolences for the loss of your children. Unlike you, I have made a poor fist of fatherhood. The career tells against it, but mostly my own shortcomings are to blame. That is why I was so keen to see Henry board his first ship. Independence will be the making of him."

"Shrugging off the apron strings, eh? Don't I know what that's about!"

"My lord, I could not possibly comment. I only know I hanker after the untrammelled camaraderie of yore."

"Come, let's drink a toast to young Henry."

"To Henry! That he may serve his country well and obtain rows of gold lace and silver stars in double quick time!" Prescott allowed the Scotch to fume his palate. "Miss Tudor is well, I take it?"

"In a delicate condition again," answered Berkeley, looking askance with a grin. "These country girls are fine breeders. Bull's eye every time!"

"I feel bound to point out the correlation between the laws of cause and effect, my lord."

"Impertinent rascal! Do I dare to comment upon your attachments?"

"I have only one, Berkeley, as I believe you do, and do not choose to speak of her here."

They went on to discuss the war and how the French were giving the British Fleet a pounding. The Admiral had no reason to expect any further allusion to Mrs Bayly and was taken aback when, upon his introduction to Mrs Price over their *apéritifs*, and within earshot of her mistress, she said in seeming innocence: "I believe you are on friendly terms with my cousin, Elizabeth Bayly, Admiral."

Prescott was ignorant of the link. Either Elizabeth was not aware of her kinswoman's movements, or thought them irrelevant.

"I know the lady, yes," he admitted rather stiffly. "We share a taste for opera."

"Dearest Beth! She has not always possessed dependable friends. We are both unfortunate creatures who benefited under the will of our Uncle, but the money did not go far, or I should not have been obliged to hire out my services," said Price, patting her chignon. "Life can be hard for females."

"Life can be hard for the mariner, the miner and the moneylender, ma'am!" retorted Prescott. He glanced with some disquiet towards Mary whose countenance was burning with indignation. Price had not mentioned her consanguinity with Mrs Bayly. "Aye, and I daresay it can be as hard for the butcher, the baker and the breadwinner, too!"

"Oh, very good, Admiral! I can tell you are an enthusiast of the *bon mot*."

From then on, Prescott relied upon a wall of deafness to keep the inquisitive Price at bay. Roaring gales and cannonade had rendered this a genuine disability, if only partial, and it was a useful screen in unpleasant situations.

"I must say, these candied peaches are aromatic. Outstanding specimens!" he enthused. A silver epergne freighted with a pyramid of sugar-frosted fruits formed the centrepiece of the table.

"That's Mary's province," said the Earl, not without pride.

"Then, congratulations, ma'am!"

"We grew them at Cranford," Mary explained. "About five years ago, we pruned the trees and trained them to fan. I had made a study of grafting in order to increase the quality and yield of fruit, so we experimented with the 'whip and tongue' method one winter."

"Most fascinating," said Prescott.

"The scion plant, that's the fruiting plant, and the rootstock plant, are cleanly cut, then dovetailed and bound until they fuse into one, creating sturdy new growth."

"The one type depending on the other? The marvels of nature!"

"We've new neighbours at Cranford, Prescott," said the Earl. "An eminent sailor like yourself!"

"I take it you mean His Highness, the Duke of Clarence. Yes, I've heard he has moved into Bushey Park."

"With Dorothy Jordan, the actress, if you please," Berkeley enlarged, knowing that his friend was too polite to do so in the society of ladies. "They have two young children."

"Oh, Dorothy Jordan!" exclaimed Mary. "You never said so, peer. My sister and I saw her play in *A Country Girl*, it must be eleven or twelve years since. She was a bang-up stunner! Most diverting!"

"Saints alive! Where did you acquire those cant locutions?" demanded his lordship. He was half-joking and half in deadly earnest. It revealed a startling part of her that was all but stifled. The diners smirked, except Price whose jaw was taut as a drum.

"It is to be hoped," Mary said, "that Prince William will do right by his lady. His brother has treated Mrs Fitzherbert unspeakably."

Berkeley was not best pleased with these comments. No one could have failed to draw a comparison between the Royal situations and their own. After the meal, when Carrington had withdrawn upon some pretext with the ladies, the Earl complained to the Admiral over their port, of Mary's gaffe. He was purple with ire.

"She is publicly taking me to task over a very private matter!"

"I find that Miss Tudor relates a great many things without thinking about them. She spills over on occasion," replied his companion in an attempt to placate him.

"I tell you, Prescott, if this pressure continues, I shall put her away!"

"Shall I tell her so, my lord?"

"Yes, you may."

Berkeley's fearsome aspect had suffered no change when, the following day, his friend called again and was shown into the Morning Room. He and Mary were in the conservatory, in the thick of a domestic argument. Prescott caught them gesticulating through the glass and was glad that his own intimate arrangements could be enjoyed at arm's length. He could not hear what was being said, but the tenor of the sentences rose and fell on an alarming gradient.

"Yesterday, you betrayed a deplorable want of education!" stormed his lordship.

"How did I?"

"You criticised the Prince of Wales, the Duke of Clarence and, by extension, me, for not sharing your plebeian virtue."

"How can the goings-on at Carlton House, among the highest in the land, be right in anyone's book? How are they more sophisticated than a farmhand who tumbles his wenches in the woods and cornfields?" A vision of James Perry, all those years ago, stunned Mary with physical pain in the solar plexus. He would have done right by her, with or without children. "There was someone who wanted to wed me once," she recollected with so wistful a sadness, it seared Berkeley's nerves. "A professional gentleman. Not rich, but of good standing. Well-respected. But you had ruined me *before the altar* and I sent him away, thinking to make your wrong right. I had no idea that I had been duped, not then."

"When? When did this happen?"

"You forsook me for months to save your reputation after we were married."

"In London? In Gloucester? You must have loved him."

"Oh, do not harangue me with these questions! Where's the point now?"

It was decided that, for a while, Mary and the children should retreat to Cranford. Prescott offered to accompany her there and, in the carriage, told her that Berkeley had threatened to put her away, 'if *it* continued'.

The Admiral would never forget the proud turn of her head, the calm self-possession, her aqueous gaze measuring the outer landscape. "He dare not!" He saw that ties lasting a round dozen years inevitably embraced truths he could not fathom. The

Admiral did not dislike Mary in the least, but her pious demands were another matter.

The echoes vanished from Berkeley House. Left alone to brood within its empty rooms, the shaky edifice of the Earl's life suddenly collapsed inwards upon him.

The future had been determined years ago! He had long sunk all he had into a joint existence with Mary. What if he had driven her away? Upon her own admission, she was not proof against the charms of other fellows. He would need to *know* how the estate was run, else be made to look very foolish. This was important in any case, the Earl realised grimly, for, while Mary was aware of his gambling, there were follies, now deeply regretted, the accounts must never reveal. He was more likely to gain Mary's goodwill, and she to trust him, if they were a team.

What stood out in bold relief was that, if Berkeley were to obtain a marriage licence, he would have to declare himself a bachelor and Mary, a spinster, thus renouncing the legend of a former ceremony and all the rights accruing to it. But as he turned this over in his mind, another audacious plan began to fizzle and spark its way to the powder barrel. Hupsman's days might not be long in the land.

A recent conversation with Mary stalked the precincts of his mind. Mrs Black, Jenner's sister, who scorned to compromise her good name, called on Miss Tudor most Thursdays and had mentioned that Hupsman had fleetingly returned to the area since being given the living of Beverstone. He was gaunt as a wraith, she reported. Mrs Black had learnt this from Mary Routh whose disabled sister at Wotton-under-Edge had one afternoon limped to answer a knock upon her door to find the revenant vicar on the step, an old and confidential friend who did not stall at giving his opinion of the Berkeleys' doings and counted them married.

Next day, Berkeley went straight to the offices of the Commissary of Surrey and swore an affidavit concerning his identity and lawful fitness, and that of his intended spouse, to be joined in Holy Matrimony. The Deputy in charge was Thomas Champion de Crespigny, son of an MP of Flemish Huguenot stock, a man with a litigious and scholarly air who made him nervous. Berkeley watched the quill etch out his signature with a bravado he did not feel. It flecked the parchment with ink like a scattering of grapeshot. What he had overlooked was the need to testify to the bride's abode and whether she had been resident in that Parish for the last four weeks. On the spur of the moment, he gave her address as Caleb Carrington's family home in Lambeth which an unmarried sister was occupying. The Almighty, *if* such presided over the affairs of men, would not hold the fact against him that he had declared this upon oath when he was trying to do the right thing by Mary and his family.

From thence, he sped to Cranford and, bursting into the Day Room where Mary sat threading a needle, just as she had the first moment he glimpsed her above the butcher's shop, he thrust away the stitchery and pulled her into his embrace, with a descant upon how miserable he had been in London. He did not know what had driven him to humiliate her for so long. At last, he had staggered to his senses and applied for a marriage licence!

Overcome, Mary chuckled and wept into his chest. "Do you really mean it, Fred? Tomorrow you might repent."

"Never! This is the sanest thing I ever did."

"Oh but, how shall I find the courage to brave society after all these years?"

"As to that," Berkeley hedged, "I have deliberated long and I do not think we should rush to publish the marriage."

"Another secret! Why? Now?"

"Consider this: In the fullness of time, we can announce that those who presumed us married were right. Hupsman's days may be numbered and, when he is gone, we shall say that you were the Countess of Berkeley all along."

"Since 1785?"

"Since March 30, 1785! I have quite a head for dates!"

"But there's no record. We have no marriage lines to corroborate the story. It won't stand up when Fitz comes to claim his dues."

"We have the Banns. There can be no dishonesty in copying a document that once existed."

"A forgery!" Mary covered her mouth with her hand in shock.

"Let's rather say a duplicate."

"Abomination!" squeaked Mary. A frisson of terror prickled along her spine. "We should forfeit our lives if it came to light!"

"And who will examine the registration for material authenticity? When Fitz is called upon to furnish the College of Heralds with proof of his lineage, there will be such a burden of surrounding proof, no one will think to quibble about a scrap of paper."

"You forget, Fred. He has never taken the courtesy title of Lord Dursley."

"To support our secret! We have publicly celebrated his birthday each year as the firstborn, the heir. We have never done so with the others."

"He was born on St. Stephen's Day. It is part of the Christmas festivities for the tenants."

"The reason don't signify, Polly."

"Well, they *are* taken up with their calving heifers and blighted bean crops and know nothing of the College of Heralds," she conceded warily.

Berkeley took her by the shoulders and pressed his lips to her forehead. He sounded like a person who was in full control of his destiny, someone on whose bosom she might rest. "Don't worry your head about it. We shall be quietly married and take each day as it comes. Meanwhile, circumspection!"

"Then I am still to be Miss Tudor?"

"For now. Trust me. We might yet make the first marriage stick!"

Mr Carrington was taken aside and the plan to marry outlined. The need for reticence was stressed. Berkeley would be obliged for his services as a witness. William Tudor, who had returned from a tour of duty on the Continent, was the obvious choice for a second witness. In his view, this was a new start which would ensure economic security. The earlier farce was a lost cause and should be buried without trace if they all meant to keep their heads!

While this was going on, the governess' antennae were twitching. The scent of intrigue hung about the Cranford rooms and she correctly guessed what was afoot. On the sixteenth of May, at Spring Gardens, she recorded in her journal that Miss Tudor appeared in the late morning dressed in emerald silk with silver crewel work. She wore a short pelisse and shoes to match and the heels were slightly raised, which was uncommon for the mistress.

"Dear Miss Tudor! How elegant you look. I should not want to brush the dust of a warehouse on those clothes!"

It was Mary's stated intention that day to buy furniture for a house in Littlehampton she had taken for the summer. The South Gloucesters were stationed in the area and the whole family would benefit from the sea air.

"Why, thank you, Price." Mary bestowed upon her an enigmatic smile, then turned and walked to the waiting barouche with the merest flounce. She was alone, but Price wasn't fooled. Lord Berkeley was not at home. There would be a hallowed venue and the most important rendezvous of their lives. Price nodded slyly to herself. Mr Carrington was also absent.

To enter the parish of Lambeth on the south side of the River Thames was to step back in time, away from the hurly-burly of the West End. Lamhytha, it was called in the Domesday Book. The landing place for lambs. What could have been more in keeping for a butcher's daughter who had been sold to her warder, and whose patron saint was the Blessed Virgin, to be married in St. Mary-at-Lambeth? A knot garden commemorated the Tradescants, father and son, who had ranged far and wide to find exotic fruits and blooms which could be established on England's soil. Anemones, tulips, cyclamen, hyacinths, quinces, mulberries, cherries and vines. Such detail delighted Mary.

Billy was waiting on the cobbled pavement outside gates gleaming with new paint. He dashed forward to help his sister alight from the carriage. Linking her arm through her brother's, Mary inhaled deeply and strolled into the porch and down the nave to be deposited on the left side of Berkeley. The curate, Mr Lloyd, commenced. Berkeley saw his lips form the time-honoured phrases and heard his own assent as from another space.

Within a few short minutes, the promises were made. There were no bells, no fugues, no fanfares. The bride carried no flowers, but the altar was radiant with Madonna lilies. Billy produced the ring Berkeley had given him and placed it on a prayer-book for a blessing. It glinted with a peculiar sentience. To her astonishment, Mary saw that it was the old ring, the first ring, long forgotten in a casket, the one artfully recorded by the jeweller who sold it as a 'golden seal'. Never was an article more fatefully described!

This is truly the last time I shall sign my name *Mary Cole*, thought the new Countess. Even as the pen swept through the peaks and curves of her signature, a fleeting presentiment caused her to shiver. She passed the tomb of Archbishop Tenison who had consoled the Duke of Monmouth at his execution for High Treason in 1685. Further, the Primate was known to have preached the sermon at the funeral service for Nell Gwynn whose portrait by Kneller hung on the staircase walls at Berkeley. The knowledge stole about Mary's psyche like ectoplasm. It had to be cancelled with positive thought. She was the Countess of Berkeley. Now she could travel light! The children would not go hungry, or see their mother cast out in favour of an heiress.

Berkeley kissed his bride and decamped with Carrington via the vestry door to his waiting chariot, a mode of exit that was so in keeping with his character! Mary set off in the carriage to seek examples of Sheraton's craft, while Billy walked home to Lydia and the baby, William Henry. Idly, it occurred to him that he had written William Tudor in the register, whereas he had been moved to give his full name *William Henry Tudor* as witness to Susan's wedding. All the signatures had been expansive on that certificate. Everyone seemed glad to subscribe to the union. What a prosaic thing a signature was to tow such momentous weight!

The Knot of Heracles

Thirteen

The first child born to the Earl and Countess of Berkeley on October 19, 1796, was a son. Berkeley was in a quandary as to how he should be registered. He understood from Lilibet that Hupsman had suffered a disorder of the liver which had laid him low for over a year, but that his health appeared greatly restored. This was attributed to the therapeutic effects of tincture of Milk Thistle and a bland diet. Hupsman was the Earl's contemporary: nature might not foreclose for decades. Bowing to circumstance, and with many misgivings, the parents went ahead and christened the child Thomas Moreton Fitzhardinge *(Lord Dursley)* at St. Martin-in-the-Fields a month later. The line thus far was safe.

Upon returning to Gloucestershire, the Earl sat down at his desk to inform Cranfield that he had broken his vow of bachelorhood and that an heir slept the sleep of innocents in the Castle nursery.

The war in Europe was not going well for England. Peace talks were disintegrating. British morale was at its nadir and sailors who had not been ashore for years were turning mutinous. The Captain's brief was to ensure a blockade of the Iroise channel out of Brest on the north-west coast of France. Eire was a tinderbox, its people ready to do Napoleon's work for him against the Union Jack.

Against this background, Sir George Cranfield Berkeley RN kt. received his brother's tidings.

"Upon my oath, I was never more amazed! I have a new sister! Well, well! The wolf and the lamb lie down together and a little child leads them. We might hope for peace in the land yet!"

The Earl of Berkeley was no less astounded when he received his brother's reply which, after a note of chagrin that he had not been taken into confidence, turned out to be a panegyric of Mary's virtues. Cranfield loved her and admired her many qualities. He noted that she possessed honour, religion and a most attentive love of their children and had been a zealous guardian of his brother's interests. If Frederick had chosen from a throne, he might not have fared better. Cranfield closed by declaring that he meant to do everything in his power to earn Mary's affection as a sister.

His sentiments could not have been warmer. This, from a quarter which had every reason to be hostile. Mary sighed profoundly and tears sprang to her eyes. "Thank you, Ma," she whispered. "Your wisdom is my dowry."

The Prince of Wales pined for Maria. All his high-flown ideals had been dragged through the mire. The turn of events which had constrained him to take a wife in accordance with British law and wipe out his debts, disgusted him. When Caroline was in his company, the Prince was revolted and had advised the King that the nation was best served if the fiend was given her own house. He could never achieve happiness with this heavy-bred German *frau*. Melodramatically, he penned his Last Will and Testament, leaving the Princess of Wales one shilling and requesting that the picture of his beloved wife in the eyes of God, who was and ever would be such in his, his Maria Fitzherbert, be interred with him. The protuberant Hanoverian eyes fastened on Berkeley hopelessly.

"*Tout est fini entre nous.* I am within an ace of ending it all. My duty is surely done."

"I'm dismayed to see your Royal Highness so distraught. Thought you'd be riding a cock horse once you'd come about."

"How can you say that, Fred, when I have betrayed my one and only love? It's all right for you. You have your shepherdess and your delightful children. Do I understand the silence has now been lifted, by the way?"

"I think I might safely say so, sir. We aren't making a song and dance when the marriage has been concealed for longer than was anticipated at the start."

The words, entirely in keeping with Berkeley's history as the Prince was meant to perceive it, came out of his mouth as unthinkingly as blinking. He was dimly aware it was rash to have committed himself to this version of events.

"Your sister-in-law is gone to the New World, I collect. Your grandfather could not have accomplished it with more despatch! A rich and prominent husband to boot!"

"Better than I had dared hope."

"A fortunate meeting, *n'est-ce pas?*" The Prince was drumming his fingers on his flabby buckskin-sheathed thigh, as if stopping himself from saying more. "I gather John Farmer, the barrister, introduced them."

"The husband of one of the Baring girls?"

"Miss Catherine as was." The Prince's brow beneath the tumbling, boyish forelock was puckered with cares. "We shall have cause for deep gratitude to Sir Francis Baring and his kidney for their patriotism if this crippling war is drawn out. They have promised Pitt funds. We ought to have seen off Frog years ago. When my turn comes, monarchy will be defunct!"

In the scorching summer of 1797, His Majesty agitated to be breathing the ozone of his beloved Dorset coast and the Royal Court removed to Gloucester House in the little port of Weymouth, along with menservants and maidservants, a train of acolytes and half the *beau monde*. The King's brother, the Duke of Gloucester, had built the residence (some years before the Earl of Berkeley espied the butcher's daughter) in response to the enthusiasm of that arbiter of good living, Ralph Allen of Bath. Allen delighted in the place and its freely available panacea which he enjoyed from his trend-setting bathing machine. The Duke of Kent was present that year and two of his brothers. A notable absentee was the Prince of Wales. He had been lampooned out of Brighton and his office as Colonel of the Light Dragoons, ridiculed. Worse still, invective had been hurled in the streets of London over his treatment of the Princess Caroline and there were calls for an Exclusion Bill to disqualify him from the Succession. He had gone into retreat at Critchell House, some miles from Weymouth, and from there made expeditions into the town in his phaeton, eluding his parents as best he could.

The South Gloucesters were based outside Weymouth and the Berkeleys took a house overlooking the bay. It was an ideal opportunity for Mary to intermingle with society and for her face to become familiar.

The minute they arrived in Gloucester Row, Mary tossed off her bonnet and hoisted up a sash window. The sky was Mediterranean blue, not a wisp of cloud. The natural crescent of the shore described a safe harbour. Gulls were gliding on thermals and swooping on titbits scattered by promenaders, as clamant as the species which fastened on the plough.

"Oh, Fred, we shall be happy here, I know it!"

The Earl fell into pensive vein. "My dear, I know it is a lot to ask – but you are quite equal to it – I wish to invite HRH to dine as soon as you are settled in."

"We are to host the Prince! I see I am to be launched at the deep end!"

"He is a good-natured buffoon, a rag-bag of fine feeling and talent. If he accepts our situation, others will follow. He has

225

always been well-disposed towards us and we must preserve that."

"He is not in good odour at present."

"With the people, no. But, it is not *they* who shape the nation's charter. That is why we're in head-to-head conflict with France."

"'Tis hard to remember we're fighting a war," sighed Mary.

Innumerable scenarios engrossed Berkeley's waking hours to do with Fitz negotiating his path to the peerage. The prelude must be carefully orchestrated. "The Prince of Wales is the future, Polly. The King will lose his wits, or die, his day will be done. With His Highness as our ally, the children stand the best chance of obtaining their rights." Besides, thought Berkeley, we may already owe him more than we know!

Learning that Colonel John West's regiment was stationed on the isle of Jersey, Mary had written to invite him to spend his leave with them in Weymouth. She told him Berkeley had a secret to communicate. "Twould be a fine idea," Fred had said, "to let him disseminate our news. He may till the ground, as it were."

The Colonel arrived exuding health and vigour. He beamed with pleasure to be re-united with cherished friends and exclaimed what a fine set of cubs they were rearing! Gus scaled his back and went charging around the garden at a rollicking pace with shouts of glee. Fitz could only roll his eyes and deplore the imbecility of adults, which, now that he was nearer eleven than ten, struck him more frequently than was comfortable. They breakfasted late the first morning and the Colonel found himself alone with his hosts. He reminded Mary she had said there was something important to relate.

"Do tell West the secret now," she besought Berkeley.

The Earl caught up his wife's hand as delicately yet intricately as if they were dancing a minuet. "Allow me to introduce you to the Countess of Berkeley!"

"My lord, I am overcome. It gives me the greatest satisfaction and delight to know your lady is the Countess. Pray forgive my boundless curiosity: when could you have done this? When could you have introduced her by that title?"

"Eleven or twelve years since! Did I not promise that in time you would know more of the business?"

"Indeed so, my lord. Then I am to understand that your eldest son is legitimate?"

"I mean you to understand that is positively the case."

"That is the best news I've heard in years! Will you allow me to talk of it abroad?"

The Earl's eyes were blazing with amusement. He inclined his head in noble condescension. "You may, West."

The Colonel could hardly contain himself and made off without finishing his dish of chocolate. He knew the Prince of Wales was in town, staying with the doughty Frederick of York. When he knocked at the door and presented his card, he was admitted to the drawing room where a small gathering was assembled around the royal brothers, one of whom was Madame D'Arblay, *née* Fanny Burney, indefatigable scribbler and former lady's maid of the Queen's retinue. She had married a General of the French Artillery and had been interned with her husband for some years.

"Ah, West!" cried the Prince in bumptious form (as was always the case when he and Frederick put their heads together). "This is a signal honour! What tidings from the Channel Isles? Have you routed the knavish Gauls?" He turned to Frances D'Arblay who took the comment in good part. "Beggin' pardon, ma'am. The fence ain't a comfortable place to sit, I am sure."

The Colonel bowed low before the Princes and acknowledged the rest of the company. "Your Royal Highness. Prince Frederick. I bring no news of surrender, at least not by our foes. But here's a devilish thing: the Earl of Berkeley tells me he is married and has been covertly so these twelve years! The eldest son is Lord Dursley!"

Astonishment rippled around the circle of friends. The Prince of Wales opened his mouth to speak, thought better of it, then declared: "You mean Fred Berkeley has hoodwinked us all these years?"

"It rather seems that way."

"That surely cannot be!" exclaimed Lady Pitt.

"Poor Miss Tudor! To have sustained a most awkward façade for so long!" remarked Colonel Addenbrooke, West's particular friend.

"I beg you will tell us what reasons," demanded the Prince, "were cogent enough to warrant a ruse so injurious to his family."

"I am not party to them, Your Royal Highness. I have to say that Miss Tudor has been accorded the respect of the Countess in every particular. I have observed it all along."

"A decorative little piece, it is rumoured," said Sir William Pitt, shrinking under his wife's glare.

"She is more than that, I assure you. The lady has close supervision of the nursery and reveals a powerful acumen in managing the estates. Many's the time I have ridden out with her when staying at Berkeley and Cranford. She knows all the cottagers' names, every timber and stone, and which phase of the lunar cycle to plant wheat. She knows prices per bushel and cider by the firkin."

"Trade!" snorted Lady Pitt.

"Trade!" concurred her spouse. His eyes lit up. "By Jove, a matron with brains *and* beauty! How did the old rake contrive that?"

"More to the point, how can he have kept it under his coronet?" wondered Madame D'Arblay. "It is an unconscionable period of time! Before the Revolution!"

The Prince of Wales felt a surge of equatorial heat. There were aspects of the Berkeley affair, George did not wish to ponder. It was too near a replication of the Maria conundrum. He neatly rallied attention, veering away from the topic.

"*À propos* of the French, I am greatly exercised as to how we can keep them from getting into Ireland by the back door while the country is in ferment."

"Ah, the eternal Catholic question," said Sir William.

"Infernal would be more of an operative word," said the Prince.

"An uninterrupted British presence in Dublin would need to be guaranteed, Your Highness," put in Colonel Addenbrooke.

"Exactly. And while you fellows are straining to beat back the enemy, I have proposed to His Majesty and Mr Pitt that civil constraints upon Catholics there be lifted. I have offered to undertake the Government of Ireland." Heroic deeds in this vein would impress Maria!

"Our father which art on the Throne has not deigned to reply," Frederick informed them.

"Neither has the scoundrel, Pitt," added his brother. "I ask you, what am I to do?"

There was nothing constructive to engage the Prince's energies and an invitation to be fêted by the Berkeleys came at just the right point to help repair his ego and boost his spirits.

Mr Carrington had gone down to Weymouth with the family for those first weeks of the vacation and received an invitation to his lordship's grand fête in the tents of the South Gloucesters. Mrs Price, on the other hand, was not invited. One reason was that she had made plans to spend her allowed leave with her cousins near Bristol, but her employers could be forgiven for thinking this fortuitous: her social skills were not finely tuned and a certain discontent was festering beneath her tight-laced form. It was the consummate slight to find that her colleague was to be presented to His Royal Highness when she was not.

"They must know very well that I would be willing to postpone my visit for a contingency of that magnitude! She has always had it in for me, Mr Carrington, I do not exaggerate. Her slack standard of honesty does not accord with my forthright views. And he, he is her mouthpiece. He does as he is told!"

"If I were you, dear lady," advised the cleric, "I would bridle my tongue. It is impolitic to bite the hand that feeds."

Mrs Price stormed off to her kin in an uppity frame of mind. The dust settled upon the cornices and the spiders scuttled out from their bullet-hole webs outside the sash windows.

Lord Berkeley's reception for the Prince of Wales went off without a hitch. It was a refulgent day. The band of the South Gloucesters struck up their martial tunes arousing morale in every patriot breast. A quartet played chamber music while His Highness partook of the multifarious delicacies laid out to tempt the gourmand. Mary was formally presented to the Prince for the first time and found him impossible to dislike.

"Your ladyship's hospitality is something to behold," he enthused. "And I have ever maintained that your husband's cellar is better than mine! A heart-warming occasion."

"Your Highness is too gracious," Mary replied, bestowing upon him a breathtaking smile. The earnest blue eyes caught hers in a glint of intimate appreciation. I may observe that his lordship's discernment of the vine is capped only by that of wives! Ah, but I see I am making you blush most becomingly. Tell me, ma'am, is that Lord Dursley entering the tent over there?"

"It is, sir. Perhaps Your Highness would be good enough to allow us to introduce him." Caleb Carrington was leading the boy towards the Prince accompanied by Lord Berkeley who made the introductions.

"So you are the Younker," said the Prince (meaning the youngster who is to inherit the family honours). "Fine boy! You will do the line proud. Any tips for Epsom next week?"

"No, sir, but I have a mare called Phoebe who's a fine goer!"

The Prince exploded raucously and punched the boy's shoulder. "Son of your pater, eh? To say the truth, young fellow, I don't have the blunt to go to the Races any more. Can't even afford to punt upon tick!" He turned to the Earl. "He'll do, Berkeley! A spell at Eton will finish him off!"

"Fitz has musical abilities and a fine singing voice," said his mother.

"Then I would esteem it a privilege if he would give us an air or two. What say you, Lord Dursley?"

"That would make me very happy, Your Highness. Your wish is my command," said Fitz, a tad precociously. "I have just the song, sir."

Freddy was summoned to the oyster-walnut clavichord and wriggled about on the seat in front of the keyboard. His fingers plunged into a chord and his brother began to unleash a confident treble voice with all the innocence of a heavenly chorister.

> On Richmond Hill there lives a lass
> More bright than Mayday morn,
> Whose charms all other maids' surpass
> A rose without a thorn,
> This lass so neat
> With smiles so sweet
> Has won my right goodwill
> I'd crowns resign to call thee mine,
> Sweet lass of Richmond Hill.
>
> Sweet Lass of Richmond Hill,
> Sweet Lass of Richmond Hill,
> I'd crowns resign to call thee mine,
> Sweet Lass of Richmond Hill!

Applause broke out on all sides when he had run the gamut of three full verses. The Prince wiped a tear from his cheek. "Bravo! A most sprightly rendering! Berkeley, your children are accomplished out of the common way. I hope they may pay regular visits to the Opera."

The day was a resounding success. Doubts were being diluted. The fable was nailed to the wallchart of history. The Prince had endorsed the Berkeley version of their genealogy.

The King was less persuaded when his Heir apprised him of the story. "Your Majesty should know that Berkeley did confide in me years ago and enjoined upon me the necessity of silence. He stated that Miss Tudor was his wife and the worst used woman in the world."

"Smells fishy," said the King. "What! If the woman was ill-used years ago, she must be a thousand times more so by now! Don't believe a word of it! We have noticed his temerity in trailing his dubious establishment under our nose. Most improper!"

"Even the King may not fly in the face of a gentleman's solemn word. The house of Berkeley is an ancient and noble one. It stands for our English heritage and all the values we endeavour to safeguard so zealously."

His Majesty would not be moved. When Mary drove out in a curricle upon the sands, he did not salute her. The Berkeley crest was screened from his vision and members of his Court were encouraged to follow his lead. The Berkeleys knew this reaction was only to be expected. Time would acquit them.

Mary refused to be insulted or deterred. There were marriage lines to support her now. Nothing, but nothing, was going to stand in the way of Fitz's inheritance.

But her husband began to dither. Their domestic life was as vibrant a theme in the Clubs and *salons* as the Prince's marriage and the progress of his *rapprochement* with Maria. People were more minutely interested than Berkeley had counted on. They wanted details. If his bride had been as ugly as sin and the daughter of a foreign dignitary, the announcement would probably have fallen flat, but Mary was beginning to attract attention. Who was she? Her provenance was maddeningly obscure. It was as if she had been borrowed from the gods.

As the Prince had suggested, visits to the Opera would promote Fitz's love of music. *The Magic Flute* was regarded by his father as a suitable diversion. It could be enjoyed on several levels and would advance the concept of freemasonry which was widespread among the Earl's set. The Marchioness of Salisbury happened to be sitting in the next box when they attended Covent Garden. She was a lady of redoubtable character whose companionship delighted the Prince of Wales. She was an expert archer and the foundress of a club at Hatfield House where His Highness had helped to refine the rules of contest. Thinking that Fitz would find this interesting, Berkeley sought permission to present his eldest son, Viscount Dursley, to her. At the end of the evening, when the Marchioness had taken her leave, Fitz noticed an article under her seat which proved to be an ivory pomander on a tassled silk cord. It had a beastly smell of camphor. One whiff was enough to wipe out the stench of the stews.

"You can return it to Lady Salisbury in the morning with a note," his mother said. "It would be a nice gesture."

"I'd sooner cannonball the French with it, Mama!"

Next day, before he had recited Archimedes' Principle and considered the Theorem of Pythagoras, the lad applied himself to writing to the Marchioness in his neatest hand. Mary smiled fondly to see his tongue appear at the corner of his mouth in fierce concentration.

"I think you are of an age to start signing yourself by your proper title," she told him.

"You mean *Viscount Dursley*?" he groaned.

"No," interjected the Earl. "Let him remain *Fitz Berkeley* for the time being."

"How in the world is he to remain *Fitz Berkeley* when you have introduced him as your heir?"

"Dear heart, this is painful, I know. It will take time for folk to get used to us."

"Then we must not waver.... Oh, you are piqued because our neighbours at Badminton cut us at the Opera!"

"His Grace of Beaufort is a man of consequence."

"My lord, though this may surprise you, I am not ignorant of the origins of the Beaufort line! They were born the wrong side of John o' Gaunt's blanket!"

The Earl sighed. "That is my point, I think. Tradition has dignified them."

The boy was leaning dejectedly on the back of his chair while his parents argued above his head. His cornflower irises swung from one to the other. Grown-ups didn't have a clue how to behave!

"We don't have centuries if he is to gain his birthright!"

"Fitz, leave your letter," ordered his father, "and go to Mr Carrington. I wish to speak with your mother." When the door had closed, Berkeley went on: "I am beginning to feel uneasy, Polly, that I declared you a spinster and myself a bachelor to acquire a marriage licence. I had no choice then. When the time comes, the College of Heralds will demand to see a copy of it."

A light but uncharacteristic growl of rage issued from the region of Mary's throat. "We both know that, but we are committed to overcoming it in whatever way we can. We did take the precaution of having Thomas baptised at Berkeley as well as in London, remember, so that we could produce a certificate with his courtesy title omitted."

"I wonder if that is strong enough evidence to substantiate our story."

"The word of the Earl of Berkeley must count for something! Does a second marriage invalidate a first? I am going to seek counsel on this."

"No! It will blow such cover as we have!"

"I will do it *incognito*. There are some advantages to being a nonentity, you observe!"

Mary had her way and Fitz wrote *Lord Dursley* under his message. Boudicca leading the Iceni into battle was not more staunch! It was this adamantine perseverance that had brought her through hardship. She was masterly at turning self-pity upon its head. She was not aware, however, that his lordship had commandeered the note and sent Fitz without it.

During the summer of 1798, the Earl bought a smart phaeton and betook himself to Tattersall's for a pair of horses. As he was coming away, he was hailed by Samuel Lysons who appeared eager to chat.

"What a catalogue of errors the cutting of the new canal has been! The dismissal of one engineer after another! Disputes over wages! Changes to the line!"

"I've heard the project lists in the doldrums. Can't say I'm surprised," said Berkeley.

"There'll be no progress without funds."

"I put it to you, Lysons, who will buy shares in a pipe-dream?"

"There have been severe losses, 'tis true. Nicholas Hickes is made bankrupt over it."

"A hazard of speculation."

"He has amassed a pile of debts against others, too. Between ourselves, my lord, I understand that the Reverend Mr Hupsman has failed to redeem vowels to quite a tidy tune. The unlucky fellow is mortally ill and I daresay Hickes will not pursue him to the grave."

"Is that so?" said Berkeley guardedly. "I've had no recent contact with Hupsman."

"One never knows how far Hickes will go. A fertile spouse has sharpened his mettle. He has turned his hand to farming as a safer livelihood."

"My wife swears by it! Knows a thing or two about manure!"

Lysons laughed heartily. The Berkeley chestnut had been bandied about among his colleagues. It was preposterous, of course: no one knew what to make of it. Whatever you believed,

233

it did nothing to present the Earl in a good light. "John Farmer was telling me the other day what a celebrated match her ladyship's sister has made."

Berkeley remembered that the Prince of Wales had mentioned Farmer (whose wife had been a Baring) as having first brought Heyward into Susan's purview. "Yes, indeed. A widow, nonetheless. She hadn't known Heyward above five minutes."

"One can appreciate how easy it is to be caught on the rebound after sudden grief."

"Susan is sure to attract an army of admirers."

"Well, she has found her consolation," said Lysons. Noting Berkeley's nonplussed expression, the lawyer faltered. "My lord....many apologies! The news cannot have reached you. Mrs Heyward wed Mr Charles Baring last autumn in Charleston, South Carolina."

"The bankers!"

"Yes, my lord. It came about on this wise: the lady was being pursued by Alexander Baring, Sir Francis' eldest son. She went so far as to accept his hand. He sent for his cousin Charles to draw up a marriage settlement and lo! the fellow fell for her himself, proposed on the spot and snatched her from under the poor swain's nose!"

"The barefaced jade!"

"Mrs Baring is the star of the Southern States. Her husband is vastly enamoured of her. They entertain in style, I am told. She is reputed to favour gowns of purple velvet and diamond tiaras with copious plumes. Farmer says she has proved herself a most amusing playwright and likes to dabble in amateur dramatics!"

Susan must have learned a trick or two from Sheridan! Ten to one, she had a finger in the pie of the East India Company. Were it not for her sex – but why should that stop her? – she'd be running for President before long! Susan was at the tiller of the New World!

In fact, it was the supremest of ironies that their connection with her would supply *éclat* to Mary's background.

The Earl did not guess how indiscriminately his sister-in-law had broadcast their relationship. Any link with the old aristocracy of England conferred a mystique and carried cachet. The New World was a clean slate, new credentials. Re-invention was all. It was worlds away from The Swan Tavern and the blood and gore of the shambles.

If the Earl of Berkeley's statement cast ripples upon the wider shores of society, it caused even greater bewilderment among his close friends. Colonel West was a man sensitive to nuance and, weighing one thing against another, was ready to believe his long-standing comrade. Admiral Prescott, he who 'went through the world in a straight line' and was not given to surmise upon personal matters, was not informed and found himself covered in embarrassment to learn the news secondhand when he was accosted in St. James's Street by Sir Godfrey Webster, a Colonial secretary. This gentleman had a reputation for eccentricity and was fascinated by stories of marital vagary. He had recently obtained a divorce from his wife by Act of Parliament. Elizabeth had run off in Florence with Henry Fox, nephew of the Whig statesman, and produced a child by him.

"Ah, Prescott! The very man!" exclaimed the baronet, pretending to point his cane into the Admiral's chest. "Tell me, fellow, is it true that Lord Berkeley is married to Miss Tudor? Deuced queer if you ask me!"

"Berkeley has not uttered a syllable to me, I assure you, sir."

Webster lifted his monocle as if to inspect this reply. "How extraordinary. Who can know for certain if you do not?"

To say that the Admiral was galled to have been left in the dark would be an understatement, though he was too well-bred and too proud to let it show. He went straight home and drafted a letter to Mary inviting her to shed some light on the matter. She furnished him with a prompt answer which closed with these phrases: *To those who make inquiry after me, you may say that your sincere and affectionate friend has, for a long time past, been Mary Berkeley.* With that he had to be content and toe his accustomed 'straight line'.

Elizabeth Martha Chichele Chapeau, she related to a former Archbishop of Canterbury, did not trust the cock-and-bull tale in the slightest.

"For Berkeley to stand up now and make such a claim, as if he were reciting the Creed, is the most pernicious falsehood. No doubt *she* has put him up to it."

The Reverend John Chapeau was in great torment of spirit, wanting to give his friend the benefit of any doubt and yet reasoning that it was profoundly unlikely that he had actually been married these thirteen years. Berkeley had been generous to the Chapeaus throughout a long acquaintance, allowing them to enjoy the comforts of Cranford House when the family was elsewhere, leaving money for expenses, and permitting Chapeau to shoot game.

"You do not know her," said Chapeau. "Have the goodness to reserve judgment. I am satisfied that there is a great deal of truth in Lady Berkeley."

And so it went on, until the Berkeleys realised they were in a suffocating vacuum where their name meant everything and nothing. It was worse than before. Further proof was strongly indicated. And that proof had to be openly aired.

It also had to be fabricated.

It was then that a sinister hand took control of their destiny. By the end of November, a rumour reached the Castle that Hupsman was dead. His daughter from Stone had told Mrs Jenner who told Mary Jane Price in Daniel Marklove's clothing shop in the town. The governess was puffed with self-importance to be the harbinger of this report which she imparted with some effect as Mary made to mount her horse in the stable yard. Her ladyship's countenance, she noted, blanched, then flushed a sundown hue. The eyes, kindling with a peculiar intensity, were trained on the distance.

"You say the doctor's wife told you?"

"Yes, ma'am. She had it direct from Mrs Hickes who ought to know her father's condition."

"I don't think Mrs Hickes is on good terms with her father. He has been at death's door for long enough. It may be hearsay."

"You doubt it, ma'am?"

"I will send Clark to Hare Hatch to find out the truth."

"That is a rare length to go to discover whether a man be alive or dead! What is it to you?"

Mary laughed in a faintly crowing manner and lifted her skirts to step up on the mounting-block. "What a frightful thing, Price, if he were raised like Lazarus!"

There was a blue chip reason why God had put Adam to sleep before stealing his rib to create Eve, Hupsman decided during his liverish last leg upon earth. Had he been awake, Adam would not have consented. Writers like Mary Wollstonecraft could turn the whole female race against their husbands! They reduced the intercourse between men and women to politics and manipulation. And for what? She had recanted in the end, married, and met an untimely death from puerperal fever. *Vanity of vanities, saith the Preacher.* As time went on, Fanny had become entrenched in the author's views. She was unable to offload the bitterness aroused by Wilmot's perfidy. Fanny felt entitled to some kind of reparation which her new lover was supposed to provide. Despite his devotion, she made Hupsman feel he was a miserable failure. She even accused him of exploiting her situation for his own designs when he could no longer hide the number of creditors to whom he owed large sums. That was before he discovered she had 'eloped' with her groom years ago. Fanny was not the sweet, helpless victim who had won his heart, and they had parted.

His quest for peace and seclusion had led him to take up an offer which had come through a neophyte cleric called Tom Fowle. This fellow was chaplain to his distant relative Major-General Lord Craven. (Craven was the son of the Margravine of Anspach and nephew of the Earl of Berkeley.) Tom Fowle had been educated by Mr George Austen before going up to Oxford and had never forgotten his tutor's striking elder daughter, Cassandra, whose sister, Jane, was showing literary promise. After graduating, he sought her hand in marriage, but determined that first he would prove himself worthy by earning a competence to support them. In the mid-nineties, he set sail with the Fleet for the West Indies where his patron owned cocoa-plantations. Whilst there, Tom contracted yellow fever and died: bereft, Cassandra was ever faithful to his memory. The Leigh-Perrots, the girls' uncle and aunt, were also in the West Indies at that time, leaving Scarlets, their elegant house at Hare Hatch in Berkshire, not far from Craven's two properties, empty. Hearing of this, the Margravine (a lady known for her bountiful nature in many departments of life) and retaining affectionate memories of her governess, Esther Hupsman, made arrangements for Hupsman to stay at Scarlets with a nurse in attendance.

It was a safe retreat. The mercenary Hickes would not find him. His family would not wish to know. The world and its doings was diminishing to an echo, 'full of sound and fury, signifying nothing'. His single eye read that Nelson, despite *his* single eye, had covered himself in glory at Aboukir Bay. The Battle of the Nile, in which Napoleon had endeavoured to break Britain's links with India, was a long-awaited triumph. In contrast, the Prince of Wales, in a fever for action, had invited further derision when he alerted the Dorset Yeomanry and rode, pell-mell, to Dorchester to lead his regiment in quelling an imminent attack. Enemy ships had been sighted in the Channel. He was soon to learn that the flotilla was as pacific and English as cricket! James Perry of the *Morning Chronicle*, and his business partner James Gray, agitators for parliamentary reform, had been found guilty (although not with intent) of libelling the House of Lords and sentenced to three months in Newgate.

Death, thought Hupsman. The last enemy that shall be defeated. He lay on his daybed, emaciated by cancer and swaddled in a blanket. His books were beside him and a beaker drained of its foul posset. It was the month of All Souls, drab skies and stagnant fogs. The spindle trees were frayed of leaves and the lucent pink seed pods that promised spring had wizened. Their bare arteries fed nothing. Miss Tudor had instructed her bean-growing tenants to cut them down, for they were an alternative host to the bean-fly.

Hupsman was ready to trace his own downfall to that lady. Oh, he had never been popular, nor brilliantly academic – his union with Miss Lambe had been a vapid undertaking – but it was not until that act of obliteration, at Lord Berkeley's behest, that decay set in. That bogus record of vows made before God had been his undoing. A sheet of toning vellum had been inserted in the register, with the inner edge sparingly pasted, giving the appearance of a new leaf, and had been effortlessly removed when the charade was over. Hupsman had not dared take it to the parsonage hearth. Instead he screwed it up and placed it in a cinerarium kept for the use of penitents whose misdeeds were listed at the Confessional and symbolically burned before they received Absolution. The tinder box he used to ignite the pyre was not one of the blessed utensils of St. Mary the Virgin, nor dare he use a taper from the sanctuary lamp, or prayer candle. He produced his own, inlaid with luminescent enamel. It was decorated with a white phoenix rising from serpent-tails of fire. As the flint sparked, his hand quivered. Liquid flame began to consume the edges of the paper. It charred and curled, reducing the sentences scribed by his own hand to flakes of carbon. It was over in seconds. Since childhood, he had known what it was to wear the outsider's shoes. This was the chill of exile. He had just become the incumbent of the Berkeley living after many years roaming the wilds of curacy. Would he have changed the course of history had he put his beliefs on the line?

There were moments when he actually thought he would have been better off staying with his wife, preserving the beautiful Fanny in the aspic of illusion. When he was with Fanny, he couldn't get Elizabeth out of his head, for all he loathed her icy aura. It was a Hebrew's fate to belong everywhere and nowhere.

The diaspora was not only one of historical times and locations; it was a fact of pilgrimage. Perhaps he had betrayed his Jewish roots by making his career in the Christian church. He had certainly lost his compass.

November. Night foreclosing on the day at a premature hour. Ahead, the Advent season with its revelation of light. Epiphany! He wondered whether he would see his mother again, or if she was lost to him for all eternity.

Perhaps an open confession would help to absolve him?

John Clark returned to the Castle with news that Hupsman had died on the last day of November. His funeral was held at Cranford on December 6th with none of his family present. His final years were shrouded in obscurity – a reek of infamy hung about them – so that his demise passed largely unlamented.

"Today is the feast of St. Nicholas," said the Countess, "and this is our Christmas gift. We are being given a chance to put things in order."

On January 14th 1799, Carrington was instituted to the parish of Berkeley which redoubled the security of his tenure. Working alongside him would be the curate who had taken over from William Davis, the Revd John Lewis.

It was on the one hundred and fiftieth anniversary of Charles, King and Martyr, executed for the Church, that Berkeley broached the subject of his first marriage.

"I am bedevilled, Carrington, by this dastardly tax Pitt is perpetrating to pay for Napoleon's vanity."

"Would that be Income Tax, my lord?"

"It would. I am entitled to an abatement for the children, but I can make no claim against four of my sons because the registry of the first ceremony in 1785 is lost."

"A most unhappy circumstance, my lord."

"For family reasons, the late Mr Hupsman was urged in the strongest terms to keep it secret and, I fear, may have destroyed the evidence in his fervour to obey. It would have been unthinkable to expose the dilemma whilst he was alive, lest he incur the full penalty of the law. As time went on, I felt it prudent to essay a second marriage, as you are aware."

"May I suggest that a thorough search of all the Books be made? Suppose he had concealed it by placing it out of sequence?"

"That would be a most tedious undertaking."

"One can perfectly sympathise with Mr Hupsman's wish to keep your instructions, my lord, but to imperil his own life and risk disgrace upon the House of Berkeley...! The registry might yet be discovered."

"You think so?" said Berkeley, clutching his chin in an attitude of deep meditation worthy of the Kembles. "Of course, I do not have access to the Registers. I am not certain where or how they are kept."

"Mr Lewis keeps the current one at his house and makes the entries himself. The rest, I apprehend, are under lock and key at the parsonage as the law prescribes."

"Might they, do you think, be brought up to the Castle and kept in the Muniment Room for the time being, now that Mrs Hupsman has vacated the Vicarage?"

Carrington was uneasy, but was prepared to believe that no real harm would be done. "If you so choose, my lord."

"I shall ask Boodle, my London solicitor, to send a man down to superintend the search. There can then be no allegation of improper procedure with government records. But first, I desire you to bring the Registers to the Castle."

"Very good, my lord."

"Get Simmonds to assist you. He is a reliable fellow. I don't need to impress upon you, I am sure, the confidential nature of this task."

"You have my word and that is my bond," said Carrington somewhat superfluously. Was he likely to disclose that he was complicit in an illegal act? He was turning to go, when he paused. "I vaguely recall, my lord, forgive me if I am in error, but lines, I believe, are not essential to the proving of a marriage if the witnesses are still alive."

"You could be right, Carrington. However, since Hupsman is no longer with us and one of the witnesses might be reckoned to be biased, it is not satisfactory. It would be nigh impossible to trace the second party after this lapse of time."

"Then a thorough search is of cardinal importance. It might also be helpful to seek counsel's opinion. Allow me to make some discreet enquiries on your lordship's behalf."

Fourteen

Sir James Mansfield was no conventional lawyer drawing a clientèle from the aristocracy and the flower of the professions. In his sixty-fifth year, he had served two terms as Solicitor General for the Crown and was on his way to becoming Lord Chief Justice of the Court of Common Pleas, the capacity in which John Wilmot's father had aggrandised himself. There were few higher offices in the land.

No stranger to the convolutions of the human mind, Sir James confessed himself baffled by a new case which had been brought to his attention by a reverend gentleman, one Caleb Carrington. The cleric had written to him in concise terms, if a little sycophantically, outlining the perplexities of an unnamed Earl who was unable to establish his marriage in 1785 because no record could be found. The writer presumed upon the goodness of the barrister to forgive the concealment of identity and hoped he would be agreeable to a consultation with the Countess at his chambers. Clearly, the lady was confident that she would not be recognised!

Sir James was filled with a quiet exasperation. He reminded himself that the law was a theoretical and abstract discipline that had to be translated into practical application and was moved to allot some time to an interview.

She entered the room with an understated but well-grounded presence and offered him a gloved hand. "Sir James, thank you for seeing me. Your time is precious, I am sure," she said in a way which rather suggested that hers was, too. Her figure fitted her elegant black garments trimly, a veil over her bonnet keeping her features in shadow. Perhaps she was hiding eyes swollen by tears of mourning, or a complexion pock-marked by disease.

"I beg your ladyship will take a seat," he said, indicating an all-embracing wing chair. He re-situated the oil lamp upon his desk the better to gauge the creature under the veil. She was no middling charmer, he could tell. The cheekbones were classically high, the nose straight, the chin delicate and the ample mouth contoured by humour rather than pessimism. The voice had a rich timbre and a hint of a West Country burr.

"You have, I believe, been primed as to the purpose of my visit," said she. She was tugging off her gloves gracefully, finger by finger.

"I have, ma'am." Mansfield surveyed the letter before him written in Carrington's methodical script. "First, let me assure you that nothing would give me greater pleasure than to be able to help you, but this is a most unusual case."

"That I understand, sir. If you could venture an opinion...."

He leaned back in his chair and made a steeple of his fingers. "It will be easier if I speak by hypothesis.... A marriage is not void for want of registration, if there be no other objection to it; but it is void if it was not performed in a Parish Church, or if there performed without Banns, or a licence, either being necessary to make a marriage valid."

"All the formalities were complied with, I declare."

"That being so, the witness now surviving may be sufficient to prove it."

"The problem is, Sir James, that the only living witness is my brother and in a situation which, as you say, is unusual, he could be deemed to be partial. My husband and I have considered the prudence and propriety of a second marriage. That would not be an illegal step, I believe?"

"There is nothing to prevent anyone marrying the same person as many times as he chooses, but in the instance you cite, I am inclined to feel that a second marriage might indeed cast doubt upon the existence of the first."

At this, the Countess showed signs of agitation. She fiddled with the chain upon her embroidered purse. "Oh dear! What have we done...? I am afraid it has already taken place...!"

"Calm yourself, dear lady, I beg. May I offer you a dish of tea? A nip of brandy?"

"A glass of water, if you please."

Mansfield rang the bell for his clerk and gave instructions. "That being the case, we must hope and pray that the earlier documentation is found. I take it that every chest, shelf, drawer and crevice have been scoured?"

"In the ordinary way, yes. There are the late Mr Hupsman's papers."

"Have you, I wonder, made enquiry of the Diocesan Office? They will have copies of the Parish Registers covering the year in question."

"Oh, I do not know! I only wish I did! I think it cannot be so, for his lordship was most anxious at that period, for personal reasons, to keep the matter quiet."

"Yes, I see. If he wishes to confer with me in the strictest confidence, my lady, I should be happy to oblige. Opinions given in the absence of a rounded picture can lead to error."

The clerk came in with a glass of water on a tray and set it down with a tentative bow. The Countess smiled gratefully and consented to lift her veil. Mansfield's expression was of one tantalised by dim recollection. After taking a sip, she said: "The Earl – my husband – is of the belief that if statements are signed where the Baptisms of our children born before the second marriage have been recorded, it will help to preserve the testimony of any witness."

"When was that marriage?"

"Three years ago."

"So it took place *prior* to the death of the clergyman you were protecting."

"Yes, it did. It was for our own peace of mind."

A long sigh underscored Mansfield's thoughts. "It seems to me that filing a Bill, or making a Declaration, can be of little use, though it cannot, I think, do any harm and, if made, it should express not only the fact of the first marriage, but why it was supposed not to be valid. The same sort of Declaration should be made where the baptism of the children born since the *second* marriage is entered, in order to explain the differences."

The Countess took another sip of water, flicked down her veil and drew on her gloves with a flexure of the hand. "I will make representations to my husband, Sir James."

"Do so, ma'am. It can only help if I discuss it with him. Concerns entailing inheritance can be notoriously fickle and riddled with idiosyncrasy."

Sir James glanced at the portrait of the late Lord Chief Justice, Sir John Eardley Wilmot, who had been unable to make good an entitlement to his deceased brother's estates.

"I can see that a second ceremony was ill-advised," the client concluded as she made to leave. Her tone was uptight and breathless, close to tears.

While the lawyer's instinct was to deal out consoling phrases, he nursed strong reservations about this case. It did not hang together as it ought. "I will look forward to speaking with his lordship." He was guiding the Countess towards the door, when she turned to him, her frustration vented in dire distress.

"I will do all in my power to obtain justice for my eldest son. He is his father's true heir. It would be a terrible thing to go to my grave knowing that I had failed him."

243

She swept through the outer office stacked high with its scrolls and ledgers testifying to tradition as a foursquare foundation of society, past the row of clerks bent over their correspondence, and down the stairs. Muffled sobs echoed up the stairwell. Startled, Bunduck, the waistcoated clerk who had provided the glass of water, looked up. "Not your average customer, that lady, Sir James."

Mansfield's gaze was slanted down upon the pavement below. He watched her tripping, almost running across the road in the thick of traffic, to where a carriage awaited in a side street. It was tawny yellow and black. An allusion Lysons had made chimed in his head. (Lysons was a prize quidnunc, one seldom heard above half he said.)

He turned away to find the intrigued clerk hovering close behind him with only a feather between their faces. "Back to your station, Bunduck. And mark this: *A goose-quill is more dangerous than a lion's claw!*"

It was a Sunday morning at the beginning of Lent. They had chosen Sunday because most of the servants would be at Parish Mass in the Minster. Mr Carrington would be conducting the service and Price would superintend the boys in the family pew. The Countess had pleaded a headache. She showed all the signs of being on the cusp of an ague.

As it happened, the governess did not go to church, but left the children in the charge of their Nurse. Five years old Francis Henry eloquently threatened to be sick. He did not like the smell of incense, nor the doleful, breast-beating phrases, and finding that his mother was not to accompany them, thought he might be let off, too, if he kicked up a dust. He would rather be arranging his wooden mosaics into a Roman viaduct, or propelling marbles around his bagatelle board. One of his favourite books was a children's version of a famous tale, *Gulliver's Travels in Lilliput*, set in a land of tiny people. Dean Swift, its author, had been chaplain to his great-grandpapa, long before Mr Carrington was born.

Her ladyship had retired to an inner chamber adjoining the bedroom and requested that she be not disturbed. It boded no good, then, when the Earl and his brother-in-law crossed the courtyard below and, ascending an outside staircase, were admitted to the sanctum. The door closed with a click. Price noticed all this from the room on the other side of the chamber.

She could hear the rumble of subdued conversation, the cadences waffled by collusion. No one had said William Tudor was coming. He had turned up after breakfast, a provisional air about him, as if he were on his way elsewhere. Price bent her ear to the wall but could barely distinguish a word.

"I don't mind telling you, Berkeley," said William, "that I am not easy about lending my hand to this. I don't relish losing my skin for my nephew. I have a wife and offspring who depend upon me."

Berkeley was in no mood for dissension in the ranks. "Let me remind you, Tudor, that all you have is from my hand. You were free to make your own way in the world, but you chose to milk me instead."

"Gentlemen!" hissed Mary. "Please desist. This is profitless. Let us do the deed and be gone!"

"I cannot see," protested her brother, "that we shall ever get away with this. The records of the Parish of Lambeth state you to be Mary Cole, spinster, and your lordship, a bachelor. Thereafter, at the baptism of Thomas Moreton, your sixth child, you pronounced him Lord Dursley."

"On paper," the Earl reminded William.

"Ain't that what the Heralds will see? They are entries you cannot doctor."

"These are my anxieties, not yours," said the Earl imperiously. "When it comes to light, there will be a full explanation given. By then, evidence of an antecedent rite will have been discovered and will support the statement."

"Tis a blundering, ham-fisted way to go about things and I don't like it above half," William deplored, "but it would please Mary to see Fitz gain his dues."

"This is a chance to show that, in truth, I have not lived dishonourably. We have the original Banns, even if Hupsman did not publish them. All we are doing is creating a facsimile of the registry. It did once exist, Billy. You know it! You saw it! You signed it!"

"I signed it *William Cole* as I recall. It was afterwards your lordship suggested the name of Tudor."

"Sign it *Tudor* now," ordered the Earl, thinking of what he had said to Carrington. "In this context, *Cole* smacks of conspiracy. The Countess must sign herself *Cole*, since that is the maiden name declared at the second marriage. How it strikes the eye is important."

245

William noted he had prevailed in the dispute over written testimony, but forbore to say so. His signature had been Tudor for the past fourteen years. He had built a new identity upon it, was employed upon it, married upon it and had attested fatherhood upon it. It was his children's surname. The notion of Billy Cole of Barnwood was unreal at this distance.

Two or three sheets of parchment were scattered over the desk in the corner of the room with writing tools, tracing paper, a pot of glue and an oil-paint brush. A half page had been cut from one of the old, unruled and incomplete Parish Registers. The Earl had refined his brainchild whilst watching Freddy make a brass-rubbing of the fourteenth century Thomas, Lord Berkeley and his wife, Margaret. He had followed the contours of Hupsman's signature again and again until he was satisfied that in freehand it appeared reasonably authentic. *Augustus Thomas Hupsman*. The late vicar had inspired the measure and his restless spirit brooded over it now, clutching at straws for exculpation. He had never deviated from the belief that the Earl of Berkeley and Mary Cole were married on the thirtieth day of March in the year of Grace one thousand, seven hundred and eighty-five. If that were not quintessentially the case, he believed he would be everlastingly damned for blasphemy.

Upon brief inspection, the text in the body of the registration might be worthy of comparison with that of the Banns, but in many ways was unlike it. In the first instance, it had no printed lines or words where information might be filled in. Also, the ink had faded on the Banns: that had been written with a very fine quill, whereas Berkeley's was cut to a more assertive thickness, the ink blacker. His was a wholly confident, not to say arrogant, hand. There was a calculated inconsistency in the way of forming a capital A which might imply to the reader that the record had been prepared by a clerk. The A of Frederick Augustus in the opening words was in a different style to the A of Augustus in Hupsman's moniker the end. In any case, Berkeley reasoned, there *had been* a space of approximately four months between the first and second documents. Another pen would have been used. If he were to make a fresh copy of the Banns, suspicion might be aroused. A vestige of truthfulness made him stall at further forgery. The doings of this day were ominous enough!

The Earl ceased shifting from boot to boot, and resuming his seat at the desk, scored a curt and irascible autograph under the deposition. *Berkeley.* Mary and William were leaning over him with bated breath.

"Now you, Mary." He rose and delivered the pen into her hand.

Mary sat down. Electricity crackled along her nape. She recalled that strange moment in St. Mary-at-Lambeth on the day of her marriage and strove to control her shaking hand. *Mary Cole.* With the last stroke of the pen, there was a knock at the door so that the tail of the E jerked a fraction. In much consternation, she hurried to answer it.

"Price! I gave explicit instructions that I was not to be disturbed!"

"A thousand apologies for the intrusion, your ladyship. I would not have inconvenienced you, but Henry is not at all well. A bilious attack coming on, I suspect. I wonder, should I give him a little bicarbonate of soda in warm water? Or a spoonful of brimstone and treacle, perhaps?" The governess peered over Mary's shoulder into the room with a defiant curiosity at variance with her air of servitude. Her penetrating eye took in the muddled paperwork, and the calf tomes with marbling. The sunblinds had been drawn down against the ditchwater light of February, as if to prevent being spied upon from the upper rooms on the other side of the courtyard. A pillar candle on the desk wavered and streamed in the draught from the open door, casting huddled silhouettes in torsion upon the walls.

"Give him a teaspoon of Nux Vomica, well-shaken," bade Mary and pushed the door shut, accidentally stubbing Price's toes.

William took a quill with a needle-like point and wrote a miserly *W. Tudor* with the barest touch of Rococo flamboyance. No generous *William Henry Tudor* here lending himself to felicitation of the couple. The mark of the nomad Richard Barns was easy to improvise.

Berkeley sanded his handiwork, blew upon the paper and laid it down carefully to dry. Meanwhile, the Banns were secreted in a long redundant Book of Banns. They were placed between two blank pages whose edges were finely pasted together and at a quick glance looked like a single page. The records began immediately after Lord Hardwicke's Act and had been abandoned around the year 1780, leaving a quantity of unused folios, when a new book had been brought into commission, perhaps under the auspices of a new curate.

On the upper part of the same page as the forged Berkeley marriage, the Earl had copied the record of a marriage between William Varnham of Berkeley and Mary Chapman King which had been solemnised on March 20th, 1785. It would have been the wedding preceding their own and was numbered 73. It was logical therefore that he should number theirs, 74, notwithstanding that another couple had been entered under that number on the correct page in the corresponding Marriage Book. The Book was then turned upside down and the counterfeit record secured, face downwards, to the binding inside the pasteboard cover, after which the last (or first!) real page was fastened to the cover with wafers with the intention of making the cover appear intact. Nothing except the slight ridge of the wafers would be remarked.

"What a serpentine mind Hupsman's was," laughed the Earl, anticipating that the stunt would be quickly forgotten. "He contrived most cunningly to hide the proof, did he not?"

"You could not have done it better yourself, my lord," said William dully, humouring him, though only a little!

"Well, sir, shall we see you at dinner?"

"Thank you, I shall not partake. I must make haste to return to London. Tomorrow, I leave for the Low Countries."

Briskly, Mary set about tidying the room, burned the unwanted papers in the grate, snuffed out the candle and drew up the blinds. A disc of silver sun, no shinier than a seed-head of honesty, hung in the mist-wreathed sky. William left the room first and Berkeley a few minutes later. Mary lagged behind, deliberating upon the wisdom of what they had plotted. The irreconcilable facts on the first and second certificates haunted her. Too late! She could only hope that no scrutiny would be occasioned. The deception was in the cause of truth. Well, they would all sink or swim together!

His lordship had enlisted Carrington to return the volumes to the Muniment Room at the hour of the children's supper, when staff would be well-occupied. The keys were to be delivered into the hands of James Simmonds.

Two days later, on February 19th, the Earl and Countess left the Castle for Spring Gardens and instructed Boodle, the family's London solicitor, to institute a thorough search of the Records.

They were gathered at one end of a long refectory table of Jacobean oak in the Muniment Room at Berkeley Castle, the Steward, the Vicar, the Curate and the Scribe, Mr Scriven, Boodle's conveyancer from London whom the others did not know. Laid out before them were several weighty volumes of

Baptisms, Weddings and Burials in the Parish covering the best part of that century which was drawing to a close. After the Marriage Act in the 1750s, the number of entries per month increased and comprised extra detail. The nature of it was often minimal and seemed to emanate from a desire to comply with the law rather than to leave markers for posterity.

"Gentlemen," said Mr Carrington in the manner of one addressing a jury, "we have before us a most solemn task. The future of the great peerage of Berkeley rests on our shoulders. Our findings...."

"Or otherwise," interpolated the woodpeckerish Mr Scriven.

"Our findings will determine whether Lord Dursley can make good his claim to the College of Heralds, or whether this family is, in fact, to be divided into the sheep and the goats, thus setting one half against the other." Only Carrington was aware that Thomas Moreton stood alone in representing the 'sheep' at the present time. But the Countess was young and could go on to bear more children. "This noble pile in which we find ourselves," he went on, "for centuries the ancestral seat of the Earls and Barons of Berkeley, might well be severed from its titular owners if we fail. It is a formidable responsibility, gentlemen, and it behoves us to exercise the utmost diligence in our search."

"The words 'needle' and 'haystack' spring to mind, Mr Carrington," said James Simmonds cheerfully. "Mrs Crouch do reckon milord was secretly married to Miss Tudor long ago."

"Then why in the name of all that's commonsensical would he want to keep it secret for so long?" demanded Mr Scriven irritably.

"Ours not to question," said Mr Lewis, the curate.

"Tis Mrs Crouch's belief he needed mothering and so looked for a humble maid with no children! She says he wants his bread buttering on both sides!"

"Yes, thank you for the benefit of your homespun wisdom," said Carrington. "Do, pray, take off that baize apron, Mr Simmonds, and look as though you mean business!"

"She's a good woman, Mrs Crouch," maintained Simmonds in a hurt tone. "Understands a thing or two." Mrs Crouch was a childless widow whose cooking and housekeeperly skills were not lost upon the young Steward.

They set to work. A dozen or more cheap tallow candles burned odiferously and vied with the pale light filtering in at the dusty narrow windows. Mr Scriven, a man with a frail constitution, kept on his comforter against the draught whilst analysing every name and phrase through a large reading glass. The task was done systematically with each person taking a book in turn and passing it on. Among them, the Vicar was the only one who might not appear to an onlooker to be seeking in earnest. He was going through the motions whilst guardedly watching the process of the search.

"Nothing!" said Mr Lewis, closing the Register he had perused.

"Actually, I think, if I can charge my memory," said Carrington casting his eyes ceilingwards, "Lord Berkeley did stress that the covers of the Books should be most carefully examined. It occurred to him just before he left for London that they might offer a place of concealment."

"It would have been helpful to know that at the start," complained Mr Scriven who was decidedly bored and could not be relied upon to think for himself. Carrington, who had made a preliminary examination of the Books, had noted which volume was in the conveyancer's hands and saw him turn to the beginning, then to the fly-leaves at the end. "The bottom of one page has been cut away! Good Heavens! Yes! Upon my soul, there is something here! See! There is a thickness in the paper! There are dents!"

"Go steadily, Mr Scriven. I believe I have a penknife in my waistcoat pocket. We must take care to inflict no damage. Here, let me."

Scriven slid the book across the table towards Carrington. Lewis and Simmonds were agog. With a cautious sawing action, the blade sliced between the stuck parchment, dragging the edges a little. "There *is* something inside!" exclaimed Scriven.

"Indeed, sir. A folded paper, as far as I can make out," said Carrington.

"Well, I'm blessed!" declared the curate.

"You should be, Mr Lewis," said the Steward. His jaw dropped open as the article was gingerly evicted from its hiding-place and withdrawn between Carrington's thumbnail and forefingernail. "I'll go to the foot of our stairs!"

"Beyond a peradventure, it is the very thing!" announced Carrington. "This piece of paper fits with the excised page! March 30th, 1785! That is the date his lordship mentioned."

"Wait till I tell Mrs Crouch," cried Simmonds. "She was right all along!"

"Mr Hupsman, may he rest in peace, manifestly did not wish it to be found in a hurry," said Mr Lewis. A blanket of heat enveloped him and he wished intently he were not present. It crossed his mind that the Register had been tampered with and that the finger of suspicion might well point towards him.

"Canny old devil!" said Simmonds in awe.

"That was a flash of genius on Lord Berkeley's part," observed Scriven, "to think of the pasteboard."

Mr Carrington reserved judgment.

After that, the congress developed a natural feel for the job and it was not long before the Banns were extruded. The Books were returned to an oak strong-box and padlocked. The group forsook the Muniment Room and Simmonds locked the door behind them. Flushed with success, they repaired to The Berkeley Arms for meat and porter.

Mr Carrington laid his knife and fork together upon his empty platter, drained his beer and scrubbed foam from his walrus mandibles with a handkerchief.

"I recommend that you and I, Mr Scriven, should return to London without delay. There is a coach at five-o-clock. His lordship will wish to know that perseverance has been favourable to our labours."

Mr Scriven consulted his timepiece and stuffed it back into an inner pocket. "I cannot conceive the frame of Mr Hupsman's mind to have gone to such lengths on his patron's behalf, nor Berkeley's in bringing it about."

"The rights and wrongs of it do not concern us," replied Carrington.

"Folk have been hanged for less!" said James Simmonds.

"Quite," said Mr Carrington, mopping his brow. "By Jove, that tripe was over-peppered!"

Three days after the 'good news' had been received, the Earl and Countess went down to Cranford where the family would join them for Easter. They were feeling serene and able to bask in a satisfying sense that their house was in order and that what was just and right-minded would follow.

On their first morning, Mr Chapeau trotted up the drive for a chinwag with his lordship. This was accompanied by cheesecakes and some fine ruby port bottled in the autumn of the Treaty of Versailles which had drawn a line under the American War of Independence. Chapeau's riding cape was hardly off when Berkeley gaily acquainted him with the 'find'.

The Reverend frowned. Delight and puzzlement wrestled upon his countenance. "That is a most adventitious blessing! Makes your marriage only a little younger than this excellent port," he said, inspecting the label of the decanted bottle in a desire to submerge his confusion.

"As I explained before, the registration was believed to have been destroyed."

"I never thought Mr Hupsman could have done such a thing! Even if he was wicked enough to perpetrate the crime, it is hard to accept that he would have been fool enough to put his life in jeopardy."

"Those were the exact sentiments of Sir James Mansfield when I consulted him. What a coil we have been in all these years!"

Chapeau plumped himself down in a chair and tugged his coat from his nether regions. "Well, well. That is a turn up, to be sure." He called to mind a deeply affecting conversation with Miss Tudor in the room next door when she had poured out her story and had used the graphic phrase: *I have been as much sold as any lamb that goes to the shambles.* He remembered also how she had admonished Fitz for some naughtiness when he arrived. *You little dog! Though I may not be your father's wife, I will let you know through life that I am your mother!* "I have to say, my lord, I always pitied Lady Berkeley's situation. She has performed her role with the utmost credit. I have sometimes wondered whether you deserved her."

Berkeley guffawed at his friend's plain speaking. "Never one to keep the buttons on the foils, were you, Chapeau?"

Chapeau squinted into the facets of the cut crystal. "I take it this means that Fitz will inherit the title?"

"No reason why he shouldn't," said Berkeley. He was holding his glass in an odd, tentative way, between his thumb and third finger, with the palm of his other hand supporting it underneath.

"Forgive me if I presume to know your business better than you do, Berkeley, but if I were you, I should lodge some sort of affidavit with the College of Heralds sooner rather than later. Lord Dursley will not attain his majority for several years and wish to take up his seat in the House, but anything could happen to you."

"My days of dicing with danger are over, whatever reputation says of me," laughed Berkeley. "It will take plague or famine to do away with me."

"'Tis good to know you have lost your proclivity for combat with highwaymen."

"Told Chesterfield some years back when he asked me if I'd taken any highwayman lately: 'Not since you hanged y'tutor!'"

"Dear me, that was a terrible business. The hanging of Dr Dodd for forging bonds. A revered preacher. Saviour of the fallen. Public benefactor extraordinaire. A divine of the first water."

"Debt did for him. It may drive a man to dubious practices he would not normally consider," said Berkeley soberly.

"At least poor Hupsman succeeded in keeping the right side of the law."

"As far as is known," agreed Berkeley.

A jarring silence fell. His lordship got up to pace to the window. Why had he said that? Sight of the placid acres beyond gave him oxygen. Chapeau was not aware that he had uttered anything untoward and was left to contemplate his host's rear in vague discomfiture. The next moment, a thunder-clap of intuition broke through his thoughts. Talk of Dr Dodd was the catalyst. He shied from allowing his mind to roam along an ugly vista.

"Forgery is a heinous transgression for which William Dodd paid the full price," he said.

"Don't forget, *his* was a crime against the Treasury. No court can show leniency for such. The exchequer was depleted by the American Wars."

"Dodd's Christian benevolence and status as spiritual advisor to the King went against him, I believe, rather than the reverse."

"So it should, Chapeau. But these are grim reflections when the grass begins to green and the sun to show its face!"

Chapeau tried to respond to these sanguine tones. He must slay the craven idea that had waylaid him with all the crudity of Berkeley's highwayman.

"Yes, indeed, I am glad for your lordship. Nonetheless, I do urge you to bear the Countess in mind. She is much younger than you and in the natural way of things will very likely be left to bear the brunt of any battle alone."

"There won't be a battle!" insisted Berkeley, retracing his steps to his chair by way of the decanter. "Now that evidence has come to light, who will contest it?"

The question hung in the air. This overweening dependence on the power of the Berkeleys was foolhardy in the extreme. Chapeau raised the port to his lips with the steadiness of one taking the Communion chalice. "Is that little Thomas Moreton I see capering in the daffodil beds out there? My word, he has grown!"

That Chapeau was an old fussbudget, Berkeley had often remarked. There were moments when the fellow so exasperated him that between themselves he was crude and rude enough to address him as 'Crapeau' and was left wondering why the longsuffering Reverend, ever solicitous of his welfare, should be offended. It implied that so fond an animadversion from a high-ranking Berkeley was some sort of accolade.

Still, Chapeau's patient counsel hit home. His lordship began to dwell on a posthumous theme. He was set to make amends for his fraudulence fourteen years ago and sought Mary's help in gathering together the documents detailing his ancestry, their marriages, the children's births and baptisms. These were sent to Garter King-at-Arms, Sir Isaac Heard, at the College of Heralds. Alongside them, the Earl furnished an explanation of the inconsistencies in the records. Because he had feared that the registry would not be found, the precaution had been taken of espousing his good lady a second time, soon after Hupsman had died. He vowed that he had acted upon professional assurance that a further rite could in no way nullify the first.

If, hitherto, the Berkeley imbroglio had raised eyebrows and caused a simmering sensation among the *haut ton*, it now reached a full rolling boil and lifted a lid that would never be replaced on their household affairs.

The clandestine nature of the first marriage did nothing to assuage the doubts that naturally arose out of this canard. No reason was volunteered for concealment. The Earl's attempt at clarification was farcical: the College of Heralds could do no other than refer the whole distasteful chapter to the Committee of Privileges of the House of Lords. His lordship was duly informed.

"Tarnation!" thundered Berkeley. "Do they dare challenge my word! They've no pedigree! Not a sinner among them knew his father!"

He emerged from the library grasping his hair with one hand, in the other a letter. It was headed by a decorated escutcheon branded with a red cross. For one awful moment, all the heraldic beasts of Revelation seemed mobilised to expel him from the Kingdom. He was the wrong side of the pale. His claim was being rejected by his own kind! Why? For what? Milord Pourquoi was in a daze of disbelief.

Mary was hustling the boys from the breakfast table and stopped in her tracks. She reached for a chair and slid down upon it as Berkeley catapulted into the room. *Hush, the whole universe will hear you,* she wanted to remonstrate. Instead, she said weakly: "What shall we do? What does it mean?"

"It means that there will be a hearing before their lordships. I shall have to testify. They will summon witnesses."

Mary rested her elbow on the table and leaned her forehead against her hand. "All because of a scrap of paper, we are to be put on trial? Why won't they accept your word?"

"It is patently absurd! Half the aristocracy of Britain is in masquerade. Nugent always refused to believe my youngest sibling, Louisa, was his own. And with good reason! There has been no cuckoo in my nest!"

The future was suddenly shuttered. "That means Billy will be arraigned before the Lords," Mary said. "You know how disgruntled he has become. He will not acquit himself well, I know it. And who else might they want to cross-examine?"

"Carrington. They will want to question him. Mr Lewis, perhaps, and Mr Scriven."

"Will they ask for Cranfield, do you suppose?"

"'Tis as well he is trying to scupper the French off the shores of Brittany," said Berkeley sombrely. He suspired slowly and shrugged. "I daresay it is a formality and will be open-and-shut within the hour. This must be the most trifling business on the Lord Chancellor's agenda."

Mary was not reassured. If it was so trivial, why go to these lengths? The phrase 'Occasion of Sin' came repeatedly into her mind. The Earl, increasingly ashamed of his cowardly hoax in 1785, was determined his sons should not suffer, nor think ill of him, while Mary in addition to that was pitched against the rules of a caste she saw as obsessed with wealth and power rather than respect for underived truth.

The enquiry opened on the twenty-seventh of May with a plaintive oration from the Earl. It was designed to appeal to the compassion and better nature of his listeners. He told the well-worn story which, by now, was a fully rationalised account in his brain. He had ordered total silence regarding his first marriage and his late chaplain had sworn to obey. *I was not aware of the latitude I had given him until afterwards, when he wanted money. I heard from him that he had risked his life for me in destroying the Register; until that moment I knew not the penalty.* Berkeley went on to explain that he could not in honour do anything that might endanger the clergyman. The manner in which the baptisms of his children were recorded was a necessary consequence of secrecy. *If the least doubt should remain in the breast of any noble Lord as to the fact of my first marriage, Lady Berkeley and myself are willing to give our personal testimony....* He pressed the Committee for a prompt decision. Further evidence which might be called was so marginal that Berkeley trusted their lordships would come to a ruling that day.

They heard him out with polite deference, schooling their features to withhold judgment, as they tried to follow the deflecting arabesques of his mind. Inconsistency forced some thorny queries. His doctrinaire assumptions ruffled a few feathers. The whole farrago bred doubt by the page. Lord Thurlow moved that, in the interests of all the children, the matter should be 'sifted through to the bottom.' He adjured the Earl to reconsider before bringing forward the Countess to the Bar. The Earl said that he was acting upon Counsel's advice and that it had been maturely considered. Lady Berkeley was able to elucidate the chain of events. Lord Thurlow replied that it was contrary to all the fundamental principles of law that a wife should be allowed to give evidence in favour of her husband: it was still more repugnant to law that a wife should be a witness against her husband. Without his having recourse to names, their lordships would call to mind a comparative instance before the Courts some years ago. (He alluded to the case of the adventuress, Elizabeth Chudleigh, Duchess of Kingston, a former Maid of Honour to Augusta, Princess of Wales with the Earl of Berkeley's mother. The Duchess was said to have interfered with her marriage records, first to remove them and, later, to have them reinstated when circumstances changed!) The Duke of Norfolk, a pragmatic man, pointed out that a delay was inevitable in order to keep the gallant Admiral informed of what went forward. Lord Walsingham, in the Chair, concurred. The hearing into the 5th Earl of Berkeley's pedigree would not be over that day, nor the next. The legal machine was cranked to run its course.

The Earl and Countess were dismayed. Neither imagined the individuals that would be requisitioned to tell what they knew. Scouts were sent out to compare the vital dates of copies with original entries. The Bishop of Gloucester's secretary, Mr Thomas Rudge, was asked whether, following a Visitation to the Parish of Berkeley, the transcripts that were drawn from the

Registers covering the year in question, contained any intimation of a marriage between the Earl of Berkeley and Miss Cole. A herald was commissioned to discover the date of the Reverend Mr Hupsman's death. Theodore Gwinnett, from Billy's early schooldays, was winkled out to confirm that the witness, William Tudor, was the same person as the William Cole he had known long ago as Mary Cole's brother. It was an attempt to elicit when and why Billy had changed his name. There was no straightforward answer and waffling about conciliating an old aunt of that name, from whom he had expectations, did not cut the mustard with their lordships. Billy flatly denied having known Gwinnett, or anyone from the family, though he shrewdly conceded the surname was not uncommon in the Vale of Gloucester. Brook Watson and Haviland le Mesurier, under whom Billy had worked at the Commissariat, were challenged upon his character and honesty. The Committee wanted to know how he had obtained a recommendation for the post in the first place. The barrister, John Harriott Roe, who had witnessed Susan's marriage to James Heyward, was questioned upon what he had learned of Mary's situation during his years of acquaintance with Billy, but, bizarrely, appeared to confuse her with Susan and there was no telling the source of that misconception! Mrs Routh stepped forward to tell the Court how Hupsman had told her and her sister, as far back as 1786, that Miss Tudor would eventually be known for the Countess of Berkeley. John Allen was a notorious shyster from Barnwood, who poached game from the Berkeley estates and had routinely found outlets with the Farren brothers and Mary's father. He had been sought on account of reputed business dealings with William Cole Sr. over many years and quoted lines from the Parish Register which revealed that 'Tudor' was not one of Billy's baptismal names. Allen's father was known to have been detained in the House of Correction and both to have been fined. Poaching game was a repeated offence: evading tithes was another, together with manifold breaches of the peace. This calibre of witness could hardly be said to underpin the cause of the claimant, William Fitzhardinge Berkeley. Mr Carrington vouchsafed as little information as possible upon oath, but had to admit, under minute interrogation, that it was his patron who had drawn attention to the covers of the Register when the search began.

The broadsheets wallowed in it and the cauldron of gossip bubbled merrily. Mary's history was teased out and reworked with all the authority of hard fact.

"I tell you, no good can come of it, Mr Carrington," said the sibyl, Price, noting his worried aspect. "I knew long ago *that pair* were up to no good. Why, it beggars belief that they think to parade such a fanciful tale in front of their lordships!"

"I may remind you that the outcome is pending. To discuss the case is forbidden."

"One thing is certain: I shall not be called as a witness. I should speak my mind. The testimony is shot through with humbug."

"Forgive me, you could not be expected to know anything material to the line of enquiry."

"Hogwash and fakery, sir! I could cite the day and the hour!"

So saying, the governess stalked off to her duties, leaving Carrington to stare after her in alarm. Suppose she were invited to testify, they might all swing! Price did not fear to articulate the unspoken narrative behind everyone's lips. It behoved the chaplain to alert Lord Berkeley.

"I am aware, Carrington, that we are nursing a viper," his lordship said in a steely undertone, "but to dismiss her now on some pretext would be foolish."

"Not an exercise in damage limitation, I own."

"This gruelling business in the House must soon draw to a close. The tiresome dame is sure to overstep the mark again."

"It is most regrettable that no one has come forward to answer for Richard Barns," said Carrington empirically. "It might turn the tide for your lordship."

"If that was indeed the fellow's name," Berkeley said. "Hupsman procured him. Anonymity was all-important at the time."

"There was a soldier of that surname, fathered a bastard child on a woman in the town." Seeing his patron's brows arch, the cleric added: "A priest gleans a lot of idle information, my lord."

"He was no stripling! I doubt it could be the same fellow."

The Committee of Privileges had gone to great lengths to find the missing witness to the 1785 marriage. Thousands of handbills were distributed at turnpikes offering a reward of twenty guineas for information leading to his whereabouts. Posters were pinned up and advertisements placed in the major newspapers of Gloucester, Bath and Bristol. It was labour in vain. What no one remembered was that Richard Barns had been married at Stone in the summer of 1740 to one, Mary Giles. They removed to

Thornbury the following year where they fell on hard times and lost their first child. The crops were sparse that Lammastide owing to a dry spell which had lasted three seasons. In the fullness of time, the Barns' migrated to Shropshire to be near some of Mary's relatives. There, they scratched a living from a smallholding to keep body and soul together. Mary died about fifteen years later and her husband found it hard to set his heart to anything for long. He tried soldiering, peddling and carrying goods. By 1787, two years after he had been paid to witness a wedding at Berkeley, Richard Barns of Ludlow lay in a common grave. When the House of Lords sought him, he had been dead for twelve years. Some said they knew all along that he had not existed.

During the last week of June, the Committee of Privileges assembled to review the evidence and close the proceedings which had stalled. One salient omission was the Earl of Berkeley's key statement to the College of Heralds. Lord Thurlow, in his summing up, pronounced it a 'tedious investigation which must have occasioned anxiety'. The Earl and Countess' feelings were probably best consulted were he to adjourn the case *sine die*.

Their *unmentionables* had been laundered outdoors to no purpose! The question was left hanging mid-air. Small consolation that Lord Thurlow was known to be a 'hard-liner' and might have taken the case into the realms of criminality had he felt it deserved further probing.

The Berkeleys scurried from the courtroom with their heads down, the Earl poker-faced and the Countess biting back scalding tears. All she could think of was Fitz. *I have betrayed my firstborn son who was the only light in my distress and loneliness, the thread that kept me clinging to his father's coat-tails.*

"Who do they think they are?" raged Berkeley in the carriage.

"No! Who does Fitz think he is! If you had been a man of honour and worthy of your title, you would not have allowed this to happen! My brother risked his life for you, so did your chaplain! I am traduced and ridiculed because of my birth! My poor mother is labelled a common prostitute because she hired herself out as a wet-nurse! Their lordships would not think such a woman too low to suckle their offspring! And your children, your dear children, *our* children, are now divided into two camps and there will be contention between them for the rest of their lives! I hope you are satisfied, Fred, because I..."

"Silence, woman! Did I not raise you from a miserable station? You entered the stage with a high opinion of your virtue."

"I know you did not really love me." Mary fumbled for her handkerchief and sniffled heartily into it.

"You needed someone to bring you down to earth! They are nobodies, the Coles. What did they ever do for the nation?"

"They purveyed good honest victuals! Pa and Will Farren and Farren's brother, Ellis. Why, the Duke of Norfolk who is now deaf to your pleading, gave Ellis the Freedom of the City of Gloucester!"

This distinction had been granted to Ellis Taylor Farren for supplying His Grace's board at Eagle House, Westgate Street, with well-fed hogs and mutton, venison sausages and barons of beef. Under the auspices of the Duke, Berkeley had tried to gain for his three eldest sons the same Freedom as a mark of respect for their birth. The whole procedure was bedevilled by lack of proof of the children's legitimacy and had been the smallest foretaste of the dispute that was set to roll for the next three or four generations. Though Charles, Duke of Norfolk and Earl Marshal of England was a Whig of democratic views, not overly concerned with the genesis of the Berkeley children at the time, the City Fathers closed ranks in opposing the claim.

The Duke was known to have widespread progeny born out of wedlock. He had lost his first wife and child in childbirth. His second, Frances Scudamore, an heiress from Herefordshire, was interned in an asylum at Holme Lacy. This gave the Duke a keen interest in the affairs of the border country with Wales and, in particular, with the thriving port of Gloucester where he held gourmet turtle dinners for the Mayor and Corporation. The 'Drunken Duke' was a popular, larger than life figure, coarse, noisy and extrovert, who paid no attention to personal appearance and was a stranger to soap and water.

"Well, he is lost to our cause, you may depend. And if he, then many others of import. Who will make a bridge of gold for us?"

They made the rest of the journey in tense silence. The Westminster streets smelled of dust and ordure. The team pounded the old cobbles, resigned to duty and familiar with the route.

Reynolds greeted them and took the Earl's hat. "Your friends are already here, my lord. Admiral Prescott and Mr Chapeau. I have shown them into the drawing room. Colonel West sent word that he is dining with Lord Uxbridge, but begs leave to call upon you in the morning."

The Earl made some surly excuse and went off to attend to his ablutions. Mary, still in her bonnet, rushed into the drawing room and flung herself down on a sofa, blurting out: "No more iniquity for me! My children shall go to church and read their bibles, and they shall learn to tread the path of truth and virtue!"

The two gentlemen swapped significant looks. The Admiral's response was to sink a deep breath. Chapeau's gaze dwelt upon the Countess with intense pity. "I take it things did not go well, your ladyship?"

"The House ignored every word Fred said! Can you believe it?"

Distressingly, Chapeau found that he could. "You were not called to shed light on the matter?"

"As a wife in the case, any evidence of mine is supposedly 'repugnant to law'! What do you make of that, Mr Chapeau?"

"Dear me, so they were not persuaded?"

"A disappointing end to a terrible ordeal," said the Admiral. "Most unfortunate for yourself and his lordship, but especially for young Fitzhardinge."

Mary clawed at her bonnet strings and tossed off the item. "Oh, do not remind me! How shall I look him in the eye? He is at that very difficult stage of puberty, you know, and inclined to rebel when he does not get his way."

The Earl was not communicative over dinner. Mary worked hard to keep the tempo raised, but soon wilted with weariness. She was glad to leave the gentlemen to their port.

When she had gone, Chapeau removed his napkin and rose from the table.

"That was an excellent dinner, my lord, I thank you. And, indeed, for your generosity over a span of what must be, let's see, some thirty-odd years of intimate acquaintance. It grieves me to declare that this is the last meal I shall share with you."

His host was thunderstruck. "Why, Chapeau, what is this? What's eating you?"

"I fear, my lord, I can no longer accept the hospitality of a man against whom I may one day be called to witness. I may say that I believe your good lady has been abominably ill-used."

"This is nonsensical! You would kick a man when he is down? We have known one another since God was in breeks!"

"My mind is made up," replied the clergyman, raising his palm. "There is no more to be said. I will bid you 'good evening', gentlemen, and see myself out."

The Earl's countenance was ashen. The Admiral's, remarkably impervious. "Well, did you ever see such a display, Prescott? The fellow's bats in the belfry! I daresay he'll come about."

"Not if Mrs Chapeau has anything to do with it."

"At all events, I trust you won't have second thoughts about my suitability as a comrade."

"No, my lord. I am not a deserter. However, I feel it would be prudent to destroy my journals! Where there is no recorded proof, sound evidence cannot be required."

"This devilish situation is proving a sore trial of friendship. I note Buckingham has absconded to the country," observed his lordship grimly. He wondered what His Royal Highness, the Prince of Wales, whom he had not seen in months, was making of the hullabaloo.

"I sink, wiz your Majesty's permission," said the Queen, "I will write to her, entreating her to come to some accommodation wiz Wales. He tries to do his duty, but is so forlorn wizout her. I fear he will not mend."

"Catholic!" returned the King.

"Mrs Fitzherbert is a goot woman."

"Comely," conceded the King. "Fine buxom figure. What!"

"*Homely*," said the Queen. "She truly cares for him and has not ze passion for politicking."

"Damned Catholic," pronounced the King again. "All Ireland will run loose. Side with the French. Revolution by the tradesmen's entrance!"

"Mr Pitt vould have somesing to say!"

"Smythes giving quarter to refugees. Throckmortons, nest of treason! Percys, Jerninghams, Radclyffes! Stuarts all over again! Foreigners to our way of thinking, Madam!"

The Queen sighed in an impatient manner. "Yes, ve are sober Protestants who know how to keep our heads! Vhy, pray, did Your Majesty condescend to visit Mr Veld at Lulworth Castle last summer?"

"Diplomacy, what! Must show solidarity with all sections of society in these turbulent times. Keep 'em sweet. Centre of percussion!"

"Is Your Majesty sure it vas not a vish to appease Mrs Fitzherbert and ze family of her first husband?"

"If it were, Madam, it appears to have failed. She is resisting Wales."

"I sink so vould I in zhese circumstances, yah!" said the Queen. "She must seek ze sanction of her Pope."

"Eternal incineration! Not a happy prospect! Still, it didn't stop Norfolk's apostasy when seeking a seat in the House."

"Mrs Fitzherbert vill not abandon her religion, Sire."

"Fellow's a tramp," grumbled the King. "Sides with the Great Unwashed. All the pumps of Arundel cannot sweeten him! Wife's more *mopsimus* than I am!"

The King reflected upon what the Queen had said. They both liked Mrs Fitzherbert and agreed she was blessed with many admirable qualities. Even a Catholic might fill a role in the stability of the nation, thought His Majesty.

"You have our approbation, Madam. Write to her! Set our stamp upon the thing!"

The King prorogued Parliament on the Glorious Twelfth of August and an informal dinner was held at Uxbridge House, a fine columned mansion in Burlington Gardens. Henry Paget, 1st Earl of Uxbridge, was a man of ripened years whose largesse and widespread interests were famed. This was an annual event for a cluster of male friends where the constraints upon conversation observed in mixed company were lifted. Fellows were apt to buzz off to their estates and one might not run into them for months.

The lake-like surface of his table gave off soft reflections from Waterford chandeliers pendent above lily-pads of Queen's Ware porcelain and candescent silverware. Among the guests were Prince William, Duke of Clarence, His Grace of Norfolk and ditto of Beaufort, the Earl of Egremont, Colonel McMahon of the Prince of Wales' Household, Admiral Prescott and Colonel West, Samuel Lysons, Charles James Fox and the MP Philip Champion de Crespigny. Mr Champion de Crespigny had several days ago buried his son, Thomas, a victim of smallpox. (This bright young Advocate of Doctors' Commons was he before whom Lord Berkeley had sworn his affidavit at the Surrey Commissariat before the Lambeth marriage.) The assembly offered condolences.

"A harrowing experience," said Mr Fox.

The bereaved father shook his head sadly. "So pointless. Diamond-sharp brain. Everything before him."

"Broadside cannonade!" submitted the Duke of Clarence.

Thomas had married Augusta Charlotte Thelusson, a Huguenot of Swiss-French extraction, whose brother was a director of the Bank of England. "Poor Lottie is expecting their first child. Eighteen and a widow!"

"A virulent enemy, smallpox, against which we have little defence," commented the Duke of Beaufort. "I take it he had received no inoculation?"

"No, your Grace. Thomas had always a fragile make-up. Feeling out of sorts, he'd gone down to Aldeburgh where he took a mortal fever."

"Thank God for Dr Jenner who is giving us hope of a cure," said Lysons.

"To my mind," said Beaufort, "it is not sufficiently proven. William Woodville of the Smallpox Hospital appears to have followed Jenner's method and succeeded in infecting hundreds of people with the disease!"

"I wonder that the same lancets should be used for variolation, when the cowpox lymph is taken, as for vaccination," remarked Uxbridge. "It is also critical to rule out confusion between cowpox and the early stages of smallpox."

Jenner's findings had been fiercely slated by some who were jealous of his discoveries and by others who had adopted them without appreciating his disciplines. He concluded that lymph extracted from actual smallpox pustules could be dried and preserved in a glass or quill without losing its potency.

"The fellow is a true benefactor," declared Norfolk. "Deuced if I don't give a ball in his honour and raise a subscription for further research! You shall see how the new wing goes forward at Arundel."

"Stupendous scheme!" endorsed Lord Egremont, Norfolk's Sussex 'neighbour', a gentleman noted for his benevolence towards the local poor. "I have corresponded with Jenner for some time and not a more self-effacing being walks the earth."

"The local people have every faith their hero," Lysons said. "The Berkeleys were among the first to have their eldest sons vaccinated."

The chatter ebbed. The diners gave way to something like a corporate groan. "Where is he, by the way?" asked Fox, who was used to seeing Lord Berkeley under his host's roof.

"Out of town if he has any sense," murmured Norfolk, "which he don't."

"His lordship is down at Cranford for the shooting," explained Uxbridge. "Keen to cull the best game himself. They've a deal of trouble with gangs of poachers."

"Don't he know how to set a gin-trap?" asked Colonel McMahon.

"He knows how to set the town by the ears," chortled Clarence, sucking his white soup with gusto.

"Very handy with the barking-iron when it comes to highwaymen," said Fox. "As soon shoot 'em as look 'em in the eye!"

"Berkeley's in his natural element when courting danger," said Norfolk.

"To speak the truth," said Beaufort, "I find it irksome to sup with the man. If he expects us to believe that Canterbury tale of two marriages, he does himself a serious disfavour. What think you, Prescott?"

"What's that, your Grace?" said Prescott, cupping his ear. "Berkeley? Ah yes, a most generous friend, but I am the last person to fathom the family tree."

"His Royal Highness, the Prince of Wales," said the Irish Colonel McMahon, "gained the impression that Berkeley plighted his troth about the same time as himself and Mrs Fitz."

"What's your opinion, West?" demanded Fox. "You know them inside out."

"For years, I cherished the notion that the bond between them was sealed in some private way."

"Most singular!" responded Beaufort. "Then you don't think it moonshine?"

"If pressed, your Grace, I would have to say that knowledge of a second marriage did occasion doubt of the first."

"Admiral Berkeley speaks highly of her," said Clarence. "Avers she is every inch the lady. Lord knows what he thinks of his brother's conduct."

Prescott, having picked up the thread of the conversation, informed them: "I understand Lady Berkeley to have excellent connections. Her sister is the wife of Mr Charles Baring. Before that she was the widow of Thomas Heyward's brother. Her ladyship's eldest sister is married to an American Judge."

"You don't say!" said Norfolk, sending forth an arc of spittle over the marzipan novelties. "And Berkeley has dubbed his mummer all this time!"

Samuel Lysons indulged in a secret smile, but ventured no comment.

"Smacks of Bluebeard's castle," said Lord Egremont who had a taste for the Gothic vogue. "A touch of the possessive case."

"I don't rate the eldest boy's chances when he comes of age," said Beaufort, an old rival of Berkeley's in fielding Parliamentary candidates. "Or when his pater hops the twig, come to that!"

"He goes by the courtesy title," Lysons told them, "but Gloucestershire folk are of the opinion the story will not stick."

"I trust you will invite them to your ball, Duke," said Uxbridge. "We can hardly celebrate Jenner's work without them when his laboratory is in their cabbage patch!"

"If the Berkeleys come, I shall be hard put to countenance the pair," grumbled Beaufort.

"They must come!" said Norfolk. "I shall also invite His Royal Highness and Mrs Fitzherbert. It will be a step towards restoring harmony between them. And Prince Ernest, now that he is in England."

"The new Duke of Cumberland," revised Clarence.

"You must bring the divine Dora. I supported her company years ago in the North, long before you, sir, crossed the Jordan to the Promised Land! She held her audiences spellbound."

"A lass from the Liffey," said the dewy-eyed Colonel McMahon, "a daughter o' Dublin."

"The land of Peru is her haunt at present," Clarence told them. "Sheridan's, *Pizarro*, draws the crowds to bursting point nightly. Dora shines as Cora and more than holds her own beside the stellar Siddons."

"Is it true, Your Highness, that you 'deign to skim her profits' as they say!" quizzed Fox. "Tell us, do you keep her, or does she keep you?"

"I cannot say the King was tight-fisted when he gave me Bushey, but you've no notion how maintaining it runs through the blunt when you've a growing family! I suffered Dora to manage on half her allowance and wrote to her when she was on tour, telling her so. And do you know what the saucy minx did? She sent me the cut-off bottom of a playbill which read: *No money returned after the rising of the curtain!*"

At this, the diners fell about in riotous mirth.

"Gentlemen, I give you Dora," cried Norfolk, raising his glass. "The *belle* of the boards!"

"Dora!" came the resounding echo, and the excuse for toasting and competitive quaffing had begun.

When the sweatmeats and Stilton had been plundered, some of the gentlemen took their liqueurs in the garden. It was a warm evening and the French doors had been wide open throughout the meal. The Duke of Clarence, listing to starboard by now, went out to pace the terrace quarterdeck, as though he expected enemy craft to appear over Uxbridge's ruddy brick wall.

Admiral Prescott and Colonel West followed him out, a few paces behind. "The call of Neptune," smiled Prescott. "Spot it a league off!"

"What a pity insubordination has made a land-lubber of him."

"Mr Walpole used to eulogise his manly attributes, but unruliness will not recommend him to His Majesty's Navy." Prescott abruptly changed tack. "I was rather hoping to see Berkeley here."

"He never misses Uxbridge's dinners if he can help it."

"Well, it is too bad of him to slope off to Cranford. I have something important to relay."

The Admiral hesitated, on the apex of disclosure. The Colonel was a man of eminent discretion. It was why Berkeley had used him as a conduit for news.

"West, I am concerned about this woman, Price, in his lordship's employ. Loose cannon, if I'm any judge. On some sort of moral crusade. She has written to Mrs Bayly virtually accusing the Berkeleys of forgery. She claims to know things she cannot tell. Now, whatever you make of the *débâcle* in the Lords, that is very dangerous ground. It also seems that she and Mrs Chapeau are hugger-mugger."

"I'll warrant the Berkeleys are not aware of it."

"Mm. I tell you this, and for nothing," Prescott said in foreboding accents, "I see a right royal showdown brewing!"

A light wind stirred the horsechestnuts fringing the western boundary of Uxbridge House. They rocked like ships at anchor, bearing a heavy cargo of prickly fruit. A copper sun dazzled the garden through the boughs and brought a blush to the uncorseted roses. That moment, a white barn owl swooped ethereally from the stables' clocktower.

Clarence poised an imaginary telescope at an absurd tangent. "Great heavens! What was that?"

"To be sure, twas an albatross, Your Highness," quipped Colonel McMahon. "Won't you be adding a flush more gin to your port now?"

Nothing could dispel the melancholy surrounding the Prince of Wales. He had been unable to lure Maria back to his arms, despite overtures conveyed by Prince Ernest. Oblique points of Catholic dogma stood between himself and ineffable bliss, like pikemen ready to skewer the intrepid martyr. The waters of Bath had done little to revive his zest for life.

The Earl and Countess of Berkeley heard that the Prince was at an easy distance from the Castle and invited him to stay. They had returned to Gloucestershire in time for the Three Choirs Music Festival held annually between the cities of Gloucester, Worcester and Hereford. 1799 being the turn of Gloucester, the Earl seized the chance to be seen at a civic event where he and his wife might confound their detractors and embark upon a conjoined life of unabridged respectability.

"It seems that a visit from His Royal Highness, the Prince of Wales, is in the wind," said Carrington to Mrs Price.

"I trust I shall sit at table with him, Mr Carrington," Price cut in. "Believe me, if I suffer exclusion a second time, I shall pack my valise. That I will!"

"You will do nothing reckless, I am confident, dear lady."

"Let us speak frankly. Our position in this house is untenable. We know too much."

Carrington would not have wished to surrender his living, but it would ease his mind to be relieved of his tutorship. Restless nights had followed the disclosure in the House of Lords that his employer had led him to inspect the covers of the Registers. It was a dormant volcano that was marked for eruption in the fullness of time. Fitz Berkeley himself was not to be underrated. He was poised for a fight and was intensely aware of adult ineptitude. *They* didn't understand that the broadsheets reached Eton and the older fellows ribbed him and made him do twice the fagging for being a 'by-blow' with high-flown aspirations. It couldn't be squared with his parents' categorical insistence that this wasn't true. He and Freddy had asked some knotty questions of their tutor which Carrington had brushed aside with a revealing embarrassment. Their next recourse was that doyenne of forthright candour, Price, who left them with a robust impression that there was scope for doubt.

"Your parents were united in the spring before Thomas was born," she told them. "That is the beginning and end of it."

"They found the other record!" cried Freddy.

"That, young sir, is a mystery some will carry to grave."

"Papa wouldn't have let Mama keep the accounts if he hadn't been married to her," protested Fitz. "She wouldn't have allowed him to do wrong."

"Her ladyship is a paragon of all the virtues, I dareswear!"

"Crouch says they *were* married," said Freddy with a pout.

"Then the woman is more gullible than I imagined!"

When the gist of this conversation came to the notice of the Countess, Price was ordered to the library and apprised of her displeasure in ear-chafing terms.

"You have taken upon yourself an unconscionable degree of licence. That a member of this household should disdain its reputation...! And in the hearing of my sons!"

"I answered the queries of intelligent young creatures as straightforwardly as I knew how. As a governess, that is my remit."

"To undermine family unity is not! You had no place to vent your opinions before the children. You have no right to ignore Lord Dursley's title!"

Price was going to stand her ground. The Countess had risen from rustic obscurity to a rank the governess could only attain vicariously. "It has oft escaped your attention, madam, that I was bred a gentlewoman. I am not an inferior citizen simply because Almighty God has not seen fit to grant me fortune such as your own."

"What is it that you have against me, Jane?" asked Mary, inclining towards arbitration. It was deeply upsetting to be wrongfooted by an upper servant .

"My notions of honour do not coincide with those of this house. I do not choose to explain myself further."

"Well, then, I can only invite you to tender your resignation."

"Do you dare to turn me off, madam?"

"My lord will pay your salary for the remainder of the year. Sadly, I should be hard put to provide you with a character."

Price clenched her fists. Her gimlet eyes were black as molten tar. Without leave, she turned on her heel. "I shall quit forthwith! But let me inform you, my lady, that it is in my power to be your greatest enemy!"

The Earl conducted the transaction in gravid silence one hour later. Price signed that she had received seven guineas for the balance of that year, but his lordship gave her twelve, allegedly to help with travel expenses. He had no intention of probing the argument further. The words *in full of all demands* were written on the receipt and a clear impression left upon the carbon copy.

In the morning, bent on heading for London, she was taken to meet the mailcoach. Mary heard the curricle clatter across the courtyard around dawn and hopped out of bed to part the window drapes. The stiff-necked form of Mary Jane Price, clad in corvine black, swept under the archway, out of sight. Mary expected to feel relief, but instead, the dawn sky was ringing with omens. I fear I have not seen the last of that woman, she said to herself.

Fifteen

In the late summer of 1799, Captain John Manley was sent to take over the *Mars*, Rear-Admiral Sir George Cranfield Berkeley's seventy-four gun ship.

After a spell at Bosham Manor with Emily and his children, the Admiral thought it high time he compared notes with his elder brother and wrote to him accordingly at Cranford. He had been informed through various agencies of events in the House of Lords, but Fred had preserved a sulky silence.

"I don't want him to come! I won't see him!" shouted Fitz as soon as he heard of the proposed visit.

"You most certainly will," decreed Mary. "You will behave like a gentleman and be civil and engaging towards the Admiral, or you'll answer to me!"

"You can't make me!"

"Speak to him, Fred. Please! Exert your fatherly rule, for I am a fallen woman in his eyes!"

"What's all this to-do, Fitz?" huffed Berkeley. "I won't have you showing disrespect to your mother, or to your Uncle Cranfield."

"He's only *half* my Uncle!"

"Where in heaven's name did you get such a notion!" exclaimed Mary.

"Well, what I mean is, I ain't proper family. You can't say I am, Mama. Nor's Freddy, nor Gus, nor Henry."

"That is the stupidest thing I ever heard from an intelligent young man."

Fitz was not to be mollified and flew into a full-blown rage, fiercely controlling his irrigated vision. "Look at me, Mama! Look at me! Who do you see?"

"Why, I see William, my firstborn lamb, my special one. I see Viscount Dursley."

"You know they won't let me take that title. I won't inherit what I should. It will all go to Uncle Cranfield, or Ge...orge," whined the boy, distorting the vowels of his cousin's name. The pantomimicry helped to cover the perturbing crack in his voice through which Fitz was convinced he lost a good deal of clout.

"What nonsense!" said Mary, exchanging glances with her husband. "In any case, Tom would be next in line."

"Ugh! That's worse! He's just a daft baby. He's always snuffling. He could die!"

"And, who knows, he might not be the last," Mary said, unable to resist a smile.

"Bam me," exclaimed Fitz, "things go from bad to worse!" His mental processes refused point blank to construe this disgusting clue. "I'm going to give some pigeons a whiff of the grapeshot! And rabbits! And stoats! And weasels! And badgers, if any get in the way!"

The boy made to slink off, but his mother, turning to Berkeley, cried: "Do not, my lord, stand there and let him eradicate the county's natural history!"

The Earl's gaze flared with fury. "Come back this instant, Fitz!"

"But I'll end up a gamekeeper, so I might as well practise."

"Don't think you're too old for a caning, sir. You will put a stop to this disgraceful exhibition at once! And I want your solemn assurance that impeccable conduct will be the order of the day when the Admiral arrives. You will make yourself agreeable to him as a cultivated young fellow ought."

"I hardly know him, Papa."

"Well, then, this is your chance to become better acquainted because, by my life, you *are* Lord Dursley and *will* come into your own! When you wish to occupy a seat in the House, your Uncle will be your best sponsor. Now take off that sullen visage!"

Duly chastened, Fitz left the room, looking askance at his mother to see how she was taking it. Anguish smote at her heart. He was a product of the shadow-world in which she had been a hostage to his father's impulses. To have Billy on the distaff side as his Uncle, who had no presence to speak of and came across as defensive when challenged, and to have Admiral Berkeley on the other, who was well-bred and whose life had tone and character, must be confoundedly confusing. Add to that the stormy straits of adolescence....

On the day of his brother's arrival, Lord Berkeley was not at home. The previous night he had been a guest of Henry Percy at Syon House and drove back in his phaeton through rain and gale, heartily wishing he had made use of the carriage.

The Admiral divested himself of his own damp hat and cape and allowed Reynolds to conduct him to the drawing room where Mary sat tinkering with the keys of the harpsichord. The scent of sweet peas pervaded the room.

"Admiral Sir George Berkeley, your ladyship."

She started out of her daydream and jumped up to greet him warmly. Unexpectedly, the sight of her caused the dauntless mariner's knees to turn to marrow. Gone was the shepherdess of yore. This was a lady worthy of a King's Court! The Admiral drew her gently towards him and planted a soft kiss on either cheek. "Mary! How you are blooming! Now I may call you 'sister', mayn't I?"

"Tis very pretty in you, sir. Do make yourself comfortable and I will send for some tea."

"You were far away when I came in. Wistful phrases, if I may say so."

"Signore Alessandro Scarlatti is quite a taskmaster. Freddy is the virtuoso of the keyboard here, although his father plays creditably when he's a mind."

"I find you all in health and spirits? Tell me, is that impious brother of mine treating you as he ought?"

Mary gestured despair. "Well, you know Fred.... To say the truth, he is as blue as megrim since the *Inquiry* did not unpack as we'd hoped."

"It was always the way with him, to act outrageously and come off unscathed."

"Oh, Cranfield, I cannot tell you how I dread being known!" Mary unlocked the caddy and doled out spoonfuls of Black Oolong. "I ride the storm as bravely as I can, but it puts his lordship in a miff. His manner towards me is harsh and cruel. He thinks he is made to look foolish by my management. But his pocket leaches money and he has no idea of the new ways in farming. I fear," Mary ended tearfully, "he is planning to put me away!"

The next moment she found herself wrapped in her brother-in-law's embrace. He folded her head into his shoulder and gently patted her back. "My dear girl, nothing could be more wrong-headed, I swear. Whatever his follies, I do not think him capable of *that*."

Beneath the tumult of her racing thoughts, Mary found herself relaxing into this sweet consolation, but recoiled gently, sensing that the Admiral was moved more than was comfortable.

"The poor harvest cannot be helped! The tithings are growing apace. Fred wants to mortgage manors and farmsteads, Cranford. *Again!* He has no cause to criticise my stewardship. I have ten thousand pounds floating at present and none but an untried young man to assist with the accounts."

What a contrast her life was to Emily's, who spent his absences among the tranquil parklands of Goodwood with her family.

"Good grief!" said the Admiral thickly. "I am all at sea and I am on *terra firma*!" There was a commotion in the hall. The door burst open. "Why, Frederick, speak of the devil!"

"Cran!"

Mary wiped her fingertips under her lower lids in a discreet gesture. "We were about to drink tea, Fred. Would you like some?"

"Is the pot big enough for three?" the Earl asked unnecessarily. His apparel was mapped with rain and mud. "Blasted horse threw a shoe. Had to nurse him for miles. Must change the rigging, Cran. I trust you had better luck?"

"I had matters to attend at the Admiralty and came from Town by chaise along the Bath Road. No bridle-culls to speak of!"

During dinner the atmosphere relaxed and the three eldest boys joined their parents and Uncle around the table with Mr Carrington. The talk was of Nelson's conquest of the French in Egypt which fully engaged the boys' attention. The Admiral made imaginative use of cutlery and condiments to illustrate manoeuvres. *"We waited for a fair wind to blow us out of the Channel...."* he began. *"We were cruising off Brest when...."*

"I want to be in the Navy like you, Uncle Cranfield," said Freddy when his uncle had finished. "You wouldn't have to press-gang me!"

"I'm pleased to hear it! Well, you know, Freddy, you could take the King's Shilling quite soon and learn the mariner's art from bottom to top."

"As long as I get my quota of grog," said Freddy, thoughtfully addressing himself to slices of capon.

"Do you not think him a little young to leave home?" asked Mary, gazing dotingly upon her second child.

"No better way, Mary, if he's truly set upon a naval career."

"I *should* join, too," offered Fitz, in a lacklustre manner. "There's not much to keep me here. Eton is for jellyfish. I don't like it."

"Oh, but you must complete your education as befits the eldest. We need fellows like you to keep the country on its feet. So when does term begin, Fitz?"

"Tuesday next, sir. I have a new coat. The old one is outgrown."

"Tuesday next?" repeated Berkeley who intended to accompany his son back to College. "I thought it was Wednesday."

"No, Papa, that is the first day of term."

"Deuced if I haven't a dining engagement in Town on Tuesday at Carlton House. I could have sworn it was Wednesday the carriage would be needed."

"My lord, do not concern yourself. I am more than willing to go," said Mary. "You have other means of transport."

"By yourself?" demanded Berkeley.

She gave him an indulgent smile, remembering journeys long past and how women at the foot of the social ladder were no strangers to independence.

"Perhaps I might resolve the difficulty," offered the Admiral, "and escort her ladyship and Fitz myself. It would be no small honour."

"Steady on, Cran," laughed Berkeley.

"I don't have your valour when it comes to 'gentlemen of the road', Frederick, though I tangled with the French in mid-Atlantic, when I was Captain of the *Marlborough*, and came off the worse for it!"

On the day of his departure, a dewy September morning breathing hints of quince and cider apple, Fitz's trunk was loaded on to the box of the landau. The boy elected to sit up alongside the driver whom he hoped to persuade to hand over the ribbons.

A concourse of vehicles was waiting to cross Windsor Bridge. The bridge at Datchet had fallen into disrepair, only a few years after the Crown had paid for it to be rebuilt and there was a long-winded debate about whether the ratepayers of Buckinghamshire and Berkshire, whose county boundaries met midstream, should share the cost of renewal. The tired horses were hot and could smell the water.

The carriages inched forward, rumbling over the wooden laths at a similar pace to the flow of traffic in the opposite direction, so that there was a clear view of the travellers leaving the Eton College and Castle bank of the river.

"By all that's famous! Viscount Dursley in charge of the family chariot!" (Fitz was anxious to demonstrate his prowess and his status by rolling up to the College doors in a fully emblazoned carriage.)

Mary started from her reverie. That masculine voice was familiar and associated with pleasant things. "West?" Leaning towards the window, she saw that it was indeed him. An immaculate spider phaeton aligned with her narrowed vision. It was drawn by a pair of Arab horses and tooled by a high-ranking military man sporting gold epaulettes and medals. He did not look of an age to have collected such distinctions. When he drew level and halted, it was plain that his bravery had cost him an eye.

"Colonel West!" she cried. "How delightful to see you! .....Oh!" She took in the full significance of his companion's regalia, with the winking Star of the Garter, and automatically lowered her head.

"Lady Berkeley! Ah, Sir George!" West peered into the carriage naturally expecting to find that his lordship was with her. "Permit me to introduce to you His Royal Highness Prince Ernest, the Duke of Cumberland!"

"Your Royal Highness," Cranfield had his back to the team and half-turned to perform his acknowledgement. Mary silently bowed again and gave the Prince the benefit of an engaging smile. His stiff façade relaxed a little. Saying nothing, he bent forward and stretched out his hand as if requesting hers. The moustachioed mouth hovered overlong upon her fingers. She perceived the trace of colour high upon his pale, polished cheekbone while his knowing eye pinioned her. It took her breath like a dash of icy water. It was over in a flash. The Berkeley carriage moved forward. Prince Ernest saluted and moved on.

Mary blinked in disbelief and hastily remarked the bridge's worn timbers to disguise her embarrassment. Dark water, confounded by an undertow, sparkled between its spars. Frederick was going to have to mend his ways, Cranfield decided. Mary was sprung from seclusion and would be exposed to the temptations of others, if not her own. If she were put in a position of refusing a Prince, there could be unpleasant ramifications in respect of the Berkeley 'cause'. The Admiral was unacquainted with this fifth son of the King, but he had heard that Ernest Augustus did not suffer fools and had no time for the bumbling idiocy of his brothers. Where they were voluble, he held aloof and did not bestir himself to put people at ease. Even in looks and stature, he did not resemble them. Had his mother been any other than Queen Charlotte, one might have been forgiven for supposing His Majesty had been cuckolded!

On the way back to St. James's Palace where Cumberland had his apartments, he said: "Sir George Berkeley is an Admiral, I see. Away from home for long spells. I wonder who consoles that pretty wife, West? Upon my life, someone will!"

The Colonel gulped and turned a greenish hue. "Not his wife. Not *his* wife."

"Did I not hear you address her as Lady Berkeley?"

"Your Highness, that is the *Countess*, the Admiral's sister-in-law."

"You mean that old *roué*, Fred Berkeley, who has caused such controversy in the House, is *her* husband? Good God! I don't wonder at the rumours he has turned into a hermit! Organise for me an *entrée* to Berkeley Castle, or wherever it is they reside."

West was in danger of stuttering and strove to command his tongue. "A chaste wife. Devoted mother. Religious principles. Not good form, sir. Trust me!"

"An introduction, man!"

The Colonel cast about for an excuse and was suddenly seized of inspiration. "No need, Your Highness. The Berkeleys will be present at the Arundel ball in honour of Dr Jenner."

"Will they, by Jove? Then I shall await it with alacrity."

That day, Colonel John West, soldier, patriot, man of honour, knew what it was to be a traitor.

Sixteen

Tickets for the Duke of Norfolk's ball, inviting the recipients to promote Dr Jenner's research into smallpox, found their way to Cranford House early in September. As etiquette dictated, Mr Dalloway, His Grace's secretary, had addressed them to The Rt. Hon. Mary, Countess of Berkeley and that good gentleman could not be expected to guess how they lifted her spirits and caused at the same time a tremor of unease. The day Fitz returned to Eton, Fred had dined informally at Carlton House where he was pleased to find the Duke one of his fellow guests. The Prince proved loyal to his old friend Berkeley and set the mood of the meeting by ignoring what had passed in the House of Lords.

During Michaelmas week, the Earl and Countess returned the Admiral to Bosham Manor. Having spent the night there, they moved on to Arundel on the day appointed for the ball. Mary was delighted with the town set among wooded slopes evocative of Claude Lorraine and Jean-Honoré Fragonard. The lower meadows were enclosed by neat hedges and knapped flint walls. Animals could safely graze, the harvest could be garnered and the quay conduct its busy custom. Red Deer browsed the parks. The elders of the herd had been a gift from the Duke of Beaufort and had travelled from Badminton by canal.

Arundel Castle was as archaic as its cousin of Berkeley and its families were interknit. Its motte post-dated the Battle of Hastings by one year only. Never having been favoured as the chief ducal seat of the Norfolks, it had fallen into dilapidation. By 1799, Charles Howard, the 11th Duke, was a decade into a makeover which was to absorb the rest of his life. Shunning Wyatt's drawings, he decided to chance his arm solo in a curious amalgam of Norman and Gothic styles. This was designed to suspend the visitor in a long-lost world of chivalry, but the mirage had been hijacked by his republican sympathies. The Duke's arched front door was flanked by twice life-size figures of Liberty and Hospitality rendered in ceramic Coade stone.

"A flight of indulgence," scoffed the Dowager Lady Sefton to her friend Mrs Fitzherbert. "The Earl Marshal can be no more a radical than His Majesty the King!"

James Dallaway welcomed the house-guests and made sure they were led up the zig-zag staircase to their rooms. His Grace would greet them over tea in the Library, but had been unavoidably detained.

"Not in his bath-tub, I'd lay odds," said Berkeley drily.

Sight of the castle interior revealed that the Duke's enterprise in reviving the feudal splendours of Arundel was far from completion. Work had recently begun on the Elizabethan Long Gallery which he planned to turn into a Library. A skeletal frame of pillars and vaults in the Perpendicular style had been crafted from Honduras mahogany with lifelike carvings of leaves and berries.

"The place deserves an eclectic mix of authors," declared the Duke. "Mary's cousin's *magnum opus* needs to be housed for one thing!"

Mary Ann Gibbon was his 'official' mistress and the mother of two small sons by him. They had been introduced through his antiquarian interests by her kinsman Edward Gibbon whose colossal work on *The History of The Decline and Fall of the Roman Empire* was praised in academe.

"A worthy offering," Berkeley said, "but I am bound to observe that were it half the length, its readership might be doubled!"

The Duke caught sight of a handsome couple entering the room. "Ah, Lord Dashalong and his better half!" This was Isabella Sefton's son, the 2nd Earl of Sefton, a 'whip hand' and a gambler, and her daughter-in-law, Lord Berkeley's niece.

"Maria!" cried Berkeley. "Didn't think to see you here!"

"Struth, Berkeley," said Sefton, "ain't clapped eyes on you since we tied the proverbial. Thought you was dead. We've a half-dozen brats rampaging about Croxteth Hall by now. Aiming to keep pace with you!"

"Impudent scoundrel! Do spare the ladies' blushes, Sefton. Permit me to introduce the Countess to you." Berkeley was seized of a terrible thought. "Don't tell me your Mama is invited to this frolic, Maria?"

"Indeed, I hope not," said Maria in alarm. "Oh, never say so! Duke?"

"I rather think the Margravine has invited herself and that the Margrave will come on leading strings," replied His Grace. "The rumour that she was touring her empires is anecdotal. I always thought delegation an overrated art myself."

"Oh no! I shall cut her! After the horrid way she treated our poor Papa!"

An Irishman materialised at the Duke's elbow and peered around his shoulder with a comic grimace. "Sheridan! Ought I to present to you this gracious lady on my left? I am in two minds."

"Then allow me to unite them, Your Grace!"

"You are unacquainted with Lady Berkeley, I take it?" Sheridan received Mary's fingers in an exaggeratedly gentle fashion. "Ah, I see humour dimples the cheek and points the beaming eye! You bear a marked resemblance to your sister, if I may say so, yet there is something altogether more demure. Won't you come into the garden? I would like the roses to see you."

"You know my sister, sir? Susan?"

"Knew, ma'am. *Knew.* Her flight from this island leaves many unconsoled!"

"She is unlikely to leave America now that Mr Baring has retrieved her from widowhood."

"She has become a celebrated hostess of that war-torn land, I hear. The lady was ever known for the breadth of her hospitality."

"Certainly she enjoys good company."

"A writer of plays to boot! Many's the time she amused us with a pithy turn of phrase. Ah, yes! None can dispute Mrs Baring's gift for fiction."

Mary worked her fan. She wished she were discussing coppicing or the sale of timber from Coaley Woods. Fred was drifting further and further away from her. It was all too plain he was used to attending parties alone.

"Forgive me, Mr Sheridan. I think I must take a little air."

"Lady Berkeley! What a pleasure to see you!" Mary was intercepted by 'the eyebrow Mr Fox', as his agent, the Duchess of Devonshire, called him. That lady been known to trade kisses for votes in order to keep him in Parliament. Fox dressed like an aging macaroni. His sallow shirts and food-stained waistcoats made Her Grace thankful it was unnecessary to offer such a *douceur* to the candidate. "We met many years ago on the river at Hampton Court," he reminded her, bowing low. It must have been in 1785, for I remember Pitt's Sinking Fund being talked of!"

Mary got the better of a blush. She had been 'Miss Tudor' in those days. "Yes, I do recall that day, Mr Fox."

"You may be aware that I am related to your husband and, therefore, also to you! The blood of the Stuart Kings runs in your children's veins. The Merry Monarch applied himself most energetically to populating the Kingdom with peers, it has to be said! Now, Lady Berkeley, do let's inspect the new stained glass of bold, bad barons and Hebrew kings."

Fox made to lead Mary away to the Medieval Hall. He was aware that several pairs of eyes were trained upon him, not least her husband's. Passing Sheridan, he heard the playwright's aside to Lady Aylesford (who had lifted her lorgnette to inspect the Countess' undeniably patrician profile). "'Tis believed she was under his protection before the match, that is such protection as vultures give to lambs!"

"I can't think," trumpeted the matron, "where he found her! She must have co-nnections, must she not?"

"The mercantile affluence and legislature of the United States would not be quite what they are without her ilk," said Sheridan airily.

"American? I thought her accent to the west of us."

"Absolutely, ma'am, but not so far it bestrides the Bristol Channel!"

The sight of his Countess escorted from the room by a foremost rebel statesman, who drank back-handed toasts to 'Our sovereign! The people!' stirred a ferment of emotions within the Earl of Berkeley's breast. He had always known that, let loose upon the hounds of society, she would become the focus of attention.

When she returned to their apartments, he was dozing upon his dressing-room couch. "What a relief that Mr Fox saved me from Sheridan's toils," she declared.

"You have a rapport with Fox evidently...."

"I thought Mr Sheridan condescending and silly."

"He is the wit of the century!"

"He is not so very droll. His humour is *passé*. Times are changing. Can you not feel it? Who would have guessed that when my sisters and I paddled in the Ousel, and picked fleece off the hawthorns in the Wotton lanes, we were destined to be Continents apart?"

"A fine thing you are!"

"You did not tell me Sheridan knew Susan. I thought his remarks snide."

"Your sister," said Berkeley with feeling, "is fair game."

Mary's blue-green eyes flashed with indignation. "Oh, and how exactly is *your* sister, Anspach, superior to mine when she has alienated all her children with her outrageous behaviour and don't give a fig for anyone's opinion?"

"Elizabeth has centuries of breeding and knows what she's doing."

"She is frowned upon by the Prince's set, that I do know! I have suffered the utmost disgrace these fourteen years and our children's future is threatened because of your squeamish attitude to Susan!"

"Your sister, damn her," swore Berkeley, "is a harpy! She is a criminal times over! She.... " He tightened with such torque, his knuckles were white. "She kept house for a couple of.... I cannot tell a lady! Tis a profane thing!"

"I find it hard to believe that Susan kept house for anyone!"

"I do not mean she was a housekeeper. She was a tenant living Scot-free of expense. She used the address as a cover for two....*gentlemen.*"

The ticking of the mantel-clock echoed in a sudden, dreadful hiatus. Pale as winter, Mary lowered herself on to the couch. "You mean that thing for which Edward II endured the vilest torture in our Castle, do you not?" she said weakly. "Dear God!"

"You see the coil I was in," Berkeley reasoned. "We could all have gone to perdition!"

"I shall never lift my head again," Mary said in an anaemic, strangled tone.

"Nonsense! If *I* must, so must you!"

"All I have striven for....a decent reputation....a birthright for Fitz...."

"What of *my* name!"

"They'll be whispering about it behind their fans and in the alcoves of their Clubs...."

"They do not know, not of *that.* Luckily, such pursuits require fastidious stealth."

"No one?"

"Well, to tell the truth, Prinny knows, but he is the acme of circumspection."

"The Prince! I cannot attend the ball. I am unwell. Pray, excuse me."

"The devil, I will! This is your first sally into the heart of society. I *demand* you will put on a fine frock and your diamonds and conduct yourself like the Countess of Berkeley!"

Mary intended to wear a plain black high-waisted gown that disguised her condition, but there wasn't the faintest chance she would blend into the background tonight. Notoriety would guarantee a simmering interest. Lord Berkeley was also to give an encomium on the work of Dr Jenner who must miss the revels because his wife had fallen sick.

"My lord, how shall I face them!" she cried. "If it hadn't been for you, Susan would never have mounted the ladder of vice!"

In the Medieval Hall, Elizabethan music rang around the hammerbeams, inventing jollity in doleful keys. The Berkeleys joined the congregating guests and presently reached the threshold. The Earl caught up his wife's fingers in his gloved hand and placed their invitation upon the footman's salver.

"The Earl and Countess of Berkeley!" bellowed the page above the hubbub. In one split second, a lull fell upon the assembly. Many turned to the doorway in a twinkling explosion of gems and an airy riffle of plumes. The chatter recovered momentum; the madrigals played on. No verdict appeared to have been passed.

"Berkeley! Your ladyship!" Norfolk met them. "Lysons and Banks were just discussing the Rosetta Stone. What a find!" The Duke moved on to the people behind. The Berkeleys were plied with champagne and Lysons introduced Sir Joseph Banks. The botanist was an old friend of Edward Jenner. They had been on an expedition together with Captain Cook. Banks had the supervision of the Royal Gardens at Kew where he had propagated many rare plants from distant climes.

"The spoils of war, eh?" said Berkeley, referring to the Egyptian slab which Napoleon's soldiers had excavated by accident in the course of laying foundations for a fort.

"The French found it, but the trophy rightly belongs to the victors," said Lysons, prouder of that than of Nelson's feat. "Just think of it, two thousand years old!"

"And does its antiquity make it so greatly prized?" asked Mary.

"That's not the half of it, Lady Berkeley. It describes the achievements of the Pharaoh, Ptolemy V, upon the first anniversary of his coronation. Scholars know this because as well as being written in hieroglyphs and in the vernacular of the region, there is a Greek translation. It means we might begin to decipher ancient Egyptian picture language."

"And will it affect the Three Percent Consols?" queried Berkeley.

Lysons grinned. "There speaks a philistine. Now Bonaparte has a grasp of what possession of such artefacts means."

"Your lordship does, however, have an exquisite understanding of the horse and hound, I am told," chortled Sir Joseph.

"Her ladyship's interests are more in line with your own, Sir Joseph," Lysons said. "She is an expert upon crop plants."

"Aye," said Berkeley, "tell the gentlemen about your mangold-wurzels, my love."

"I cannot think they would find it at all diverting! Sir Joseph, I'd be glad of some advice about my nectarine vines.... Oh!" Prince William and Mrs Jordan were making an entrance and, in their wake, a person whose ramrod stature and haughty looks Mary recognised. Prince Ernest, Duke of Cumberland.

Cumberland's monocular gaze swept over the room in one penetrating beam. It fastened upon Mary. She was the only person in the room for him, as he was for her. An invisible thread linked them. It was a psychical imposition she could not shake off. He piloted his way among the guests to keep her in his sightlines, over a shoulder here, reflected in a mirror there, a sidelong glance down a breaking avenue between the crowd. She noticed that he stood awkwardly, with his left hand bent behind his back.

A blast from the herald cornets announced the Prince of Wales. The Elizabethan polyphony vaulted two hundred years and broke briefly into Handel's anthem, *Zadok, the Priest*, foretelling a coronation. The women curtsied in unison, the men bowed low. The Prince was elated to spot Maria Fitzherbert. Maria Sefton sidled up to her Uncle Fred and whispered behind her Oriental fan: "I don't think Mama can be coming after all, thank God!"

"Bad form if she's later than Prinny, but ain't that her style, my dear?"

Scarcely had he spoken and the musicians were launched into a pavanne, than the Margrave and Margravine of Anspach, swept in, all gracious smiles, with tales of molestation on the King's highway. The Margravine had been forced to surrender a priceless brooch and several guineas, but apparently not such of her virtue as remained. Her husband, bless his silken hose, had required medicinal fortification at a wayside tavern. He was not equipped with her brother's mettle in matters of self-defence. Dear Christian's timid soul took refuge in hers!

The Margrave looked like nothing so much as a stuffed life-size puppet, his features stamped with a leer of benign humour. "*Guten Abend, Königliche Hoheit*, ladies and chentlemen! Apologies *für die verzögerung. Straßenräuber! Bettler haben keine wahl!*" His wife's verbosity had little impact upon the

Margrave's English which served that lady well. He came packaged with high distinction and, in addition to being his consort, she was formally known in her own right as Princess Berkeley of the Holy Roman Empire which absurd handle plunged both her brothers into fits of hilarity.

"Pray, don't genuflect, good people. We are among friends!"

Maria Sefton cowered behind the potted palms.

"Your Noblenesses might consider outriders in future," suggested Norfolk.

"Fie, Duke," said the Margravine, "and deprive us of excitement!"

"You presume upon the good nature of His Royal Highness, the Prince of Wales," replied Norfolk, sensible of the slight from her nonchalance more than from the lateness of hour. He did not for an instant believe the given reason.

"Don't be so stuffy, Earl Marshal! That is for virgins with no light to bring!"

"If that were the case, I might well stand indicted!"

"Monsieur Voltaire," declared the Margravine charmingly, "believes it a superstition of the human mind to imagine that virginity could be a virtue! But there! Frenchmen are blessed with superior discernment."

Berkeley groaned to see his sister by-passing the Prince of Wales with an acknowledgement of sober brevity and advancing towards *him*. They had been at loggerheads since her second marriage. She still had the same doe-eyes, the same sweet, heart-shaped face, unsagging, but now viewed as through creased tiffany. She had drunk many strings of pearls in her time, all dissolved in champagne, to nourish the complexion immortalised by George Romney. Berkeley was relieved that her husband had been foisted upon Cumberland who was no conversationalist but could speak German.

"Lilibet! Why take the room by stealth when you can take it by storm?" Blandishments were delicately negotiated. Mary could veritably smell the history behind these two people from which she was excluded. "Ain't seen you since you went on that *Reconnaissance* Tour, spreading your affections in your usual democratic manner and bagging a husband! You were the death of poor Mama!"

"I think Mama was mightily pleased to see that *I* had exalted the family name, Frederick. God knows, someone had to provide counterpoise!"

Mary rode this cheerful snub with just as cheerful dignity, determined to out-do the Margravine in gracious good breeding. "Yes, I might suppose it to have been a spur in your canon of motives for engineering a match of some lustre for yourself."

"*Touché!*" Berkeley struck his thigh, his eyes brilliant with startled energy. "Go to it, Polly! I can see I am in for some excellent sport!"

"I hear you had a run in with the Old Lion," Elizabeth said, not to be put down.

"Lord Thurlow? Yes, I recall you had a close encounter of your own with him, to conjure a euphemism. Craven thought twice before citing him in the Spiritual Court, though the alternative of citing the Archbishop of York could not have embarrassed him any the less!"

"Ah, my lawn-sleeved Phaon!"

"No wonder your husband, poor gudgeon, pickled himself to death!"

The Margravine flicked her fan shut and used it to tap her brother's arm. "You will never make good your ludicrous claim. It drove poor Hupsman to his doom. He went into hiding at Scarlets because Hickes, from Stone, was dunning him. Hickes will gain his dues, I warn you!"

The Duke of Clarence was standing nearby and noticed Mary's discomfiture. He turned to the Margravine. "It appears the natives ain't as hospitable as they was used. Take yourself off to Tartary, ma'am, and feast on sheep's eyes there!" As the Margravine flounced off, Mary offered him an indebted smile, unsuspecting that circumstances would so assort themselves in the future, that he would seek to marry her and would reign as King William IV. "Berkeley! 'Tis high time we introduced our ladies to one another."

Dorothy Jordan was as full of infectious laughter and mischief as the roles she played. The breaking folds of her skirt confided that she, too, was with child and in the vanguard of Mary.

"I'd be glad to sit down to supper, to say the truth, Countess. Me back is plaguing me with the cramps. I'll not sit with the old biddies. They quiz like the Spanish, so they do."

Flemish needlework chairs and sofas of the Louis Quatorze period furnished the outskirts of the room where turbanned Duchesses and Dowagers viewed the gathering with the bittersweet detachment of spent years. Mrs Harcourt, a Colonel's wife, who had been chatting to one of them, turned towards Mary and her new friend:

"I see Clarence managed to release your ladyship from the Margravine's toils."

"I am indebted to him."

"Cumberland won't brook her airs and graces, either. His manners are not English, alas. Do you know, when we were stationed in Flanders, I accompanied him to the English Convent in Ghent where he made a display of kissing the Abbess and ogled the nuns the whole time we were there. Wild to a fault!"

"He'd give the devil the creeps," shuddered Dora. "Clarence reckons he's frittered a fortune on mirrors for his bedroom!"

"Shocking! Quite shocking! Methinks," sang Mrs Harcourt, a touch ironically, "he must be sweet on you, Dora, for he keeps glancing in this direction! Why, Lady Berkeley, how disconcerted you look!"

In another part of the Medieval Hall, a counterpoint discussion was taking place.

"Yes, it has caused an unholy furore. What do I make of it, sir? An ungainly swindle!" declared the Margravine.

"Unless you mean to wreak the utmost revenge upon your brother, I'd not put *that* about it if were you," cautioned Cumberland.

"Berkeley is putty to be moulded. She....her ladyship....has a parochial turn of logic. If fornication were tantamount to marriage, it would make us all thoroughgoing polygamists!"

"The lady has been quarantined too long."

"*Gott in Himmel*, if Mary Harcourt spends any longer bending her ear, Lady Berkeley will be invited to Portland Place to admire the green flock wallpaper and the octagon closet!"

"She is too fine a bird to be caged."

"And do you mean to broaden her horizons, Highness?" demanded the Margravine archly.

"Allies, I am persuaded, would not be unwelcome."

"You'll draw Frederick's cork first!"

"The fellow's a trifler, well past his prime."

"I certainly won't take it upon myself to introduce you."

"Pray don't exert yourself, madam. The deed is already done. I make a point of never choosing my women or my linen by candlelight!"

The Prince of Wales saluted Mary and presented Maria which occasioned a lot of head-turning. Mary sensed a kindred spirit in the lady in whom maternal qualities seemed united with those of goddess.

"My dear, how glad I am to meet you at last! His Highness has spoken of you tenderly. You must bring your little ones up to Richmond soon. I should like of all things to see them."

"I will, ma'am, thank you," Mary promised.

"Before you leave Sussex, "said the Prince, "be sure to cut along to Brighton. Do me the honour of being my guest at Grove House. I suppose you must bring that scamp of a spouse! Clarence and Mrs J will be there, and one or two others keen to befriend you."

Mary dropped a second curtsy and assured him that nothing would give them greater pleasure. One did not refuse the Prince of Wales, or the chance of winning apostles in the wake of scandal. This was to be her life now. She was going to have to meet Fred on new ground.

Her head was swimming and the music thrummed in her skull.

Cumberland's shadow was never far away but, mercifully, he made no move to speak to her. At the first chance, Mary slipped into the Picture Gallery. This corridor connected all the main reception rooms of the southern wing.

In the shadow of marble Kings and elder statesmen, posted like ghostly sentinels between the lampstands, Mary recognised Samuel Lysons talking to two gentlemen who had their backs to her. "Lady Berkeley, I beg you'll come and meet these affable fellows."

His companions turned together. The younger had a pleasing face with curbed silver-gilt locks, not tossed and tweaked *á la mode* like the Prince of Wales'. His name was Thomas Creevey, barrister, witty correspondent and diarist, who was hopeful of making his way into Parliament. But it was the sight of the other which caused Mary to gasp and her eyes to widen. Not since 1787 had she glimpsed that finely-tooled cranium, its side-curls having stolen further away from the crown.

"Mr Perry! James! How... how unexpected this is!" She fluttered her fan at an *accelerando* pace.

"I note," said Lysons, "that only Creevey needs introduction."

"We are old friends, her ladyship's family and I," Perry told them. "I am a godparent to her niece."

Lysons and Creevey were prepared to be engrossed, but the conversation fragmented into small talk and they made polite excuses to be off, aware of a fine tension between the Countess and the editor of the *Morning Chronicle*.

"I....I little thought to see *you* tonight...." Mary looked down at her fan. She found herself surprisingly overcome.

"The Duke of Norfolk is my benefactor. When I bought the *Chronicle* from Mr Woodfall, His Grace was kind enough to offer sponsorship. He is a man of emancipated views."

"I heard you reported from Paris during the Revolution."

"'Tis so, but I'm no Republican. No, nor High Tory, either. Human welfare, however, demands that a thousand injustices be tackled."

"You will probably know that my sisters are gone to the New World. Your goddaughter remains in Gloucester with my mother."

Perry nodded but did not dilate upon any contact with them. "And you? What of you, Mary?"

As he spoke, Mary caught sight of Cumberland's form at the far end of the passage. "I could swear we are being watched. Thank heavens the music has stopped, for I have a fearful headache."

"Come, we will go into the Quadrangle and take a breath of air."

The Hall doors stood open and a few guests had wandered into the garden. An Indian summer day had given way to the burnished dusk of September and there was a tinge of decay in the damp salt air. Swallows darted about the parapets, massing for flight to the great African Continent. *L'hirondelle* was an ancient heraldic emblem of Arundel and, some said, where it acquired its name. Perry and the Countess strolled along the gravel paths and into the copse below the motte of the Norman Keep.

"The seasons are turning," Mary said. Spectral fire glanced off the diamonds lacing her throat.

"I still see the lass in white dimity," Perry said. "Tell me you are happy." He could not wring the intimacy from his voice. He had lived in London many years and the Scots accent was by now less turgid with poignant romanticism.

"Happiness? Have I not more than any woman could reasonably want?"

"Ah, the rhetorical evasion. I'm sure the Earl has truly engaged your affections."

"He is the father of my children."

"It is good that you have no regrets."

Mary remembered those frank, intelligent eyes, clear as a Highland burn. "Will you believe I did what I thought honourable?"

Perry quickly recalled himself. "I'm sorry, I had no right...."

"I was sold," Mary blurted out, "like a sheep at the market. He paid a hundred guineas! My sister abetted him in a most crude stratagem to kidnap me."

"Susan!"

"She counted it a favour. I was so sick and distraught, it terrified Berkeley into an offer of marriage.... I tell you all this so that you do not think ill of me, or disparaging of your affection. Dear God, if only you knew how I set my face towards Jerusalem when I found out that I had been tricked! Not until after William was born did my sorry condition become fully apparent. But I was married, you know. *I was. We both made vows in front of a parson.*"

Perry had followed the Berkeley debate, but had put any conclusion in abeyance. His own newspaper, a political organ rather than a scandal-sheet, had not commented upon it. Notably, it refrained from gloating over the plight of unfortunate women.

"Then there was a certificate?" he said.

"Of course....*at the beginning.*" Dismayed that she had implied more than was prudent, Mary continued hastily: "Do you remember an occasion when Susan and I went with you to Drury Lane, at the time I lived in the Brompton Road and seldom saw her? We saw Mrs Siddons as the blighted *Jane Shore*? That was the last time we spoke and I think of it with utter pain. I was sure that beneath your amiable manner you had cast me as a woman of easy virtue with Berkeley, for I had then to go by the name of 'Miss Tudor'."

"The matter was troublesome, for I could not make the picture fit to one frame. I was waiting...."

"You would have saved me from shame?" said Mary in surprise.

Perry let go a dispirited breath. "My dear, dear Countess, I have loved you since you would wear no mask at the Lenten Ball and hated the familiarity of admirers and longed only to make hay in meadows of Glevum."

Now the tears started to seep from her lashes and to fall hotly upon his hands which Mary absently noted were badly scarred. Last winter, Perry's quick thinking had rescued his new wife from living flame when a candle fell into her skirts, but this was not the moment to speak of either thing. His anger with Berkeley was a dragon's corpse that had stirred to virulent life and must be slain a second time. He dabbed Mary's tears and drew her against his breast while a light wind disturbed the ivy mantling the Keep gatehouse.

"We must go our ways and be thankful," he whispered. "I feel sure that your children are beautiful."

"They are my life," she said.

The rustle and stiff recoil of cypress plumes at the edge of the Quadrangle shattered their last precious moments.

"That was no listing breeze," said Perry under his breath. "Ah, I think I hear supper being announced. Allow me to escort your ladyship."

Lord Berkeley was at odds with his surroundings. No one knew what to make of him.

Far worse than anything he might have prophesied, was a gnawing fear that he had lost Mary. He bitterly regretted losing his temper. Elizabeth had warned him that Cumberland was on the prowl. It was foolish to take the cavalryman lightly who would have been handsome had he not been disfigured. Such valour might enlist the sympathies of a female. What was more, he had youth on his side, and was the Sovereign's son.

But when he saw her with a stranger, despair set in. "Lysons, who is that going into the garden with my wife?"

The antiquarian glanced over his shoulder. "Oh *him*, your lordship. That is Perry of the *Morning Chronicle*. An old friend of Lady Berkeley's, I understand."

"Indeed. He runs a plain-spoken outfit, don't he?"

Lysons gaze was bright with quiescent humour. "Lord Mulgrave was saying the other day that he thought Perry a cut above the run of editors, a man of sense and manners and without that slighting propensity common among such."

"I believe her ladyship recommends him also," replied Berkeley. His voice was pitched between wistfulness and admiration.

She had come in from the garden, tongue-tied, thinking of all the things she had meant to say before they were interrupted by an eavesdropper.

He parted from her in a formal manner to seek his own place at the table and Mary quickly discovered she was condemned to spend supper beside the Duke of Cumberland. The abrupt contrast between one presence and another came sharp as a wound. Fortunately, the loquacious Mr Creevey was seated on her other side and put her at ease. "I consider myself most fortunate, Lady Berkeley," he whispered in her ear. "You won't get more than two words out of the Duke which means I shall be required to make good the shortfall!"

"Does he not believe himself under obligation to be sociable?"

"He might as well be a statue. Don't care for the fellow above half."

Mary viewed her gooseberry and goats' cheese tartlets glumly. The Duke and his occult influence should not win! She would not allow him to make her wait (as long as he chose!) to be addressed. She turned to him. She had been placed on his 'good' side, either by a random etiquette or by design.

"Your Highness is on leave from active service, I gather?"

"I have been in Germany, under Frederick's command. I was thrown from my horse and broke several ribs in the spring. The animal had to be shot."

"Oh dear. You are mended now, I trust, sir."

"Good as new. I await His Majesty's pleasure in giving me the command of English Cavalry. Its officers need some Teutonic discipline: they are apt to forget themselves. Our dynasty has ruled the plains of Middle Europe for as long as the Berkeleys have been in the West Country. The very name Guelph means 'wolf'. I myself am not only a wolf, I am considered the black sheep of the family! Does that not intrigue your ladyship?"

"Then I should think you your own worst enemy, sir!"

"I am looking to you, Lady Berkeley, to redeem me."

Mary frowned in mounting distress. "How so?"

"Are you not the lady who has tamed the wolf?

"You are speaking in riddles, sir."

"That is what some say of you. I hesitate to incarnadine your cheek, my dear, but you cannot be unaware of your husband's predatory reputation," Cumberland hissed.

Mr Creevey, who had cocked an astonished ear, now gallantly cut in: "What a novel refectory Norfolk's chapel has made since he turned out his priest. Unorthodox yet inspired!"

"He says he will open the Keep, Gatehouse and Grounds next year," said Mary, grasping the chance to forsake Cumberland's thread.

"I was thinking just now that the upkeep of a pile like this must render Midas indigent." A sought-after guest, the diarist now spread his attention to the lady on his right.

"And what of you, Countess? Would you admit the enthralled visitor?" murmured Cumberland in Mary's ear.

"I imagine I should not be in transports, sir. Berkeley Castle has been home to our family for centuries."

"You might be in grave danger of confusing friend and foe, madam. In your very pretty shoes, I should want to step carefully."

"I do not think I understand Your Highness."

"A word in the right ear would close the case upon the Berkeley Peerage for good. I am not without influence, I promise you."

Lord Berkeley, on the opposite side of the table, itched to deal the pestiferous soldier a bunch of fives. He could not hear was what being said, but Mary's eyes were softly-sharp with contained fear. Many a time as a huntsman he had seen that look in his quarry.

For the remainder of the meal, the Duke was laconic to the point of rudeness as Creevey had predicted. Mary promised herself that she would plead an excuse to retire for the night when the dancing began again. Lord Berkeley gave his speech while the Sussex Yeoman cheese was being served. The diners dispersed soon afterwards, the younger element to trip minuets, gavottes and reels in the Medieval Hall, the rest mostly to gossip in the Drawing Room, or play cards in the Anteroom.

The Prince performed a token dance with the Duchess of Devonshire. A little winded, he thankfully surrendered to the highlight of the evening, a sedentary game of whist. He was teamed with Lord Berkeley against Clarence and Norfolk and it provoked no embarrassment when the Countess pleaded fatigue and bade them 'goodnight'.

A sleeping-draft took no effect. The fluttering within Mary's abdomen told her that the baby shared her disquiet. The undercurrent of sound from the junketing downstairs would continue for hours. Fred would be at his stupid cards till dawn, risking stall and stable.

A peremptory rap on the door made her jump. She sat bolt upright and slid from the bed, dragging a robe about her shoulders. Something fidgeted. In the dying glow of the fire, she made out a pale rectangle gravitating across the floor with an animus of its own. She opened the door to admit a sliver of lamplight. The corridor was deserted. Hastily, she bent towards the embers and fumbled to relight a candle. The document was folded and fixed with the thinnest of seals and came unstuck with handling. It was written in manuscript lettering which seemed to divorce the sentiments from authorship.

One last farewell. Come to the Keep, I beg. Fashion and folly may dictate alteration, neglect may despoil, but the Keep remains forever. J.

James! He would realise she was alone while her husband was playing cards with the gentlemen. Mary knew it was foolhardy, perhaps wicked, to go, but she could not bring herself to let him down. Her heart was bursting with things she wanted to explain. She wriggled into her day clothes, fastening them haphazardly in her haste, and lifted her cloak off its peg. This was the kind of madcap thing that forged tales of apparitions wandering the parapets! No! It was for James Perry who had loved her faithfully and unselfishly all the years he had known her and had never harmed a hair of her head, and had done her only good.

The Prince of Wales was on the careless side of 'tipsy'. Likewise the Duke of Norfolk. Clarence regretted that he had not stayed sufficiently sober for the dancing, but opined that Dora would not mind seeing as she was in the rotund phase of expectancy! It then behoved Lord Berkeley to own that his family was in the process of expansion. Wine had not quite deluged the moodiness which had befallen him since he pondered consignment to that league of husbands obliged to look the other way when royal personnel selected their wives for reciprocal favours.

Prinny's face suddenly clouded. "You may well thank heaven for that, Berkeley," he muttered. "I would swear Ernest has designs upon her."

"By Jupiter, he does!" agreed Clarence in tactless awe. "Saw it myself!"

"Unparliamentary," said Norfolk.

"There was never a father well with his son, or husband with his wife, or lover with his mistress, or friend with his friend," reflected Prinny, "that he did not try to make mischief between them."

"Hope you remembered your fowling-piece, Berkeley!" roared Clarence.

"Many would consider our brother a fair target. Your cut for the deal, I think, Norfolk."

"Ye gods!" cried Norfolk. "Tis a civilised Shoot planned for the morning while the ladies tour the gardens and enjoy a little botanical instruction. That will especially appeal to Lady Berkeley."

"I bet Ernest won't!" roared Clarence again.

"He won't waste his powder on pheasant and woodcock, that's for sure," said Prinny.

"Prefers Frogs! Broke his sabre on a French Dragoon once! Made mincemeat of him!"

"Sort of curmudgeon you prefer on your side to theirs," Norfolk said.

"By and by, our respected father will relent and Ernest will be off to the Wars. You'll be shot of him, Berkeley. I say, Norfolk, this is excellent Calvados."

"It don't have to travel far. Purchase it by the cask, Your Highness."

"So he can lay down under the spigot and cut out the butler!" Clarence hooted.

"Had the good fortune to come by some unrivalled wines a while back. The labels make better reading than Rousseau."

Prinny looked down his nose at an unpromising hand of cards. "Then let us repair to the cellar forthwith and inspect them!"

"To the Undercroft!" seconded Clarence. "We must sample them!" The King's third son scrambled to his pins with heroic instability and slithered in an undignified heap between the chairs. A spinsterish *grande dame* of the Queen's household, who was entering the room at that moment, puffed up her chest and wondered tartly why the race of men deemed itself fit to rule the seas. "Hold you your potato jaw, my dear! Sailors like me keep you *virgo intacta*! You have my word upon it!"

"Land or water, William's in his element half seas over," chuckled Prinny.

Mary stole down the servants' stairs in her dancing slippers to the South Passage, hoping to gain an exit through the Undercroft, a route by which she was least likely to be seen. This cellar below the drawing room was intended as a dungeon when the castle was built, but had never been used for the purpose. Arundel had been a minor palace of Henry II's in those days (that sovereign whose crusades Robert Fitzhardinge had helped to finance) and its dungeon had done duty as a store-room ever since.

On reaching the passage, she paused and listened. It was unnervingly quiet and the sounds of merry-making above, remote. Deep Gothic doorways recessed the walls, leading to a series of domiciliary offices, the stillroom, the butler's pantry, the china cupboards and those cobwebbed crannies where unused lengths of carpet, old ironmongery and torn Holland covers lay forgotten. With its barrel-vaulted ceiling, the hallway appeared tunnel-like and presented a longer aspect than it measured. At the far end, a window gave on to the courtyard and light from flaring torches slanted across the flagstones. *What am I doing?* she thought. *What folly has consumed me when I have five sons and a child coming before the swallows return? I have a safe haven in Gloucestershire, away from the world, and a husband who will do his best by my children.* She began to hurry past the glittering watch of stuffed birds in full plumage, the trophy heads of hunted creatures and the vainglorious, unsheathed swords clinging to the walls. The light was growing bigger; it promised to engulf her. Instead, night! A blanket of darkness swirled around her. An iron-sinewed arm made a noose about her neck, while a stark-white gloved hand smelling of a repugnant pomade stifled her mouth and pushed back her head. She found herself staring into the hawkish features of her wounded suitor, rendered even more formidable in the half-light.

"And is your husband aware of your trysting, you little cockteaser! Spurn me, would you? Well, you shall learn the unwisdom of that!"

That minute, the clamour of raised voices rebounded upon the dusty wine-racks in the Undercroft. The beam of a swinging pole-lantern washed over the vaulting and projected a company of shadows. Turning sharply, Mary's captor inadvertently loosened his hold upon her mouth and she set up a piercing scream.

"By God, what was that! Who goes there?" boomed Norfolk.

"Avast!" shouted Clarence, cupping his hands to his mouth. "Avast in the King's name!"

The Prince of Wales was the first to recognise the reedy outline of his brother. Horrified stupefaction made a gargoyle of his countenance. Berkeley's veins were instantly engorged with scalding adrenalin. His body was fired with that old exultation in youth. It did not occur to him to wonder what the Countess was doing there, for Cumberland was implicated. In one accusing flashback, he saw his own abduction of her and how and why he had gone to such lengths, and the pain it had caused. He sprang forward and, wrenching a rapier from its bracket, held it at a perilous arm's length an inch from the Duke's throat, his chin jutting in the meanest snarl he could invent.

"Cumberland, you blackguard! You limb of Satan! Let go my wife! I'll see you in Hell for this!"

"Ernest, I beg you...!" cried the Prince. "Abandon this unseemly spectacle! The lady is with child!"

"Oh, Fred, Fred," cried Mary, "take me home, take me back to our dear old castle!"

The tip of the sword quivered under superhuman restraint "Name....your....friend, *sir*."

"B....Berkeley....!" the Prince stuttered. "Can't...!"

"I choose Clarence," said the Duke coolly.

"I will send Sefton to wait upon him and see you in Rewell Wood at dawn!"

"Fred!" shrieked Mary. "Recollect yourself, I beg!"

Roughly, the Duke shoved his hostage aside and brushed his cape of imaginary dust. He strode off, calling back: "Rewell Wood, Berkeley. Make peace with your God before you come! Either way, it cannot go well for you."

Panting from unaccustomed exertion, the Earl threw down his sword and scooped the Countess into a sumptuous embrace. "Polly, my love! My life! I can't let you out of my sight for a second!"

"Oh dear," groaned Clarence, "I fancy a little precipitation is within sight."

Mary screwed her lids tight-shut. At last she knew what she had always longed to know and what she had hoped was the *ultimate* truth.

"You cannot call him out, Fred!" she wailed. "He is a Prince of the Blood!"

"Then I might as well be hanged for a sheep as a lamb!"

Acknowledgements

The Berkeley story is woven from **The Minutes of Evidence taken before the Committee of Privileges on the Earl of Berkeley's Pedigree - 1799** and **1811** and *A Narrative of the Minutes of Evidence respecting the claim to The Berkeley Peerage, 1811.*

Regrettably, it would be impossible to list all the sources consulted and cross-referenced. Here are some of them:

Mary Cole, Countess of Berkeley – *Hope Costley-White*
The Berkeleys of Berkeley Square – *Bernard Falk*
Royal Dukes – *Roger Fulford*
George The Fourth – *Roger Fulford*
George, Prince & Regent – *Philip W. Sergeant*
The Life and Times of George IV – *Alan Palmer*
Caroline, The Unhappy Queen – *Lord Russell of Liverpool*
The Prince of Pleasure – *J. B. Priestley*
Maria Fitzherbert – *James Munson*
Mrs Fitzherbert – *Shane Leslie*
My Life and Recollections – *Hon. Grantley Berkeley*
Old Q, The Rake of Piccadilly – *Henry Blyth*
William Pitt, The Younger – *William Hague*
Life of Edward Jenner – *F. D. Drewitt*
Edward Jenner – *E. Ashworth Underwood*
A Letter to the Women of England – *Mary Robinson*
A Vindication of the Rights of Woman – *Mary Wollstonecraft*
The Times
British History Online
The National Archives
Access to Archives
Berkeley Muniments
Berkshire Record Office
Birmingham City Archives
Centre for Buckinghamshire Studies
Centre for Kentish Studies
Derbyshire Record Office
Gloucestershire Record Office
Lancashire Record Office
Middlesex Archives

Northamptonshire Record Office
Nottinghamshire Archives
Warwickshire County Record Office
West Sussex Archives
Scribe's Alcove Parish Archives (*excellent website!*)
Ancestral Notes of Orlando Mansfield
Inner Temple Admissions Database
Middle Temple Alumni
Oxford DNB
1911 Encyclopedia (based on E. Brittanica)
Wikipedia
The Farington Diary, 8 vols. 1793 -1821
Life of Lord Chancellor Eldon (3 Vols) – *Horace Twiss*
Memoirs of Harriette Wilson (2 Vols)
The Dukes of Norfolk – *John Martin Robinson*
Arundel Castle – *John Martin Robinson*
Mrs Jordan's Profession – *Claire Tomalin*
Goddess of the Green Room – *Jean Plaidy*
Perdita's Prince – *Jean Plaidy*
Sweet Lass of Richmond Hill – *Jean Plaidy*
Devil Water – *Anya Seton*
Katherine – *Anya Seton*
Agriculture of Gloucestershire – *Thomas Rudge*
History of Waterways – *Jim Shead*
Portrait of Gloucestershire – *T. A. Ryder*
The Great Road to Bath – *Daphne Phillips*
The Gentlemen's Clubs of London – *A. Lejeune & M. Lewis*
London Clubs – *Ralph Nevill*
Royal Navy 1793 -1815
Naval History of Great Britain – *William James*
National Maritime Museum
Journal for Maritime Research
Letters and Dispatches of Horatio Nelson
Royal College of Physicians Heritage Centre
Institute of Historical Research
Rossbret Institutions Online
The Country House Database
The Clergy of the Church of England Database
Spartacus Educational
BBC History
The Mists of Time
The Georgian Index
Peelweb

Web of English History
Dukes of Buckingham & Chandos Online
National Portrait Gallery
Government Art Collection
Digital Library of Historical Directories
Gendocs: Ranks, Professions, Occupations and Trades
Ancestry.com. British Origins. Rootsweb. Jewish Virtual Library.
Genuki. Familysearch. Maximilian Genealogy. E-familytree.net.
UK Genealogy, Heraldry & History. thePeerage.com. Burke's
Peerage. Stirnet. GLOSGEN.
Alf Beard for tombstone transcription
Hickes Family Tree courtesy of *Neil Ghosley.*
The late *Arthur Sadler* of Cranford, a descendant of Thomas
Moreton Fitzhardinge Berkeley, 6th Earl *de jure* for the loan of
books
Mr David Smith, now Berkeley Castle Archivist
The Society of Authors *for patient advice*

THE BERKELEY TRILOGY

Book 2 The Sheep and The Goats *(to follow)*
Book 3 The Ivy and The Violet *(to follow)*

Please see www.pilgrimrose.com for details of other books in
print.

Lightning Source UK Ltd.
Milton Keynes UK
UKOW051932121211

183641UK00002B/41/P